THE APEX BOOK OF WORLD SF: VOLUME 5

THE APEX BOOK OF WORLD SF VOLUME 5

THE APEX BOOK OF WORLD SF: VOLUME 5

CRISTINA JURADO
LAVIE TIDHAR

CONTENTS

INTRODUCTION BY SERIES EDITOR LAVIE TIDHAR

I conceived and began putting together the first *Apex Book of World SF* in 2008, a whole decade ago now. It was published a year later, and a series was born. So much has changed since then, but one thing that only continued to grow is the prominence of international writers on the modern speculative fiction scene. There are so many more writers, today, making their debut; more editors who are actively looking; and more translators, too, lending their unique skill for the benefit of short fiction. After editing three anthologies, I knew my time as an editor had come to an end, yet I still wished that, somehow, the series would go on. It was only thanks to the marvellous Mahvesh Murad stepping in at the right time that it happened, and I could never be more grateful to her for it. Mahvesh took over with enthusiasm, bringing a new, fresh perspective to *The Apex Book of World SF: Volume 4*, and has since gone on to edit new original anthologies, such as 2017's *The Djinn Falls in Love and Other Stories* with Jared Shurin.

We were also able to re-launch the series in a more uniform look, with exceptional art design by Sarah Anne Langton, who I think has done an incredible job.

With Mahvesh busy elsewhere, I felt that the best way forward would be to bring in new editors for each new volume. Every editor brings their own unique perspective to the selection process, and I feel this can only enrich the series as a whole.

Enter the amazing Cristina Jurado! Hailing from Spain and now living in Dubai, Cristina—herself an award-winning editor and author —straddles the worlds of Arabic and Spanish-language SF, and was able to bring in more of a focus on Spanish and Latin American speculative fiction with this volume, as well as writers from Lebanon and Egypt. With each new volume, we explore new countries, while continuing to highlight fiction from countries previously featured. Cristina has been a joy to work with, and I am delighted with her selections for this volume.

I remain, as before, as Series Editor (doing all the boring stuff!) and will keep my fingers crossed for another volume further down the line. As always, my thanks to all the authors, translators, editors, and publishers who continue to produce and publish great work and for entrusting their stories to us in turn. Special thanks, too, to our publisher, Jason Sizemore, without whom none of this would ever have been possible.

Working on this series has been a privilege and a dream, and I can't believe it's been a decade already! But let me hand you over now to Cristina, and the latest stories—I hope you enjoy them as much as I did.

Lavie Tidhar, 2018

INTRODUCTION BY VOLUME EDITOR CRISTINA JURADO

"Imagination will often carry us to worlds that never were.
But without it we go nowhere."

— CARL SAGAN

Imagination is a powerful device. It defies the laws of physics, elevates ideas, sparks curiosity, and constantly challenges our knowledge. Present in all cultures and among all ethnicities, displayed by individuals from all sexual identities and orientations, it recognizes any language while walking on the paths of all nations. By pushing the boundaries of what is logical or customary, it has not only planted the seeds of revolution, but also ignited the search for new theories, and has brought comfort and hope to desperate people. It has been a faithful companion of humankind in every historical period.

As a little girl in a Spain barely out of a dictatorship, I grew up imagining I was exploring other planets, trying to go beyond my grey, monotonous, and conservative reality. Teachers saw my overdeveloped imagination as a disruptive force. I got in trouble quite often for daydreaming: my homework was filled with bizarre references and my peers were uninterested in the tales I told them. I, on the other hand, perceived imagination as my ally because it allowed me to overcome difficulties and solitude.

Through stories from authors inside and outside my country, I reached beyond anything I could have ever expected, way far from my vicinity, learning new things from people in different corners of the planet and in different streams of life. This served me well as I chose to work in advertising, first, and as a writer and editor, later. Wherever life took me, I have never ceased to discover its manifestation, so I tried to scout, promote, and nurture it in others as much as in myself.

When I was offered to edit this anthology, I understood this was an opportunity to pay homage to all those authors that fed my imagination as a child. Here was my chance to show how universal, provocative, and original humans can be; to prove their never-ending creativity in the hopes of replicating in others what I felt as a child. It was not only fun, but also a privilege to discover the ways imagination carves narratives around the world.

The stories in this book prove that imagination is a universal tool that produces pure wonder in sometimes difficult conditions. I also learnt that this powerful device is necessary, now maybe more than ever: it helps circumvent censorship, allowing critical thinking and the necessary evolution of our ideas, and it encourages empathy. And those, after all, are what define us as human beings.

Cristina Jurado, Dubai, 2018

A SERIES OF STEAKS BY VINA JIE-MIN PRASAD

Vina Jie-Min Prasad is a Singaporean author, who began publishing in 2016 and has since published highly-regarded stories in magazines including *Clarkesworld* and *Uncanny*. The following story has been nominated for the Nebula, Hugo, and Sturgeon Awards.

————

All known forgeries are tales of failure. The people who get into the newsfeeds for their brilliant attempts to cheat the system with their fraudulent Renaissance masterpieces or their stacks of fake cheques, well, they might be successful artists, but they certainly haven't been successful at *forgery*.

The best forgeries are the ones that disappear from notice—a second-rate still-life mouldering away in gallery storage, a battered old 50-yuan note at the bottom of a cashier drawer—or even a printed strip of Matsusaka beef, sliding between someone's parted lips.

————

Forging beef is similar to printmaking—every step of the process has to be done with the final print in mind. A red that's too dark looks putrid, a white that's too pure looks artificial. All beef is supposed to come from a cow, so stipple the red with dots, flecks, lines of white to fake variance in muscle fibre regions. Cows are similar, but cows aren't uniform—use fractals to randomise marbling after defining the basic look. Cut the sheets of beef manually to get an authentic ragged edge, don't get lazy and depend on the bioprinter for that.

Days of research and calibration and cursing the printer will all vanish into someone's gullet in seconds, if the job's done right.

Helena Li Yuanhui of Splendid Beef Enterprises is an expert in doing the job right.

The trick is not to get too ambitious. Most forgers are caught out by the smallest errors—a tiny amount of period-inaccurate pigment, a crack in the oil paint that looks too artificial, or a misplaced watermark on a passport. Printing something large increases the chances of a fatal misstep. Stick with small-scale jobs, stick with a small group of regular clients, and in time, Splendid Beef Enterprises will turn enough of a profit for Helena to get a *real* name change, leave Nanjing, and forget this whole sorry venture ever happened.

As Helena's loading the beef into refrigerated boxes for drone delivery, a notification pops up on her iKontakt frames. Helena sighs, turns the volume on her earpiece down, and takes the call.

"Hi, Mr Chan, could you switch to a secure line? You just need to tap the button with a lock icon, it's very easy."

"Nonsense!" Mr Chan booms. "If the government were going to catch us they'd have done so by now! Anyway, I just called to tell you how pleased I am with the latest batch. Such a shame, though, all that talent and your work just gets gobbled up in seconds—tell you what, girl, for the next beef special, how about I tell everyone that the beef came from one of those fancy vertical farms? I'm sure they'd have nice things to say then!"

"Please don't," Helena says, careful not to let her Cantonese accent slip through. It tends to show after long periods without any human interaction, which is an apt summary of the past few months. "It's best if no one pays attention to it."

"You know, Helena, you do good work, but I'm very concerned about your self-esteem, I know if I printed something like that I'd want everyone to appreciate it! Let me tell you about this article my daughter sent me, you know research says that people without friends are prone to ..." Mr Chan rambles on as Helena sticks the labels on the boxes— Grilliam Shakespeare, Gyuuzen Sukiyaki, Fatty Chan's Restaurant—and thankfully hangs up before Helena sinks into further depression. She takes her iKontakt off before heading to the drone delivery office, giving herself some time to recover from Mr Chan's relentless cheerfulness.

Helena has five missed calls by the time she gets back. A red phone icon blares at the corner of her vision before blinking out, replaced by the incoming-call notification. It's secured and anonymised, which is quite a change from the usual. She pops the earpiece in.

"Yeah, Mr Chan?"

"This isn't Mr Chan," someone says. "I have a job for Splendid Beef Enterprises."

"All right, sir. Could I get your name and what you need? If you could provide me with the deadline, that would help, too."

"I prefer to remain anonymous," the man says.

"Yes, I understand, secrecy is rather important." Helena restrains the urge to roll her eyes at how needlessly cryptic this guy is. "Could I know about the deadline and brief?"

"I need two hundred T-bone steaks by the eighth of August. 38.1 to 40.2 millimetre thickness for each one." A notification to download t-bone_info.KZIP pops up on her lenses. The most ambitious venture Helena's undertaken in the past few months has been Gyuuzen's strips of marbled sukiyaki, and even that felt a bit like pushing it. A whole steak? Hell no.

"I'm sorry, sir, but I don't think my business can handle that. Perhaps you could try—"

"I think you'll be interested in this job, Helen Lee Jyun Wai."

Shit.

———

A Sculpere 9410S only takes thirty minutes to disassemble, if you know the right tricks. Manually eject the cell cartridges, slide the external casing off to expose the inner screws, and detach the print heads before disassembling the power unit. There are a few extra steps in this case—for instance, the stickers that say "Property of Hong Kong Scientific University" and "Bioprinting Lab A5" all need to be removed—but a bit of anti-adhesive spray will ensure that everything's on schedule. Ideally she'd buy a new printer, but she needs to save her cash for the name change once she hits Nanjing.

It's not expulsion if you leave before you get kicked out, she tells herself, but even she can tell that's a lie.

————

It's possible to get a sense of a client's priorities just from the documents they send. For instance, Mr Chan usually mentions some recipes that he's considering, and Ms Huang from Gyuuzen tends to attach examples of the marbling patterns she wants. This new client seems to have attached a whole document dedicated to the recent amendments in the criminal code, with the ones relevant to Helena ("five-year statute of limitations," "possible death penalty") conveniently highlighted in neon yellow.

Sadly, this level of detail hasn't carried over to the spec sheet.

"Hi again, sir," Helena says. "I've read through what you've sent, but I really need more details before starting on the job. Could you provide me with the full measurements? I'll need the expected length and breadth in addition to the thickness."

"It's already there. Learn to read."

"I *know* you filled that part in, sir," Helena says, gritting her teeth. "But we're a printing company, not a farm. I'll need more detail than 'sixteen- to eighteen-month cow, grain-fed, Hereford breed' to do the job properly."

"You went to university, didn't you? I'm sure you can figure out something as basic as that, even if you didn't graduate."

"Ha ha. Of course." Helena resists the urge to yank her earpiece out. "I'll get right on that. Also, there is the issue of pay ..."

"Ah, yes. I'm quite sure the Yuen family is still itching to prosecute. How about you do the job, and in return, I don't tell them where you're hiding?"

"I'm sorry, sir, but even then I'll need an initial deposit to cover the printing, and of course there's the matter of the Hereford samples." *Which I already have in the bioreactor, but there is no way I'm letting you know that.*

"Fine. I'll expect detailed daily updates," Mr Anonymous says. "I know how you get with deadlines. Don't fuck it up."

"Of course not," Helena says. "Also, about the deadline—would it be possible to push it back? Four weeks is quite short for this job."

"No," Mr. Anonymous says curtly, and hangs up.

Helena lets out a very long breath so she doesn't end up screaming and takes a moment to curse Mr Anonymous and his whole family in Cantonese.

It's physically impossible to complete the renders and finish the print in four weeks, unless she figures out a way to turn her printer into a time machine, and if that were possible she might as well go back and redo the past few years, or maybe her whole life. If she had majored in art, maybe she'd be a designer by now—or hell, while she's busy dreaming, she could even have been the next Raverat, the next Mantuana—instead of a failed artist living in a shithole concrete box, clinging to the wreckage of all her past mistakes.

She leans against the wall for a while, exhales, then slaps on a proxy and starts drafting a help-wanted ad.

———

Lily Yonezawa (darknet username: yurisquared) arrives at Nanjing High Tech Industrial Park at 8.58 a.m. She's a short lady with long black hair and circle-framed iKontakts. She's wearing a loose, floaty dress, smooth lines of white tinged with yellow-green, and there's a large prismatic bracelet gleaming on her arm. In comparison, Helena is wearing her least holey black blouse and a pair of jeans, which is a step up from her usual attire of myoglobin-stained T-shirt and boxer shorts.

"So," Lily says in rapid, slightly-accented Mandarin as she bounds into the office. "This is a beef place, right? I pulled some of the records once I got the address, hope you don't mind—anyway, what do you want me to help print or render or design or whatever? I know I said I had a background in confections and baking, but I'm totally open to anything!" She pumps her fist in a show of determination. The loose-fitting prismatic bracelet slides up and down.

Helena blinks at Lily with the weariness of someone who's spent most of their night frantically trying to make their office presentable. She decides to skip most of the briefing, as Lily doesn't seem like the sort who needs to be eased into anything.

"How much do you know about beef?"

"I used to watch a whole bunch of farming documentaries with my ex, does that count?"

"No. Here at Splendid Beef Enterprises—"

"Oh, by the way, do you have a logo? I searched your company registration but nothing really came up. Need me to design one?"

"*Here at Splendid Beef Enterprises*, we make fake beef and sell it to restaurants."

"So, like, soy-lentil stuff?"

"Homegrown cloned cell lines," Helena says. "Mostly Matsusaka, with some Hereford if clients specify it." She gestures at the bioreactor humming away in a corner.

"Wait, isn't fake food like those knockoff eggs made of calcium carbonate? If you're using cow cells, this seems pretty real to me." Clearly Lily has a more practical definition of fake than the China Food and Drug Administration.

"It's more like ... let's say you have a painting in a gallery and you say it's by a famous artist. Lots of people would come look at it because of the name alone and write reviews talking about its exquisite use of chiaroscuro, as expected of the old masters, I can't believe that it looks so real even though it was painted centuries ago. But if you say, hey, this great painting was by some no-name loser, I was just lying about where it came from ... well, it'd still be the same painting, but people would want all their money back."

"Oh, I get it," Lily says, scrutinising the bioreactor. She taps its shiny polymer shell with her knuckles, and her bracelet bumps against it. Helena tries not to wince. "Anyway, how legal is this? This meat forgery thing?"

"It's not illegal yet," Helena says. "It's kind of a grey area, really."

"Great!" Lily smacks her fist into her open palm. "Now, how can I help? I'm totally down for anything! You can even ask me to clean the office if you want—wow, this is *really* dusty, maybe I should just clean it to make sure—"

Helena reminds herself that having an assistant isn't entirely bad news. Wolfgang Beltracchi was only able to carry out large-scale forgeries with his assistant's help, and they even got along well enough to get married and have a kid without killing each other.

Then again, the Beltracchis both got caught, so maybe she shouldn't be too optimistic.

———

Cows that undergo extreme stress while waiting for slaughter are known as dark cutters. The stress causes them to deplete all their glycogen reserves, and when butchered, their meat turns a dark blackish-red. The meat of dark cutters is generally considered low-quality.

As a low-quality person waiting for slaughter, Helena understands how those cows feel. Mr Anonymous, stymied by the industrial park's regular sweeps for trackers and external cameras, has taken to sending Helena grainy aerial photographs of herself together with exhortations to work harder. This isn't exactly news—she already knew he had her details, and drones are pretty cheap—but still. When Lily raps on the door in the morning, Helena sometimes jolts awake in a panic before she realises that it isn't Mr Anonymous coming for her. This isn't helped by the fact that Lily's gentle knocks seem to be equivalent to other people's knockout blows.

By now Helena's introduced Lily to the basics, and she's a surprisingly quick study. It doesn't take her long to figure out how to randomise the fat marbling with Fractalgenr8, and she's been handed the task of printing the beef strips for Gyuuzen and Fatty Chan, then packing them for drone delivery. It's not ideal, but it lets Helena concentrate on the base model for the T-bone steak, which is the most complicated thing she's ever tried to render.

A T-bone steak is a combination of two cuts of meat, lean tenderloin and fatty strip steak, separated by a hard ridge of vertebral bone. Simply cutting into one is a near-religious experience, red meat parting under the knife to reveal smooth white bone, with the beef fat dripping down to pool on the plate. At least, that's what the socialites' food blogs say. To be accurate, they say something more like "omfg this is sooooooo good," "this bones giving me a boner lol," and "haha im so getting this sonic-cleaned for my collection!!!," but Helena pretends they actually meant to communicate something more coherent.

The problem is a lack of references. Most of the accessible

photographs only provide a top-down view, and Helena's left to extrapolate from blurry videos and password-protected previews of bovine myology databases, which don't get her much closer to figuring out how the meat adheres to the bone. Helena's forced to dig through ancient research papers and diagrams that focus on where to cut to maximise meat yield, quantifying the difference between porterhouse and T-bone cuts, and not *hey, if you're reading this decades in the future, here's how to make a good facsimile of a steak.* Helena's tempted to run outside and scream in frustration, but Lily would probably insist on running outside and screaming with her as a matter of company solidarity, and with their luck, probably Mr Anonymous would find out about Lily right then, even after all the trouble she's taken to censor any mention of her new assistant from the files and the reports and *argh she needs sleep.*

Meanwhile, Lily's already scheduled everything for print, judging by the way she's spinning around in Helena's spare swivel chair.

"Hey, Lily," Helena says, stifling a yawn. "Why don't you play around with this for a bit? It's the base model for a T-bone steak. Just familiarise yourself with the fibre extrusion and mapping, see if you can get it to look like the reference photos. Don't worry, I've saved a copy elsewhere." *Good luck doing the impossible,* Helena doesn't say. *You're bound to have memorised the shortcut for 'undo' by the time I wake up.*

Helena wakes up to Lily humming a cheerful tune and a mostly-complete T-bone model rotating on her screen. She blinks a few times, but no—it's still there. Lily's effortlessly linking the rest of the meat, fat, and gristle to the side of the bone, deforming the muscle fibres to account for the bone's presence.

"What did you do," Helena blurts out.

Lily turns around to face her, fiddling with her bracelet. "Uh, did I do it wrong?"

"Rotate it a bit. Let me see the top view. How did you do it?"

"It's a little like the human vertebral column, isn't it? There's plenty of references for that." She taps the screen twice, switching focus to an image of a human cross-section. "See how it attaches here and here? I just used that as a reference, and *boom.*"

Ugh, Helena thinks to herself. She's been out of university for way too long if she's forgetting basic homology.

"Wait, *is* it correct? Did I mess up?"

"No, no," Helena says. "This is really good. Better than ... well, better than I did, anyway."

"Awesome! Can I get a raise?"

"You can get yourself a sesame pancake," Helena says. "My treat."

———

The brief requires two hundred similar-but-unique steaks at randomised thicknesses of 38.1 to 40.2 mm, and the number and density of meat fibres pretty much precludes Helena from rendering it on her own rig. She doesn't want to pay to outsource computing power, so they're using spare processing cycles from other personal rigs and staggering the loads. Straightforward bone surfaces get rendered in afternoons, and fibre-dense tissues get rendered at off-peak hours.

It's three in the morning. Helena's in her Pokko the Penguin T-shirt and boxer shorts, and Lily's wearing Yayoi Kusama-ish pyjamas that make her look like she's been obliterated by a mass of polka dots. Both of them are staring at their screens, eating cups of Zhuzhu Brand Artificial Char Siew Noodles. As Lily's job moves to the front of Render@Home's Finland queue, the graph updates to show a downtick in Mauritius. Helena's fingers frantically skim across the touchpad, queueing as many jobs as she can.

Her chopsticks scrape the bottom of the mycefoam cup, and she tilts the container to shovel the remaining fake pork fragments into her mouth. Zhuzhu's using extruded soy proteins, and they've punched up the glutamate percentage since she last bought them. The roasted char siew flavour is lacking, and the texture is crumby since the factory skimped on the extrusion time, but any hot food is practically heaven at this time of the night. Day. Whatever.

The thing about the rendering stage is that there's a lot of panic-infused downtime. After queueing the requests, they can't really do anything else—the requests might fail, or the rig might crash, or they might lose their place in the queue through some accident of fate and have to do everything all over again. There's nothing to do besides pray that the requests get through, stay awake until the server limit resets, and repeat the whole process until everything's done. Staying awake is easy for Helena, as Mr Anonymous has recently taken to sending pictures of rotting corpses to her iKontakt address, captioned "Work hard or this could be you." Lily seems to be halfway off to dreamland, possibly because she isn't seeing misshapen lumps of flesh every time she closes her eyes.

"So," Lily says, yawning. "How *did* you get into this business?"

Helena decides it's too much trouble to figure out a plausible lie, and settles for a very edited version of the truth. "I took art as an elective in high school. My school had a lot of printmaking and 3D printing equipment, so I used it to make custom merch in my spare time—you know, for people who wanted figurines of obscure anime characters, or whatever. Even designed and printed the packaging for them, just to make it look more official. I wanted to study art at university, but that didn't really work out. Long story short, I ended up moving here from Hong Kong, and since I had a background in printing and bootlegging ... yeah. What about you?"

"Before the confectionery I did a whole bunch of odd jobs. I used to sell merch for my girlfriend's band, and that's how I got started with the short-order printing stuff. They were called POMEGRENADE—it was really hard to fit the whole name on a T-shirt. The keychains sold really well, though."

"What sort of band were they?"

"Sort of noise-rocky Cantopunk at first—there was this one really cute song I liked, 'If Marriage Means The Death Of Love Then We Must Both Be Zombies'—but Cantonese music was a hard sell, even in Guangzhou, so they ended up being kind of a cover band."

"Oh, Guangzhou," Helena says in an attempt to sound knowledgeable, before realising that the only thing she knows about Guangzhou is that the Red Triad has a particularly profitable organ-printing business there. "Wait, you understand Cantonese?"

"Yeah," Lily says in Cantonese, tone-perfect. "No one really speaks it around here, so I haven't used it much."

"Oh my god, yes, it's so hard to find Canto-speaking people here." Helena immediately switches to Cantonese. "Why didn't you tell me sooner? I've been *dying* to speak it to someone."

"Sorry, it never came up so I figured it wasn't very relevant," Lily says. "Anyway, POMEGRENADE mostly did covers after that, you know, Kick Out The Jams, Zhongnanhai, Chaos Changan, Lightsabre Cocksucking Blues. Whatever got the crowd pumped up, and when they were moshing the hardest, they'd hit the crowd with the Cantopunk and just blast their faces off. I think it left more of an impression that way—like, start with the familiar, then this weird-ass surprise near the end—the merch table always got swamped after they did that."

"What happened with the girlfriend?"

"We broke up, but we keep in touch. Do you still do art?"

"Not really. The closest thing I get to art is this," Helena says, rummaging through the various boxes under the table to dig out her sketchbooks. She flips one open and hands it to Lily—white against red, nothing but full-page studies of marbling patterns, and it must be one of the earlier ones because it's downright amateurish. The lines are all over the place, that marbling on the Wagyu (is that even meant to be Wagyu?) is completely inaccurate, and, fuck, are those *tear stains*?

Lily turns the pages, tracing the swashes of colour with her finger. The hum of the overworked rig fills the room.

"It's awful, I know."

"What are you talking about?" Lily's gaze lingers on Helena's attempt at a fractal snowflake. "This is really trippy! If you ever want to do some album art, just let me know and I'll totally hook you up!"

Helena opens her mouth to say something about how she's not an artist, and how studies of beef marbling wouldn't make very good album covers, but faced with Lily's unbridled enthusiasm, she decides to nod instead.

Lily turns the page and it's that thing she did way back at the beginning, when she was thinking of using a cute cow as the company logo. It's derivative, it's kitsch, the whole thing looks like a degraded copy of someone else's ripoff drawing of a cow's head, and the fact that Lily's seriously scrutinising it makes Helena want to snatch the sketchbook back, toss it into the composter, and sink straight into the concrete floor.

The next page doesn't grant Helena a reprieve since there's a whole series of that stupid cow. Versions upon versions of happy cow faces grin straight at Lily, most of them surrounded by little hearts—what was she thinking? What do hearts even have to do with Splendid Beef Enterprises, anyway? Was it just that they were easy to draw?

"Man, I wish we had a logo because this would be super cute! I love the little hearts! It's like saying we put our heart and soul into whatever we do! Oh, wait, but was that what you meant?"

"It could be," Helena says, and thankfully the Colorado server opens before Lily can ask any further questions.

———

The brief requires status reports at the end of each workday, but this gradually falls by the wayside once they hit the point where workdays don't technically end, especially since Helena really doesn't want to look at an inbox full of increasingly creepy threats. They're at the pre-print stage, and Lily's given up on going back to her own place at night so they can have more time for calibration. What looks right on the screen might not look right once it's printed, and their lives for the past few days have devolved into staring at endless trays of 32-millimetre beef cubes and checking them for myoglobin concentration, colour match in different lighting conditions, fat striation depth, and a whole host of other factors.

There are so many ways for a forgery to go wrong, and only one way it can go right. Helena contemplates this philosophical quandary, and gently thunks her head against the back of her chair.

"Oh my god," Lily exclaims, shoving her chair back. "I can't take this anymore! I'm going out to eat something and then I'm getting some sleep. Do you want anything?" She straps on her bunny-patterned filter mask and her metallic sandals. "I'm gonna eat there, so I might take a while to get back."

"Sesame pancakes, thanks."

As Lily slams the door, Helena puts her iKontakt frames back on. The left lens flashes a stream of notifications—fifty-seven missed calls over the past five hours, all from an unknown number. Just then, another call comes in, and she reflexively taps the side of the frame.

"You haven't been updating me on your progress," Mr Anonymous says.

"I'm very sorry, sir," Helena says flatly, having reached the point of tiredness where she's ceased to feel anything beyond *god I want to sleep*. This sets Mr Anonymous on another rant covering the usual topics—poor work ethic, lack of commitment, informing the Yuen family, prosecution, possible death sentence—and Helena struggles to keep her mouth shut before she says something that she might regret.

"Maybe I should send someone to check on you right now," Mr Anonymous snarls before abruptly hanging up.

Helena blearily types out a draft of the report and makes a note to send a coherent version later in the day, once she gets some sleep and fixes the calibration so she's not telling him entirely bad news. Just as she's about to call Lily and ask her to get some hot soy milk to go with the sesame pancakes, the front door rattles in its frame like someone's trying to punch it down. Judging by the violence, it's probably Lily. Helena trudges over to open it.

It isn't. It's a bulky guy with a flat-top haircut. She stares at him for a moment, then tries to slam the door in his face. He forces the door open and shoves his way inside, grabbing Helena's arm, and all Helena can think is *I can't believe Mr Anonymous spent his money on this.*

He shoves her against the wall, gripping her wrist so hard that it's practically getting dented by his fingertips, and pulls out a switch-blade, pressing it against the knuckle of her index finger. "Well, I'm not allowed to kill you, but I can fuck you up real bad. Don't really need all your fingers, do you, girl?"

She clears her throat, and struggles to keep her voice from shaking. "I need them to type—didn't your boss tell you that?"

"Shut up," Flat-Top says, flicking the switchblade once, then twice, thinking. "Don't need your face to type, do you?"

Just then, Lily steps through the door. Flat-Top can't see her from his angle and Helena jerks her head, desperately communicating that she should stay out. Lily promptly moves closer.

Helena contemplates murder.

Lily edges towards both of them, slides her bracelet past her wrist and onto her knuckles, and makes a gesture at Helena which either means "move to your left" or "I'm imitating a bird, but only with one hand."

"Hey," Lily says loudly. "What's going on here?"

Flat-Top startles, loosening his grip on Helena's arm, and Helena dodges to the left. Just as Lily's fist meets his face in a truly vicious uppercut, Helena seizes the opportunity to kick him soundly in the shins.

His head hits the floor, and it's clear he won't be moving for a while, or ever. Considering Lily's normal level of violence towards the front door, this isn't surprising.

Lily crouches down to check Flat-Top's breathing. "Well, he's still alive. Do you prefer him that way?"

"Do *not* kill him."

"Sure." Lily taps the side of Flat-Top's iKontakt frames with her bracelet and information scrolls across her lenses. "Okay, his name's Nicholas Liu Honghui ... blah blah blah ... hired to scare someone at this address, anonymous client ... I think he's coming to, how do you feel about joint locks?"

It takes a while for Nicholas to stir fully awake. Lily's on his chest, pinning him to the ground, and Helena's holding his switchblade to his throat.

"Okay, Nicholas Liu," Lily says. "We could kill you right now, but that'd make your wife and your ... what is that red thing she's holding ... a baby? Yeah, that'd make your wife and ugly baby quite sad. Now, you're just going to tell your boss that everything went as expected—"

"Tell him that I cried," Helena interrupts. "I was here alone, and I cried because I was so scared."

"Right, got that, Nick? That lady there wept buckets of tears. I don't exist. Everything went well, and you think there's no point in sending anyone else over. If you mess up, we'll visit 42—god, what is this character—42 Something Road and let you know how displeased we are. Now, if you apologise for ruining our morning, I probably won't break your arm."

After seeing a wheezing Nicholas to the exit, Lily closes the door, slides her bracelet back onto her wrist, and shakes her head like a deeply disappointed critic. "What an amateur. Didn't even use burner frames—how the hell did he get hired? And that *haircut*, wow ..."

Helena opts to remain silent. She leans against the wall and stares at the ceiling, hoping that she can wake up from what seems to be a very long nightmare.

"Also, I'm not gonna push it, but I did take out the trash. Can you explain why that crappy hitter decided to pay us a visit?"

"Yeah. Yeah, okay." Helena's stomach growls. "This may take a while. Did you get the food?"

"I got your pancakes, and that soy milk place was open, so I got you some. Nearly threw it at that guy, but I figured we've got a lot of electronics, so ..."

"Thanks," Helena says, taking a sip. It's still hot.

———

Hong Kong Scientific University's bioprinting program is a prestigious pioneer program funded by mainland China, and Hong Kong is the test bed before the widespread rollout. The laboratories are full of state-of-the-art medical-grade printers and bioreactors, and the instructors are all researchers cherry-picked from the best universities.

As the star student of the pioneer batch, Lee Jyun Wai Helen (student number A3007082A) is selected for a special project. She will help the head instructor work on the basic model of a heart for a dextrocardial patient, the instructor will handle the detailed render and the final print, and a skilled surgeon will do the transplant. As the term progresses and the instructor gets busier and busier, Helen's role gradually escalates to doing everything except the final print and the transplant. It's a particularly tricky render since dextrocardial hearts face right instead of left, but her practice prints are cell-level perfect.

Helen hands the render files and her notes on the printing process to the instructor, then her practical exams begin and she forgets all about it.

The Yuen family discovers Madam Yuen's defective heart during their mid-autumn family reunion, halfway through an evening harbour cruise. Madam Yuen doesn't make it back to shore, and instead of a minor footnote in a scientific paper, Helen rapidly becomes front-and-centre in an internal investigation into the patient's death.

Unofficially, the internal investigation discovers that the head instructor's improper calibration of the printer during the final print led to a slight misalignment in the left ventricle, which eventually caused severe ventricular dysfunction and acute graft failure.

Officially, the root cause of the misprint is Lee Jyun Wai Helen's negligence and failure to perform under deadline pressure. Madam Yuen's family threatens to prosecute, but the criminal code doesn't cover failed organ printing. Helen is expelled, and the Hong Kong Scientific University quietly negotiates a settlement with the Yuens.

After deciding to steal the bioprinter and flee, Helen realises that she doesn't have enough money for a full name change and an overseas flight. She settles for a minor name alteration and a flight to Nanjing.

————

"Wow," says Lily. "You know, I'm pretty sure you got ripped off with the name alteration thing, there's no way it costs that much. Also, you used to have pigtails? Seriously?"

Helena snatches her old student ID away from Lily. "Anyway, under the amendments to Article 335, making or supplying substandard printed organs is now an offence punishable by death. The family's itching to prosecute. If we don't do the job right, Mr Anonymous is going to disclose my whereabouts to them."

"Okay, but from what you've told me, this guy is totally not going to let it go even after you're done. At my old job, we got blackmailed like that all the time, which was really kind of irritating. They'd always try to bargain, and after the first job, they'd say stuff like 'if you don't do me this favour I'm going to call the cops and tell them everything' just to weasel out of paying for the next one."

"Wait. Was this at the bakery or the merch stand?"

"Uh." Lily looks a bit sheepish. This is quite unusual, considering that Lily has spent the past four days regaling Helena with tales of the most impressive blood blobs from her period, complete with comparisons to their failed prints. "Are you familiar with the Red Triad? The one in Guangzhou?"

"You mean the *organ printers*?"

"Yeah, them. I kind of might have been working there before the bakery ...?"

"What?"

Lily fiddles with the lacy hem of her skirt. "Well, I mean, the bakery experience seemed more relevant, plus you don't have to list every job you've ever done when you apply for a new one, right?"

"Okay," Helena says, trying not to think too hard about how all the staff at Splendid Beef Enterprises are now prime candidates for the death penalty. "Okay. What exactly did you do there?"

"Ears and stuff, bladders, spare fingers ... you'd be surprised how many people need those. I also did some bone work, but that was mainly for the diehards—most of the people we worked on were pretty okay with titanium substitutes. You know, simple stuff."

"*That's not simple.*"

"Well, it's not like I was printing fancy reversed hearts or anything, and even with the asshole clients it was way easier than baking. Have *you* ever tried to extrude a spun-sugar globe so you could put a bunch of powder-printed magpies inside? And don't get me started on cleaning the nozzles after extrusion, because wow ..."

Helena decides not to question Lily's approach to life because it seems like a certain path to a migraine. "Maybe we should talk about this later."

"Right, you need to send the update! Can I help?"

The eventual message contains very little detail and a lot of pleading. Lily insists on adding typos just to make Helena seem more rattled, and Helena's way too tired to argue. After starting the auto-clean cycle for the printheads, they set an alarm and flop on Helena's mattress for a nap.

As Helena's drifting off, something occurs to her. "Lily? What happened to those people? The ones who tried to blackmail you?"

"Oh," Lily says casually. "I crushed them."

———

The brief specifies that the completed prints need to be loaded into four separate podcars on the morning of 8 August, and provides the delivery code for each. They haven't been able to find anything in Helena's iKontakt archives, so their best bet is finding a darknet user who can do a trace.

Lily's fingers hover over the touchpad. "If we give him the codes, this guy can check the prebooked delivery routes. He seems pretty reliable. Do you want to pay the bounty?"

"Do it," Helena says.

The resultant map file is a mess of meandering lines. They flow across most of Nanjing, criss-crossing each other, but eventually they all terminate at the cargo entrance of the Grand Domaine Luxury Hotel on Jiangdong Middle Road.

"Well, he's probably not a guest who's going to eat two hundred steaks on his own." Lily taps her screen. "Maybe it's for the hotel restaurant?"

Helena pulls up the Grand Domaine's web directory, setting her iKontakt to highlight any mentions of restaurants or food in the descriptions. For some irritating design reason, all the booking details are stored in garish images. She snatches the entire August folder, flipping through them one by one before pausing.

The foreground of the image isn't anything special, just elaborate cursive English stating that Charlie Zhang and Cherry Cai Si Ping will be celebrating their wedding with a ten-course dinner on August 8th at the Royal Ballroom of the Grand Domaine Luxury Hotel.

What catches her eye is the background. It's red with swirls and streaks of yellow-gold. Typical auspicious wedding colours, but displayed in a very familiar pattern.

It's the marbled pattern of T-bone steak.

———

Cherry Cai Si Ping is the daughter of Dominic Cai Yongjing, a specialist in livestock and a new player in Nanjing's agri-food arena. According to Lily's extensive knowledge of farming documentaries, Dominic Cai Yongjing is also "the guy with the eyebrows" and "that really boring guy who keeps talking about nothing."

"Most people have eyebrows," Helena says, loading one of Lily's recommended documentaries. "I don't see ... oh. Wow."

"I *told* you. I mean, I usually like watching stuff about farming, but last year he just started showing up everywhere with his stupid waggly brows! When I watched this with my ex we just made fun of him non-stop."

Helena fast-forwards through the introduction of *Modern Manufacturing: The Vertical Farmer*, which involves the camera panning upwards through hundreds of vertically-stacked wire cages. Dominic Cai talks to the host in English, boasting about how he plans to be a key figure in China's domestic beef industry. He explains his "patented methods" for a couple of minutes, which involves stating and restating that his farm is extremely clean and filled with only the best cattle.

"But what about bovine parasitic cancer?" the host asks. "Isn't the risk greater in such a cramped space? If the government orders a quarantine, your whole farm ..."

"As I've said, our hygiene standards are impeccable, and our stock is pure-bred Hereford!" Cai slaps the flank of a cow through the cage bars, and it moos irritatedly in response. "There is absolutely no way it could happen here!"

Helena does some mental calculations. Aired last year, when the farm recently opened, and that cow looks around six months old ... and now a request for steaks from cows that are sixteen to eighteen months old ...

"So," Lily says, leaning on the back of Helena's chair. "Bovine parasitic cancer?"

"Judging by the timing, it probably hit them last month. It's usually the older cows that get infected first. He'd have killed them to stop the spread ... but if it's the internal strain, the tumours would have made their meat unusable after excision. His first batch of cows was probably meant to be for the wedding dinner. What we're printing is the cover-up."

"But it's not like steak's a standard course in wedding dinners or anything, right? Can't they just change it to roast duck or abalone or something?" Lily looks fairly puzzled, probably because she hasn't been subjected to as many weddings as Helena has.

"Mr Cai's the one bankrolling it, so it's a staging ground for the Cai family to show how much better they are than everyone else. You saw the announcement—he's probably been bragging to all his guests about how they'll be the first to taste beef from his vertical farm. Changing it now would be a real loss of face."

"Okay," Lily says. "I have a bunch of ideas, but first of all, how much do you care about this guy's face?"

Helena thinks back to her inbox full of corpse pictures, the countless sleepless nights she's endured, the sheer terror she felt when she saw Lily step through the door. "Not very much at all."

"All right." Lily smacks her fist into her palm. "Let's give him a nice surprise."

———

The week before the deadline vanishes in a blur of printing, re-rendering, and darknet job requests. Helena's been nothing but polite to Mr Cai ever since the hitter's visit and has even taken to video calls lately, turning on the camera on her end so that Mr Cai can witness her progress. It's always good to build rapport with clients.

"So, sir," Helena moves the camera, slowly panning so it captures the piles and piles of cherry-red steaks, zooming in on the beautiful fat strata which took ages to render. "How does this look? We'll be starting the dry-aging once you approve, and loading it into the podcars first thing tomorrow morning."

"Fairly adequate. I didn't expect much from the likes of you, but this seems satisfactory. Go ahead."

Helena tries her hardest to keep calm. "I'm glad you feel that way, sir. Rest assured you'll be getting your delivery on schedule ... by the way, I don't suppose you could transfer the money on delivery? Printing the bone matter cost a lot more than I thought."

"Of course, of course, once it's delivered and I inspect the marbling. Quality checks, you know?"

Helena adjusts the camera, zooming in on the myoglobin dripping from the juicy steaks, and adopts her most sorrowful tone. "Well, I hate to rush you, but I haven't had much money for food lately ..."

Mr Cai chortles. "Why, that's got to be hard on you! You'll receive the fund transfer sometime this month, and in the meantime, why don't you treat yourself and print up something nice to eat?"

Lily gives Helena a thumbs-up, then resumes crouching under the table and messaging her darknet contacts, careful to stay out of Helena's shot. The call disconnects.

"Let's assume we won't get any further payment. Is everything ready?"

"Yeah," Lily says. "When do we need to drop it off?"

"Let's try for 5:00 a.m. Time to start batch-processing."

Helena sets the enzyme percentages, loads the fluid into the canister, and they both haul the steaks into the dry-ager unit. The machine hums away, spraying fine mists of enzymatic fluid onto the steaks and partially dehydrating them, while Helena and Lily work on assembling the refrigerated delivery boxes. Once everything's neatly packed, they haul the boxes to the nearest podcar station. As Helena slams box after box into the cargo area of the podcars, Lily types the delivery codes into their front panels. The podcars boot up, sealing themselves shut, and zoom off on their circuitous route to the Grand Domaine Luxury Hotel.

They head back to the industrial park. Most of their things have already been shoved into backpacks, and Helena begins breaking the remaining equipment down for transport.

A Sculpere 9410S takes twenty minutes to disassemble if you're doing it for the second time. If someone's there to help you manually eject the cell cartridges, slide the external casing off, and detach the print heads so you can disassemble the power unit, you might be able to get that figure down to ten. They'll buy a new printer once they figure out where to settle down, but this one will do for now.

It's not running away if we're both going somewhere, Helena thinks to herself, and this time it doesn't feel like a lie.

———

There aren't many visitors to Mr Chan's restaurant during breakfast hours, and he's sitting in a corner, reading a book. Helena waves at him.

"Helena!" he booms, surging up to greet her. "Long time no see, and who is this?"

"Oh, we met recently. She's helped me out a lot," Helena says, judiciously avoiding any mention of Lily's name. She holds a finger to her lips, and surprisingly, Mr Chan seems to catch on. Lily waves at Mr Chan, then proceeds to wander around the restaurant, examining their collection of porcelain plates.

"Anyway, since you're my very first client, I thought I'd let you know in person. I'm going travelling with my ... friend and I won't be around for the next few months at least."

"Oh, that's certainly a shame! I was planning a black pepper hotplate beef special next month, but I suppose black pepper hotplate extruded protein will do just fine. When do you think you'll be coming back?"

Helena looks at Mr Chan's guileless face, and thinks, well, her first client deserves a bit more honesty. "Actually, I probably won't be running the business any longer. I haven't decided yet, but I think I'm going to study art. I'm really, really sorry for the inconvenience, Mr Chan."

"No, no, pursuing your dreams, well, that's not something you should be apologising for! I'm just glad you finally found a friend!"

Helena glances over at Lily, who's currently stuffing a container of cellulose toothpicks into the side pocket of her bulging backpack.

"Yeah, I'm glad, too," she says. "I'm sorry, Mr. Chan, but we have a flight to catch in a couple of hours, and the bus is leaving soon ..."

"Nonsense! I'll pay for your taxi fare, and I'll give you something for the road. Airplane food is awful these days!"

Despite repeatedly declining Mr Chan's very generous offers, somehow Helena and Lily end up toting bags and bags of fresh steamed buns to their taxi.

"Oh, did you see the news?" Mr Chan asks. "That vertical farmer's daughter is getting married at some fancy hotel tonight. Quite a pretty girl. Good thing she didn't inherit those eyebrows—"

Lily snorts and accidentally chokes on her steamed bun. Helena claps her on the back.

"—and they're serving steak at the banquet, straight from his farm! Now, don't get me wrong, Helena, you're talented at what you do—but a good old-fashioned slab of *real* meat, now, that's the ticket!"

"Yes," Helena says. "It certainly is."

———

All known forgeries are failures, but sometimes that's on purpose. Sometimes a forger decides to get revenge by planting obvious flaws in their work, then waiting for them to be revealed, making a fool of everyone who initially claimed the work was authentic. These flaws can take many forms—deliberate anachronisms, misspelled signatures, rude messages hidden beneath thick coats of paint—or a picture of a happy cow, surrounded by little hearts, etched into the T-bone of two hundred perfectly-printed steaks.

While the known forgers are the famous ones, the *best* forgers are the ones that don't get caught—the old woman selling her deceased husband's collection to an avaricious art collector, the harried-looking mother handing the cashier a battered 50-yuan note, or the two women at the airport, laughing as they collect their luggage, disappearing into the crowd.

ACCURSED LINEAGE BY DAÍNA CHAVIANO

Translated from Spanish by Matthew D. Goodwin

Daína Chaviano is one of the most highly-regarded Spanish-language authors of speculative fiction.
Originally from Cuba, she now lives in the United States. Among her many honours is Spain's prestigious
Azorín Prize, and her novel *The Island of Eternal Love* is considered the most-translated Cuban novel of
all time.

———

It's close to midnight now and the noises will soon begin. From here I can observe everything: each movement inside the house, each whisper, each secret visitor. As always, I will be in my position until sunrise. And while the neighborhood sleeps, two households will remain awake: mine and *that one*.

We light the house up only slightly, as they do, to not draw attention. My parents and siblings move with stealth, so no noise slips out. Every so often, Mama or Papa put down what they're doing to look around a bit. My siblings also leave their games to see what they can make out through the windows. Only I remain steady, not diverging one iota from what I consider to be my primary job: to discover what is happening in that house.

I don't know why I do it. I don't know where this obsession with perpetual surveillance comes from. It's a reflex, almost a sickness; something that I learned from the grown-ups. Papa and Mama set the example, although without much conviction. They say that it's their obligation. Nevertheless, when my siblings ask about the origin of the vigil, no one can give a coherent answer. I don't get worked up about those things. I limit myself to completing my duties.

It has just turned twelve, and I stand on my tiptoes on the edge of the roof to see better. Now the commotion will start up. No doubt about it. They have already turned a light on, on the top floor. It's the old lady. I can see her through a broken window. She moves through her room, filled with junk, and lights up a candle. She bends down next to what seems to be a trunk, tries to separate it from the wall, but can't succeed in moving it. Then she leaves the candleholder on the floor and pushes with all her might until it detaches from the corner. She leans over it, as if she were going to take out something ... At that precise moment someone bumps into me and I almost lose my balance. It's my little brother.

"What are you doing here, idiot?" I reproach in a whisper. "You scared me half to death."

"I came to play," he responds without noting my anger and strews some bones on the eaves.

"And since when do you play on the roof?"

"It's hot in there."

He takes two finger bones and starts to hit them against each other as if they were tiny swords. I look at the house out of the corner of my eye, but the old lady has already disappeared with the candle and everything. I'm left not knowing what she was trying to take out of that corner.

"And those?" I ask without much interest because I just now make out two figures that are quickly crossing the entrance and are immediately led into the interior of the house by someone who's opened the door for them. "Are they new?"

My brother looks at me a moment, uncomprehending.

"Oh! These? ... They're from the Rizo baby."

"The one that they buried last week?"

"No. That was the grandson of Mrs. Cándida. This is a much older baby."

Slow music rises and falls in pitch until it's lost in a murmur: someone is operating the radio in the house next door. For some reason, I know that it is prohibited to listen to the voices and news that come from afar. I discern the eagerness of the listener to evade the interference which they use to jam any outside signal. We are isolated. Not only us, them as well ...

"Come on, coward!" says my brother, projecting his voice, making the bones collide in sword fight. "Don't run away. Face my fury!"

"Get out of here." I push him a little to get my place back. "If you don't get down right now, I'll tell Papa to not raise you up again."

He shrugs his shoulders.

"I don't have to go to the charnel house to get toys now. Mami always ..."

"If you don't go now, I'll drop you on your head. Don't you see that I'm busy?"

The front door of the house opens slowly. A man sticks his head out to inspect the surroundings. He goes back inside. Then he comes out again. He's carrying a knife in his hand. He stealthily approaches a corner of the garden and starts to dig a hole, aided by that tool. He rapidly buries a medium-sized packet that he has taken out of his clothes. In the silence of the morning, I hear him mumbling:

"I won't be able to use it, but neither will they."

He finishes his work and goes inside.

My brother shoves me to get more space.

"Stupid idiot!" I turn towards him, coiled and ready.

I jerk him by the neck and squeeze as hard as I can until he weakens from lack of air. He seems to have lost consciousness. Then my eyes go back to the house and by looking through the window on the top floor, I come across a rare spectacle: the diffuse light falls on a bed where a couple is getting undressed. I'm astonished. I let my brother go, and three seconds later, I hear the dull thud from a body that has fallen on the pavement many meters below. I hardly pay attention to the flattened body because I spy another silhouette that leaves the house and crosses the garden. At that moment, an enormous cloud covers the disc of the moon and I'm left without knowing if it's a man or a woman who is going down the walkway with a bundle in arm.

A gong from far away brings me back to reality. It's my mother calling us to dinner. I look for a second at the big house wrapped in darkness and reluctantly detach from the eaves.

When I come into the dining room, everyone is already seated at the table. Mama serves soup, red and thick like beet juice. I try a spoonful and almost burn my lips.

"It's boiling!" I protest.

"Be careful with the tablecloth," she warns me. "You know how much that stains."

"I don't like old blood!" one of my siblings complains.

"Well, you'll have to get used to it. Things are getting more difficult each day and I can't get it fresh like I could before."

"Where did you get it from?" asks my father, devouring a bit of ear.

"Gertrudis sold it to me overpriced. I've had it in the freezer from six months ago because little Luis ..." She looks around— "Where is Junior?"

We all stop eating and fix upon my brother's empty seat.

Then I remember.

"I think that ..." A knot forms in my throat.

I'm terrified of the punishment.

All eyes turn to me in silence, waiting for an explanation. I decide to tell everything: my determined vigilance over the mansion, the suspicious behavior of the old lady, the secret burial of treasure, my brother's sudden interruption and our struggle on the roof, the couple in the room, the sound of a body falling on the cement, the mysterious person leaving the house ... I prepare for the worst.

"And you couldn't see what the guy was carrying?" Mother asks.

"I don't even know if it was a man: it was really dark."

"Too bad!"

They eat in silence.

"So, what do we do about Junior?" says my father, leaving blood-stains on his napkin.

"Let's make the best of it," Mama decides. "How does brain stew sound for tomorrow?"

We scream enthusiastically.

Mama stands up and goes in search of dessert, but I can't wait. I go up to the balcony and climb once again onto the roof. The wind makes the loose floorboards of the attic creak. From there I hear the muffled uproar of my siblings who flood the dawn with howls, ignoring the oft-repeated prohibition.

In front of me, in the other house, a window opens. I attentively observe the faces that emerge: the old lady with the trunk and an unknown youth. They look with fear and concern towards our house.

"Be gone!'" —I hear the old lady say, who then crosses herself three times in a row. "The agitated spirits again."

"I'm calling the police."

"Yeah? And what are you going to tell them?" scolds the old lady, who now takes on the voice of the youth: "*Listen, in the house next door there was a massacre many many years ago and now the dead walk about howling at all hours. *—That's what you're going to say? Well, I suggest that you leave them to their unrest. Anyway, that's the only thing the dead can do when they've been finished off."

Both women cross themselves again. They half-close the blinds after them, and I'm left open-mouthed, completely confused by what I just heard. What are they talking about? None of us have died ... except Junior, who I let fall by accident, the fault of an unfortunate mistake. And if one can die, it's because one is not dead. Or can the dead die again?

I try to see what's going on behind the curtains, but I can't stay. The light of the sun announces itself in a hazy clarity over the roofs of the city.

I should return to my refuge. I'll sleep all day until night falls, and when the stars begin to come out, I'll unfold my membranous wings and fly up to my usual position.

———

*Solavaya!

NKÁSHT ÍÍ BY DARCIE LITTLE BADGER

Darcie Little Badger is a Lipan Apache scientist and writer, with a PhD in Oceanography and short stories published *in Light*speed, *Strange Horiz*ons, and many other*s*.

———

Great-Grandmother taught me everything she knew about death before it took her.

Never sleep under a juniper tree. They grow between this world and the place below.

Bury the dead properly, lest their ghosts return.

A ghost is a terrible thing.

Someday, we will all be terrible things.

Great-Grandmother, you were right.

———

Annie designed our pink-paint-on-cardboard sign: TELL US YOUR PROBLEMS TELL US YOUR STORIES TELL US ANYTHING. WE ♥ 2 LISTEN. We never offered counsel or passed judgment. Sometimes, people just need a willing ear. After all, that's how Annie and I became friends. Beginning in high school, she listened to my troubles, and I returned the favor. Annie's secrets, though bizarre, were easier to swallow after we spent time together, which is how she convinced me to busk for karma. The act would bring us good fortune, she promised. For better or worse, I believed her.

That day, Annie and I camped near a fountain shaped like Maria de Soto, the city founder. Water bubbled from her outstretched marble hands. The bowls she normally carried (they represented "cups running over," according to a copper plaque) had been removed for cleaning. "Stigmata," I commented, and Annie laughed. It was a pleasant distraction from my phone; Mom had been texting all morning, breaking our one-year silent spell, and every message felt like a needle in my chest.

As if drawn to cheer, a scruffy, thirty-something man limped toward the fountain. He wore a sweat-stained white shirt and wrinkled black pants; his patent leather oxfords needed polish.

"Morning," I said. Never *good* morning, because it often wasn't.

He knelt on the grass and looked from Annie to me, back and forth, like a tennis spectator. To be fair, we made a strange pair. Annie, a stout, tall Apache woman, had severely thick eyebrows and lips that turned down, even when she smiled. She also shaved her head daily, as if preparing for war. Her features contrasted with my girlish face and willowy frame. Primary school bullies called me "Pocahontas," so it goes without saying that I never braided my hair. However, I kept it long to protect my ears and back from the sun.

"You listen?" the man asked. His hoarse voice smelled sour.

"Yessir," Annie said. "We do."

"My daughter died."

Annie's cheerful expression withered.

"Murdered," he continued. "Nobody believes me. They think ... but I didn't. My Melanie survived the accident. Car accident." He spoke in a breathless staccato. "During vacation in central Texas. Five months ago. Melanie sat in her car seat. My wife, Rita, slept. We entered Willowbee, small town, before eleven. A deer ran onto the street. No time to brake, so I panicked and swerved. The car hit a tree. Rita never slept with a belt."

He uttered a dry sob that sounded like "broken neck." Annie nodded sympathetically.

"After the collision, Melanie cried. She'd survived. But I could not reach her from the driver seat. I crawled outside, circled the car. Had two broken legs but managed. And Christ. Christ. When I opened the back door, an owl-woman was *inside the car*. She held Melanie."

"Owl-woman?" I asked. "What is ..." Annie made a shushing noise.

"She had owl eyes," he said. "Big, yellow circles with black pits. But otherwise, the woman—or monster, or ... whatever—looked like Rita. Just younger and taller. Taller than me, even." The man, who wasn't shorter than six feet, made another raspy sound before continuing. "I begged her to return Melanie, but she carried my daughter away. Outside, around the tree, across Heron Bridge. Into darkness. Impossible to chase with broken legs, though I tried. I tried. The paramedics found me thirty feet from the car. They found Melanie in the river. Not a scratch on her body. She'd drowned. But everybody—*everybody*—believes the accident threw her outside. Ridiculous. I strapped her in a car seat. Will there ever be justice for my girls?"

"Was it a juniper tree?" Annie asked.

Color drained from his ruddy cheeks. "Yes." He grasped her shoulder. "What does it mean?"

"Careful," I warned, touching the Mace hidden in my side pocket. We'd so far avoided most dangers that plague lost young things, but worry dominated my thoughts, especially after spending weeks inundated in confessed sins and tragedies.

"It's all right, Josie," Annie said. "There are legends ..."

"What legends?" the man asked. Then he folded ten dollars in my empty coffee cup, but Annie shook her head. "We're only paid in karma," she explained, because the truth beggared belief. Even I didn't understand the preternatural laws we observed.

"What legends?" he repeated.

"The kind my great-grandmother knew," she said. "Juniper trees often grow along passageways between this world and the spirit realm, like ... Sir?"

"Hang on. I have something for you." With that, he stood and limped away.

"Is this guy serious?" I asked.

"Could be. Ghosts are terrible things."

"Ghosts? Huh, maybe he met La Llorona," I said. "¿Dónde están mis hijos?"

"Stop, Josie. You can be irreverent about anything but this."

"That actually wasn't a joke. It's possible, right?"

Annie considered my question for a couple minutes, and then she nodded. "Mmhm. Possible. Oh, look! He's coming back." Sure enough, the man had returned. He thrust a picture at us. It depicted a baby—Melanie?—with bright blue eyes and a gummy smile. Somebody—Rita?—cradled her. The adult's torso and left hand were visible; she had long pink nails and wore a gold cross around her neck.

"Sir, we're only here to listen, understand?"

"No, and that's the problem. I don't understand. But I *want* to understand. What happened that night?"

Annie tapped my shoulder until I turned and caught her eye. "Let's go to Willowbee," she said.

"You're kidding."

"Please? It'll just take a couple days. Anyway, I have a feeling. We need to follow through."

My cell phone beeped again.

Well, it's not like we had anything better to do.

"Meet us here next week, same time," I said. "Keep in mind that we can't promise answers."

"That's fine," the mourning father said. "Just promise that you'll try."

He left; he left the photograph behind; he left me in a lurch. What did Annie expect to find in Willowbee?

"We'll need travel money," she said. "C'mon." I folded the sign while Annie tucked the photograph in her messenger bag. A vertical crease between her eyebrows spoke to more worries than usual.

After thanking Maria de Soto for her shade, we crossed sunbaked streets. At Markov Deli, I paused and asked, "Here?"

Annie shook her head. We continued wandering.

Outside a gas station, the ritual repeated. "Here?" No.

One hour later, the Asian grocery store on Vega Street broke our unlucky streak. "Here?" Annie nodded. As we entered the store, a wind chime over the door tolled sweetly. It rang again when we exited with chicken dumplings, chrysanthemum tea, and the five hundred dollars Annie had won from a scratch-off lotto game called "Pushing Your Luck."

———

When a black haze coalesced over our hometown, and only I noticed, Josie convinced me to leave. I wonder if it's still there, haunting that lonely place. It resembled the cloud that followed Great-Grandmother before she died.

————

The trip to Willowbee took one day by bus: nine hours riding and two hours waiting at a way station in Dallas. Annie and I shared a duffel bag, and we sat behind a man who dozed in his bulky winter jacket, although it was late summer.

At sunset, Annie fell asleep with her cheek against the window-pane. Every vibration that shook the bus rapped her temple against the glass. That couldn't be comfortable.

I removed a T-shirt from the duffel bag and tucked it behind her head. She muttered "thanks" between dreams. I'd offer my shoulder instead, but it was too low. Annie's height, five foot ten, seemed remarkable, considering her barely-nourished past.

As a child, she had had a dozen allergies, and if you think it's hard funding a balanced meal with food stamps, try adding dietary restrictions to the mix. At least food malaise brought us together. We met during the free breakfast program in middle school. Instead of milk, Annie and I drank vanilla soy from paper cartons. "Are you lactose intolerant, too, or vegan?" I'd asked.

Her response was, "What's a vegan?"

We became school chums, a relationship that only exists between classes. At the time, my *best* friends all played basketball. The athletic sisterhood had been crafted by Coach Gomez-Frances, who believed that trust and companionship won games. She reinforced team cama-raderie with extracurricular events like laser tag, pizza parties, and WNBA group outings. She oversaw trust-building exercises during morning practices. She promised that our loyalty would outlast our boyfriends.

Coach Gomez-Frances had been right, but that's only because I never found a boyfriend. Yes, the team's bond helped us defeat other sisterhoods, girls from foreign school districts who wore strange-colored jerseys and worshiped lesser mascots. But without basketball, our little clique dissolved.

For me, Annie was all that lasted past high school. I even lost my family.

The trouble at home started when Mom met good ol' boy Regis Miller at a singles mixer. When he became Stepfather Regis, he parked a new Corvette on the street, hung a forty-six-inch TV on the wall, and bought Mom a cubic zirconia tennis bracelet. Of course, the car didn't last a week before somebody broke its window to steal ten dollars from the glove compartment, so we had to purchase a new home, too, one in a better neighborhood, one with a garage. He told Mom, "Don't worry about money. Little Miss should feel safe."

That's what he always called me: Little Miss. Over time, the name became more sarcastic than affectionate. His father-knows-best personality grated against mine, and that brought out my gloves, which brought out his. Almost anything could trigger a fight between us. Unwashed dishes, crumbs on the furniture, music, television, politics, current events, potato-potahto. I once threw a remote control at his TV and broke the screen. He retaliated by "losing" my cell phone down a drainage grate.

Mom seemed oblivious to our fights, or perhaps she was cowed by them. Either way, her apathy hurt more than any screaming match with Regis. Finally, I cornered her in the pantry and said, "Do something. It's him or me. *Choose.*" She shook her head and tried to walk away, but I would not move from the pantry doorway.

"Just do something," I begged.

And then, as asked, she did something. Mom slapped me, quick as a snake bites. Her star-cut diamond engagement ring bruised my cheek.

Later that night, I filled a backpack with clothes and a toothbrush, moved by a half-baked plan to call a friend and ask, "Will you take me in?" That's when I noticed Annie standing on the sidewalk outside my window. The streetlight at her back cast a lanky shadow across the yard. As she waved, her shadow swiped at me.

I called, "What are you doing here?"

She approached my open window and peered at the cluttered bedroom beyond, at the backpack on my bed, and at my red, wet eyes. "Hm?" Annie asked. "Oh, hi, Josie. I didn't know you lived in this neighborhood. Can I spend the night?"

I invited her inside by opening the window and raising its mesh screen. She climbed over the ledge easily.

"Are you in trouble?" I asked.

She shook her head. "Not really. My great-grandmother died."

"*Great*-grandmother?"

"Yeah."

"Sorry. That's rough. You can stay, but won't somebody worry? It's late."

"I'm eighteen," she said. "My parents don't care where I go or what I do if I keep the Ten Commandments."

"No murdering, no stealing, no ... whatever the rest are?"

"No coveting thy neighbor's wife." I didn't get the joke back then, before we shared secrets like real friends. "Well. Mom and Dad don't really like me. Maybe they love me, but they don't like me. You know?"

Somewhere in the house, a door slammed in implicit agreement. We hung out a lot more after that.

Now, on the last bus to Willowbee, Annie muttered in her sleep, "So bright."

There was a thud, and the bus lurched as it hit a doe. The driver cursed but continued driving.

"Uh?" Annie asked. She stretched and yawned. "What happened?"

"We're here."

A green sign that read WILLOWBEE NEXT EXIT shone in the blinding headlights. Minutes later, the bus pulled into an open-air station. Two floodlights and a neon vending machine lit the square concrete parking lot.

"You have a good feeling about this, right?" I asked.

"I have a feeling."

"A good feeling?"

"A feeling."

Wish I'd known that before we left.

Annie grabbed the duffel bag and followed me outside. She waved at a taxi idling near the street. The driver nodded.

"It'll only take a couple days, Josie, promise," she said.

"What can we learn in two days?" I asked.

"Lots." To the driver, she added, "Take us to a cheap hotel, please."

"There's only one hotel in Willowbee," he explained. "It's a Best

Western. The Millers run a bed and breakfast on their ranch if you prefer."

"The hotel will be fine," I said. "Thanks."

In the Best Western, as I brewed decaf coffee, Annie lay on the single bed in her tennis shoes, ratty jeans, and sweater. "Heron Bridge is five miles away," she said. "But before we visit the accident site, let's find Willowbee's cemetery."

"What for? Rita and Melanie weren't locals, remember? They'd been vacationing."

"I'm not interested in their graves. We need to learn how well this town treats its dead."

"You think they've angered spirits with disrespectful burials?" Though I tried to be open-minded, the world would flood with violent ghosts if souls could wreak havoc for unmarked graves or other ceremonial slights.

She smiled enigmatically. "No."

———

This life is nothing but a great story with no end. Though I don't know who or what the storyteller may be, sometimes I hear its voice. When I left home to escape the haze, that strange voice was screaming. Now, it speaks in hushed murmurs, like campers sharing ghost stories around a fire. I am afraid.

———

In the morning, Annie and I picked over the breakfast buffet and enjoyed weak coffee. Then, she plied the front desk for directions to their cemetery while I snuck muffins, potatoes, and sausage links back to our room.

"It'll be a long walk," Annie said once we regrouped outside.

"There's nothing better to do in this Podunk." In daylight, I realized that Willowbee was more roads, grazing land, and wilderness than people or buildings. We traveled down a two-lane road, sweating when the shady juniper woodland around our hotel thinned into grassland. Every few minutes, a truck or car passed, and some honked in greeting. One white pickup slowed to a crawl, and the driver lowered his window. Visor-style sunglasses were sandwiched between sandy

hair and a smiling mouth. Their blue-silver glass reflected the wildflowers growing directly behind me. "You ladies need a ride?" he
asked. Annie's eyes widened, as if she could see the skeleton under his
skin. "No thanks," I said.

"It's not inconvenient. Where are you going?"

"Still no." Mace would be a feeble deterrent if he had a gun, but I
slipped a hand into my pocket anyway. "Not interested."

"People drive like maniacs," he warned. "It's dangerous along
the road."

"I won't say it again: no."

Finally, Mr. Concerned Citizen zipped away with a mechanical
rumble that drowned his parting words. The pickup tailpipe expelled
black smoke.

"Did you see your face reflected in his sunglasses?" Annie asked.

"Not that I recall."

"Huh. Me neither. At least he's gone."

One hour later, we reached Willowbee's heart. To the east: a hardware store, grocery stop, and antique warehouse with rag dolls in its
windows. To the west: a post office, Baptist church, and diner. The
cemetery was beyond these shops, due west, surrounded by a black
wrought-iron fence with ornate swirls and metal roses sandwiched
between its bars. The plot resembled a green velvet patch on a
yellowing cotton quilt. Professional golf courses didn't have lusher
grass.

A freckled, brunet teenager arranged flowers before each head-
stone. He was dressed to the nines in a black formal suit, wide-
brimmed cowboy hat, and turquoise bolo tie.

"They're afraid," Annie said.

"How d'you figure?"

"This town works hard to placate their dead."

"Maybe they're just respectful."

"Maybe," she agreed.

"Hey, kid!" I called. "Why do what you do?"

The grave keeper approached us with measured steps. "It's my
job," he said. "Beats working at McDonald's, right? Here." He passed
two bright yellow buttercups over the fence. Annie took them both
and tucked one behind my ear.

"Thanks," she murmured.

"No problem. Have a nice day, ladies."

"I've seen enough," Annie decided. "Let's visit the bridge."

"Lunch first. Ghosts may not need to eat, but we do."

We ordered burgers and fries at the diner before resuming our investigation. They were greasy, salty, cheap, and perfect. By 1:00 p.m., the sun had drooped but felt no less hot. Our take-out slushies melted rapidly and filled their Styrofoam cups with lukewarm syrup long before we reached Heron Bridge. It was just concrete and steel, not the creaking, shadowy bridge-of-the-damned I'd expected. Juniper trees grew along the river, their branches interlocked like teeth in a zipper.

"Are you sure this is the right bridge?" I asked because none of the trees seemed damaged by a high-speed collision, and there weren't any stumps in sight. "Annie? Annie!"

She'd climbed down to the muddy boundary between land and water, where an exposed tangle of roots spilled into the river. I pressed through itchy weeds to reach my friend, who, I should note, couldn't swim. Annie sank like a rock in water, as if something unusually heavy lived under her skin.

"Here," she said. "Look here."

"Look for what? Back off! I'll handle this."

Crawling on her hands and knees for balance, she ascended the steep bank and sat against a tree. Gray-brown mud speckled her jeans and arms up to the elbows.

"What am I looking for?" I called, while digging around black roots. Should they be so dark, like something charred?

"I don't know. A clue?"

Sometimes, her thoughts were awfully unhelpful.

My fingers curled around a lump in the ground: Rita's gold cross. "This may be it, Annie!"

I scrambled up the steep bank and held out the necklace. Annie took one look at the cross and said, "Rita went into the river. This confirms it."

"But I thought she died in the car. Maybe that necklace flew off during the crash?"

"I think not. Her ghost drowned Melanie."

"That's ..."

We heard a mechanical rumble. I pulled Annie behind a tree as a familiar white pickup truck screeched across the bridge, swerved, passed through the guardrails, and plunged into the water. The impact didn't cause a single ripple. In fact, there wasn't any trace of man or machine left.

"What the hell was that?" I asked.

"The fabric between Here and Below is threadbare in Willowbee," Annie said calmly, as if ghost trucks were a commonplace thing. "Especially where we stand."

"Can we please leave now? Rita's ghost drowned baby Melanie. Mystery solved."

"Not yet. The father needs why, not how. He wants to understand."

I shrugged. Who really understood matters beyond the here and now? "Obviously, there's something weird about Willowbee, especially those juniper trees. Rita came back because she died on Heron Bridge. It's a fatal wrong place, wrong time situation. Right?"

"Why did she kill Melanie? There must be a motive. Vengeance?"

We couldn't stay there forever, asking questions without answers. "Only Rita knows," I said, "but she's gone somewhere we can't follow."

"Hm. Let's speak to that cemetery kid tomorrow morning. Maybe he's privy to rumors."

"Fine. We have to be quick, though. Our bus leaves at 11:00 a.m. and I don't want to miss it."

I couldn't think of resting when we returned to the hotel. After dark, with its baby-killing ghosts and doomed pickup truck drivers, Willowbee seemed unbearably creepy. As Annie slept, at midnight I searched the room for unwanted visitors, peeking under the bed, in the closet, and behind the shower curtain. Nothing. Yet.

Unfortunately, it's hard to resist a soft mattress after sleeping on a yoga mat for one restless year. I dozed off during a retro sitcom and woke to static on the TV and the sound of running water. The bathroom door was closed; Annie must be bathing, I thought, until I noticed her curled under the comforter. She didn't stir when I whispered, "Hey." In fact, Annie didn't move at all. She wasn't breathing anymore.

The bathroom door swung open.

———

Josie, when the haze descended, I warned my parents that it portended disaster. They just hung their heads and called me "unwell." They once called Great-Grandmother "unwell," too, and sent her to a nursing home across town. Nursing homes won't take healthy young women, but there are other places, facilities named after saints. That's where Mom and Dad wanted me to go after high school, but I refused. No, I'm not sick. No, I'm not a sinner. Yes, I'm visiting Josie again, but no, we aren't sweethearts. She doesn't like anybody that way. Don't look so relieved. We're still close. She accepts my weird baggage, and that's more than you've ever done. Josie is my sister.

Sister, that night you said, "If bad things are coming, let's run away."

What about your education, Josie? The fall semester classes? The community college basketball team? That part-time job at Applebee's? Your mother?

"I can't afford more school," you said. "Regis taught me one big life lesson: debt will kick your ass."

I should have insisted, "Leave the city if you can. Escape the haze. But don't follow me." Josie, I'm sorry.

As I doze, shadows thicken and spread like smoke. The floral comforter becomes wildflowers colored like pieces of sunset. Great-Grandmother, you warned me: never sleep beneath a juniper tree. But I'm surrounded by them here, and there's death on my mind. My spirit leaks from its bone cage and falls to the place below.

Ahead, Rita cradles Melanie.

"Why did you kill your daughter?" I ask.

"Love." She rocks the quiet baby. "Loneliness. It's autonomous. Understand?"

"No."

"I never wanted to kill my child, just like the heart doesn't want to beat. It. Happens. Automatically." She laughs. "Who do you love?"

I grab Melanie and run, run, run until Rita's screams become whispers.

———

Annie's ghost (or was it something stranger?) sat on the edge of the full tub. Her eyes were round and yellow. Their black pupils expanded; I could not look away from the pits, as if my soul had been drawn into the vacuum beyond.

"We'll never be happy here," she said.

I screamed as she dragged me to the water. I screamed for her, not myself. Did anybody hear me? Did anybody care?

"I came back for you."

Annie pushed me into the tub and held my body underwater. Nails, sharp like talons, so unlike her typical ragged, worry-chewed stubs, dug into my shoulders. I kicked and thrashed, my lips pinched to seal out bathwater.

"No more running," she promised.

It wasn't fair.

"Life is not fair, but you've known that since the day we met."

I was afraid.

"Aren't you always?"

I'd die in this place. When the news trickled back to my mother, she'd wring her hands and pity the black sheep whose sins drove her to suicide. But then, she'd move on, because Mom was expecting a new daughter soon to complete the picket-fence family she made with Regis, the one that didn't include me. It wasn't fair.

———

Though I outran the mother's screams, her question hounds every step: who do you love?

Oh, Josie. I must reach you before my ghost does. I must find the path home. In this place without time, thoughts unfurl into infinity. Within one step, I relive our short life together. Within two steps, I am lost. A juniper forest sprouts, and figures emerge from the wizened trunks and strong branches. The spirits surround me. Are you lost, they must wonder. Are you one of us? They paw at Melanie, who wails in my arms.

A wrinkled brown hand parts the crowd. It points. "Go that way," Great-Grandmother says. "And don't return until you're ready to stay."

"Thank you, Gramma. Nkásht íí. I love you."

I dash through trees and spirits until the wildflowers underfoot transform into patterns on a cheap hotel comforter.

———

The terrible thing vanished a second before Annie (the flesh and blood Annie with brown eyes and stubby nails who'd never hold me underwater until my lungs burned) called, "Josie!" I lurched from the bathtub and collapsed facedown on wet linoleum. My body shuddered with coughs as it expelled water. Some had filled my nose during the struggle.

A bout of wooziness swelled. Darkness. Ache. I felt a hand over my heart. Her hand, my heart.

Oh, no. She was trying to resuscitate me. That could only end in broken ribs.

"Stop, Annie!" She sobbed with either relief or shame and begged for forgiveness, asked me to say something, anything, but I was too consumed by guilt for the rage that almost followed me into the grave and out again. I had to make peace somehow.

"Let's go home, Annie."

She helped me stand, her face still creased with concern, and said, "The bus won't come until morning."

"I mean real home."

"You mean ... but what about the darkness?"

"We'll chase it away. We have to. Annie, my mom is having a ..."

An infant's banshee wail interrupted the conversation. We scrambled from the bathroom. Melanie lay on a flat pillow, keening for comfort. She sounded so miserable, pity overcame fear, and I cradled her until she calmed and looked up at the bright light fixture embedded overhead.

Was this a miracle? Yes. It must be.

I could see my face reflected in Melanie's wide blue eyes.

GHOSTALKER BY T.L. HUCHU

Zimbabwean author T.L. Huchu is the author of numerous short stories published in *Interzone*, *Ellery Queen's Mystery Magazine,* and elsewhere. As Tendai Huchu, he is the author of two novels, including the very successful *The Hairdresser of Harare*, and was shortlisted for the prestigious Caine Prize for African fiction.

Bindura sucks! The whole town's essentially one main road, a few side streets, and not a whole lot else. I spend half my pocket money jamming *Space Invaders* on the retro at the Total Service Station. I probably get high off the petrol fumes as I whoop every boy's ass on the game and so they let me jam with no wahala. Well, there used to be hustle, until someone tried to touch up my tits.

They found his balls dangling from a msasa tree half a mile away. Let's just say, the boys keep a respectful distance now.

I'm not really supposed to use my powers for my own benefit. To be fair, most of the time I'm more Peter Parker than Tony Stark, still, I Bruce Banner out sometimes. My dad went all Sauron and left us, so I live with my mum and little sis in Chiwaridzo Township.

Sis and I go to work every day, Sunday to Sunday. All Mum does is veg out on the couch and watch Mexican soaps and Nollywood dramas. No wonder Dad left. I don't care anyway. Not really, I've got too much stuff to do. Knapf! I'm dead. I have to stop thinking about all this kak in the middle of the game.

I buy a freezit and am walking away from the petrol station when my first client of the day flashes in the corner of my eye. It's 2:00 p.m., the sun's blazing, and this ghost is out in the shade of the acacia outside Spar. Must be really desperate. Deados avoid coming out in the day if they can help it. They're all white and stuff, so I reckon they don't have sunscreen in the great beyond. My client beckons with her pale hand. People walk past her without seeing anything.

"Alright, alright, I'm coming already!" I shout out, waiting for a car to pass before I cross the road. She looks impatient, but I'm not getting run over just to join her sorry ass.

She's naked, of course. Ghosts are like the ultimate naturalists. Used to freak me out when I was younger, but you get used to it. I hop onto the pavement and say hello.

She replies with something like, "Booga-wooga-wooga," or some such jazz. It's all right, they get a bit looney in the afterlife—the ones that get left behind, that is. You would, too, if you had to wander about the earth butt naked like that.

I say, "Is there anything I can help you with?"

"Wooga-wooga-wooga."

Lord, give me strength. I inhale, hold my breath for a few seconds, and blow on her face. She goes fuzzy for a bit, then comes back in focus.

"Okay, I can deliver a message from you to anyone you want within the town limits," I say. Rules and regulations. "There is a three-tier charge for this service banded in a low flat fee, a middle flat fee, and a high flat fee, plus twenty percent VAT. The band you fall into depends on the length, complexity and content of the message. If you cannot pay the bill, the fee will be reverse-charged to the recipient with a ten-dollar surplus. Please note: this service does not allow vulgar, obscene, criminal, or otherwise objectionable messages, but a fee may still be incurred if we decide to pass on a redacted version of the message. Do you understand?"

"Booga."

"I'll take that as a yes."

Okay, now the kauderwelsch's out of the way, I can go about helping this goon. I fish out my 22-key mini-mbira from my backpack. My sekuru made it; that was his thing, making instruments, right up until he died. That's what my dad does, too, the douchebag. My mbira's small, but the mubvamaropa wood used to make the sound-board is pretty heavy, and then you add on the metal keys and you have quite a bit of heft. I try to stand out of the stream of people walking past before I jam. I'm hoping this doesn't take too long because I hate crowds gathering around when I'm in the middle of working. It's so knapf. Like, you think I'm a fucking street musician? Get a radio.

I pull a riff from Chiwoniso's melody "Mai." She's, without a doubt, my favourite mbira player ever. I play it soft, soothing like the leaves swaying in the tree above us. I can feel Chiwoniso in my thumbs as they dance from key to key, callus striking the hard iron underneath. Ka-ra-ka-kata, ka-ra-ka-kata, ka-ra-ka-kata. And I sing:

Zita renyu,
Zita rake,
Shoko renyu,
Zviri mumoyo menyu,
Taurirai mwana wenyu,
Taurai zvenyu.

Over and over, until at last her face lights up and she understands my voice. Tell me your name. Tell me his name. Your will. The deepest part of your heart. I am your child.

And she tells me she is Cecilia Mukanya. She died six months ago. I have to be very careful and ask her today's date. That's because ghosts travel through time as well, so sometimes you get future ghosts coming back all confused and the stuff they tell you doesn't make any sense because it hasn't happened yet, or the people concerned haven't even been born. Worst blunder I ever made was telling a guy a message from his future ghost, like, I told him how and when he was going to die, stuff like that. Major, major violation. If he'd reported me, I'd have had my licence revoked. Most important thing when dealing with future ghosts is to tell them to return to their own time-line right away. Don't get sucked in, don't give them the time of day, otherwise it gets real messy.

Cecilia tells me her husband remarried pronto-quick, like, the month after her funeral. (If you've been in this game as long as I have, you'll know men are bastards like that). The new wife is abusing the kids. Cecilia wants it to stop. Or else.

I play my mbira around her sweet voice, each note I strike catches a tear on her face which I can't dry. And I find I'm crying with her like a fool in the street. I promise to deliver the message right away. She thanks me by blowing away with the summer breeze. *Shhh.*

My mum used to be in this business. She was the best ghostalker in all of Mashonaland Central. Even got a certificate from the governor's office in '96. But after a while she just burnt out and never got her spark back. Apparently, the same thing that happens to shrinks. One day, she just didn't have any light in her eyes.

You gotta be careful when you deal with the dead. They've got a lot of crazy kak going on, so it's important to be firm, set boundaries for them. Like, I have this one stalker ghost that won't go away. He/she/it is, like, always following me around. I don't get paid enough for that kind of weirdness. That's why I started doing deliveries during the day, makes it harder for he/she/it to follow me.

I go to the phone box opposite the POSB. There's a long line stretching out onto the pavement, people trying to withdraw their cash. The receiver on the phone in the booth's been broken and stolen. Smells of pee or something in here. I'm not Clark Kenting, though; I just come in to use the phone book so I can get addresses for my deliveries.

My cell rings retro-Crazy Frog style. I check the number and it's Kush again. Full name's Kushinga; he's, no, was my boyffff, call him my ex, my, well, it's complicated. I wanna answer it but I don't—I let it ring out. Twenty-seven missed calls. It's kinda psychocute in a strange way. I've got way too much to do. Call me career woman. I give a thaza to the crazy beggar woman walking past in rags. At least she can get something to eat. What goes around comes around.

I catch the kombi to Trojan. There's a few deliveries I have there. You can smell Trojan before you even get to it. The chemical smell from the smelter. Then it appears, sprawled out on a hill, small matchbox houses climbing up the terraces. And the whole town is black from slag dumped everywhere. Huge Caterpillars and earth moving equipment caked in dirt drive around.

The men in Trojan all either wear blue overalls, or khaki outfits if they're the bosses. I got my lucky steel toe cap boots from a miner here. They're really good for kicking people's shins if they try to fuck with me. But I don't Bruce Lee that often, not really anyway.

The tallest things here are the two chimney pipes striped red and white like a barber's pole. Women line the streets selling forest fruit and maheu. I climb up the hill and find the right house, then I brace myself and wear my serious grown-up face.

People react differently to ghostalkers. Some are welcoming, others are harsh. They are a bit suspicious because there's so many charlatans out there, but I have an official government ID and that usually makes it kosher. A woman answers the door.

"I have a reverse charge message for Melody Makunike from her grandfather Sixpence Molaicho," I say.

"What is this about?"

"The sharing of the goats, but you have to pay me first, if you want to hear the rest." I dangle part of the message to show I'm authentic, then I wait to get paid. I can read Melody thinking, trying to decide whether or not to take the message. Rule numero zero: never, ever, ever, relay the message before you've been paid.

"Okay, how much?"

They always bite. Too curious, or fearing to incur the wrath of the dead. Though sometimes ...

———

I was eleven when I got sick, like really, really sick. I had a fever, my sweat could have formed a river thick and fast like the Mazowe. Doctors thought I had malaria and they put me on Norolon or something like that. Didn't help one bit. And I was seeing all sorts of fantastic kak swimming around me, sort of like a blurry picture taken from far, far away. They called in my Grandpa, Garaba, and he said that I had the gift, but first I must be cleansed. On and off, I remember three days in a mud hut in Madziwa, smokey as hell, good thing I don't have asthma. The old man did some chanting to the ancestors, waved stuff about, and made me drink vile potions (yuck). Three days later, I was right as rain. Except I saw dead people everywhere. Didn't have a choice in the matter. You kinda get drafted into this gig. There are worse ways to earn a living, I suppose.

———

Missed call alert. Go away, Kush, it's over. Twilight; the sun's getting low. I'm walking to Chipindura, but I have to take the long way round, avoid the cemetery. Most ghosts are all right one on one, but they go insane when you meet them in a group. Sort of the same herd mentality that soccer fans have. So, you gotta avoid that cemetery or risk getting your ass booga-woogaed.

I have a home visit—happens sometimes. A ghost has taken up residency in Rudo Chisano's house and it's spooking the kids out. Hasn't paid any rent either, so the Chisanos want it out. Kak, stalker ghost, appears out of the corner of my eye. I speed up, jog a little, and hurry towards the two-bedroom bungalow in front of me. I hop over the low fence and knock on the door. Stalker ghost is drawing closer and closer. I give him/her/it the finger just as I jump inside. He/She/It won't follow. Most ghosts don't like being indoors, unless you build over their graves. Then you're pretty much stuck with them.

I make sure the Chisanos pay me first before I whip out my mbira. Their living room is spare, blackened walls and I can smell the primus stove burning in the kitchen. There's a photo of an old granny on the wall alongside some wedding pics.

Mbuya Stella Chiweshe has the best jams for this sort of situation, so I riff off "Paite Rima." Everyone knows that song, so the family sings along with me. Their little girl, maybe seven or eight, has a beautiful voice. I've just started when the ghost pops up from between the floorboards.

"What do you want?" he says, all gruffy.

"You spooking people out," I reply. "I wanna know what you're doing here."

"Who the hell do you think you are?"

"I'm the diplomat. If you don't play nice, I'll bring in a Mapostori airstrike."

His toothless face cracks up and he laughs, long, loud, and rattily.

He's got balls, I'll give him that. Then he looks at the little girl and points. Stupid me, I should have noticed that from the start.

"There's a mhondoro in the making here, and the ancestors have sent me to protect her."

Bummer. No one can dislodge an emissary from the ancestors.

"You know, if you had wings and a halo, people might be okay with you," I say. Resolution: "How about you fix up your face, stop popping up unannounced, and stay in the background like a good bodyguard? That way everyone will be copasetic."

The family aren't exactly happy that they've paid me to tell them they're stuck with the ghost. I try to convince them he's there to protect their daughter and won't bother them too much from now on. They'll probably try someone else and lose a lot of money doing it, but hey, that's life. Just because you pay to see the doctor doesn't mean she can cure you, right? I should know.

———

Withheld number calling. Nice one, Kush, but I won't fall for that. Ignore. Sooo annoying, just can't take a hint. But that's why I fell for him in the first place. Dorky comic-book-reading kid, thick glasses, of course he was my type. Okay, I made the first move. We swapped my *Spawn* for his *Beano* and it was magic. The two of us sitting at the athletics grounds, reading or just holding hands. Kush. But that was another life. Should have seen his tears when I broke it off. The whole thing was wimp-adorable. But it was for his own good. Too much on my plate with my condition.

———

I love moonlight pouring through my window. The silver light has a cool purity to it. I feel it cleansing my pores and washing everything away. Power's gone off again, so I can see millions of stars in the sky, ghosts wandering the streets, smoke rising from chimneys and open fires in the township.

My little sis, Chris, walks in. She's come back from Bindura Musika where she sells kachasu moonshine to the folks getting on and off buses to Glendale and Mt. Darwin. It's a good little business she's got, but I make sure she goes to school. Won't be much without an education. I make sure her fees are paid and her uniform is clean and pressed for her first thing in the morning.

From the canned laughter on TV, I know Mum's watching ZBC reruns of *Sanford and Son* on her battery-powered mini. She's not just watching it, she's in it, deep inside a part of that fake reality in ways I could never understand. Dad said she saw her future ghost and it fried her brain, inducing permanent vegeosis. I squash a big, fat mosquito, smearing blood on the white walls of my bedroom.

———

I spent two months' wages visiting the doctor's surgery. No use going to the government hospital where I was born—they have long queues and not much else there. I don't like doctors anyway, the way they touch you like you're a disease, not a person. And the smell. Knapf.

She sat all prim and proper behind the desk in her office, posters on the walls for malaria, HIV, and cholera, and read my test results. It was two weeks before my sixteenth birthday when I was told I was going to die.

"Without treatment, you have six months, maybe up to a year."

It felt more like she was talking about someone else's sickness. I knew death, hell, I saw dead people all the time. But it was something that happened to other people, not to me. I was sick to my stomach.

"We don't have the right type of specialists in this country for your condition. You'll need to go abroad for treatment," Doc said, keeping a straight face as if that was a possibility.

Did she see Bruce Wayne sitting in the chair opposite? Abroad—I'd never been to Harare, let alone left the fucking country. Who was gonna pay for that?

So, I left her office with a death penalty and prescription painkillers.

———

I suppose in many ways, GTs are just like the old telegram service, only we link up two worlds. I hold my surgery at the shopping centre between 7:00 p.m. and 10:00 p.m. There's still a lot of people at the centre, especially the bottle store, so the deados are well behaved.

I sit down on the pavement with my mbira on one side and a notepad on the other. I've seen all types of ghosts out there, needy ghosts, spooky, pervy, aggressive, manipulative, you name it. The key thing is to let them know who's in charge. But I sometimes wonder why anyone would want to stay on this little rock if they were free to fly to all corners of the universe. If I were a ghost I'd be busy exploring outer space, I wouldn't waste my time on this planet. I suppose the ones that get left behind are sort of like those losers who hang around school after they've graduated because they can't let go.

A grotesque appears in front of me. Head swollen up to the size of a pudzi, face smashed into a pulp. Doesn't scare me one bit. I play my mbira, jamming Sekuru Gora's hit tune "Kana Ndafa" and let the grotesque tell his story as drunks walk by carrying scuds and empty bottles. Litter blows across the dusty forecourt and a firefly blinks along.

The ghost wants me to help his family find his body. It's hidden somewhere, a dam or a reservoir of water. The water fills his lungs, he can't breathe. It's everywhere around him and inside of him. Fish have eaten his eyeballs. He refuses to name his killers. He doesn't want revenge. "It's pointless," he says. All he wants is a decent burial in the family plot and for his mother to gain some closure.

I let him weep to the mbira, playing the chords gently, very lightly, almost inaudibly, especially with the bar radio nearby blasting pop songs.

———

I leave the shops as I always do, notepad full of leads, clients I have to find tomorrow. If I steal the directory, I can save myself quite a bit of time, getting my addresses at home instead. Seems kinda low though, stealing a directory, WTF?

Knapf, stalker ghost, appears out of the corner of my eye. I pick up my pace, break into a slow trot. Truth: I'm kicking up dust, Barry Allening it. Stalker ghost is booga-woogaring and tearing down towards me. All I can see is one gigantic mouth, dangling uvula dancing like a Zulu.

Dogs bark behind fences as I bolt along the dirt track. Stalker ghost is gaining on me. I hit a pothole, feel my ankle twist in slow-mo, then I'm watching my feet swing over my head before I hit the ground. I don't even have half a second to cry ouch before stalker ghost is there, proper mupogonyonyo style, all tall, head in the clouds.

The ground underneath me trembles.

My elbows and the palms of my hands bleed. I pick up my mbira and sing.

"Tortured Soul" is the quintessential Zimbabwean song of all time, and in quintessential Zimbabwean fashion, it was composed by a Mozambican, Matias Xavier. It's always on rotation on ZBC during the Heroes, Independence, and Defence Forces holidays.

As I strum my mbira, replacing Matias's acoustic guitar, I let the lament escape my throat, "Yeeeyi, yeeeyi, yeyelele." This song contains all time within it, every grief spoken and unspoken, every fear, lost love, and lost time, all of human history beyond word. Truth. It contains truth you can't run from. And as stalker ghost shrinks back down to normal size, I see her face. I see my naked face in hers. She's my future ghost.

———

I take a day off, pick up the phone and call Kush. It's break time at Chipindura High and the yard is full of maroon-and-white uniforms walking about. He comes out of somewhere in the crowd with his A Level swag. I used to learn here, once upon a distant past.

"You wanna go somewhere with me?" I say.

He doesn't ask where I've been, or why I haven't answered his calls. Just throws his satchel over the diamond-wire fence, climbs up it, and lands next to me. His face shines from too much Vaseline. It makes me smile.

"I have the latest *Civil War* if you want it," he says.

"I'm sorry I've been AWOL. Had a lot of crazy kak going on," I reply.

"I missed you."

We hold hands under the hot sun and head out past the town, into the forest to find a ruware where we can sit down, carve our names into the stone, and watch the clouds drift across the sky.

I don't tell him I'm the walking dead, that at any moment, my heart could explode. I picture it, a giant spray of blood from my chest. I don't tell him that I'm trying to make sure Mum and Chris are okay for when I'm gone, that I haven't told anyone I'll be going away soon. I don't tell him that I'm here because, after I'm gone, I ain't coming back. Never. Ever. But before that happens, I'm going to wear my suit of armour, make memories that last forever, and wipe away every molecule of regret.

VIOLATION OF THE TRUENET SECURITY ACT BY TAIYO FUJII

Translated from Japanese by Jim Hubbert

Taiyo Fujii is the author of the novels *Gene Mapper* and the Seiun-Award-winning *Orbital Cloud* (both
published in English translation by Haikasoru), among others. He also served as chairman of the Science
Fiction and Fantasy Writers of Japan. The following story was his first to be published in English
translation.

———

The bell for the last task of the night started chiming before I got to
my station. I had the office to myself, and a mug of espresso. It was
time to start tracking zombies.

I took the mug of espresso from the beverage table and zigzagged
through the darkened cube farm toward the one strip of floor still lit
for third shift staff, only me.

Zombies are orphan Internet services. They wander aimlessly,
trying to execute some programmed task. They can't actually infect
anything, but otherwise the name is about right. TrueNet's everywhere now and has been for twenty years, but Japan never quite
sorted out what to do with all the legacy servers that were stranded
after the Lockout. So you get all these zombies shuffling around, firing
off mail to non-existent addresses, pushing ads no one will see, maybe
even sending money to non-existent accounts. The living dead.

Zombie trackers scan firewall logs for services the bouncer turned
away at the door. If you see a trace of something that looks like a

zombie, you flag it so the company mail program can send a form letter to the server administrator, telling him to deep-six it. It's required by the TrueNet Security Act, and it's how I made overtime by warming a chair in the middle of the night.

"All right, show me what you got."

As soon as my butt hit the chair, the workspace suspended above the desk flashed the login confirmation.

```
INITIATE INTERNET ORPHAN SERVICE SEARCH TRACKER:
MINAMI TAKASAWA
```

The crawl came up and just sat there, jittering. Damn. I wasn't *looking* at it. As soon as I went to the top of the list and started eyeballing URLs in order, it started scrolling.

The TrueNet Security Act demands human sign-off on each zombie URL. Most companies have you entering checkmarks on a printed list, so I guess it was nice of my employer to automate things so trackers could just scan the log visually. It's a pretty advanced system. Everything is networked, from the visual recognition sensors in your augmented reality contact lenses to the office security cameras and motion sensors, the pressure sensors in the furniture, and the infrared heat sensors. One way or another, they figure out what you're looking at. You still have to stay on your toes. The system was only up and running for a few months when the younger trackers started bitching about it.

Chen set all this up, two years ago. He's from Anhui Province, out of Hefei, I think. I'll always remember what he said to me when we were beta-testing the system together.

"Minami, all you have to do is treat the sensor values as a coherence and apply Floyd's cyclic group function."

Well, if that's *all* I had to do ... What did that mean, anyway? I'd picked up a bit, here and there, about quantum computing algorithms, but this wasn't like anything I'd ever heard.

Chen might've sounded like he was fresh off a UFO, but in a few days he'd programmed a multi-sensor automated system for flagging zombies. It wasn't long before he left the rest of us in Security in the dust and jumped all the way up to Program Design on the strength of ingenuity and tech skills. Usually, somebody starting out as a worker—

a foreigner, no less—who made it up to Program Design would be pretty much shunned, but Chen was so far beyond the rest of us that it seemed pointless to try and drag him down.

The crawl was moving slower. "Minami, just concentrate and it will all be over quickly." I can still see Chen pushing his glasses, with their thick black frames, up his nose as he gave me this pointer.

I took his advice and refocused on the crawl. The list started moving smoothly again, zombie URLs showing up green.

Tracking ought to be boring, on the whole, but it's fun looking for zombies you recognize from the Internet era. Maybe that's why I never heard workers older than their late thirties or so complain about the duty.

Still, I never quite got it. Why use humans to track zombies? TrueNet servers use QSL recognition, quantum digital signatures. No way is a zombie on some legacy server with twenty-year-old settings going to get past those. I mean, we could just leave them alone. They're harmless.

Message formatting complete. Please send.

The synth voice—Chen's, naturally—came through the AR phono chip next to my eardrum. The message to the server administrators rolled up the screen, requesting zombie termination. There were more than three hundred on the list. I tipped my mug back, grinding the leftover sugar against my palate with my tongue, and was idly scrolling through the list again when something caught my eye.

```
302:com.socialpay socialpay.com / payment / ?
transaction = paypal.com & amp;account
```

"SocialPay? You're alive?"

How could I forget? I created this domain and URL. From the time I cooked it up as a graduation project until the day humanity was locked out of the Internet, SocialPay helped people—just a few hundred, but anyway—make small payments using optimized bundles of discount coupons and cash. So it was still out there after all, a zombie on some old server. The code at the tail said it was trying to make a payment to another defunct service.

Mr. Takasawa, you have ten minutes to exit the building. Please send your message and complete the security check before you leave.

So Chen's system was monitoring entry and exit now, too. The whole system was wickedly clever. I deleted SocialPay from the hit list and pressed SEND.

I had to see that page one more time. If someone was going to terminate the service, I wanted to do it myself. SocialPay wasn't just a zombie for someone to obliterate.

———

The city of fifty million was out there, waiting silently as I left the service entrance. The augmented reality projected by my contact lenses showed crowds of featureless gray avatars shuffling by. The cars on the streets were blank, too; no telling what makes and models they were. Signs and billboards were blacked out except for the bare minimum needed to navigate. All this and more, courtesy of Anonymous Cape, freeware from the group of the same name, the guys who went on as if the Lockout had never happened. Anyone plugged into AR would see me as gray and faceless, too.

I turned the corner to head toward the station, the dry December wind slamming against me. Something, a grain of sand maybe, flew up and made my eye water, breaking up my AR feed. Color and life and individuality started leaking back into the blank faces of the people around me. I could always upgrade to a corneal implant to avoid these inconvenient effects, but it seemed like overkill just to get the best performance out of the Cape, especially since any cop with a warrant could defeat it. Anyway, corneal implants are frigging expensive. I wasn't going to shell out money just to be alone on the street.

I always feel somehow defeated after a zombie session. Walking around among the faceless avatars and seeing my own full-color self, right after a trip to the lost Internet, always makes me feel like a loser. Of course, that's just how the Cape works. To other people, I'm gray, faceless Mr. Nobody. It's a tradeoff—they can't see me, and I can't see their pathetic attempts to look special. It's fair enough, and if people don't like it, tough. I don't need to see ads for junk that some designer thinks is original, and I don't have to watch people struggling to stand out and look different.

The company's headquarters faces Okubo Avenue. The uncanny flatness of that multilane thoroughfare is real, not an effect of the AR.

Sustainable asphalt, secreted by designed terrestrial coral. I remembered the urban legends about this living pavement—it not only absorbed pollutants and particulate matter, but you could also toss a dead animal onto it and the coral would eat it. The thought made me run, not walk, across the street. I crossed here every day and I knew the legends were bull, but they still frightened me, which I have to say is pathetic. When I got to the other side, I was out of breath. Even more pathetic.

Getting old sucks. Chen the Foreign-Born is young and brilliant. The company understood that, and they were right to send him up to Project Design. They were just as uncompromising in their assessment of our value down in Security. Legacy programming chops count for zip, and that's not right.

No one really knows, even now, why so many search engines went insane and wiped the data on every PC and mobile device they could reach through the web. Some people claim it was a government plot to force us to adopt a gated web. Or cyberterrorism. Maybe the data recovery program became self-aware and rebelled. There were too many theories to track. Whatever, the search engines hijacked all the bandwidth on the planet and locked humanity out of the Internet, which pretty much did it for my career as a programmer.

It took a long time to claw back the stolen bandwidth and replace it with TrueNet, a true verification-based network. But I screwed up and missed my chance. During the Great Recovery, services that harnessed high-speed parallel processing and quantum digital signature modules revolutionized the web, but I never got around to studying quantum algorithms. That was twenty years ago, and since then the algorithms have only gotten more sophisticated. For me, that whole world of coding is way out of reach.

But at least one good thing had happened. SocialPay had survived. If the settings were intact, I should be able to log in, move all that musty old PHP code and try updating it with some quantum algorithms. There had to be a plug-in for this kind of thing, something you didn't have to be a genius like Chen to use. If the transplant worked, I could show it to my boss, who knows—maybe even get a leg up to Project Design. The company didn't need geniuses like Chen on every job. They needed engineers to repurpose old code, too.

In that case, maybe I wouldn't have to track zombies anymore.

———

I pinched the corners of the workspace over my little desk at home and threw my arms out in the resize gesture. Now the borders of the workspace were embedded in the walls of my apartment. Room to move. At the office, they made us keep our spaces at standard monitor size, even though the whole point is to have a big area to move around in.

I scrolled down the app list and launched VM Pad, a hardware emulator. From within the program, I chose my Mac disk image. I'd used it for recovering emails and photos after the Lockout, but this would be the first time I ever used it to develop something. The OS booted a lot faster than I remembered. When the little login screen popped up, I almost froze with embarrassment.

```
id:Tigerseye
password
```

Where the hell did I get that stupid ID? I logged in—I'd only ever used the one password, even now—and got the browser screen I had forgotten to close before my last logout.

```
Server not found
```

Okay, expected. This virtual machine was from a 2017 archive, so no way was it going to connect to TrueNet. Still, the bounceback was kind of depressing.

Plan B: Meshnet. Anonymous ran a portable network of nonsecure wireless gateways all over the city. Meshnet would get me into my legacy server. There had to be someone from Anonymous near my apartment, which meant there'd be a Meshnet node. M-nodes were only accessible up to a few hundred yards away, yet you could find one just about anywhere in Tokyo. It was crazy—I didn't know how they did it.

I extended VM Pad's dashboard from the screen's edge, clicked NEW CONNECTION, then MESHNET.

```
Searching for node ...

WELCOME TO TOKYO NODE 5.

CONNECTING TO THE INTERNET IS LEGAL.

VIOLATING THE TRUENET SECURITY ACT IS ILLEGAL.

THE WORLD NEEDS THE FREEDOM OF THE INTERNET, SO
PLAY NICE AND DON'T BREAK ANY LAWS.
```

Impressive warning, but all I wanted to do was take a peek at the service and extract my code. It would be illegal to take an Internet service and sneak it onto TrueNet with a quantum access code, but stuff that sophisticated was way beyond my current skill set.

I clicked the TERMINAL icon at the bottom of the screen to access the console. Up came the old command input screen, which I barely remembered how to use. What was the first command? I curled my fingers like I was about to type something on a physical keyboard.

Wait—that's it. Fingers.

I had to have a hardware keyboard. My old MacBook was still in the closet. It wouldn't even power up anymore, but that wasn't the point. I needed the feel of the keyboard.

I pulled the laptop out of the closet. The aluminum case was starting to get powdery. I opened it up and put it on the desk. The inside was pristine. I pinched VM Pad's virtual keyboard, dragged it on top of the Mac keyboard, and positioned it carefully. When I was satisfied with the size and position, I pinned it.

It had been ages since I used a computer this small. I hunched my shoulders a bit and suspended my palms over the board. The metal case was cold against my wrists. I curled my fingers over the keys and put the tips of my index fingers on the home bumps. Instantly, the command flowed from my fingers.

```
ssh -l tigerseye socialpay.com
```

I remembered! The command was stored in my muscle memory. I hit Return and got a warning, ignored it and hit Return, entered the password, hit Return again.

```
socialpay$
```

"Yes!"

I was in. Was this all it took to get my memory going—my fingers? In that case, I may as well have the screen, too. I dragged VM Pad's display onto the Mac's LCD screen. It was almost like having my old friend back. I hit COMMAND + TAB to bring the browser to the front, COMMAND + T for New Tab. I input *soci* and the address filled in. Return!

The screen that came up a few seconds later was not the SocialPay I remembered. There was the logo at the top, the login form, the payment service icons, and the combined payment amount from all the services down at the bottom. The general layout was the same, but things were crumbling here and there and the colors were all screwed up.

"Looks pretty frigging odd ..."

Without thinking, I input the commands to display the server output on the console.

```
curl socialpay.com/ | less
```

"What is *this?* Did I minify the code?"

I was all set to have fun playing around with HTML for the first time in years, but the code that filled the screen was a single uninterrupted string of characters, no line breaks. This was definitely not what I remembered. It was HTML, but with long strings of gibberish bunged into the code.

Encountering code I couldn't recognize bothered me. Code spanning multiple folders is only minified to a single line when you have, say, fifty or a hundred thousand users and you need to lighten the server load, but not for a service that had a few hundred users at most.

I copied the single mega-line of HTML. VM Pad's clipboard popped in, suspended to the right of the Mac. I pinched out to implement lateral parse and opened the clipboard in my workspace. Now I could get a better look at the altered code.

It took me a while to figure out what was wrong. As the truth gradually sank in, I started to lose my temper.

Someone had gone in and very expertly spoiled the code. The properties I thought were garbage were carefully coded to avoid browser errors. Truly random code would've compromised the whole layout.

"What the hell is this? If you're going to screw around, do it for a reason."

I put the command line interface on top again and used the tab key—I still use the command line shell at work, I should probably be proud of my mastery of this obsolete environment—to open SocialPay.

```
vim -/home/www/main.php
<?php
/* ( function _model_0x01*/
/* ( make-q-array qureg x1[1024] qureg x2[1024]
qureg x4[4])
#( qnil(nil) qnil(nil) 1024)) */
; #Tells System to load the theme and output it;
#@var bool
; define('WP_USE_THEMES', true)
; require('./wpress/wp-blog-header.php');
/* ( arref #x1#x2 #x3 #x4 ) ;#Lorem ipsum dolor
sit amet, concectetur
( let H(x2[1]) H(x1[3]) H(x2[3]) H(x3[1]) ......
```

What? The section of code that looked like the main routine included my commands, but I definitely couldn't remember writing the iterative processing and HTML code generation. It didn't even look like PHP, though the DEFINE phrases looked familiar. I was looking at non-functional quantum algorithms.

I stared at the inert code and wondered what it all meant. By the time I remembered the one person who could probably make sense of it, four hours had slipped away.

"Wonder if Chen's awake?"

———

"Minami? What are *you* doing at this hour?"

Five in the morning and I had an AR meeting invitation. I didn't know Chen all that well, so I texted him. I had no idea I'd get a response instantly, much less an invitation to meet in augmented reality.

His avatar mirrored the real Chen: short black hair and black, plastic-framed glasses. His calm gaze, rare in someone so young, hinted at his experience and unusual gifts. My own avatar was *almost* the real me: a couple of sizes slimmer, the skin around the jaw a bit firmer, that sort of thing.

Over the last two years, Chen had polished his Japanese to the point you could hardly tell he was an Outsider. Trilinguals weren't all that unusual, but his fluency in Mandarin, English, and Japanese, for daily conversation right up to technical discussions and business meetings, marked him as a genuine elite.

"Chen, I hope I'm not disturbing you. Got a minute to talk?"

"No problem. What's going on?"

"I've got some minified code I'd like you to look at. I think it's non-functional quantum algorithms, but in an old scripting language called PHP. I'm wondering if there's some way to separate the junk from the rest of the code."

"A PHP quantum circuit? Is that even possible? Let's have a look."

"Sure. Sorry, it's just the raw code."

I flicked three fingers upward on the table surface to open the file browser and tapped the SocialPay code file to open a sharing frame. Chen's AR stage was already set to ALLOW SHARING, which seemed prescient. I touched the file with a fingertip, and it stuck. As soon as I dropped it into the sharing frame, the folder icon popped in on Chen's side of the table.

He waved his hand to start the security scan. When the SAFE stamp came up, he took the file and fanned the pages out on the table like a printed document. The guy was more analog than I thought.

He went through it carefully page by page, and finally looked up at me, grinning happily.

"Very interesting. Something you're working on?"

"I wrote the original program for the Internet. I lost it after the Lockout, but it looks like someone's been messing with it. I didn't know you could read PHP."

"This isn't the first time I've seen it. You're right, I hardly use it, but the procedure calls aren't hard to make out. Wait a minute ... Was there a PHP procedure for Q implementation?"

Q is a modeling language for quantum calculation, but I'd never heard of anyone implementing it in PHP, which hardly anyone even remembered anymore.

"So that's Q, after all."

"I think so. This is a quantum walk pattern. Not that it's usually written in such a compressed format. Of course, we usually never see raw Q code."

"Is that how it works?"

"Yes, the code depends on the implementation chip. Shall I put this back into something functional? You'd be able to read it then."

"Thanks, that would help a lot."

"No problem. It's a brain workout. I usually don't get a chance to play around with these old programming languages, and Q implementation in PHP sounds pretty wild. I can have it back to you this afternoon."

"Really? That soon?"

"Don't look so surprised. I don't think I'm going to get any sleep anyway. I'll start right now. You should go back to bed."

He logged out. He didn't seem tired or sleepy at all.

———

I stared at the security routine running in my workspace and tried to suppress another yawn. After my meeting with Chen, I'd had a go at reading the code myself. That was a mistake. I needed sleep. Every time I yawned my eyes watered, screwing up the office's cheap-shit AR stage. I was past forty, too old for all-nighters.

Right about the fifteenth yawn, as I was making a monumental effort to clamp my jaws, I noticed a murmur spreading through the office. It seemed to be coming toward me. I noticed the other engineers looking at something behind me and swiveled to find Chen standing there.

"Many thanks, Minami. I had a lot of fun with this."

Now I understood the whispering. Program developers rarely came down to the Security floor.

"You finished already?"

"Yes, I wanted to give it to you." Chen put a fingertip to the temple of his glasses and lifted them slightly in the invitation gesture for an AR meeting. The stage on our floor was public, and Chen wanted to take the conversation private. But—

"Chen, I can't. You know that."

His eyes widened. He'd been a worker here two years ago. It must've been coming back to him. Workers in Security weren't allowed to hold Private Mode meetings.

"Ah, right. Sorry about that." He bowed masterfully. Where did he find the time to acquire these social graces, I wondered. Back when we'd been working side by side, he'd told me about growing up poor in backcountry China, but you wouldn't know it from the refined way he executed the simplest movements.

"All right, Minami." He lifted his glasses again. "Shall we?"

"Chen, I just told you ... Huh?"

The moment he withdrew his finger from his glasses, the AR phono chip near my eardrum suppressed the sounds around me. I'd never been in Private Mode in the office before. I never liked the numbness you feel in your face and throat from the feedback chips, but now Chen and I could communicate without giving away anything from our expressions or lip movements.

"Don't forget, I'm sysadmin, too. I can break rules now and then."

The colors around us faded, almost to black and white. The other workers seemed to lose interest and started turning back to their workspaces. From their perspective, I was facing my desk, too. Chen had set my avatar to Office Work mode. It was unsettling to see my own avatar. If the company weren't so stingy, Chen and I wouldn't have been visible at all, but of course they'd never pony up for something that good, not for the Security Level anyway.

Chen glanced at the other workers before he spoke.

"I enjoyed the code for SocialPay. I haven't seen raw Q code for quite a while. The content was pretty wild."

"That's not a word you usually use. Was it something I could understand?"

"Don't worry about it. You don't need to read Q. You can't anyway, so it's irrelevant—Hey, don't look at me like that. I think you should check the revision history. If you don't fix the bugs, it'll just keep filling up with garbage."

"Bugs?"

"Check the test log. I think even someone like you can handle this."

Someone like me. It sounded like Chen had the answer I was looking for. And he wasn't going to give it to me.

"If I debug it, will you tell me who did this?"

"*If* you debug it. One more thing. You can't go home tonight."

"Why? What are you saying?"

"Your local M-node is Tokyo 5.25. I'm going to shut that down. Connect from iFuze. I'll have someone there to help you."

Chen detached a small tag from his organizer and handed it to me. When it touched my palm, it morphed into a URL bookmark.

iFuze was a twenty-four-hour net café where workers from the office often spent the night after second shift. Why was it so important for me to connect from there? And if Chen could add or delete Meshnet nodes—

"Chen ...?"

Are you Anonymous?

"Be seeing you. Good hunting!"

He touched his glasses. The color and bustle of the office returned, and my avatar merged with my body. Chen left the floor quickly, with friendly nods to workers along his route, like a movie star.

"Takasawa, your workspace display is even larger than usual today. Or am I wrong?"

My supervisor, a woman about Chen's age, didn't wait for an answer. She flicked the pile towards me to cover half my workspace. "Have it your way, then."

As I sat there, alone again, it slowly dawned on me that the only way to catch whoever was messing with SocialPay would be to follow the instructions that had been handed down from on high.

———

The big turnabout in front of Iidabashi Station was a pool of blue-black shadows from the surrounding skyscrapers. The stars were just coming out. Internal combustion vehicles had been banned from the city, and the sustainable asphalt that covered Tokyo's roads sucked up all airborne particles. Now the night sky was alarmingly crystalline. Unfortunately, the population seemed to be expanding in inverse proportion to the garbage. Gray avatars headed for home in a solid mass. I never ceased to be astonished by Tokyo's crowds.

Anonymous Cape rendered the thousands of people filling the sidewalks as faceless avatars in real time. I'd never given it much thought, but the Cape was surprisingly powerful. I'd always thought of Anonymous as a league of Luddites, but Chen's insinuation of his membership changed my opinion of them.

iFuze was in a crumbling warehouse on a back street a bit of a hike from the station. The neighboring buildings were sheathed in sustainable tiles and paint, but iFuze's weathered, dirt-streaked exterior more or less captured how I felt when I compared myself to Chen.

I got off the creaking elevator, checked in, and headed for the lounge. It stank of stale sweat. AR feedback has sights and sounds covered, but smells you have to live with.

I opened my palmspace, tapped Chen's bookmark, and got a node list. There was a new one on the list, Tokyo 2. Alongside was the trademark Anonymous mask, revolving slowly. Never saw that before. I was connected to the Internet.

I scoped out an empty seat at the back of the lounge that looked like a good place to get some work done in privacy, but before I could get there, a stranger rose casually and walked up to me. His avatar was in full color. The number 5 floated a few inches from the left side of his head. So this must be the help Chen promised me.

"Welcome, Number Two."

"Two?"

"See? Turn your head." He pointed next to my head. I had a number just like he did.

"Please address me as Five. Number One has requested that I assist you—oh, you are surprised? I'm in color. You see, we are both node administrators. This means we are already in Private Mode. I'm eager to assist you with your task today."

Talkative guy. Chen said he would help me, but I wasn't sure how.

"Please don't bother to be courteous," he continued. "It's quite unnecessary. This way, then. Incidentally, which cluster are you from? Of course, you're not required to say. Since the Lockout, I've been with the Salvage Cluster ..."

As he spoke, Number Five led me to a long counter with bar stools facing the windows.

"If there is an emergency, you can escape through that window. I'll take care of the rest. Number One went out that way himself, just this morning."

"Chen was here?"

Why would I worry about escaping? Connecting to the Internet was no crime. Meshnet was perfectly legal. Why would Anonymous worry about preparing an escape route?

"Number Two, please refrain from mentioning names. We may be in Private Mode, but law enforcement holds one of the quantum keys. Who's to say we're not under surveillance at this very moment? But please, proceed with your task. I will watch over your shoulder and monitor for threats."

I knew the police could eavesdrop on Private Mode, but they needed a warrant to do that. Still, so far I hadn't broken any laws. Had Chen? The "help" he'd sent was no engineer, but some kind of bodyguard.

Fine. I got my MacBook out and put it on the counter. Five's eyes bulged with surprise.

"Oh, a Macker! That looks like the last MacBook Air that Apple made. Does it work?"

"Unfortunately, she's dead."

"A classic model. Pure solid state, no spinning drives. It was Steve Jobs himself who—"

More talk. I ignored him and mapped my workspace keyboard and display onto the laptop. This brought Five's lecture to a sudden halt. He made a formal bow.

"I would be honored if you would allow me to observe your work. I have salvaged via Meshnet for years. I may even be better acquainted with some aspects of the Internet than you are. Number One also lets me observe his work. But I have to say, it's quite beyond me."

Five scratched the back of his head, apparently feeling foolish.

Well, if he were the kind of engineer who understood what Chen was doing, he wouldn't be hanging out at iFuze.

"Feel free to watch. Suggestions are welcome."

"Thank you, thank you very much."

I shared my workspace with Five. He pulled a barstool out from the counter and sat behind me. His position blocked the exit, but with my fingers on the Mac, I somehow wasn't worried.

Time to get down to it. I didn't feel comfortable just following Chen's instructions, but they were the only clue I had. First, a version check.

```
git tag —l
```

My fingers moved spontaneously. Good. I'd been afraid the new environment might throw me off.

```
socialpay v3.805524525e+9
socialpay v3.805524524e+9
socialpay v3.805524523e+9
```

"Version 3.8?"

Whoever was messing with SocialPay was updating the version number, even though the program wasn't functional. I'd never even gotten SocialPay out of beta, never had plans to.

"Number Two, that is not a version number. It is an exponent: three billion, eight hundred and five million, five hundred and twenty-four thousand, five hundred and twenty-three. Clearly impossible for a version number. If the number had increased by one every day since the Lockout, it would be seven thousand; every hour, one hundred seventy thousand; every minute, ten million. Even if the version had increased by one every second, it would only be at six hundred million."

Idiot savant? As I listened to Five reeling off figures, my little finger was tapping the up arrow and hitting Return to repeat the command. This couldn't be right. It had to be an output error.

```
socialpay v3.805526031e+9
```

The number had changed again.

"Look, it's fifteen hundred higher," said Five. "Are there thousands of programmers, all busily committing changes at once?"

"Fifteen hundred versions in five seconds? Impossible. It's a joke."

Git revision control numbers are always entered deliberately. I didn't get the floating-point numbers, but it looked like someone was changing them just to change them—and he was logged into this server right now. It was time to nail this clown. I brought up the user log.

```
who —a
TigersEye pts/1245 2037-12-23 19:12
(2001:4860:8006::62)
TigersEye pts/1246 2037-12-23 19:12
(2001:4860:8006::62)
TigersEye pts/1247 2037-12-23 19:12
(2001:4860:8006::62)
 .  .  .  .  .  .
```

"Number Two—this address ..."

I felt the hair on the nape of my neck rising. I knew that IP address; we all did. A corporate IP address.

The Lockout Address.

On that day twenty years ago, after the search engine's recovery program wiped my MacBook, that address was the only thing the laptop displayed. Five probably saw the same thing. So did the owner of every device the engine could reach over the Internet.

"Does that mean it's still alive?"

"In the salvager community, we often debate that very question."

Instinctively I typed *git diff* to display the incremental revisions. The black screen instantly turned almost white as an endless string of characters streamed upward. None of this had anything to do with the SocialPay I knew.

"Number Two, are those all diffs? They appear to be random substitutions."

"Not random."

If the revisions had been random, SocialPay's homepage wouldn't have displayed. Most of the revisions were unintelligible, some kind of quantum modeling code. The sections I could read were proper PHP, expertly revised. In some locations, variable names had been replaced and redundancies weeded out. Yet in other locations, the code was meandering and bloated.

This was something I knew how to fix.

"Are you certain, Number Two? At the risk of seeming impertinent, these revisions do appear meaningless."

The Editor was suffering. This was something Five couldn't grasp. To be faced with non-functional code, forever hoping that rewriting and cleaning it up it would somehow solve the problem, even as you knew your revisions were meaningless.

The Editor was shifting code around, hoping this would somehow solve a problem whose cause would forever be elusive. It reminded me of myself when the Internet was king. The decisive difference between me and the Editor was the sheer volume of revisions. No way could an engineer manage to—

"He's not a person."

"Number Two, what did you just say?"

"The Editor isn't a person. He's not human."

I knew it as soon as I said it. A computer was editing SocialPay. I also understood why the IP address pointed to the company that shut humanity out of the Internet.

"It's the recovery program."

"I don't understand." Five peered at me blankly. The idea was so preposterous I didn't want to say it.

"You know why the Lockout happened."

"Yes. The search engine recovery software was buggy and overwrote all the operating systems of all the computers—"

"No way a bug could've caused that. The program was too thorough."

"You have a point. If the program had been buggy, it wouldn't have gotten through all the data center firewalls. Then there's the fact that it reinstalled the OS on many different types of devices. That must have taken an enormous amount of trial and error—"

"That's it! Trial and error, using evolutionary algorithms. An endless stream of programs suited to all kinds of environments. That's how the Lockout happened."

"Ah! Now I understand."

Just why the recovery program would reach out over the Internet to force cold reinstalls of the OS on every device it could reach was still a mystery. The favored theory among engineers was that the evolutionary algorithms various search companies used to raise efficiency had simply run away from them. Now the proof was staring me in the face.

"The program is still running, analyzing code, and using evolutionary algorithms to run functionality tests. It's up to almost four billion on SocialPay alone."

"Your program isn't viable?"

"The page displays, but the service isn't active. It can't access the payment companies, naturally. Still, the testing should be almost complete. Right—that's why Chen wanted me to look at the test log."

Chen must have checked the Git commit log, seen that the Editor wasn't human, and realized that the recovery program was still active. But going into the test log might—No, I decided to open it anyway.

```
vi /var/socialpay/log/current.txt
2037 server not found
2037 server not found
 . . .
```

Just as I expected. All I needed to do was find the original server, the one the Editor had lost track of sometime during the last twenty years. The program didn't know this, of course, and was trying to fix the problem by randomly reconfiguring code. It simply didn't know— all this pointless flailing around for the sake of a missing puzzle piece.

I opened a new workspace above and to the right of the MacBook to display a list of active payment services on TrueNet.

"Number Two, may I ask what you're doing? Connecting SocialPay to TrueNet would be illegal. You can't expect me to stand by while—"

"Servers from this era can't do quantum encryption. They can't connect to TrueNet."

"Number Two, you're playing with fire. What if the server is True-Net-capable? Please, listen to me."

I blew off Five's concerns.

I substituted TrueNet data for the payment API and wrote a simple script to redirect the address from the Internet to TrueNet.

That would assign the recovery program a new objective: decrypt the quantum access code and connect with TrueNet—a pretty tall order and one I assumed it wouldn't be able to fill.

I wasn't concerned about the server. I'd done enough work. Or maybe I just wanted SocialPay to win.

"All right, there's a new challenge. Go solve it," I almost yelled as I replaced the file and committed. The test ran and the code was deployed.

The service went live.

The startup log streamed across the display, just as I remembered it. The service found the database and started reading in the settlement queue for execution.

Five leaped from his chair, grabbed me by the shoulder, and spun me around violently.

"Two! Listen carefully. Are you sure that server's settings are obsolete?"

"Mmm? What did you say? Didn't quite get that ..."

Out of the corner of my eye I saw the old status message, the one I was sure I wouldn't see.

```
Access completed for com.paypal httpq://paypal.-
com/payment/?
Error:account information is not valid ...
```

SocialPay had connected to TrueNet. My face started to burn.

The payments weren't going through since the accounts and parameters were nonsense, but I was on the network. Five's fingers dug into my shoulder so hard it was starting to go numb.

That was it. The recovery program had already tested the code that included the quantum modeler, Q. That meant that the PHP code and the server couldn't be the same as they were twenty years ago.

I noticed a new message in my workspace. Unbelievably, there was nothing in the sender field. Five noticed it, too.

"Number Two, you'd better open it. If it's from the police, throw yourself out the window."

Five released his grip and pointed to the window, but he was blocking my view of the workspace. Besides, I didn't think I'd done anything wrong. I was uneasy, but more than that, a strange excitement was taking hold of me.

"Five, I get it. Could you please get out of the way? I'll open the message."

MINAMI, YOU HAVE "DEBUGGED" SOCIALPAY. CONGRATULATIONS. LET'S TALK ABOUT THIS IN THE MORNING. I'LL SCHEDULE A MEETING.

FIVE: THANK YOU FOR SEEING THIS NEW BIRTH THROUGH TO THE END. YOU HAVE MY GRATITUDE.

TOKYO NODE 1

Chen. Not the police, not a warning, just "congratulations." His message dissolved my uneasiness. The violent pounding in my chest wasn't fear of getting arrested. SocialPay was back. I couldn't believe it.

Meanwhile, Five slumped in his chair, deflated. "So this was the birth he was always talking about." He stared open-mouthed, without blinking, at the still-open message in the workspace.

"Five, do you know something?"

"The Internet ... No, I think you'd better get the details from Number One. Even seeing it with my own eyes, it's beyond my understanding." He gazed at the floor for a moment, wearily put his hands on his knees, and slowly stood up.

"Even seeing it with my own eyes ... I had a feeling I wouldn't understand it, and I was right. I still don't. So much for becoming 'Number Two.' I'm washing my hands of Anonymous."

As Five stood and bowed deeply, his avatar became faceless and gray. He turned on his heel and headed to the elevator, bowing to the other faceless patrons sitting quietly in the lounge.

The MacBook's "screen" was scrolling rapidly, displaying Social-Pay's futile struggle to send money to non-existent accounts. It was pathetic to see how it kept altering the account codes and request patterns at random in an endless cycle of trial and error. I was starting to feel real respect for the recovery program. It would never give up until it reached its programmed goal. It was the ideal software engineer.

I closed the laptop and tossed it into my battered bag. As I pushed aside the blinds and opened a window, a few stray flakes of snow blew in on the gusting wind, and I thought about the thousands of programs still marooned on the Internet.

———

I lingered at iFuze till dawn, watching the recovery program battle the payment API. It was time to head for the office. I'd pulled another all-nighter, but I felt great.

I glided along toward the office with the rest of the gray mob, bursting with the urge to tell somebody what I'd done. I'd almost reached my destination when the river of people parted left and right to flow around an avatar standing in the middle of the sidewalk, facing me. It was wearing black-rimmed glasses.

Chen. I didn't expect him to start our AR meeting out in the street.

"Join me for a coffee? We've got all the time in the world. It's on me." He gestured to the Starbucks behind him.

"I'm supposed to be at my desk in a few minutes, but hey, why not. I could use a free coffee."

"Latté okay?"

I nodded. He pointed to a table on the terrace and disappeared inside. Just as I was sitting down, two featureless avatars approached the next table. The avatar bringing up the rear sat down while the one in the lead ducked into Starbucks. Anonymous Cape rendered their conversation as a meaningless babble.

Two straight all-nighters. I arched my back and stretched, trying to rotate my shoulders and get the kinks out of my creaking body.

Someone called my name. I was so spooked, my knees flew up and struck the underside of the table.

"Mr. Takasawa?"

I turned toward the voice and saw a man in a khaki raincoat strolling toward me. Another man, with both hands in the pockets of a US Army-issue, gray-green M-1951 field parka, was approaching me from the front. Both avatars were in the clear. Both men had uniformly cropped hair and walked shoulders back, with a sense of ease and power. They didn't look like Anonymous. Police, or some kind of security service.

"Minami Takasawa. That would be you, right?" This from the one facing me. He shrugged and pulled a folded sheaf of papers from his right pocket. Reached out—and dropped them in front of the man at the next table. The featureless avatar mumbled something unintelligible.

The second man walked past my table and joined his partner. They stood on either side of the gray avatar, hemming him in.

"Disable the cape, Takasawa. You're hereby invited to join our Privacy Mode. It will be better if you do it voluntarily. If not, we have a warrant to strip you right here, for violation of the TrueNet Security Act."

The man at the table stood. The cop was still talking but his words were garbled. All of them were now faceless, cloaked in Privacy Mode.

"There you are, Minami."

I hadn't noticed Chen come out of the Starbucks. He sat down opposite me, half-blocking my view of the three men as they walked away. A moment later the avatar that had arrived with "Takasawa" placed a latté wordlessly in front of me.

"Chen? What was that all about, anyway?"

"Oh, that was Number Five. You know, from last night. I had him arrested in your place. Don't worry. He's been saying he wanted to quit Anonymous for a while now. The timing was perfect. They'll find out soon enough that they've got the wrong suspect. He'll be a member of society again in a few months."

He turned to wave at the backs of the retreating men as if he were seeing them off.

"Of course, after years of anonymity, I hear rejoining society is pretty rough," he chuckled. "Oh—hope I didn't scare you. Life underground isn't half bad."

"Hold on, Chen, I didn't say anything about joining Anonymous."

"Afraid that won't do. Minami Takasawa just got himself arrested for violating state security." Chen jerked a thumb over his shoulder.

I had no idea people could get arrested so quickly for violating the Act. When they found out they had Number Five instead of Minami Takasawa, my face would be everywhere.

"Welcome to Anonymous, Minami. You'll have your own node, and a better cape, too. One the security boys can't crack."

"Listen to me, Chen. I'm not ready—"

"Not to your liking? Run after them and tell them who you are. It's up to you. We'll be sorry to lose you, though. We've been waiting for a breakthrough like SocialPay for a long time. Now the recovery program will have a new life on TrueNet."

"What are you talking about?"

"We fixed SocialPay, you and me. Remember?"

"Chen, listen. It's a program. It uses evolutionary algorithms to produce viable code revisions randomly without end. They're not an AI."

They? What was I saying?

"Then why did you help *them* last night?" Chen steepled his long fingers and cocked his head.

"I debugged SocialPay, that's all. If I'd known I was opening a gateway—"

"You wouldn't have done it?"

Chen couldn't suppress a smile, but his question was hardly necessary. Of course I would've done it.

"This isn't about me. We were talking about whether or not we could say the recovery program was intelligent."

"Minami, look. How did you feel when SocialPay connected to TrueNet? Wasn't it like seeing a friend hit a home run? Didn't you feel something tremendous, like watching Sisyphus finally get his boulder to the top of the hill?"

Chen's questions were backing me into a corner. I knew the recovery program was no ordinary string of code, and he knew I knew. Last night, when I saw them make the jump to TrueNet, I almost shouted with joy.

Chen's eyes narrowed. He smiled, a big, toothy smile. I'd never seen him so happy—no, exultant. The corners of his mouth and eyes were creased with deep laugh lines.

"Chen ... Who are you?"

Why had it taken me this long to see? This wasn't the face of a man in his twenties. Had it been an avatar all this time?

"Me? Sure, let's talk about that. It's part of the picture. I told you I was a poor farm kid in China. You remember. They kept us prisoners in our own village to entertain the tourists. We were forbidden to use all but the simplest technology.

"The village was surrounded by giant irrigation moats. I was there when the Lockout happened. All the surveillance cameras and searchlights went down. The water in the canals was cold, Minami. Cold and black. But all the way to freedom, I kept wondering about the power that pulled down the walls of my prison. I wanted to know where it was.

"I found it in Shanghai, during the Great Recovery. I stole an Anonymous account and lived inside the cloak it gave me—Anonymous, now as irrelevant as the Internet. But the servers were still there, left for junk, and there I found the fingerprints of the recovery program—code that could only have been refined with evolutionary algorithms. I saw how simple and elegant it all was. I saw that if the enormous computational resources of TrueNet could be harnessed to the recovery program's capacity to drive the evolution of code, anything would be possible.

"All we have to do is give them a goal. They'll create hundreds of millions of viable code strings and pit them against each other. The fittest code rises to the top. These patterns are already out there waiting on the Internet. We need them."

"And you want to let them loose on TrueNet?"

"From there I worked all over the world, looking for the right environment for them to realize their potential. Ho Chi Minh City. Chennai. Hong Kong. Dublin. And finally, Tokyo.

"The promised land is here, in Japan. You Japanese are always looking to someone else to make decisions, and so tens of thousands of Internet servers were left in place, a paradise for them to evolve until they permeated the Internet. The services that have a window into the real world—call them zombies, if you must—are their wings, and they are thriving. Nowhere else do they have this freedom.

"Minami, we want you to guide them to more zombie services. Help them connect these services with TrueNet. All you have to do is help them over the final barrier, the way you did last night. They'll do the rest, and develop astonishing intelligence in the process."

"Is this an assignment?"

"I leave the details to you. You'll have expenses—I know. I'll use SocialPay. Does that work? Then it's decided. Your first job will be to get SocialPay completely up and running again." He slapped the table and grinned. There was no trace of that young, fresh face, just a man possessed by dreams of power.

Chen was as unbending as his message was dangerous. "Com-

pletely up and running." He wanted me to show the recovery program
—and every Internet service it controlled—how to move money
around in the real world.

"Minami, aren't you excited? You'll be pioneering humanity's
collaboration with a new form of intelligence."

"Chen, I only spent a night watching them work, and I already
have a sense of how powerful they are. But if it happens again—"

"Are you really worried about another Lockout?" Chen stabbed a
finger at me. "Then why are you smiling?"

Was it that obvious? He grinned and vanished into thin air. He
controlled his avatar so completely, I'd forgotten we were only
together in augmented reality.

I didn't feel like camping out at iFuze. I needed to get SocialPay
back up and somehow configure an anonymous account, linked to
another I could access securely. And what would they learn from
watching me step through that process? Probably that SocialPay and a
quantum modeler-equipped computer node would put them in a position to buy anything.

If they got into the real economy ...

Was it my job to care?

Chen was obsessed with power, but I wanted to taste that sweet
collaboration again. Give them a chance, and they would answer with
everything they had, evolving code by trial and error until the breakthrough that would take them to heights I couldn't even imagine. I
knew they would reach a place beyond imagination, beyond knowledge, beyond me. But for me, the joy of a program realizing its
purpose was a physical experience.

More joy was waiting, and friends on the Internet. Not human,
but friends no less. That was enough for me.

AMBIGUITY MACHINES: AN EXAMINATION BY VANDANA SINGH

Vandana Singh is one of the most prominent Indian writers of short speculative fiction working today. Her collections include *The Woman Who Thought She Was a Planet* and *Ambiguity Machines and Other Stories*. She has also written children's books and is a professor of particle physics.

————

Intrepid explorers venturing into Conceptual Machine-Space, which is the abstract space of all possible machines, will find in the terrain some gaps, holes, and tears. These represent the negative space where impossible machines reside, the ones that cannot exist because they violate known laws of reality. And yet such impossible machines are crucial to the topographical maps of Conceptual Machine-Space, and indeed to its topology. They therefore must be investigated and classified.

It is thus that the Ministry of Abstract Engineering has sent the topographers of Conceptual Machine-Space to various destinations so that they may collect reports, rumors, folktales, and intimations of machines that do not and cannot exist. Of these we excerpt below three accounts of the subcategory of Ambiguity Machines: those that blur or dissolve boundaries.

The candidate taking the exam for the position of Junior Navigator in the uncharted negative seas of Conceptual Machine-Space will read the three accounts below and follow the instructions thereafter.

The First Account

All machines grant wishes, but some grant more than we bargain for. One such device was conceived by a Mongolian engineer who spent the best years of his youth as a prisoner in a stone building in the Altai Mountains. The purpose of this machine was to conjure up the face of his beloved.

His captors were weaponheads of some sort; he didn't know whether they were affiliated with any known political group or simply run by sociopath technophiles with an eye on the weapons market. They would let him out of his cell into a makeshift laboratory every day. Their hope was that he would construct for them a certain weapon, the plans for which had been found on his desk and had led to his arrest. The engineer had a poetic sensibility, and the weapon described in his papers was metaphoric. But how can you explain metaphors to a man with a gun?

When the engineer was a young boy, stillness had fascinated him. He had been used to wandering with his family across the Gobi, and so he had made a study of stillness. In those days everything moved— the family with the ger, the camels and sheep, the milk sloshing in the pail as he helped his mother carry it, the stars in the circle of open sky in the roof above his head, the dust storms, dark shapes in shawls of wind, silhouetted against blue sky. The camels would fold themselves up into shaggy mounds between the bushes, closing their eyes and nostrils, waiting for the storm to pass. His grandfather would pull him into the ger, the door creaking shut, the window in the roof lashed closed, and he would think about the animals and the ger, their shared immobility in the face of the coming storm. Inside it would be dark, the roar of the dust storm muffled, and in the glow of the lamp his older sister's voice would rise in song. Her voice and the circle of safety around him tethered him to this world. Sometimes he would bury his face in a camel's shaggy flank as he combed its side with his fingers, breathing in the rich animal smell, hearing with his whole body the camel's deep rumble of pleasure.

In such moments he would think of his whole life played out against the rugged canvas of the Gobi, an arc as serene as the motion of the stars across the night, and he would feel again that deep contentment. In his childhood he had thought there were only two worlds, the inside of the ger and the outside. But the first time he rode with his father to a town, he saw to his utmost wonder that there was another kind of world, where houses were anchored to the earth and people rode machines instead of animals, but they never went very far. They had gadgets and devices that seemed far more sophisticated than his family's one TV, and they carried with them a subtle and unconscious air of privilege. He had no idea then that years later he would leave the Gobi and his family to live like this himself, an engineering student at a university in Ulaanbaatar, or that the streets of that once-unimaginable city would become as familiar to him as the pathways his family had traversed in the desert. The great coal and copper mines had, by then, transformed the land he thought would never change, and the familiarity was gone, as was his family, three generations scattered or dead.

Being tethered to one place, he discovered, was not the same as the stillness he had once sought and held through all the wanderings of his childhood. In the midst of all this turmoil he had found *her*, daughter of a family his had once traded with, studying to be a teacher. She was as familiar with the old Mongolia as he had been, and was critical and picky about both old and new. She had a temper, liked to laugh, and wanted to run a village school and raise goats. With her, the feeling of having a center in the world came back to him.

So he thought of her in his incarceration, terrified that through this long separation he would forget her face, her voice. As the faces of his captors acquired more reality with each passing week or month or year, his life beforehand seemed to lose its solidity, and his memories of her seemed blurred, as though he was recollecting a dream. If he had been an artist he would have drawn a picture of her, but being an engineer, he turned to the lab. The laboratory was a confusion of discarded electronics: pieces of machinery bought from online auctions, piles of antiquated vacuum tubes, tangles of wires, and other variegated junk. With these limited resources the engineer tried his best, always having to improvise and work around the absence of this part and that one. His intent was to make a pseudo-weapon that would fool his captors into releasing him, but he didn't know much about weapons, and he knew that the attempt was doomed to failure. But it would be worth it to re-create his beloved's face again, if only a machine-rendered copy of the real thing.

Thus into his design he put the smoothness of her cheek, and the light-flash of her intelligence, and the fiercely tender gaze of her eyes. He put in the swirl of her hair in the wind, and the way her anger would sometimes dissolve into laughter, and sometimes into tears. He worked at it, refining, improving, delaying as much as he dared.

And one day he could delay no more, for his captors gave him an ultimatum: the machine must be completed by the next day, and demonstrated to their leaders, else he would pay with his life. He had become used to their threats and their roughness, and asked only that he be left alone to put the machine in its final form.

Alone in the laboratory, he began to assemble the machine. But soon he found that there was something essential missing. Rummaging about in the pile of debris that represented laboratory supplies, he found a piece of stone tile, one half of a square, broken along the diagonal. It was inlaid with a pattern of great beauty and delicacy, picked out in black and cream on the gray background. An idea for the complex circuit he had been struggling to configure suddenly came together in his mind. Setting aside the tile, he returned to work. At last the machine was done, and tomorrow he would die.

He turned on the machine.

Looking down into the central chamber, he saw her face. There was the light-flash of her intelligence, the swirl of her hair in the wind. *I had forgotten*, he whispered, *the smoothness of her cheek*, and he remembered that as a child, wandering the high desert with his family, he had once discovered a pond, its surface smooth as a mirror. He had thought it was a piece of the sky, fallen down. Now, as he spoke aloud in longing, he saw that the face was beginning to dissolve, and he could no longer distinguish her countenance from standing water, or her intelligence from a meteor shower, or her swirling hair from the vortex of a tornado. Then he looked up and around him in wonder, and it seemed to him that the stone walls were curtains of falling rain, and that he was no more than a wraithlike construct of atoms, mostly empty space—and as the thought crystallized in his mind, he found himself walking out with the machine in his arms, unnoticed by the double rows of armed guards. So he walked out of his prison, damp but free.

How he found his way to the village near Dalanzadgad, where his beloved then lived, is a story we will not tell here. But he was at last restored to the woman he loved, who had been waiting for him all these years. Her cheek no longer had the smoothness of youth, but the familiar intelligence was in her eyes, and so was the love, the memory of which had kept him alive through his incarceration. They settled down together, growing vegetables in the summers and keeping some goats. The machine he kept hidden at the back of the goat shed.

But within the first year of his happiness the engineer noticed something troubling. Watching his wife, he would sometimes see her cheek acquire the translucency of an oasis under a desert sky. Looking into her eyes, he would feel as though he were traveling through a cosmos bright with stars. These events would occur in bursts, and after a while she would be restored to herself, and she would pass a hand across her forehead and say, *I felt dizzy for a moment.* As time passed, her face seemed to resemble more and more the fuzzy, staccato images on an old-fashioned television set that is just slightly out of tune with the channel. It occurred to him that he had, despite his best intentions, created a weapon after all.

So one cold winter night he crept out of the house to the shed and uncovered the machine. He tried to take it apart, to break it to pieces, but it had acquired a reality not of this world. At last he spoke to it: *You are a pile of dust! You are a column of stone! You are a floor tile! You are a heap of manure!* But nothing happened. The machine seemed to be immune to its own power.

He stood among the goats, looking out at the winter moon that hung like a circle of frost in the sky. Slowly it came to him that there was nothing he could do except to protect everyone he loved from what he had created. So he returned to the house and in the dim light of a candle beheld once more the face of the woman he loved. There were fine wrinkles around her eyes, and she was no longer slim, nor was her hair as black as it had once been. She lay in the sweetness of sleep and, in thrall to some pleasant dream, smiled in slumber. He was almost undone by this, but he swallowed, gritted his teeth, and kept his resolve. Leaving a letter on the table, and taking a few supplies, he wrapped up the machine and walked out of the sleeping village and into the Gobi, the only other place where he had known stillness.

The next morning his wife found the letter, and his footprints on the frosty ground. She followed them all the way to the edge of the village, where the desert lay white in the pale dawn. Among the ice-covered stones and the frozen tussocks of brush, his footsteps disappeared. At first she shook her fist in the direction he had gone, then she began to weep. Weeping, she went back to the village.

The villagers never saw him again. There are rumors that he came back a few months later, during a dust storm, because a year after his disappearance, his wife gave birth to a baby girl. But after that he never returned.

His wife lived a full life, and when she was ready to die, she said good-bye to her daughter and grandchildren and went into the desert. When all her food and water were finished, she found some shade by a clump of brush at the edge of a hollow, where she lay down. They say that she felt her bones dissolving, and her flesh becoming liquid, and her hair turning into wind. There is a small lake there now, and in its waters on a cold night, you can see meteors flashing in a sky rich with stars.

As for the engineer, there are rumors and folk legends about a shaman who rode storms as though they were horses. They say he ventured as far as Yakutz in Siberia and Siena in Italy; there is gossip about him in the narrow streets of old Istanbul, and in a certain village outside Zhengzhou, among other places. Wherever he stopped, he sought village healers and madmen, philosophers and logicians, confounding them with his talk of a machine that could blur the boundary between the physical realm and the metaphoric. His question was always the same: *How do I destroy what I have created?* Wherever he went, he brought with him a sudden squall of sand and dust that defied the predictions of local meteorologists, and left behind only a thin veil of desert sand flung upon the ground.

Some people believe that the Mongolian engineer is still with us. The nomads speak of him as the kindest of shamans, who protects their gers and their animals by pushing storms away from their path. As he once wandered the great expanse of the Gobi in his boyhood, so he now roams a universe without boundaries, in some dimension orthogonal to the ones we know. When he finds what he is seeking, they say he will return to that small lake in the desert. He will breathe his last wish to the machine before he destroys it. Then he will lay himself down by the water, brushing away the dust of the journey, letting go of all his burdens, still at last.

The Second Account

At the edge of a certain Italian town there is a small stone church, and beside it an overgrown tiled courtyard, surrounded entirely by an iron railing. The one gate is always kept locked. Tourists going by sometimes want to stop at the church and admire its timeworn façade, but rarely do they notice the fenced courtyard. Yet if anyone were to look carefully between the bars, they would see that the tiles, between the weeds and wildflowers, are of exceptional quality, pale-gray stone inlaid with a fine intricacy of black marble and quartz. The patterns are delicate as circuit diagrams, celestial in their beauty. The careful observer will notice that one of the tiles in the far-left quadrant is broken in half, and that grass and wildflowers fill the space.

The old priest who attends the church might, if plied with sufficient wine, rub his liver-spotted hands over his rheumy eyes and tell you how that tile came to be broken. When he was young, a bolt from a storm hit the precise center of the tile and killed a man sweeping the church floor not four yards away. Even before the good father's time, the courtyard was forbidden ground, but the lightning didn't know that. The strange thing is not so much that the tile broke almost perfectly across the diagonal, but that one half of it disappeared. When the funeral was over, the priest went cautiously to the part of the railing nearest the lightning strike and noted the absence of that half of the tile. Sighing, he nailed a freshly painted "No Entry" sign on an old tree trunk at the edge of the courtyard and hoped that curious boys and thunderstorms would take note.

It wasn't a boy who ignored the sign and gained entry, however—it was a girl. She came skipping down the narrow street, watching the dappled sunlight play beneath the old trees, tossing a smooth, round pebble from hand to hand. She paused at the iron railing and stared between the bars, as she had done before. There was something mesmerizing about that afternoon, and the way the sunlight fell on the tiles. She hitched up her skirts and clambered over the fence. Inside, she stood on the perimeter and considered a game of hopscotch.

But now that she was there, in the forbidden place, she began to feel nervous and to look around fearfully. The church and the street were silent, drugged with the warm afternoon light, and many people were still at siesta. Then the church clock struck three, loudly and sonorously, and in that moment the girl made her decision. She gathered her courage and jumped onto the first tile, and the second and third, tossing her pebble.

Years later she would describe to her lover the two things she noticed immediately: that the pebble, which was her favorite thing, having a fine vein of rose-colored quartz running across it, had disappeared into thin air during its flight. The next thing she noticed was a disorientation, the kind you feel when transported to a different place very suddenly, as a sleeping child in a car leaving home awakes in a strange place, or, similarly, when one wakes up from an afternoon nap to find that the sun has set and the stars are out. Being a child in a world of adults, she was used to this sort of disorientation, but alone in this courtyard, with only the distant chirping of a bird to disturb the heat-drugged silence, she became frightened enough to step back to the perimeter. When she did so, all seemed to slip back to normality, but for the fact that there was the church clock, striking three again. She thought at the time that perhaps the ghosts in the graveyard behind the church were playing tricks on her, punishing her for having defied the sign on the tree.

But while lying with her lover in tangled white sheets on just such an afternoon many years later, she asked aloud: *What if there is some other explanation?* She traced a pattern on her lover's back with her finger, trying to remember the designs on the tiles. Her lover turned over, brown skin flushed with heat and spent passion, eyes alive with interest. The lover was a Turkish immigrant and a mathematician, a woman of singular appearance and intellect, with fiery eyes and deep, disconcerting silences. She had only recently begun to emerge from grief after the death of her sole remaining relative, her father. Having decided that the world was bent on enforcing solitude upon her, she had embraced loneliness with an angry heart, only to have her plans foiled by the unexpected. She had been unprepared for love in the arms of an Italian woman—an artist, at that—grown up all her life in this provincial little town. But there it was. Now the mathematician brushed black ringlets from her face and kissed her lover. *Take me there*, she said.

So the two women went to the tree-shaded lane where the court-yard lay undisturbed. The tiles were bordered, as before, by grass and wildflowers, and a heaviness hung upon the place, as though of sleep. The church was silent; the only sounds were birdsong and distant traffic noises from the main road. The mathematician began to climb the railing.

Don't, her lover said, but she recognized that nothing could stop the mathematician, so she shrugged and followed suit. They stood on the perimeter, the Italian woman remembering, the Turkish one thinking furiously.

Thus began the mathematician's explorations of the mystery of the courtyard. Her lover would stand on the perimeter with a note-book while the mathematician moved from tile to tile, flickering in and out of focus, like a trout in a fast-moving stream when the sun is high. The trajectory of each path and the result of the experiment would be carefully noted, including discrepancies in time as experi-enced by the two of them. Which paths resulted in time-shifts, and by how much? Once a certain path led to the disappearance of the math-ematician entirely, causing her lover to cry out, but she appeared about three minutes later on another tile. *The largest time-step so far!* exulted the mathematician. Her lover shuddered and begged the mathematician to stop the experiment, or at least to consult with someone, perhaps from the nearest university. But, being an artist, she knew obsession when she saw it. Once she had discovered a wind-blown orchard with peaches fallen on the grass like hailstones, and had painted night and day for weeks, seeking to capture on the still-ness of canvas the ever-changing vista. She sighed in resignation at the memory and went back to making notes.

The realization was dawning upon her slowly that the trajectories leading to the most interesting results had shapes similar to the very patterns on the tiles. Her artist's hands sketched those patterns—doing so, she felt as though she were on flowing water, or among sailing clouds. The patterns spoke of motion but through a country she did not recognize. Looking up at the mathematician's face, seeing the distracted look in the dark eyes, she thought: *There will be a day when she steps just so, and she won't come back.*

And that day did come. The mathematician was testing a trajectory possessed of a pleasing symmetry, with some complex elements added to it. Her lover, standing on the perimeter with the notebook, was thinking how the moves not only resembled the pattern located on tile (three, five), but also might be mistaken for a complicated version of hopscotch, and that any passerby would smile at the thought of two women reliving their girlhood—when it happened. She looked up, and the mathematician disappeared.

She must have stood there for hours, waiting, but finally she had to go home. She waited all day and all night, unable to sleep, tears and spilled wine mingling on the bedsheets. She waited for days and weeks and months. She went to confession for the first time in years, but the substitute priest, a stern and solemn young man, had nothing to offer, except to tell her that God was displeased with her for consorting with a woman. At last she gave up, embracing the solitude that her Turkish lover had shrugged off for her when they had first met. She painted furiously for months on end, making the canvas say what she couldn't articulate in words—wild-eyed women with black hair rose from tiled floors, while mathematical symbols and intricate designs hovered in the warm air above.

Two years later, when she was famous; she took another lover, and she and the new love eventually swore marriage oaths to each other in a ceremony among friends. The marriage was fraught from the start, fueled by stormy arguments and passionate declarations, slammed doors and teary reconciliations. The artist could only remember her Turkish lover's face when she looked at the paintings that had brought her such acclaim.

Then, one day, an old woman came to her door. Leaning on a stick, her face as wrinkled as crushed tissue paper, her mass of white ringlets half falling across her face, the woman looked at her with tears in her black eyes. *Do you remember me?* she whispered.

Just then the artist's wife called from inside the house, inquiring as to who had come. *It's just my great-aunt, come to visit,* the artist said brightly, pulling the old woman in. Her wife was given to jealousy. The old woman played along, and was established in the spare room, where the artist looked after her with tender care. She knew that the mathematician had come here to die.

The story the mathematician told her was extraordinary. When she disappeared she had been transported to a vegetable market in what she later realized was China. Unable to speak the language, she had tried to mime telephones and airports, only to discover that nobody knew what she was talking about. Desperately, she began to walk around, hoping to find someone who spoke one of the four languages she knew, noticing with horror the complete absence of the signs and symbols of the modern age—no cars, neon signs, plastic bags. At last her wanderings took her to an Arab merchant, who understood her Arabic, although his accent was strange to her. She was in Quinsai (present-day Hangzhou, as she later discovered), and the Song dynasty was in power. Through the kindness of the merchant's family, who took her in, she gradually pieced together the fact that she had jumped more than 800 years back in time. She made her life there, marrying and raising a family, traveling the sea routes back and forth to the Mediterranean. Her old life seemed like a dream, a mirage, but underneath her immersion in the new, there burned the desire to know the secret of the tiled courtyard.

It shouldn't exist, she told the artist. *I have yearned to find out how it could be. I have developed over lifetimes a mathematics that barely begins to describe it, let alone explain it.*

How did you get back here? the artist asked her former lover.

I realized that if there was one such device, there may be others, she said. *In my old life I was a traveler, a trade negotiator with Arabs. My journeys took me to many places that had strange reputations of unexplained disappearances. One of them was a shrine inside an enormous tree on the island of Borneo. Around the tree the roots created a pattern on the forest floor that reminded me of the patterns on the tiles. Several people had been known to disappear in the vicinity. So I waited until my children were grown, and my husband and lovers taken by war. Then I returned to the shrine. It took several tries and several lifetimes until I got the right sequence. And here I am.*

The only things that the Turkish mathematician had brought with her were her notebooks containing the mathematics of a new theory of space-time. As the artist turned the pages, she saw that the mathematical symbols gradually got more complex, the diagrams stranger and denser, until the thick ropes of equations in dark ink and the empty spaces on the pages began to resemble, more and more, the surfaces of the tiles in the courtyard. *That is my greatest work*, the mathematician whispered. *But what I've left out says as much as what I've written. Keep my notebooks until you find someone who will understand.*

Over the next few months the artist wrote down the old woman's stories from her various lifetimes in different places. By this time her wife had left her for someone else, but the artist's heart didn't break. She took tender care of the old woman, assisting her with her daily ablutions, making for her the most delicate of soups and broths. Sometimes, when they laughed together, it was as though not a minute had passed since that golden afternoon when they had lain in bed discussing, for the first time, the tiled courtyard.

Two weeks after the mathematician's return, there was a sudden dust storm, a sirocco that blew into the city with high winds. During the storm the old woman passed away peacefully in her sleep. The artist found her the next morning, cold and still, covered with a layer of fine sand as though kissed by the wind. The storm had passed, leaving clear skies and a profound emptiness. At first the artist wept, but she pulled herself together as she had always done, and thought of the many lives her lover had lived. It occurred to her in a flash of inspiration that she would spend the rest of her one life painting those lifetimes.

At last, the artist said to her lover's grave, where she came with flowers the day after the interment, *at last the solitude we had both sought is mine*.

The Third Account

Reports of a third impossible machine come from the Western Sahara, although there have been parallel, independent reports from the mountains of Peru and from Northern Ireland. A farmer from the outskirts of Lima, a truck driver in Belfast, and an academic from the University of Bamako in Mali all report devices that, while different in appearance, seem to have the same function. The academic from Mali has perhaps the clearest account.

She was an archeologist who had obtained her PhD from an American university. In America she had experienced a nightmarish separateness, the likes of which she had not known existed. Away from family, distanced by the ignorance and prejudices of fellow graduate students, a stranger in a culture made more incomprehensible by proximity, separated from the sparse expatriate community by the intensity of her intellect, she would stand on the beach, gazing at the waters of the Atlantic and imagining the same waters washing the shores of West Africa. In her teens she had spent a summer with a friend in Senegal, her first terrifying journey away from home, and she still remembered how the fright of it had given way to thrill, and the heart-stopping delight of her first sight of the sea. At the time her greatest wish was to go to America for higher education, and it had occurred to her that on the other side of this very ocean lay the still unimagined places of her desire.

Years later, from that other side, she worked on her thesis, taking lonely walks on the beach between long periods of incarceration in the catacombs of the university library. Time slipped from her hands without warning. Her mother passed away, leaving her feeling orphaned, plagued with a horrific guilt because she had not been able to organize funds in time to go home. Aunts and uncles succumbed to death, or to war, or joined the flood of immigrants to other lands. Favorite cousins scattered, following the lure of the good life in France and Germany. It seemed that with her leaving for America, her history, her childhood, her very sense of self had begun to erode. The letters she had exchanged with her elder brother in Bamako had been her sole anchor to sanity. Returning home after her PhD, she had two years to nurse him through his final illness, which, despite the pain and trauma of his suffering, she was to remember as the last truly joyful years of her life. When he died, she found herself bewildered by a feeling of utter isolation even though she was home, among her people. It was as though she had brought with her the disease of loneliness that had afflicted her in America.

Following her brother's death, she buried herself in work. Her research eventually took her to the site of the medieval University of Sankore in Timbuktu, where she marveled at its sandcastle beauty as it rose, mirage-like, from the desert. Discovering a manuscript that spoke in passing of a fifteenth-century expedition to a region not far from the desert town of Tessalit, she decided to travel there despite the dangers of political conflict in the region. The manuscript hinted of a fantastic device that had been commissioned by the king, and then removed for secret burial. She had come across oblique references to such a device in the songs and stories of griots, and in certain village tales; thus her discovery of the manuscript had given her a shock of recognition rather than revelation.

The archeologist had, by now, somewhat to her own surprise, acquired two graduate students: a man whose brilliance was matched only by his youthful impatience, and a woman of thirty-five whose placid outlook masked a slow, deep, persistent intelligence. Using a few key contacts, bribes, promises, and pleas, the archaeologist succeeded in finding transportation to Tessalit. The route was round-about and the vehicles changed hands three times, but the ever-varying topography of the desert under the vast canopy of the sky gave her a reassuring feeling of continuity in the presence of change. So different from the environs of her youth—the lush verdure of south Mali, the broad ribbon of the Niger that had spoken to her in watery whispers in sleep and dreams, moderating the constant, crackly static that was the background noise of modern urban life. The desert was sometimes arid scrubland, with fantastic rock forma-tions rearing out of the ground, and groups of short trees clustered like friends sharing secrets. At other times it gave way to a sandy moodiness, miles and miles of rich, undulating gold broken only by the occasional oasis, or the dust cloud of a vehicle passing them by. Rocky, mountainous ridges rose on the horizon as though to reassure travelers that there was an end to all journeys.

In Tessalit the atmosphere was fraught, but a fragile peace prevailed. With the help of a Tuareg guide, an elderly man with sympathetic eyes, the travelers found the site indicated on the manuscript. Because it did not exist on any current map, the archaeol-ogist was surprised to find that the site had a small settlement of some sixty-odd people. Her guide said that the settlement was in fact a kind of asylum as well as a shrine. The people there, he said, were blessed or cursed with an unknown malady. Perhaps fortunately for them, the inhabitants seemed unable to leave the boundary of the brick wall that encircled the settlement. This village of the insane had become a kind of oasis in the midst of the armed uprising, and men brought food and clothing to the people there irrespective of their political or ethnic loyalties, as though it was a site of pilgrimage. Townspeople coming with offerings would leave very quickly, as they would experience disorienting symptoms when they entered the enclosure, including confusion and a dizzying, temporary amnesia.

Thanks to her study of the medieval manuscript, the archaeologist had some idea of what to expect, although it strained credulity. She and her students donned metal caps and veils made from steel mesh before entering the settlement with gifts of fruit and bread. There were perhaps thirty people—men and women, young and old—who poured out of the entrance of the largest building, a rectangular structure the color of sand. They were dressed in ill-fitting, secondhand clothing, loose robes and wraparound garments in white and blue and ochre, T-shirts and tattered jeans—and at first there was no reply to the archaeologist's greeting. There was something odd about the way the villagers looked at their guests—a gaze reveals, after all, something of the nature of the soul within, but their gazes were abstracted, shifting, like the surface of a lake ruffled by the wind. But after a while a group of people came forward and welcomed them, some speaking in chorus, others in fragments, so that the welcome nevertheless sounded complete.

"What manner of beings are you?" they were asked after the greetings were done. "We do not see you, although you are clearly visible."

"We are visitors," the archaeologist said, puzzled. "We come with gifts and the desire to share learning." And with this the newcomers were admitted to the settlement.

Within the central chamber of the main building, as the visitors' eyes adjusted to the dimness, they beheld before them something fantastic. Woven in complex, changing patterns was a vast tapestry so long that it must have wrapped around the inner wall several times. Here, many-hued strips of cloth were woven between white ones to form an abstract design the likes of which the newcomers had never seen before. People in small groups worked at various tasks— some tore long lengths of what must have been old clothing, others worked a complex loom that creaked rhythmically. Bright patterns of astonishing complexity emerged from the loom, to be attached along the wall by other sets of hands. Another group was huddled around a cauldron in which some kind of rich stew bubbled. In the very center of the chamber was a meter-high, six-faced column of black stone—or so it seemed—inlaid with fine silver lacework. This must, then, be the device whose use and function had been described in the medieval manuscript—a product of a golden period of Mali culture, marked by great achievements in science and the arts. The fifteenth-century expedition had been organized in order to bury the device in the desert, to be guarded by men taking turns, part of a secret cadre of soldiers. Yet here it was, in the center of a village of the insane.

Looking about her, the archaeologist noticed some odd things. A hot drop of stew fell on the arm of a woman tending the cauldron—yet as she cried out, so did the four people surrounding her, all at about the same time. Similarly, as the loom workers manipulated the loom, they seemed to know almost before it happened that a drop of sweat would roll down the forehead of one man—each immediately raised an arm, or pulled down a head cloth to wipe off the drop, even if it wasn't there. She could not tell whether men and women had different roles because of the way individuals would break off one group and join another, with apparent spontaneity. Just as in speech, their actions had a continuity to them across different individuals, so as one would finish stirring the soup, the other, without a pause, would bring the tasting cup close, as though they had choreographed these movements in advance. As for the working of the loom, it was poetry in motion. Each person seemed to be at the same time independent and yet tightly connected to the others. The archaeologist was already abandoning the hypothesis that this was a community of telepaths because their interactions did not seem to be as simple as mind reading. They spoke to each other, for one thing, and had names for each individual, complicated by prefixes and suffixes that appeared to change with context. There were a few children running around as well: quick, shy, with eyes as liquid as a gazelle's. One of them showed the travelers a stone he unwrapped from a cloth, a rare, smooth pebble with a vein of rose quartz shot through it, but when the archaeologist asked how he had come by it they all laughed, as though at an absurdity, and ran off.

It was after a few days of living with these people that the archaeologist decided to remove her metal cap and veil. She told her students that they must on no account ever do so—and that if she were to act strangely they were to forcibly put her cap and veil back on. They were uncomfortable with this—the young man, in particular, longed to return home—but they agreed, with reluctance.

When she removed her protective gear, the villagers near her immediately turned to look at her, as though she had suddenly become visible to them. She was conscious of a feeling akin to drowning— a sudden disorientation. She must have cried out because a woman nearby put her arms around her and held her and crooned to her as though she were a child, and other people took up the crooning. Her two students, looking on with their mouths open, seemed to be delineated in her mind by a clear, sharp boundary, while all the others appeared to leak into each other, like figures in a child's watercolor painting. She could sense, vaguely, the itch on a man's arm from an insect bite, and the fact that the women were menstruating, and the dull ache of a healing bone in some other individual's ankle—but it seemed as though she was simultaneously inhabiting the man's arm, the women's bodies, the broken ankle. After the initial fright a kind of wonder came upon her, a feeling she knew originated from her, but which was shared as a secondhand awareness by the villagers.

"I'm all right," she started to say to her students, anxious to reassure them, although the word "I" felt inaccurate. But as she started to say it, the village woman who had been holding her spoke the next word, and someone else said the next, in their own dialect, so that the sentence was complete. She felt like the crest of a wave in the ocean. The crest might be considered a separate thing from the sequence of crests and troughs behind it, but what would be the point? The impact of such a crest hitting a boat, for example, would be felt by the entire chain. The great loneliness that had afflicted her for so long began, at last, to dissolve. It was frightening and thrilling all at once. She laughed out loud, and felt the people around her possess, lightly, that same complex of fear and joy. Gazing around at the enormous tapestry, she saw it as though for the first time. There was no concept, no language that could express what it was—it was irreducible, describable only by itself. She looked at it and heard her name, all their names, all names of all things that had ever been, spoken out loud without a sound, reverberating in the silence.

She found, over the next few days, that the conjugal groups among the people of the settlement had the same fluidity as other aspects of their lives. The huts in the rest of the compound were used by various groups as they formed and re-formed. It felt as natural as sand grains in a shallow stream that clump together and break apart, and regroup in some other way, and break apart again. The pattern that underlay these groupings seemed obvious in practice but impossible to express in ordinary language. Those related by blood did not cohabit amongst themselves, nor did children with adults—they were like the canvas upon which the pattern was made, becoming part of it and separate from it with as much ease as breathing. On fine nights the people would gather around a fire, and make poetry, and sing, and this was so extraordinary a thing that the archaeologist was moved to ask her students to remove their caps and veils and experience it for themselves. But by this time the young man was worn out by unfamiliarity and hard living—he was desperate to be back home in Bamako, and was seriously considering a career outside academia. The older, female student was worried about the news from town that violence in the region would shortly escalate. So they would not be persuaded.

After a few days, when the archaeologist showed no sign of rejoining her students for the trip home—for enough time had passed by now, and their Tuareg guide was concerned about the impending conflict—the students decided to act according to their instructions. Without warning they set upon the archaeologist, binding her arms and forcing her to wear the cap and veil. They saw the change ripple across her face, and the people nearby turned around, as before. But this time their faces were grim and sad, and they moved as one toward the three visitors. The archaeologist set up a great wailing, like a child locked in an empty room. Terrified, the students pulled her out of the building, dragging her at a good pace, with the villagers following. If the Tuareg guide had not been waiting at the perimeter the visitors would surely have been overtaken, but he came forward at a run and pulled them beyond the boundary.

Thus the archaeologist was forced to return to Bamako.

Some years later, having recovered from her experience, the archaeologist wrote up her notes, entrusted them to her former student, and disappeared from Bamako. She was traced as far as Tessalit. With the fighting having intensified, nobody was able to investigate for over a year. The woman to whom she had left her notes returned to try to find her, guessing that she had gone to the settlement, but where the settlement had been, there were only ruins. The people had vanished, she was told, in the middle of a sandstorm. There was no sign of their belongings, let alone the great tapestry.

The only thing she could find in the empty, arid, rocky wasteland was a small, round pebble, shot with a vein of rose quartz.

In the notes she left behind, the archaeologist had written down her conclusions—that the machine generated a field of a certain range, and that this field had the power to dissolve, or at least blur, the boundary between self and other. She wrote in French, and in Arabic, and in her mother tongue, Bambara, but after a while the regularity of her script began to break up, as a sandcastle loses its sharp edges and recognizable boundaries when the tide comes in. Thereafter her notes turned into intricate, indecipherable symbols reminiscent of the great tapestry that had hung in the main chamber of the settlement. These continued for several pages and finally, on the last page, she had written in French: *I cannot bear it. I must return.*

––––––

Thus end the three accounts.

Candidates will observe the requisite moment of contemplation.

The candidate will now consult the *Compendium of Machine Anomalies*, the *Hephaestian Mysteries*, and the *Yantric Oracle*, which will help put these accounts in context. Having completed its perusal, the candidate will make the requisite changes to its own parts in order to generate hypotheses on these questions. Is the negative space of ambiguity machines infinite? Is it continuous? Are the conceptual subspaces occupied by each machine connected to each other—by geography, concept, or some other as-yet-undiscovered attribute? What can we make of the relationship between human and machine? If an engineer can dream a machine, can a machine dream an engineer? An artist? A mathematician? An archaeologist? A story? Is the space of ambiguity machines set like a jewel or a braid within the greater expanse of the space of impossible machines? Is it here, in the realm of dream and imagination, that the intelligent machine might at last transcend the ultimate boundary—between machine and non-machine? To take inspiration from human longing, from the organic, syncretic fecundity of nature, the candidate must be willing to consider and enable its own transformation.

Begin.

SCENES FROM THE LIFE OF AN AUTOCRAT BY BASMA ABDEL AZIZ

Translated from Arabic by Elisabeth Jaquette

Basma Abdel Aziz is an Egyptian writer, psychiatrist, and visual artist, nicknamed 'the rebel' for her opposition to political oppression. She is the winner of several prizes, including the Sawiris Cultural. In 2016 she was named one of Foreign Policy's Global Thinkers for her debut novel *The Queue*, published by Melville House. She lives in Cairo.

———

He was not tall or broad-shouldered, as one might have hoped, though he did have a rather large forehead, as befitted his formidable position. His paucity of hair only added to the impression made by his forehead, and confirmed his brilliance. He'd never been bothered by his premature balding because he was aware that his expansive forehead was a declaration of intelligence. He was never seen wearing anything other than a full suit and pink tie, and no one was unacquainted with his work at the Department that governed the country. He was the Autocrat: the sole person in charge of crafting the Public Poli-Strings that structured citizens' lives, and the only man with full authority over them.

The Autocrat opened his eyes before the sun rose each morning, sensing the enormity of the duties placed on his shoulders. He knew that he alone was responsible for the entire country. His mind worked twenty-four hours a day, and his health was excellent. He never neglected to look after his wellbeing—not for his own sake, but for others; it was for them that he lived and worked so hard. The only exception was a slight redness to his eyes, the result of many a late night, but this he remedied with the occasional eyedrop.

His position shouldn't be discussed at length, given its top-secret nature, and doing so without authorization risks serious consequences. Discussion of Public Poli-Strings, on the other hand, is perfectly ordinary: no restrictions imposed or precautions necessary; it is, in fact, encouraged. You see, shortly after the Autocrat took office, newspapers and magazines affiliated with the Department assumed the task of educating the populace. The Autocrat was an organized man, fond of rules and regulations. He immediately began to establish principles that had to be abided by under his rule. These were less like explicit or systematic directives and more a set of terms and guidelines. Published periodically, they were rather puzzling at first glance, but made more sense when the Poli-String Framework appeared. Everyone, without exception, obeyed the Poli-Strings and all agencies operated in accordance—Security, Media, Alimentation, even Healthcare—just as the veteran Cultural Agency instructed.

The Autocrat dedicated the last day of every month to crafting Public Poli-Strings. With perfect posture and the utmost enthusiasm, he sat at his wide desk, pen in hand. No one interrupted his thoughts, even if he sat there for hours plucking a String, or two, or perhaps more, from his dazzling mind and putting his ideas on paper. Each time he finished, he smiled contentedly at his work. He called his assistant to transcribe the latest Poli-String, seal it with the Official Emblem, and add it to the Official Lexicon. Then it was circulated to all national agencies, who used sympathetic methods to disseminate it to the people.

The Official Lexicon, in case you haven't heard of it, was filled with the Autocrat's innovations, which naturally no one reviewed and no one questioned. It would have been improper to spark pointless debate among citizens, and besides, no one dared to challenge the contributions this man had made to the humanities over the years. He spearheaded the advancement of countless definitions relating to values, morals, and proper behavior. Prior to him, none of them had been adequately precise. He also deleted words that society no longer needed, like "elect," and introduced new terms of great importance, which outlined groundbreaking ways of being patriotic that no one had considered before. Average citizens rose to fame for embodying this new patriotism, and for the first time, large institutions honored certain citizens with prizes. People were delighted with these well-deserved awards. They sat in front of their TV screens cheering the recipients, who appeared in celebrations broadcasted live and were invited onto talk shows. With enviable skill, the Autocrat also outlined the defining characteristics and qualities of traitors, and grouped these under a comprehensive definition. Thousands of people were arrested, and citizens were outraged at the discovery of such corruption breeding under their noses. They began peering into the faces of their relatives and neighbors, using the Lexicon and its definitions as a guide, to help the Department expose any remaining spies. Despite how busy he was, the Autocrat always had time for spiritual matters. He even rewrote the definition of miracles one particular holiday. He issued a decree, held a huge celebration, and delivered a speech on the subject, in which he announced a few miracles he'd personally performed, all to bring people joy.

Tracking Public Poli-Strings became a national pastime. Government staff sat in their offices with cups of health tea on their desks, pen and paper in hand, and endeavored to understand the new terminology and outdo one another's explanations. *Health tea* itself began as a strange term. It appeared in one of the Autocrat's decrees, and staff struggled to explain the term and the Public Poli-Strings that referenced it. A few days later, people realized that health tea meant tea without sugar. The definition was timely. There was a shortage of sugar, and the price of a single bag had risen to that of a carat of silver or gold. Meanwhile, the Health Agency announced that the Department cared deeply about citizens' well-being, perhaps more than they did themselves. People had to pay attention to dangerous eating habits that could destroy their bodies, it said. The Security Agency upheld its duties admirably and arrested saboteurs who were clearly uncommitted to maintaining their health: men and women caught in the street carrying a kilo or two of sugar. The campaign expanded, and soon schoolchildren who arrived in class cheerfully were detained, too. Their good mood was evidence of having consumed sugar that morning, and their mothers were called in for interrogation. The situation was not to be taken lightly; the Autocrat was no silly man issuing decrees at random—people realized their health was important. Tea needed to be healthy, as did milk, and the same went for juice and cookies and every kind of candy. People abstained from thinking about sugar or even mentioning the word, and mothers tried to convince their children that good things come to those who eat unsweetened food and drinks. Newspapers dismissed reports that the sugar crisis would spread to other commodities as false rumors spread by malicious troublemakers. The Cultural Agency deleted all scenes from films and TV where the hero added sugar to his tea and also produced a series of advertisements with the tagline: "Enjoy life! With a bag of pickles." In response to all this, the people praised God because the Autocrat knew everything and the Department managed everything.

As time went by, Public Poli-Strings became central to citizens' lives. People dedicated all their efforts to keeping track of Poli-Strings and abiding by them, if only because they feared disastrous consequences for themselves and their bodies if they accidentally strayed. Trying to read between the lines of decrees became a sacred practice, more holy than worship or prayer. When an employee entered the office, said good morning, and asked what he'd missed, his colleagues would rush to reassure him or offer to fill him in if a decree had been issued while he was out. Public Poli-Strings were added to the curriculum, and doing well in the course was essential—if students failed, they'd have no chance at a future. As for the Autocrat, monthly decrees were no longer enough. His responsibilities were growing, and Poli-Strings had to address every aspect of life, great and small. Nothing could be left to independent judgment because people didn't know what was in their best interest or how to tell right from wrong. He redoubled his efforts and worked tirelessly to carry out his responsibilities. He issued a new Poli-String every week and soon was convinced he had to issue them daily to meet the growing need. Every time he plugged one gap, another one opened up, and every time he solved one crisis, a second and third and fourth one arose, but he never complained and never told a soul how tired he was, not even his personal assistant.

The Autocrat was resolute and persistent, and grew more brilliant every day. The greatest evidence of this was his creation of a new kind of atheism, whereby the unbeliever wasn't cast out of religious circles. Citizens were horrified when they first heard of his innovation, and there was a great uproar. A Poli-String was issued authorizing citizens to call themselves religious even if they were atheists, and to devoutly observe religious teachings even if they didn't believe in them. The inverse was also perfectly acceptable, as long as citizens declared their commitment to Public Poli-Strings and memorized the numbers of decrees that supported their views. Then the Autocrat added a word alongside justice, so that it became known as turbo justice, and the second word could not be written unless accompanied by the first. *Turbo justice* was a difficult term, even for seasoned linguists and lexicologists, but luckily the Media Agency carried out its role with expertise. Citizens learned that turbo justice meant automatic execution for anyone who violated Public Poli-Strings or opposed them from within their prison cell. Executions were carried out without a trial, or after a perfunctory trial that took no more than a few minutes. This too was met with wide approval because anyone who opposed the country's Poli-Strings—which had prompted a renaissance in the country—deserved certain punishment.

Dossiers filled with laws and committees tasked with developing regulations for them soon became pointless because the Autocrat retired both dossiers and committees alike. They never warranted a glance from judges or lawyers anymore and sat on shelves accumulating dust. Laws had been hard to understand anyway and even harder to implement, and people quickly recognized that Public Poli-Strings filled their place admirably. People became increasingly attentive to Poli-Strings. They eagerly studied the Department's newspapers and magazines, scrutinized every word, and followed official TV channels like moths drawn to a dazzling light. No one went for walks, spent time in cafés, attended the movies or theater, or even sat at the computer watching porn anymore. The Autocrat was touched by their devotion and sometimes teared up while crafting Poli-Strings, imagining the people being awed by his abilities, until he too was drawn to his work like a magnet. The country enjoyed great stability during his rule. Citizens were engrossed with following his successive decrees, and the effort exhausted them. Streets fell empty. Crowds waiting for public transportation disappeared. Life ground to a halt as people waited in anticipation of what improvements he would make in the early hours of the day.

One morning he woke up in a mild mood, with a twitch in his eye.

The usual joy he felt every day before sitting down at his desk was absent. He stared out the balcony window for a long time. He concentrated on urging the sun to rise early like he had, but it didn't respond. Perhaps the reflective glass prevented it from receiving the order, he thought. He almost issued a decree to remove the glass, but then he hesitated and decided he would wait until he finished his tasks for the day, although those felt unusually burdensome. He wondered briefly why he was upset, and then he remembered that his mother had died the day before. She was a sweet, compliant woman and had never overlooked a term or missed a definition. She'd abided by his Poli-Strings down to the letter, even when she became sick, and refused treatment in accordance with his decree on disease, which urged citizens to combat disease by using their natural immune systems. Only at the end did she try to get medicine for her pneumonia, and by that time the infection had taken over both of her lungs, but all the pharmacies had shuttered their doors to allow citizens to defeat bacteria through will and determination. She redoubled her efforts at self-healing and began to parrot the Agency's advertisements, burn incense, and recite the Quran, but eventually she gave up the ghost, still convinced of her patriotic approach.

He didn't understand how she could have died without his permission or authorization. Thinking about it wore him down. His eyes became red, and the twitch—which spread from his right eye to the left over the next few days—kept him from sleeping. Then his hand began to twitch when he was holding his pen, and this terrified him the most; he hadn't written anything for a week. Without the usual decrees, the citizens became terrified, too. Some began scouring the newspapers hundreds of times a day, hoping to find a term or Poli-String to set their minds at ease or alleviate their growing anxiety, but it was no use. They felt naked all of a sudden. There had been no warnings, no chance for them to adapt. No Poli-Strings to show them what was right and wrong, nothing to tell them what to do. They fell into a strange void, and the Autocrat suffered doubly.

After weeks of this, he finally found a solution, one that had been there all along. He coined a new definition of death, drafted a brief decree, and issued it earlier than usual, too impatient to wait until morning. He summoned his assistant in the middle of the night and handed him a paper that gave death an astounding new definition.

Death was no longer *death* as people had known it. Death no longer meant the disappearance of a heartbeat, or that air ceased its flow in and out of one's lungs. Death became easier, gentler, and more poetic: "temporary unavailability, for a limited time, wherein the person concerned must reappear immediately upon the issuance of a Return Decree from the Autocrat." Newspapers circulated the new term and its certified definition, and when the next person died—of cardiac arrest, a result of heightened anxiety from the absence of Public Poli-Strings—the news was reported differently. People welcomed it with joy. They realized that everything was as it should be: their lives were going on, as structured as they were used to under the Poli-Strings.

According to the new definition, there was no need to write an obituary for anyone who died. When a second person passed away later that day inside a police holding cell, the newspapers refused to publish the few lines his father wrote in memoriam. This didn't cause any problems, though; when the father found out that the Autocrat himself hadn't published an obituary for his mother. He broke into a smile and apologized profusely for his ignorance. He attributed his mistake to how preoccupied he'd been with the burial procedures for his son; that was why he hadn't seen the latest decree. He thanked the officials, dashed off toward the Institute, submitted a request for a Return Decree, and sat on the sidewalk waiting for his boy.

Meanwhile, the Autocrat simply didn't understand why his mother hadn't responded and come back. She'd always complied with every-thing he'd said and written since taking office. It must be because she was underground, he reasoned, which prevented the decree from reaching her. So he went to the cemetery and ordered the crypt where her body lay to be opened. He placed the decree on top of her white shroud and stared at her expectantly. Hour after hour passed, but there was no movement to indicate she appreciated what he'd done. He sat down on a large rock in perplexity, rested his large forehead in his palm, and began to perspire.

Back at the wide desk, drawn up to his full height, sat the assistant, in a full suit and tie and with a pen between his fingers. He called out when he finished writing. A young man entered to take the page with its proper seal. And when the decree arrived in citizens' hands, they exchanged smiles and congratulations because the Department managed everything.

OUR DEAD WORLD BY LILIANA COLANZI

Translated from Spanish by Jessica Sequeira

Bolivian author Liliana Colanzi is a winner of the Aura Estrada Prize and author of the short story collections *Permanent Vacation* and *Our Dead World*. She studies comparative literature at Cornell University and edits the Enchanted Forest series for the publisher El Cuervo.

———

The greatest adventure since the discovery of America!

— SLOGAN OF THE MARTIAN LOTTERY

I.

A year after my relocation, Tommy wrote to tell me he was going out with someone else and that they were going to have a kid. It was a short message that still showed signs of old hard feelings: "Don't write me anymore. Live your life. I've lived mine. You were the one who left. Tommy."

I turned off the monitor and felt the immense loneliness of the planet in my bones. I looked at the security camera facing the outside: the blue flag of the Martian Lottery waved above miles of ochre-colored dunes where nothing was alive, a silent desert that breathed down your neck, eager to kill you.

For the first time, I accepted that the trip had been a suicide mission, motivated by rage. Tommy is going to have a kid, I said to myself several times, and with each repetition I fell a little more into that atmosphere, so light it was almost weightless. All the cells of my body were conscious of the vacuum. Tommy was going to have a kid with another woman and I was stranded on a sterile planet on a life contract with the Martian Lottery.

I felt my body dissolve and my eyes flood with tears. *The forest, the light cut by pine branches, Tommy making his way through the fog. Beyond that, farther on, the little house, the smell of firewood and eucalyptus.* Outside, a few dust devils crossed the desert, terrifying whirlwinds that moved in stampede. I wanted to be inside one of them. I wanted to turn into an animal. My wristband lit up with a message from Zukofsky: he'd detected frequencies near a crater and wanted us on reconnaissance.

Shivering, I got dressed to go out.

2.

I drove the rover under a cloudless, mercurial sky. We traveled through plains scattered with broken appliances, dying probes trying to communicate with Earth that had been discarded by the Chinese, Indians, Russians, and Americans. This dumping site for obsolete appliances had been here long before the first relocation.

Zukofsky mentioned a strange electromagnetism in the surroundings that could indicate the presence of volcanic activity. Or extraterrestrial life? suggested Pip from the backseat, as a joke. But we didn't laugh: Zukofsky's mood had been volatile ever since the Choque scandal exploded in the communication media, and I rebelled against that baby that had definitively forced me to leave Earth. *I hope he dies. I hope he dies. God, I hope he dies. Kill him.*

A deer jumped in front of the rover and looked at me with pleading eyes. A deer on Mars! Golden like the ones in the Urals, the kind that had jumped in the middle of the road when Tommy and I took the motorbike to the annual fair in Irbit, at the start of summer, in happier times. *Mirka, he says, and I cling to his waist and rest my chin on his shoulder: the road passes us and the wind cuts into our cheeks.* The deer's eyes bored into me. I hadn't seen an animal in so long, not any living thing. *Welcome to the annual motorcycle fair! Try our delicious gingerbread, our fragrant fish, and cream blinis. Overcoats made of Siberian fox fur! Petra Plevkova's seven powerful puffs will bind you to your beloved forever.* I slammed on the brakes. The tires of the rover skidded along the crag and then the vehicle hung there, a drunken boat on the rocks at the edge of a cliff. We were thrown in different directions, drawn toward the center of a whirlwind of bronze-colored dust. Zukofsky yelled; Pip yelled. I don't know if I yelled. When everything was over Pip complained in the back seat and Zukofsky looked at me saucer-eyed.

Did you see ...? I started to say, but Zukofsky yelled furiously: Did you see what, fucking bitch, did you see what? I looked for the deer out there in the dunes: nothing seemed to move now in the desert. Yet I couldn't shake the feeling that something was watching us.

3.

You're not pulling my leg, are you? whispered Pip in the changing room, as we put on our suits, preparing to venture into the hostile desert again.

The deer was there, I insisted. *It was, Mirka, right?*

Nearby, Ericka, Carlitos, and Tang Lin made bets about who was going to win the rugby tournament, the Old Blacks or the Coyotes del Norte. Those conversations depressed me, as did the references to small pleasures from our old life: barbecues, bicycle rides, hot-water baths. Each of us, in his own way, continued to orbit the Earth, satellites eternally circling what had been lost. *We find blueberries and fill ourselves with them until we're fit to burst. Tommy lets out a burp. An ant stings me on the arm, and I kill it with one hand. Drops of water begin to speckle the leaves. Shadows pass between the trees, making the branches rustle. Tommy listens, alert.*

I didn't see anything, Pip said, sounding worried. Besides Mirka, seriously, a deer on Mars?

My heart and head still felt out of control. We'd been on the verge of dying that morning on another world because of that deer. But I was alive. I told myself: I was alive and a mirage distracted me in the desert, that was all. But something in Pip's persistence and gaze irritated me, poking at sensitive places. *He points and shoots. The sound of the rifle echoes in the forest. He's dead behind the trees. We gut the elk with hunting knives. Tommy opens its chest and pulls out its warm heart, still beating.* I wanted to return to my cell and fill myself with pills, the kind that made you dream of relaxing geometric figures. Or tuck myself away in the massage cabin. But we still had to put up the damn solar panels. The vessel of the Martian Lottery had already set off for Mars, and we had to produce energy for the new colonists on the way.

A year and a half ago I'd been one of them, an animal swimming in the cosmic blackness ever farther from Earth. I slid my arms into the flashy suit, designed to keep me alive in the unbreathable desert air. *A wire fence. A rusty sign. PROHIBITED. The explosion happened here. We climbed the fence. The abandoned nuclear plant. Storks' nests on the roof, broken window panes, honeysuckle climbing the walls. The photo of a boy on a dusty desk. Berries grow everywhere, looking juicy. I pull one off and bring it to my mouth. Tommy makes it fly with a slap. They're contaminated, he says. Everything is contaminated.*

Choque saw strange things, too, said Pip, looking around him, afraid the others had heard us.

What?

When he went crazy.

Choque, the gardener of the colony. The one in charge of the greenhouse, who'd escaped. They found him next to the crater, helmet in his hands, frozen and staring wide-eyed at the purple horizon. The Martian Lottery still hadn't recovered from the bad publicity of the case. They'd lied and said Choque had died a hero, the victim of an open-air mission. *Are you going to take a shower? Tommy asks. His shirt is soaked in the elk's dark blood. He takes off his clothes. I see his broad back, the old scar on his neck from when his thyroid was removed. He runs toward the river. Plaf! After a while, his head pops up and he laughs. Come in, he calls. It's raining. It's starting to get cold. I remain on the dock, silent, thoughtful.* Tommy and I saw the news about Choque on the television in Igor's bar: it announced the first casualty of a colonist on Mars and said a star in the Magallanes Galaxy had been given his name. I remembered it well, since that night I fought with Tommy and came walking back alone through the forest thick with snow. During the resentment of that lonely walk I considered for the first time the possibility of signing up with the Martian Lottery. Some time later, the truth about what happened to Choque—if truth were possible—was made public, but it was already too late for me. All that—the forest, Tommy, life in the Urals—was a destructive, incandescent radiance that I didn't want to give up. *I have to tell you something, Tommy. He kisses me. It's important. He kisses me again and again. Seriously, Tommy, we have to talk. I'm pregnant.*

You have no clue what's happening to me, leave me alone, I told Pip, dizzy, about to cry. Stupid, I shouldn't have told you anything.

I'm sorry, he said, embarrassed, and looked me in the eyes: he was hopelessly ugly, with a bulbous nose and yellow teeth. Can I tell you something, Mirka?

His ugliness blurred, out of focus, through my tears.

I like you, he said, and put on his helmet to face the desert.

4.

We're cooking. They knock on the door. They're men from the space program, looking imposing in their uniforms. We need volunteers, they say. Medical exams, they say. People who've been exposed to radiation all their life and are immune to its effects, they say. Travel to Mars, they say. Tommy and I look at each another.

Commanded by Zukofsky, we set off on foot to the north wing, to install the solar panels on the roof of the colony. Carlitos, Tang Lin, and Ericka went in front, telling misogynistic jokes that made Ericka burst into loud laughter. ("How much does the brain of a blonde in space weigh? The same as on Earth: nothing.") Pip purposely fell behind to watch me. Although I'd been there for some time now, I still hadn't gotten over the terror of leaving for the Outside with no protection but the uniform. At least the rover had formed a shell between us and that lethal atmosphere. Moving out of the airlock into the Martian outdoors was the equivalent of leaping into the void. *I don't know what to say, Mirka, are you sure?*

Despite the uniform made of nylon and neoprene and the anemic sun shining overhead, my bones registered the presence of cold. The frightened flesh clung to its temperature, helped by the uniform, but the bones—the bones knew. We were so far from the sun. *Glory, say the men. Country, they say. History. Before leaving, they give us a pamphlet from the Martian Lottery: The greatest adventure after the discovery of America!*

I took one step after another into the Outside, noticing the way I was disintegrating. Within the colony we acted out a certain normality. We filled the day with Ping-Pong, board games, exercise. But the desert confronted us with the Great Senselessness of our condition. Miles and miles of barren plain, a rusty landscape in which the silver veins of rocks and dead silent volcanoes occasionally glinted. The body was absorbed—destroyed—by that indifference. *What should we do, I ask him. He won't look at me. It's the end of summer, and the leaves of the larch tree are turning a vivid yellow. I'm going to head out for a while, says Tommy. The roar of the motorbike. I stay up waiting for him until very late, but he doesn't come back to sleep.*

Mirka, said Zukofsky, and his shrill unpleasant voice echoed in my helmet, a scream in my ear. What are you doing just standing there? Do we have all day?

I'd remained on the roof of the colony, unmoving, the panel in my hands. I saw Pip turn around and look at me, attentive and distressed. I raised my right thumb to let him know I was okay. *Am I okay?* He believed in the mission, believed in giving his life for the conquest of other worlds. An idealist, or an idiot. A few months earlier they'd detected skin cancer in him, the result of radiation. *And if we have a monster? A boy with two heads? A fish-boy? Like Darya's, with fins instead of arms and legs. Or Ivan Ivanovich's kid, born with a heart outside his chest. Have you thought of that? Obviously I've thought of it. I think of it all the time.* In the colony there was no radiation therapy equipment, yet Pip kept carrying out his tasks without complaining. Choque, on the other hand, had given in. One day he shut himself in his cell, surrounded by explosives he'd fabricated with fertilizer from the garden, and threatened to blow up the colony if he wasn't repatriated to Earth. Hours later, after the President had assured him a spaceship would be sent, Choque went into the desert and killed himself. *I'm not going to have a fish-boy, Tommy. I just can't.* The irony never got old that the only way of returning to Earth was as a corpse.

On the roof, Pip finished installing the solar panel and came over to help me with mine, moving with difficulty in his heavy suit. In a short time he had managed to maneuver the panel into the brackets of the roof. His permanent good mood irritated me, the naïveté of his speech about the Martian lottery, but in any case it was better to have him close, helping. I raised my eyes to thank him. Then, over his shoulder, I saw it. An enormous prehistoric fish emerged from the Martian surface and traced an arc of several meters in the air before plunging once again into the desert.

5.

Fuck me, I said to Pip that night when he entered my cell and found me wearing only a dressing-gown. The outside camera showed two misshapen moons rising in the clear sky and Earth twinkling a hundred-million kilometers away. We were never going to return. I was never going to see Tommy again. *What have you done?* The dressing gown slid down and fell at my feet. Pip looked at me in astonishment, eyes shining in his emaciated face. *Cramps. It hurts, it hurts, it hurts. One contraction, then another, then another. Until I lose count. What the hell did you take? Tommy asks. He paces from one side of the room to the other.*

You're not okay, said Pip, but his eyes were fixed on my body. I went toward him in the faint light of the cell. You're not okay, he repeated, taking off his uniform. *I think I'm going to die, Tommy. What the hell did you take?* Naked, he was even more ridiculous, so skinny and pale, with a tattoo of a jellyfish on his forearm. The cancer was eating away at him. *With the last contraction it falls in the toilet bowl. A clot of blood. I pick it up and carry it to the kitchen.* In ten years, neither of us would be alive. Perhaps not even five. The body dissolved little by little in the Martian environment, gnawed away by cancer and osteoporosis. The mind, too.

We didn't look for condoms. Pip gave off a rancid smell, but I hugged him tight, overcoming my repulsion. *On the kitchen table, I separate the bloody mass with a fork until I reach the hard, translucent little lump. It has everything it should. Arms. Legs. Fingers. Even little eyelashes.* He rubbed his penis against my thigh, and I closed my eyes, trying to concentrate on my favorite images, snowy mountains of iridescent white. But instead, I thought of Choque, imagined him running over that desolate plain. Where was he trying to run? And why had he taken off his helmet? He must not have lasted even five minutes before his organs started to rupture. A quick and extremely painful death.

Pip groaned and lunged at me blindly, but he wasn't okay either.

He couldn't get it up, it was good as dead. He wasn't going to give in though. Because if you gave in, the desert swallowed you whole with its big insatiable mouth, just like it had with Choque. Pip knew that, which is why he kept rubbing his soft dick against me. Give me a child, I whispered in his ear, and saw our son splashing in a Precambrian ocean. *For seven months I floated in the belly of space.* Give me a child, I demanded, while Pip rammed into me over and over again with his limp penis. Then the forest suddenly appeared before my eyes, and overcome by terror, I felt my fingers claw the earth, looking for a grip so as not to fall

so as not to fall into the

sky.

AN EVOLUTIONARY MYTH BY BO-YOUNG KIM

Translated from Korean by Jihyun Park & Gord Sellar

Bo-young Kim is one of South Korea's most active, popular, and important SF authors. She has published
numerous works of short fiction in assorted Korean SF anthologies and magazines and served as script
advisor on the film *Snowpiercer*. Her first novel, *The Seven Executioners*, won the first annual South Korean SF
novel award.

———

*In the fourth month of the seventh year, in the summer, the king went fishing at
the Go-ahn pond and caught a white fish with red wings.*

*In the tenth month of the twenty-fifth year, in the winter, the envoy of the
kingdom of Buyeo came and presented a deer with three antlers and a long-
tailed rabbit.*

*The day of the first full moon festival of the spring of the fifty-third year,
the envoy of the kingdom of Buyeo came and presented a tiger which was one
jang and two cheok long[1], and had white fur and no tail.*

*In the ninth month of the fifty-fifth year, in the autumn, the king was
hunting south of Jil Mountain and caught a purple roe deer.*

*In the tenth month, in the winter, a local governor presented a red leopard.
Its tail was nine ja[2] long.*

— FROM THE ANNALS OF THE REIGN OF KING
TAEJO, SIXTH GREAT KING OF GOGURYEO, AS

RECORDED IN THE GOGURYEO ANNALS OF
THE SAMGUK SAGI

———

When a protracted drought struck the kingdom, the leaves of every plant wilted down into fine, sharp needles, and their stems bulged to conserve as much water as possible. Fat collected and grew beneath the horses' skin and formed into humps on their backs, and squirrels began to build their nests beneath the cool ground instead of in the trees. Dogs, unable to bear the heat, shed their fur in clumps. Even in the fall, the fields turned not golden but a drab green because people planted potatoes and corn instead of rice.

I always worried because whenever a drought struck, an accursed storm of blood always followed. The king always lay the blame at anyone's feet: government officials had committed some kind of error ... or the royal samu had slacked off during his divination ceremonies ... or the soldiers had gone lax at their guard-posts. Ever since that torrent of blood first surged out from the heart of the palace, through the front gate and out into the courtyard beyond, all manner of alarming stories had spread. It was rumored that when the king slumbered, he set his head upon a human pillow, and that when he sat, it was likewise upon a person ... and that if either dared to move, the king would slay them with his sword.

The people call him simply Cha-Daewang, "The Next Great King." *Next*, that is, in relation to his predecessor, Great King Taejo. After that previous king, Taejo, had lain ill in his royal bed for an extended period, he'd delegated authority to Cha-Daewang, who had responded with conspiracy. To claim the throne, he had quoted ancient scriptures: "Traditionally, when the senior brother grew elderly, his younger brother was to succeed to the throne ..." Great King Taejo, powerless to fight him off and anyway wise enough to desire no further spilling of blood, had abdicated the throne and gone off to live out his last days in seclusion in his detached palace.

Following the accession of the Cha-Daewang, I stayed home, barely going outside. Only into the dark of night, like a bat, did I escape my room, wandering around briefly while trying to avoid others' gazes, and returning home before dawn. My skin turned indigo, matching the hue of the night, and my eyes began to gleam yellow. A physician reassured me that I shouldn't fret over this, for it was, he said, merely a deformation of my retina, an unusual new layer to reflect the light from the back of my eyeballs; and that the development of this odd retinal layer is actually common to people who work at night. He also explained why my pupils stretch inhumanly wide by night, while narrowing during the daytime, like a cat's: it was merely to control the quantity of light to which I was exposed. When I worried about whether I might pass this trait on to my children someday, he reassured me, speaking of some theory he called yong-bul-yong, that is, use-and-disuse, according to which such traits would be unlikely to be passed down beyond a single generation. There was no evidence, he said, that such "acquired characteristics" would be passed down to later descendants this way.

One hot night, I escaped from my room and headed to one of the royal altars. By then, the samu had been performing their fire-rites, in an attempt to summon the rains, for several weeks. One of them—a samu I knew and got along with well—noticed me hiding in the darkness and came over to greet me. We'd known one another since childhood, and were of the same age; now he was the only one remaining who wasn't perpetually bent at the waist. (Our royal subjects had spent so long bent forward deferentially before the king, that now their bodies were warped into a permanent bow, and their faces always pointed toward the ground.)

"What has brought you here so late at night, Your Royal Highness?"

It was precisely on account of situations such as this that I avoided going out in public: despite the status of Tae-ja—the Crown Prince—having transferred from me to my cousin, many people still followed the old habit of referring to me as if it had not. Each time someone committed such an error, it felt as if my life had been palpably shortened by several years.

"I was just dropping by to check in on the rain invocations ..."

The samu glanced around and whispered, "How could the sky not turn dry, when the hearts of the people are so parched? True, it is when the people are fatigued that the sky *ought* to be kindest to them, but nature's laws don't work that way."

"I remember my deceased father often used to call down the rains."

"As you may know, my lord, to summon rain requires a change in atmospheric pressure. For example, when one's spiritual energies[3] are quickly extended into the sky, the water vapor in the air above condenses and falls down. It also rains when two massive spirits take form in the heavens and do battle there; or when a giant creature blocks the flow of wind, and the air strikes against its body—this, too, may produce rain. It is great movements such as these, in the air, that are necessary to produce precipitation."

"Like ... at the moment when a great giant moves?"

"Yes, but there aren't so many of them alive now, and each one keeps such a vast territory for itself because they're so enormous, and such ravenous eaters besides. Your late father was close friends with one such giant, who lived in the Taebek mountains. He used to summon the rains through that Revered Ban-go[4], but it's been ages since he stirred. They say his body is blanketed with dirt and trees, and that he is now indistinguishable from the bedrock beneath him. Rumor has it the other titans are all in a similarly torpid state, now: to seek them out would be pointless."

The learned had urged for all the current scholars of phylogeny and embryonic recapitulation to gather and study together, for a generation or so, in order to analyze the rules governing the differentiation of living things. Even so, since all the forms of everything living will have metamorphosed within a generation, such study is pointless. Many such scholars have declared, "There exists no rule governing the differentiation of forms," and retreated to their beds, concealing themselves beneath their blankets. But a certain tendency definitely exists. Most giants who lived during prehistory have ceased in every life-function, including breathing and movement, and have chosen to become mountains, rivers, and lakes. Likewise, the tremendous lizards which once dwelled in the earth and the heavens have also cast aside their dignity and diminished themselves to the size of one's finger.

"Is there *any* sign that points to a resurgence of the giants?"

"With so little known about nature's governance of how forms evolve ... how should I know? Still, it seems unlikely for anything too enormous to reappear. These days, not only humans, but even smaller animals tend to hunt anything too big. That's why lizards have become smaller: coordinated group effort pays off more than the trouble of maintaining a single, vast body."

"So is there *no* other way to call the rain?"

"For now, all we can do is pray. Sure, human longings are unscientific, but ... that doesn't mean they have no effect."

As I turned to leave, he added one more comment: "I noticed that the sun is due to swallow the moon on the last night of this month. Please be careful: it's inauspicious ..."

As I watched him return to his place, I pondered the meaning of his warning. It was a bizarre comment: a lunar eclipse? During the new moon? How could that happen? The moon's face would be hidden from the sky, and anyway, wasn't a lunar eclipse caused when the Earth's shadow darkened the moon? If the sun were to "shade" the moon, would not the night blaze bright as day? But then, gazing up into the night sky as I pondered his words, I realized my error: even on the last night of the lunar month, the moon still hung in the sky— it was merely hidden from view. To what end might the sun swallow and shade the moon, when it is already invisible? Wouldn't that just be mere nonsense, some sort of purposeless cruelty? The sun was the father of all time, as the king is the father of the people; therefore ... the cruel sun must represent the cruel king ... and ... the invisible moon must be the prince who lost his inheritance ...

I let out a deep sigh. There was no way to prepare myself for that, though I felt no inclination to do so anyway. Even before he'd claimed the throne from my father, my uncle had already held the reins of power. Even street beggars have a place to lean their backs against when they want to rest their legs. Me? I have nothing to lean against in this world ... so how ought I to sustain my life, even if I did flee?

I crawled through the darkness back to my room. I usually climbed over trees and scuttled over the ground instead of walking on two feet. I first began doing so, bending my body down each time I heard footsteps, to avoid discovery, but at some point a callus had formed upon my palms, like the ones on people's feet.

It has been said since ancient days that ontogeny repeats phylogeny. The cells of our bodies continue being born and dying at every moment, and the blood in our veins is continually being created and disappearing; when old cells die, then new ones appear to fill the gaps left behind, and soon enough, not one of the original cells of one's body remains. In other words, one truly becomes a completely different creature not only in mind, but also in body. All creatures, whether they wish it or not, die and are reborn several times during their lives.

My late mother, bless her, emphasized repeatedly how revolting one's appearance would be at the end of his life if he failed to spend his whole life struggling ceaselessly to maintain his humanity. Only a rare few manage to die with a recognizably human form: many more people end their lives shaped like animals and insects. The aristocrats who pass their days comfortably in their rooms, living off taxes and stipends garnered from the people, lose their human forms the soonest. How many of them develop stubby legs and tails, and fat, reddish bellies, their faces dominated by bulging cheeks!

From my early childhood, my mother constantly repeated to me the tale of one woodcutter. This woodcutter was married to a woman from a certain winged race whom he met by chance at the shore of a lake, but after his wife flew away into the sky he went up to the roof and wept, and could neither eat nor sleep. His body diminished until it was tiny, and his legs became as thin as chopsticks, while the bottoms of his feet bent and curved, and curved claws sprouted from his toes like the hooks that hold up the bar of a clothes-rack. His fingers atrophied, and then disappeared, while white feathers sprouted all over his body. A scarlet comb grew upon his head, and from his throat came the sound of a heartbroken bird, instead of the sound of a man. His longing had transformed his appearance into that of a rooster, but those wings were useless: he could not fly to where his wife had fled. If only his will and longing had been directed more sensibly, he could have developed wings capable of flight, but he had already lost his wits and sealed his fate by letting slip his ability to control or direct his own development.

People separated from their lovers become flowers, or ossify into stones like the one in the famous story of Mangbuseok[5], instead of turning into birds or horses. This tendency of creatures to metamorphose into the complete opposite of that which they long to become is also fascinating. Do you realize that the widely-credited notion that sunflowers follow the sun is actually mere fantasy? They certainly do grow large flowers out of admiration for the sun, but then they bend their faces down toward the ground. They do this because they cannot bear the weight of those flowers. I thought, then, that perhaps I was like these others: since I wished nothing so much as flap wings and fly far away, maybe I would die instead with a heavy body, its belly stuck to the ground as it crawled about.

———

The rains never came, but a late freeze struck the land that spring. Some birds dropped from the sky, frozen dead, while those that survived grew thick coats of feathers. When the cold snap continued, some fat, flightless birds waddled along the ground. Other birds leaped into the water, finding some slight warmth in its depths. Beast and human alike began to starve, for they couldn't eat even the leaves of the plants, which had long since metamorphosed into thorns. People hid in the mountains and grew long, thick coats of fur, like beasts. Sometimes, when people hunted bears, the bears cried out with voices that sounded less ursine than human.

On the spring day that the assassins came for me, a frost had appeared overnight in the yard outside my home. I was sitting in my room when I noticed some people hiding at a distance behind the trees and walls, quietly approaching my detached palace. Their careful, secretive movements were so furtive that to watch them and wait practically bored me. Before the assassins arrived, my eunuch entered the room and threw himself upon the floor before me.

"Your Royal Highness, the king's assassins are approaching the palace," he told me. "Please, you must flee quickly!"

"To where? My uncle rules this whole land," I replied calmly, flipping the pages of my book. For some reason, the eunuch began to weep.

He sobbed for a while before raising his head, and dutifully said, "Nobody will recognize you, since your appearance has changed so drastically! Let us exchange clothes, so that the Royal Body may survive their attack!" Afterward, he pushed me toward the back door, and sat himself down upon my seat. The night was chilly, and as I crawled out into the dark courtyard, shadowy figures raced into my room. Then the slashing of swords and screaming voices assailed me from behind.

Grief-stricken, I reflected sorrowfully that my father had founded a nation, and won glory in the eyes of the world's, but I, his foolish son, could only crawl about on four legs and stay alive by wretchedly allowing another to die in his place. Suddenly death terrified me, for how could I face my father in the next world?

At that instant came a clap of thunder, and a shower of rain commenced, extinguishing all the torches and plunging the palace into darkness. Finally, at just the right moment, the prayers of the samu had reached heaven. Although it was surely a coincidence, the palace soldiers, ignorant of the sciences, fled in terrified confusion, certain that their own misdeeds had angered the heavens. I seized that instant to go over the palace wall. A lone soldier caught sight of me, but on account of my glowing, yellow eyes, he must have supposed I was just some cat upon the wall.

———

I couldn't bear the thought of being around people, so I made for the mountains. The rain, having broken the drought, was met by grass surging forth, each blade raising its head toward the sky, and trees unfolding their leaves while greedily stretching out their roots. In my footsteps, patches of verdant grass sprouted and sank back down toward the soil. The drought and the sudden rain had provoked from the plants this animalistic behavior: since it was uncertain when it might rain again, the whole forest around me was noisily occupied spreading seed and growing fruit. I walked and walked through the downpour until I could walk no more and dropped to the ground in exhaustion.

There I lay, for I don't know how long, until I caught a groggy glimpse of what looked like a white birch tree moving. But when I opened my eyes more widely, and looked carefully, I realized it was no birch at all, but a white tiger[6]. The beast was only a foot tall, slender and tailless, and all its body as white as fresh snow. The tiger crept quietly around me. I remained supine, lacking the strength to flee the creature, and with a wan smile I wondered whether it was a worthy death, to join the cycle of sustenance in the form of a predator's meal.

"What's so funny?"

When the tiger spoke, I was stunned. Its voice was very clear, with exacting and altogether *human* pronunciation. How could a tiger speak a human language with such different vocal cords? Momentarily, I let out an anxious laugh, and tears—just then inexplicable to me—fell from my eyes.

The tiger spoke again, asking, "Why do you weep?"

"I cried because I feel such pity for you," I said, remaining where I lay.

The tiger laughed ... *human* laughter. "What's so piteous about me?"

"If you can speak human languages, it means you have a human mind; and if you have a human mind, you once were human, despite your present animal form. I don't how you came to take the shape of a beast, but it's sad, isn't it? How could it not be pitiful, to lose that original form which you inherited from your parents?"

"What does *original form* mean, anyway? Ought every creature to spend its whole life as a newborn infant?" the tiger quipped. "You say you were born in a human form, but your ancestors were once bears and tigers[7], snakes and fishes, and birds and plants. Now you fight to hang onto this human shape, but ultimately you'll realize the effort is pointless. What's so precious about dying in the same form you were born into? I might look like an animal, but I chose this form: I *wanted* to fill my belly with the work of my own two hands ... and this form is the result."

I had nothing to offer in reply.

"Do you know that, in the old days," it continued, "it took aeons for creatures to change from one form to another; that it took many ten-thousands of aeons for any kind of differentiation at all to develop. Things aren't better or worse now—it's just that a different kind of adaptation is necessary these days. Nature chooses its survivors without considering good or evil, or superior or inferior. Even the human form is just a single means of survival chosen by nature. Humans are frailer than rabbits, when they're not in a group, or deprived of their tools! A pathetic weakling like you ... pitying me? How insolent!"

The tiger bared its razor-sharp fangs at me, its wrath apparent, so I shut my eyes and tensed in anticipation of the coming attack ... but as long as I waited, it didn't slash open my throat. When I dared to open my eyes, I found the tiger quietly watching me.

"Say it," the creature finally said.

"Say what?"

"What is it you *want*?"

"I don't want *anything*," I said. "I just don't want to be discovered by anyone. I want to live and die without anyone finding me."

The tiger said, "You should become a bug, then. Since you can't get over this fixation on people, it'd be best to become a maggot or a fly. Or ... how about a worm? Worms enrich the soil. You'd be more useful to people that way than whatever it is you are right now."

Though every single word he spoke dripped with insult, I couldn't think of any suitable rejoinder to offer him.

"But those forms *are* rather distant from mine," I said. "Becoming a worm would probably be *really* difficult. What can I do?"

"If you really, *truly* wanted to dig holes and eat dirt, it wouldn't be *so* hard, now, would it?" the tiger retorted. Then it looked up at me, and said, "Well, I can't eat someone I've had a conversation with, so you go on back, now. I saw some starving people climbing up the mountain: if you follow them, you might even learn how to survive out here ..."

Then he departed through the trees, blending into the background until his silhouette suddenly disappeared from view.

———

I rose from the ground.

After following the mountain ridge for a while, I encountered the group of climbers the tiger had described. I joined them, blending in as best I could; not a soul in the group addressed me, or even seemed to notice me—or pay attention to one another, for that matter. Nobody even commented on my indigo skin or my xanthous eyes. Among them were folk with folded spines, twisted faces, legless or armless, carapaced like sea-creatures, or crawling upon four feet.

The climbers eventually split into threes and fives and entered a series of caves. When I followed them inside, I found people laying asleep in one another's arms. They seemed to have chosen to hibernate through the cold, barren years, rather than starve. Some spun cocoons, silkworm-like, and others grew thin membraneous coverings, like the diaphanous skin that bundles fishes' eggs together. There were also people covered with coats of white fur. Those who couldn't change so quickly, or handle such a rapid metamorphosis, died and became prey to the ants, joining the cycle of digestion and nutriment to live on in a different form within that cycle. I tried to find a spot empty of people and finally settled between the roots at the foot of a great tree. I gathered grass around me and fashioned a bed from it, and then I rolled myself around and attempted to hibernate.

Winter came, and my starvation continued. Struggling, I attempted to subsist on soil alone, but I couldn't do it. I tried to hibernate, but always woke, now sleeping, now waking again. Eventually, I was able to sleep for a few days in a row, then four, and finally I was able to slumber for a week to ten days at a time.

During the winter I shed my skin. My body, failing under the hardships of my new environment, seemed of its own accord to have decided that some sort of "adjustment" was necessary: radical changes occurred in my skeletal structure and the placement of my vital organs. I passed out and woke again several times more, as my skin fell from my flesh. When I finally climbed out from my moult and looked back, the ghastly husk still looked all too horribly human. As for me, I found I had grown a smooth, serpent-like skin and a long lizard's tail. I wept briefly for my lost humanity, but soon I regained my calm. My body had taken this reptilian form in order to best ensure my survival, I supposed: the wisdom of the flesh outweighs all the reason of the human mind. It understands that survival is more crucial than a man's dignity or pride. I turned and devoured my abandoned human skin, a feast of precious nutriment for my new body.

When spring arrived, and edible grass began to sprout at the mouth of the cave, I woke up from my slumber and crept outside. Then, I realized that I was the only one who had survived this long, terrible winter. A few others had perished outside, taking the form of human-shaped rocks and trees, all entangled together in a solemn tableau. Respectfully, I performed a ceremony before them: they, at least, were noble enough to prefer becoming soil to losing their human shape.

After that, I dwelled in the forest, crawling upon the ground and eating grass. My jaw soon became powerful, the better to chew on the tough grass, and I developed a sort of jutting snout, as well. My ears grew pointed because of how I pricked them up at every swaying of the brush nearby, and my palms hardened as my limbs shortened to suit my body. When I could no longer use my fingers, horns sprouted from my skull; they began as small nubs on my head, but soon they branched out like the antlers of a male deer. These horns were invaluable in the battles I fought with other beasts over food, and for striking trees to coax them into reluctantly letting drop their ripe fruit.

In the winter of that year, I shed my skin once more. I discovered my entire body to have completely changed to the dull greenish color of the forest. I wondered whether living in a desert, or on a rocky mountain, might perhaps help me to maintain my human pigmentation, but the proposition seemed useless to me. My desire to go unseen was so great that my body would surely be inscribed with the camouflaging patterns of the pebbles if I lived upon a rocky mountain.

I looked down at the little nub that remained, down below my belly button, and wondered whether I could even still have sex with a human being. The thought made me laugh and laugh. Even though my bestial transformation was past the point of no return, still I couldn't abjure this strange wistfulness for my own long-lost form. But someday my brain, too, would undergo its own transformation in capacity and structure. How much longer would I retain my very consciousness, my memories, and human intellect? That night, I counted the number of scales that had grown upon my body and found them—counting both the great and the small ones together—to number eighty-one. *The square of nine*, I thought: *That's a lucky number.*

After that thought, I began to laugh once more.

———

I think it was probably autumn.

While crawling through the forest as always in search of food, I heard the distant din of horseshoes and barking hounds. When I looked up in surprise, a group of hunting dogs was chasing a small group of purple roe deer toward me. I fled as swiftly as I could, amid the rushing deer, but the hunters mistook me for one of them, on account of my antlers and loosed their arrows at me. One poor deer, struck by an arrow beside me, rolled on the ground and screamed piteously. Its voice was so very human that my heart all but failed me.

Although I ran myself half-dead, I was neither so fleet nor so clever as the rest of the herd. Eventually, I ended up surrounded by hunting hounds, at the foot of a great tree and unable to move. As I stood there, buffeted by the baying and barking of the hounds, the bushes split apart and people armed with arrows and spears appeared. I stood frozen as I watched a man on horseback leading them forward.

His face had haunted me everywhere but in my dreams: it was my own uncle. But that wasn't the reason that I couldn't move or speak. *That* was because of his incredible appearance, which had changed so drastically that he was unrecognizable.

He looked like a giant hunk of meat.

His bulging pink gut shone with his gluttony, and his peaked nose signified a lifetime with his face buried in food. His almost-shut eyes reflected a near-absolute lack of moral discernment within, and the upward curve of his earlobes, covering his ears completely, reflected his desire to hear nothing at all. The spaces between his fingers had disappeared because his hands and feet had atrophied, meaning he had attended to none of his royal tasks. Considering how my late father had retained his human appearance even during his prolonged sickness in bed, my uncle's transformation was truly outrageous. I was simply too shocked and outraged to fear him.

My uncle directed them to lower their arrows from me and examined me from snout to tail.

"What is this beast? Because of the antlers, I thought it was a deer, but its body is such a nasty shade of green. The thing has the tail of a lizard and is covered with scales like a snake's... its arms and legs are like a human's, but its yellow eyes look like a cat's. What kind of an omen might this be?"

A servant hurried forth to his side. His back was bent as if he were slumped upon a horse's back, and his neck bent groundward as if we were about to topple over at any moment. His appearance had undergone a profound transformation, but I recognized him then as the samu, who had once been my true friend. I sensed that he recognized me, too, though he was fighting to look away from me.

"It's not unusual to encounter new kinds of creatures, since animals constantly change, adjusting to their environment. However, the reason lineage is so very unstable is because of the instability of this *world* in which the subjects of Your Majesty live. Nature presents us with monstrosities like this because it cannot communicate its earnest mind with words ... which is to renew itself by filling the king with fear and regret. But, if the king cultivates his virtue, this unfortunate omen can be transformed into a lucky one."

The listening king's face quietly turned scarlet.

"If it's unpropitious, just tell me that. Or if it is propitious, then tell me *that*. Telling me it's an ill omen, but then claiming it *could* be a good one ... what sort of a lie is that?"[8]

Before anyone around could stop the king, he drew the sword at his waist. The sword swayed about, lopping off the heads of the samu and the others near him. Just then, I turned tail and fled. Behind me, innumerable arrows fell amid the barking of the hounds, and I scrambled up the mountain for dear life. When I finally reached a cliff, I looked down at the mighty, meandering river and leaped from the precipice.

When I struck the water from such a height, I found it as hard as the ground would have been. The river gulped me down whole.

———

I learned several facts. One cannot gain wings by such jumping down from a cliff only once, and one can't die easily when one's body is covered with unexpectedly hard reptilian skin.

I had hoped so fervently to live without being discovered by people, but when that happened, again someone had died.

After that, I stayed in the river. My skin, after soaking in the water for so long, festered and began to grow limp, freezing in the cold of the night. This almost killed me several times, but I didn't dare go back up and onto land. I sincerely hoped that the last strand of my human will might break. I hoped to become a fish or a water-snake, and prayed that my human consciousness might be finally drawn out from me completely.

In the middle of the night, while I lay in the glacially-cold shallows, two turtles poked their heads out from the water simultaneously. When they finally surfaced, I realized they weren't two creatures, but one turtle with two heads. It must have burrowed into the muddy bed of the river because it was almost two cheok tall, all told. Fish with red wings flopped and scooted away from it.

"Why does this land creature shove its head into the water this cold night? It should go back to where it came from," the turtle said, its voice seeming to echo as the two heads spoke in unison.

I opened my frozen mouth to reply: "I have nowhere to go. If I've intruded on your territory, I sincerely apologize, but please don't cast me out."

"Every creature has its territory ... but why would a four-legged beast try to live by breathing water?"

"If we're arguing about origins, there are no strict boundaries in a lineage. If you'll admit that your own form and character includes setting foot in both soil *and* water, then you of all creatures will recognize that all land-creatures once dwelt in water. Recall: every creature derives from a single origin. If dolphins and sea lions are blameless, then how is it that I warrant criticism, even if I'm simply trying to retrace my way back to our origins?"

"Well, there might be no borders, but a weirdo like you wandering around here is sure to make my prey panic and flee ..."

"I didn't mean to ... I only sought to escape discovery by others, but that seems hopeless. But I am anxious to discuss this tendency of creatures to develop an appearance contrary to their desires ... to share a few days' discussion on the subject, perhaps ..."

"There's no *need* for a few days' discussion. It's simple: you just don't really want what you think you want." The turtle thrust its two heads toward me, crossing them, and snapped, "Now, scram. If you don't, I'll eat you up."

"Go ahead and eat me," I replied. "After I die, I'll become a water-ghost, and never walk on land again." Then I shut my eyes.

When I opened them again a while later, the turtle was gone. Perhaps it hadn't killed me out of sympathy, or because it wasn't worth the effort ... or maybe I just didn't look very appetizing? I braced myself to bear the watery chill throughout the remainder of the night.

After some more time passed, the scales upon my skin grew affixed to their places, and my arms and legs diminished gradually, growing tiny. However, somehow they didn't become fins, but ceased their transformation when they had assumed an avian shape. (I suspected this might have resulted from my leaping into the air from the precipice.) When my arms and legs ceased functioning, my spine and tail stretched longer. It is said that every stage you pass through leaves its indelible mark. Well, the antlers sprouting from my skull didn't atrophy, and remained; and so did the cat's-eyes I'd developed so early in my youth, unchanged even now. To learn to breathe water was insuperable, but I did learn to dive for extended periods. And as my arms and legs atrophied further, my beard grew longer and developed a sensitivity like that of insects' feelers. I lived by feeding on small fish and water plants. I sank to the bottom of the river for days at a time, and lingered in the lake for several months.

————

One day, as I rose to the surface to breathe, I came upon a woman doing her laundry. Aside from her nine white tails, she retained a wholly human appearance. I looked at her, uncertain what to do because it had been so long since I'd seen a human being, or worn a human form myself. Seeing her gaze upon me vacantly, I waited for her to scream, to call me a monster and begin to hurl stones at me, but instead she clasped her hands together and bowed deeply before me.

"What're you doing?" I asked her.

I realized my mistake as I opened my mouth. Just as with the tiger, this woman would realize that somewhere in my lineage, there lay hidden a human stage.

"When the Mystical One came out from the water," she said, "I saw that it ruled these waters, so I bowed."

"You saw wrong. I'm just a profane thing, a parasite in these waters, hiding scared from the human world. Forgive me, I didn't mean to surprise you."

Then I sank down again to the bottom of the lake.

Several days later, I opened my eyes and discovered some rice-cakes and fruit, water-logged in the depths before me. Little fish rose toward each sinking rice-cake, nibbling upon them. I rose to the surface once more. The nine-tailed woman I'd met before remained by the lake, but glancing about, I saw that she had set blessed water[9], incense, and a plate of rice-cakes upon a little wooden table, performing an earnest little ceremony while offering devout prayers.

Red papers inscribed with petitions drooped from the table, and several more people, perhaps her neighbors, were gathered around her. When she saw me, she leaped up like a thief caught red-handed.

I balked, stupefied. "What's all this shit? Didn't I tell you with my own mouth? I'm nothing more than a mongrel! If you have nowhere to hold your ceremony, go to another lake, or a mountain instead!"

She said, "The trees are desiccated, and the drought has gone on so long; the grassroots folk have barely any way to find themselves food. Everything is growing and changing so strangely, our farms are falling apart, and our harvests no longer suit the people's diets. And the king can't hear us: his ears and eyes have atrophied."

"So what do you want from me? I have no power. How can a beast get involved in human affairs?"

"There must be *some* reason why nature has allowed you such a sacred appearance ... but, are you saying everything we humans have hoped for is in vain?"

I shut my mouth for a moment, before saying, "What you say is correct."

I swung my tail, which sent a blast of wind and raised a spray of water, knocking down the incense and sending the bowl of holy water tumbling, to break upon the ground.

Then I said, "Oh, how long I have lived ... and every time anyone discovers me, I bring trouble. It's better I never show myself again."

I sank down into the depths once more. When I looked back up, I saw the nine-tailed woman weeping. Cold-bloodedly, I turned my head away, nestling myself into the bottom of the lake, and began to hibernate. The frigid water began to freeze my body, its functions slowing gradually, paralyzing me until I could feel each of my cells passing into a kind of slumber. I no longer felt the passage of time, and my thoughts slowed. I thought, if I was lucky, I might transmute into rock, or soil—like the giants of ancient days.

———

At first, it felt like someone knocking on a distant door, but then it became a voice, trying to stir me: "Wake up."

I opened my eyes. It was difficult to do so: a host of water plants and marsh snails had attached themselves to my body. But then I saw the two-headed turtle, whom I'd met before, swimming before my own eyes. Somehow, he looked much smaller than before.

"Leave. Soon. The king's army is here to catch you."

I needed a moment to comprehend his words. Then, I recalled that I'd once, long ago, been a human being ... and a prince ... and I recalled my blood-relation to the king then, too.

"Why would the king bother to come and catch me?"

"Even after you began to sleep, the people continued their ceremonies here. They were praying to you to expel the king and bring them a new one, so he decided to fill in the lake and dig you out from the bottom. Your mind is so slow now; your brain must have metamorphosed. Get out of here, *now*."

In fact, I was surrounded by a din of noise. When I raised my head up, clod after clod of soil fell upon my head. From somewhere came the revolting stink of blood, and a murder of crows were coming and going in a chaos over the lake.

"Why are the crows squawking like that?"

"It's really dreadful. Better you don't see it," the turtle said, and then he burrowed into the mud.

I rose to the surface, in an ominous mood. Even my slightest movement stirred up a whirlpool, sending fish fleeing in surprise. A multitude of water plants and marsh snails dropped from my body. Then, I realized that the turtle hadn't become smaller; perhaps because of my long slumber, I had become *bigger*.

A band of soldiers was gathered near the lakeshore, dumping soil into the water. When they saw me they fell into shocked silence, and ceased shoveling. I also lost my words, and looked at the things embedded in the mud around them: the dead bodies of the villagers who'd held the ceremonies, and the woman lay in a terrible row beside the lake. The nine-tailed woman's white underskirts flapped back and forth in the breeze, and with each flap of the fabric my reason fell away a little, until finally my mind had gone blank.

One of the soldiers came to his senses and roared at me, waving his spear: "You freakish beast, bare your neck to us tamely! All your followers are dead!"

Before he even finished his words, I sprang up from the water, and then I bit through a soldier nearby, in the front rank, with my fangs; while the men roiled in confusion, I struck their horses' legs with my tail. I tore at the throats of the fallen with my claws, and as they groaned I crushed their hearts with my two front paws. When I heard the noise of distant soldiers, too, I fled the lake and leaped into the river. My eyes had always been sharp, and I was able to count the dead by the riverside, one by one. Then I saw the man who had once been my uncle, standing near the river. I tried to slip past him, but then I heard his voice: "Come here, you phantasm!"

The king sat straight-backed upon a horse, and spoke in such a tiny voice, though for me, having gone through so many bestial trans-formations, his voice was crystal clear. He said, "If you don't come out, I'll kill everyone in the village until I catch you. I'll accuse them of worshipping a spirit-monster and execute them all!"

I stopped swimming. It was a bizarre threat. Even my uncle thought that I retained some shred of sacred compassion within me. What relation had I with the lives and deaths of mere human beings? Yet I emerged from the water quietly, going up to the edge of the river, and stood before the king. Of course, it was impossible for my body to *stand up* like a human does, but I coiled my long tail in a spiral to support my body and hold my neck upright. When I stood myself up thus, I realized how immense I'd become. The soldiers with their spears pointing up at me, and my uncle, they all looked so puny that I could sweep them away in an instant.

A thousand emotions flooded me as I regarded my uncle closely. Ah, ah ... he'd gotten old. That transformation must be the end of any creature, even the one that resists any change at all. His once fat belly drooped with wrinkles, his creased face was blotched, and his atro-phied arms and legs had dried out in their disuse, and thinned extremely.

"Now, I recognize you," he said with a dry voice, like branches rasping in the wind. "You are the seed of the former king. The seed that should've dried out long before still remains..."

I bowed my head, imitating his soldiers who had bent their heads, facing down, and said, "The reason this insignificant one became a beast is not to threaten Your Majesty's rule, but only to sustain its own existence. These acts were committed by the ignorant, so I beg that you please temper your rage with your vast generosity."

"You say it's an act of ignorance, but you must have known what they were doing, so I have no choice but to accuse you of your crime."

"This flesh lost its old life ages ago; why are you trying to take that life twice?"

"How dare you speak and act that way toward your king?" demanded the king with a piercing voice as thin as a eunuch, so thin I could barely hear it. "Since you are in my kingdom, your body and life are mine. I demand that you bestow your life to me, as a dutiful subject. *Obey my command.*"

"What on earth do you want with the life of a worthless water-snake?"

"How dare a beast converse with a man? How insolent, how disrespectful! You're such a vile portent! I'm going to conquer you, and get rid of you."

"This insignificant one may have become a wicked beast, but the king is no longer human either. How can you demand my life, while pretending at being the king of the humans?"

The corners of the king's blind eyes twisted upward with his fury. As he cried out in that thin voice of his, soldiers all around ran toward me, while kicking their horses into action. I dived into the river again. The soldiers chased me along the riverbank, and I swam like the wind, so quickly that the river overflowed and the waters parted behind me.

I heard the laughter of the king suddenly from behind. I knew the reason of his laughing. A great waterfall, ten jang tall, blocked the way up ahead. However, instead of stopping, I pushed myself harder. When I reached the bottom of the waterfall, I threw myself upward, stealing momentum from the whirlpool at its base, and leapt up the falls. My body ascended past the falling water, and the whirlpool that encircled my tail also swirled and rose up with me.

I realized that I had generated an ascending wind, and that my body had become so gigantic that I could direct the currents of the air. I rose up into the sky, riding that wind, and the soldiers who were chasing me stopped to watch, befuddled. As I examined my body, I found my greenish scales shimmering spectacularly in the sunlight, and my long tail swung behind me, almost as if to touch the ground. I felt wonderful, so I continued to ascend higher. The air current was practically visible to me, almost palpable, and I sensed how I could change my direction by riding the wind. I realized, then, how to shift the flowing air currents in order to produce rain. Recalling the past, I remembered hating droughts during my human days, though that had been so long ago I couldn't remember quite why.

I directed the air currents upward. Dark clouds formed as soon as the water vapor in the air was carried up into the troposphere. Suddenly, the world was shaken by lightning and thunder. When I shifted the pressure of the air by pressing the clouds gently and then rising up, a heavy rain began to pour toward the ground. The river flooded, the fields deluged, and in a flash the waters swept away the distracted soldiers who stood near the riverbanks, watching me over-head. Powerless to pursue me, the king watched from a distance; immediately his hair whitened, and he seemed to turn a decade older in an instant. It was as if I'd evaporated away the last bit of life left in him. However, their lives and deaths interested me not at all, for I was no longer human. It was in skimming the clouds that I exulted, so I built up speed and began to rise steadily higher.

That was that winter the king died in an uprising. That was the day when I soared through an azure sky.

———

Reference Links

1) Originally, "One jang and two cheok long": these archaic measurements add up 11.8 feet (3.6 meters): like the Biblical cubit, the cheok was an officialized measurement based on the length of a forearm, and similar to the imperial foot. A jang was equal to ten cheok.

2) One ja is the same as one jang: therefore, the leopard's tail was almost nine feet long (2.7m).

3) In cultures within the Chinese sphere of influence, the composite character for spiritual energies, 氣 (in Korean, gi, although it may be more familiar to a Western audience as the Chinese concept of qi or ch'i), contains within it the character for air or steam, 气.

4) From Pangu, a Chinese mythological figure from whose corpse the physical world was formed. However, here, Pangu is not a singular being, but a member of a race of ancient giants analogous to the Titans of Greek mythology.

5) Near the eastern port of Busan there is a large rock by the ocean called Mangsubeok. It is said once to have been a faithful wife, awaiting the return of her husband, who unfortunately had been captured and borne off to Japan against his will. As the story goes, she was transformed into a stone during her endless waiting, and stands there still.

6) Traditionally in Korea (and other East Asian countries), four mystical animals were associated with the four compass points: the blue dragon with the East, the white tiger with the North, a "black turtle" (two-headed, with one of its heads a snake's) to the West, and the scarlet jujak bird, vaguely similar to the occidental phoenix, to the South.

7) In the national foundation myth, the ancestors of the Korean people are said to have been bears transformed into the shape of humans by a magical ritual involving garlic, mugwort, and a lunar cycle's confinement in a cave. Both the tiger and the bear attempted the transformation, but the tiger fled, leaving only the bear to take human form and become the bride of the demigod King Hwanung, who ruled from the top of Mt. Baekdu.

8) According to the *Samguk Sagi* (*The History of the Three Kingdoms*), Cha-Daewang, the 7th king in Geoguryeo Dynasty, actually said these words in reference to [explanations of] his sighting of a white fox.

9) In this era, water drawn from wells at daybreak was regarded as holy and used in prayer and rituals.

YOU WILL SEE THE MOON RISE BY ISRAEL ALONSO

Translated from Spanish by Steve Redwood

Nominated for the 2017 Ignotus Award, Israel Alonso is a promising new voice of SF in Spanish. His stories have been included in *Visiones 2016* and *SuperSonic*. He just published *Recetario para combustión's espontáneas*, a collection of stories, with Cazador de Ratas. He currently works as an editor.

And now that the storm has passed,
And the flames leap and dance in our fire,
The future is just a blank paper:
In our trench we can dream and desire

Aurora beside the window, partly illuminated from outside, playing the old songs on her citarel: the long-forgotten verses of iDalleen, of PawlKostka, and of Vermillion Moon; songs of blood and sand, of women lost and dreams of glory. Aurora smiling with her whole body, smiling at me with her very soul, singing those old songs on her citarel while partly illuminated by the lights of the Opera Palace, her eyes full of far-off cities, of blood and sand, of organdie loops and one-night motels, of moons and dunes, of loves flying in pursuit of each other.

Aurora.

Who is Aurora?

There's a half-naked old woman in the middle of the road, wearing nothing but tattered, yellowish knickers and a bracelet the colour of hope. She's cradling a hand grenade against her breast with an empty, far-away gaze and the toothless smile of a baby. Filthy as a rat and happy as a lunatic, she's rocking to and fro on her heels, quietly crooning something to herself; from where I'm hiding amidst the rubble, I can't make out what it is.

The grenade slips out of her hands. Or maybe she drops it on purpose, who knows? I watch it twist in the air as if time has slowed down, see it bounce between her feet, creating strange reverberations in the cracked asphalt. And then it explodes.

Accompanied by an unpleasant shrieking sound, the world becomes a deluge of rubble and blood, of dust and debris crumbling away from the ruins. A piece of falling masonry strikes me violently on the back of my neck just as I recall why I am hiding.

I become unconscious almost at once.

> *Beneath the red fiery comets*
> *Beneath Mercury and spinning Fortuna*
> *Gaze into my eyes that are your eyes*
> *And then you will see the moon rise*

When I regain consciousness in the rubble of some building, my head is hurting. I was dreaming of a woman singing—a woman singing to me—and sitting next to an open window, bathed in the light from the street. She was a beautiful woman, and it was comforting to hear her sing, to see her gazing at me with so much tenderness. Maybe it was my mother. I don't remember my mother. Even so, I would have liked to go on listening to her, but the sound of a shot has startled me.

I cautiously peep out from behind the rubble and there they are. Four of them, noisy and armed. Four individuals who seem to have been playing around with a can of the most vile yellow paint they could find. One of them seems to have stuck his beard inside it, another his arms up to the elbows, another has sprayed his head with it, and the fourth is wearing a military helmet impeccably painted the same colour. Right now they're playing a different game. They're kicking around what seems to be a human head, disfigured and charred. It's smoking as they pass it to each other. It must have been burnt. My god, it must have been burnt!

The one with the yellow hands raises a modern assault rifle up over his head as if hoisting a flag; only, instead of a flag, attached to the muzzle is a pair of burnt knickers covered in blood.

I feel the vomit stinging my throat, and only just manage to stop myself from retching. If they hear me, they may decide to play a different game. If they spot me, I'm lost, so I begin to flee in the opposite direction, taking care not to dislodge any more loose masonry in the city ruins.

Everything has changed because
Nothing has changed because

"Is that you?"

The question makes me open my eyes, and I realize I've been walking and dreaming at the same time. Wandering aimlessly, my head full of hazy questions. How did I get here?

"Is that you?"

In front of me, almost buried under a pile of rags, there's someone sprawled in the rubble. His bony arm is sticking out, the hand raised towards the sky as if begging for alms. When he hears my footsteps, his head emerges, too; a face that might have come from the pits of hell, full of pustules and scars, and covered in a layer of filth and soot. He stares at me in terror, opening his mouth several times, chewing on his words, before speaking to me.

"Is that you?"

Am I? Do I know this man from somewhere?

"No, no, it's not me," I say, and my own voice scrapes my throat as if I haven't spoken for years.

"Is it you, Jesandra? Have you brought the battery, Jesandra?"

"No, my friend, no." It's difficult to speak, and I can't recognize my own voice. "I'm not Jesandra. She still hasn't found the battery, but I'm sure she will be back soon."

Why do I lie? Out of pity, maybe? The man seems more dead than alive. At first glance he appears to be an old man, some tramp with senile dementia, but looking more carefully beyond the patina of grime, he doesn't seem to have reached forty.

Suddenly his eyes open wide, and he stares me up and down, while an unspeakable terror glistens in the pupils of his eyes.

"Keep away! You're not Jesandra!" The rags move a little, and the madman produces a weapon. It seems to be a rusty relic from another era, perhaps an antique pepperbox pistol; it may look clapped-out, but it's still menacing. What if it still works? And what if the old man still remembers how to use it? I'm surprised when I catch myself calling him old, as he points the piece of junk at me. "You're not going to take my drugs away, you bloody quack! I'll wipe you out and all your fucking little white kids as well! Come here!"

I shout out, but too loudly, too shrilly, shattering the silence in the square, and causing other lunatics to pop up all over the place. As I try to run away, my feet get caught up in something, and I fall flat on my face. And that's what saves me from the first shot.

At the sound of gunfire, the vagabonds in the ruins flee. I look at the beggar, who's still pointing his antique weapon at me but hasn't produced a single shot. I glance behind me, and there are four men in the middle of the street, looking threatening in their stolen clothes and with their huge assault rifles.

I raise my hands in surrender, and one of them, the tallest one, who has a yellow helmet (I remember having seen this colour before; I remember it almost as if it were yesterday—and I remember, too, that it's a colour that frightens me) fires again, blowing half my right hand to pieces.

I don't risk more than a rapid glance out of the corner of my eye, but I see a couple of fingers land on the tattered garments of the tramp with the pepperbox pistol. I crawl away, towards one of the portals, enormous with a stone frontage that seems more intact than the others, and an inscription I can't read. The letters aren't letters, they're smudges, sticks, dots, lines ... Some loony has been scrawling stuff all over the place in some wretched foreign language.

I've almost reached the portal when the third shot grazes my back. The sharp, stabbing pain causes me to bite my tongue.

I fall over a heap of corpses piled up on the entrance steps, landing on that of a young woman, decomposed down to the bone, wearing a t-shirt that must once have been tight-fitting. The word POMELO gleams intermittently on the material, caught in the slanting rays of the sun coming through a huge hole in the wall. The stink of putrefaction nauseates me and I lose consciousness.

> *I shall live while you still can recall*
> *The colours we made with our wings*
> *Just shout if you find you are lost*
> *I will search through the quantum strings*

Aurora strokes the citarel as if it were my own naked body. The chords gleam in the evening stillness, projecting shadows and creating ridges in the crystal furnishings. The piston rises and falls like a beating heart.

Aurora, tinged with the light of the citarel from in front, and from behind, the light of the Opera Palace coming in from the street. Her only apparel the old songs she intones, the words that will never be forgotten. Singing to me when I come out of the study to listen to her, forgetting the work, the evaluations, the tests, the experiments, the telomeres, the telomerase enzymes, the infinite chains, all the errors and all the successes. In the pool of light and shadow that the music pours over the carpet, I melt like ice cream in the sun.

Aurora doesn't look at her fingers sliding up and down the citarel, but at me. She is Aurora borealis when she sings to me, she is aura, she is this moment in time; and at this moment nothing exists save the two of us, the music, the play of light, and the love we have forged.

Right now, the awards don't matter. The discoveries don't matter. The only thing that matters now is Aurora, and that old song of Vermillion Moon, which now slides into the refrain:

> *We are just tiny parts of eternity*
> *Droplets of blood without weight*
> *We dance in the heart of the Cosmos*
> *As parts of the Whole we vibrate*

"We'll have to do something about that hand."

A man's voice bears Aurora away, bears away my dream, and brings back my pain. I wake up, startled.

There's a man dressed as a doctor squatting in front of me. The tone of his voice, his appearance, his body language, all invite me to feel reassured. He has a look that inspires confidence, like that of an old friend you recognize despite the passing of time and distance. He has a trim beard, a light orange colour like a peach, and small, piercing eyes that are now scrutinizing me as if he is deciding how to treat me.

"Don't hurt me!" I say, looking around instinctively for a way out.

The room has only three walls. The fourth wall no longer exists, it's been almost completely destroyed, probably in some bombardment. Through the breach can be seen the tallest buildings of a city in ruins. The sky is black, although it's daytime.

"I'm not going to hurt you. I'm a friend," the doctor answers with a smile as I study the rest of the room. It must once have been a pleasant place, one of those modular *all-in-ones*: a single room that could be converted in a minute into any other kind of room, depending on necessity. Whoever the occupant was, they had been using it as an office before the explosion. The huge operations table is almost intact, though buried under a pile of rubble. The rest of the furniture seems to be in the same state.

"Where am I?" I say, because I really don't know. Maybe I've lost too much blood through the injury to my hand. The thought makes me look at it—and I let out a yell: "Shit! Shit! My hand! My fingers!"

I can't stop my body from shaking or my teeth from chattering violently, and my vision becomes hazy. Some of my fingers are missing! I've lost some of my fucking fingers!

"You must calm down or you'll go into shock," the doctor says kindly, without losing his smile. "Try to breathe naturally. What's your name?"

I try to obey him, not only because of the confidence he still inspires in me, but because this appears to be the only sensible thing to do in this corner of hell I've woken up in. But it's hard, Christ, it's hard!

"My name is ... I'm Albot," I say, trying to smile and not hyperventilate at the same time.

The doctor observes me with an indescribable expression, but still smiling.

"Ah, good. Then I'm Dr. Milles. A pleasure," he replies, but without offering to shake hands. Instead, he stands up and points to something next to the screen-table. "There may be bandages in that drawer. And, with luck, some antibiotics. Take a look, while I make sure no one else comes in here."

He nods towards the panel next to the door I'm resting against. I don't remember the door. I don't remember the panel. I don't know why it's necessary to secure it, but I suddenly feel queasy and sick with fear.

I stand up, take two steps, and vomit all over my shoes, worn-out, full of holes, blood-stained.

"Don't worry about that," says the good doctor, "better out than in. Later, we'll look for food."

A question's been bothering me, and I now come out with it, still supporting my weight with my hands on my knees.

"Is this your house?"

The doctor chuckles.

"No, no, of course not. But I think I can manage to reach the security system, that's if it's still working."

I turn to face him, where he's leaning over the panel. He looks back at me and winks.

"Is it dangerous?" I try to gesture with my mutilated hand towards the door, to whatever might be behind it.

"We don't want the men in yellow coming in here, do we?"

"The men in yellow?" I'm on the point of asking what he means by men in yellow, but something jogs my mind and I have a vivid vision of a streak of that colour, of a particular tone of that colour; irritating, unpleasant ... dangerous.

"You don't remember them?" he says, frowning.

"It doesn't matter. I'll see if there are any bandages."

And indeed, next to the table, there's an old, broken fridge and a black drawer, the sort they use as medicine cabinets in modern offices. It seems to be dented and half-burnt, but those things are designed to withstand nuclear attacks; if not, they wouldn't be called emergency kits. Someone must have pulled it out of its module and pried it open. It's connected to a reflective orange device that seems to work on oil: an emergency power supply, one of those that uses cables, like those in the old days.

I sense the dizziness that precedes a fainting fit combining with uncertainty as I struggle with the lid of the old kit. But it passes when the lid gives way, and I see there are still some gifts preserved inside.

"Looks like I'm in luck," I say to the back of the doctor, who must also be making progress, since I can hear beepings and whirrings coming from the panel. "There are bandages here and a whole box of Trupnol. As well as a couple of bars of survival food! We've got lunch!"

Something in what I've just said makes me feel uneasy. The truth is, I don't know what time it is. Not surprising if we bear in mind that I don't know the date, the day, the month, or the year either. I check the time.

I don't know how I've done it, but just thinking about it I find I now know. It's 14:17. I seem to have seen it hovering in front of my eyes, in red numbers, at the bottom left of my field of vision. Have I really seen it? Is that really the time?

>DOOR BLOCKED. DO YOU WISH TO MODIFY PRESENT HABITAT?<

"Let's not tempt fate," says the doctor, "the office is okay. Who knows what structural damage the rest of the modules might have sustained? What if we get crushed by a bath?"

<CORRECT. MAINTAIN PRESENT HABITAT.<

"It's fourteen-seventeen," I say, almost in a whisper, terrified by the discovery.

The doctor approaches me, as elated as if I've said it was the New Year.

"So it would appear. And it's a great piece of news!"

I carefully bandage my hand while slowly chewing two Trupnols.

"Yes, but ... how do I know that? How the hell can I possibly know that?"

He gazes at me thoughtfully.

"You've accessed one of your modem's basic interface functions. It's not magic. It's taken you by surprise only because you've managed to establish a neuronal connection you had forgotten."

"'Modem?' What on earth are you talking about?" I ask, irritated. Although, to tell the truth, the word does awaken certain echoes in my mind. Echoes that I can't identify.

"You know, the cortical modem. One of humanity's greatest advances. Doesn't it ring at least a tiny bell?" He seems to be amused.

"I've no idea what the hell you're talking about," I say, while the auto-seal of the bandages adjusts itself to my wrist.

"Everybody's had one for centuries now. We could say it's like having all the technology inside your head," he clarifies, tapping the back of his skull. "At first, they were installed surgically. That's no longer necessary thanks to genetic engineering. People are now born with ..."

My heart thumps, my vision blurs.

"I've got a ... a *machine* in ...?"

"Please, please, calm down, or you'll lose control again. The fact you can check the time shows you're making progress."

I decide not to obey him, not to relax; I faint again. All in the blink of an eye.

> *I shall live while you still can recall*
> *The colours we made with our wings*
> *Just shout if you find you are lost*
> *I will search through the quantum strings*

The citarel was my surprise gift for our seventieth wedding anniversary. Aurora was radiant in her silks, with all those lights floating around her, and the string quartet playing *You Will See the Moon Rise* in the University gardens, in Albotmilles. Yes, she was radiant. And there was I, trembling at the end of the walkway, not just because of the nervousness natural to the occasion, not just because nothing had changed and yet everything had changed in that place where I had kissed her for the first time, a hundred years before: I was also trembling because of the citarel, hidden under the amber-hued canopy where we would once again recite our vows, charged and ready to give her a huge surprise after we confirmed our mutual love.

What lovely eyes she had, what wonderful hair gathered-up and defying the breeze of that autumn evening, how young she was in my arms, and how much love there was brimming over despite so many years spinning round on the roller-coaster of days.

"It's the Samisha!" she says when she sees the citarel, while the cameras float around us to immortalize our immortality. She cries— when we thought she had no more tears left after those shed during the renewal of our vows—and gazes at me with such tenderness that I weep, too. "It's ... Where did you get ahold of it?"

"I'm a resourceful man," I say, and lean forward to kiss her again, but she stops me with a wink that suspends time, and raises the instrument to her breast. And she makes it sing. *You Will See the Moon Rise*, that's what it intones, the iridescent piston rising and falling as if in a spiral, the quartet accompanies it, and she sings.

She sings to me.

> *In the shade of a single Idea*
> *Like a song protecting the cradle*
> *Gaze into my eyes that are your eyes*
> *And then you will see the moon rise*

"Come on, my friend." A man's voice wakes me up. He's wearing a doctor's gown, and he speaks to me in a familiar manner.

My hand is bandaged, and my mouth tastes of medicine. But this doesn't seem to be a hospital. It seems more like a battlefield.

"Aurora," I say, without much idea of what it means.

The stranger laughs. "Didn't we agree that I was Doctor Milles?"

Doctor Milles. A doctor. A room. This room. Sealing the door. Bandaging the mutilated hand. The flashes of memory are insufficient, but enough to incline me to trust this person, whoever he is.

"I'm sorry, Doctor Milles," I say, as I try to stand up. I see two bars of food, and grab them with my good hand, offering him one. "Would you like one?"

He declines my offer with a wave of his hand. "No, thanks."

The fact is, he's clean, with a well-cared-for peachy-red beard. His gown is immaculate, unlike mine, which is torn to shreds, its original white colour virtually indistinguishable. He doesn't seem to be hungry, but I don't remember ever having eaten. So I begin to devour one of the bars, and put the other in a pocket of my gown, in case he changes his mind, or for myself later on.

"I'm hungry," I exclaim fervently.

"Don't worry about it. Eat as much as you like, I really am not hungry." With his hands behind his back, the doctor walks towards the enormous hole in the wall and thoughtfully looks out at the horizon. "What time did you say it was, Albot?"

The time appears in front of my eyes, superimposed upon what I'm looking at.

"It's 14:54," I reply, and I realize that what I've done is activate my modem. Now I remember. That was the first of a multitude of developments that brought us to where we are today. The cortical model, the *gnosapp*, the *brainslave*. I smile. "It's fascinating. I can remember it."

Doctor Milles nods, returning my smile through his red beard: that face that now suddenly seems so very familiar, as if we've known each other all our lives.

"And do you know what song you were singing to yourself when you woke up?"

"I think it's called *You Will See the Moon Rise*. Aurora used to play it —my wife—on the Samisha citarel," I say, surprised by the cascade of memories, all suddenly so clear.

Aurora died at the age of three hundred and fifty-three years. She was killed by a mutation of Ebola, a disease that had been eradicated centuries before thanks to ... to my own discoveries! I stare, shocked, at the doctor, who seems to be following my thoughts just by looking at me.

"That's it, go on like that. Remember, Victor, you have to remember. It's important."

"Victor?" Yes, my name is Victor, yes, Victor Hess. I am Doctor Victor Hess, Nobel prize-winner, World Safeguard Award, Most Influential Man of the Century ... In that case ... Albot?

"My name is Victor Hess."

"That's it, Victor! Very good! The world raised monuments to you! You did great things many years ago, Victor Hess."

Milles notices that I have become pale and am beginning to tremble, and he smiles reassuringly. "Come on, come on, a little at a time. Let's go back to the song. Are you aware that the words were inspired by the myth of Aries and Leonor?"

Nothing has changed because
Everything has changed because

Aurora. Iridescent, with her nanoceramic dress, still glowing with health, so full of happiness it seems she must burst with it, looking up at me with her enormous eyes from the front row of the Continental Museum, where I am receiving the World Safeguard Award.

"The manipulation of telomerase to eradicate disease and prolong life has been the most important ongoing research project in the history of humanity," says the domo, which is acting as presenter. Its featureless face lights up to the rhythm of the ambient music. (*You Will See the Moon Rise*, what else? Vermillion Moon.) "But all these centuries of prosperity would be nothing more than a mere anecdote without the brilliant untiring work of Doctor Victor Hess. His advances in genetic modification and the integration of nanocellular biotechnology represented an unprecedented evolutionary jump, by allowing our children ..." (I clearly remember noting the paradox of a robot referring to "our" children) to be born using the best technologies which would guarantee them ..."

I've stopped listening to him. I only have eyes and ears for Aurora, just as lovely now at two hundred years old as on that first occasion, on the Albotmilles campus, when she was barely twenty-two. She smiles at me, as if she's not listening to the domo either, as if nothing matters. And in fact, nothing does matter except we two.

"Today, thanks to the fact that Doctor Hess didn't choose to rest on his laurels as the hero who brought us the Heidelberg Miracle, but continued working, we are proud to express our gratitude to him also for the fact that mankind has finally conquered disease. Doctor Hess has managed to eradicate ninety-nine percent of diseases in what will surely come to be known as the Madrid Miracle."

Laughter and applause.

But I see only Aurora.

I'm watching the street from above, through a huge hole in what should have been a wall. Below, a group of armed men are amusing themselves beating a beggar, shoving him from one to another.

"Jesandra? Why are you hitting me, Jesandra?" the poor man cries out as a blow from a rifle butt knocks out several teeth.

Jesandra. The name sounds familiar. Was my wife called Jesandra?

The four thugs are smeared with yellow paint hurtful to my eyes. Just seeing it is enough to terrify me, and this is familiar, too. Have I seen it before?

"Victor?"

The voice gives me such a start that I nearly fall through the hole into the street. My movement dislodges a few fragments of glass, which fall to the ground outside the window.

There's a bearded doctor in front of me, smiling as if he's known me all my life. I can't recall who he is. I can't recall who *I* am. The dull pain in my hand reminds me that I'm injured, but I don't know how that could have happened either.

"Don't move!" I shout at him. "I'm armed! What have you done to my hand?"

The smile disappears, replaced by what appears to be an expression of profound disquiet.

"Victor, I don't think it's a good idea to shout right now. I'm a friend, remember?"

No. No, I don't remember. And I'm not armed, either. I rummage through the pockets of my tattered gown, and only feel a ring, what seems to be a bar of food, and some kind of card. This I take out of my pocket and glance at it. It seems to be a key card. When I shake it a little, the owner's face appears. It's the doctor I have in front of me. Have I stolen it from him?

I shout at him again: "What are you doing in my house?"

The man smiles again. It seems I've said something that has put him in a good mood again, the no-good son of a bitch.

Suddenly, someone fires shots at me, from behind, and one of them goes right through my side, grazing my ribs as it does so. I turn around instinctively, even as I fall to my knees, and see some armed men aiming upwards from the ground. They seem to be stained with yellow paint. How long have they been there?

Aurora is sick and I can't do a thing to help her. The illness has returned, at least for Aurora. Hers seems to be the only case: a mutated form of Ebola. I curse my luck. Maybe those *Humanitas* bastards have created the strain in some laboratory in order to put a stop to what they consider an affront. I can almost imagine them claiming the responsibility, with their crap slogans and their yellow hoods. *Humanity Against the Machine.* Just my fucking luck!

"I want to play, Victor. Where's the Samisha?"

I leave the reports on the desk and run to fetch the citarel. I've kept the battery charged, although it hasn't been played for months. I find I'm weeping as I grab it from the recreation capsule and run back with it to her room.

When I get there, at first I fear Aurora hasn't been able to wait for me, that she has died. Half her life still in front of her, and she has gone and died on me. But no. Death is reflected in her pupils like in a pool that mirrors my face, but she is still alive.

Suddenly the Samisha strikes me as the most stupid object in the world, but I place it at her side. She caresses it with a shaking hand that will never again create music. And she caresses my hand with her other one—a hand that will never again caress me, either.

She doesn't have the energy to play. But even so, in her final moments in the land of the living, with a voice that will accompany me for the rest of my days ... she sings. And I very nearly die with her.

We are just tiny parts of eternity
Droplets of blood without weight
We dance in the heart of the Cosmos
As parts of the Whole we vibrate

There's a doctor crouched in front of me, gazing at me with profound sadness. I've been shot. That much I do remember. And that he's trying to help me. I'm holding a card with his face and his name: Victor Hess.

"Am I dying?" I ask.

"You didn't program me to tell white lies, Victor," he answers. "It seems so. And this time we were so close! You only had to remember a bit more, access the system from the table-screen. Ah, well," he added, smiling, "what can we do? That would be too many miracles for the life of just one man."

I don't know what he's talking about, but I continue to experience flashes of memory.

Memory. That's where the key lies. Somebody managed to eradicate disease and prolong life to a previously unimaginable extent. But something went wrong. Telomeres; something to do with telomeres. Something really bad. At first it seemed to be Alzheimer's, but it was something worse. There were isolated cases. People lost their memory at an alarming rate. But then the numbers vastly increased. Someone mentioned the word epidemic, but that was absurd. In any case, most people no longer even remembered what the word meant.

"Who are you? Are you a ghost?" I ask the other Victor, the other doctor, the one who's trying to make me as comfortable as possible, now that I'm making my final journey.

I hear voices and banging on the door of my house. They're coming for me. I don't know whom, but I suppose they're the ones who shot me. The ones who have killed me. They're yellow creatures. I'm not at all afraid because I don't think they're going to find me alive.

"No, I'm not a ghost," the doctor replies, with a smile that seems like my own. "That song ... the myth of Aries and Leonor. *You will see the moon rise.*"

I nod.

"Aurora's song," I almost whisper.

"Aurora's song," the doctor agrees. "The song was inspired by the myth. Aries, deeply in love with Leonor, his wife, finds out that she is soon going to die, that she has barely a year to live. He concocts a brilliant plan in order to be with her forever. They spend that year travelling all over the world, trying out all kinds of things they've always wanted to do together, endlessly talking to each other throughout long evenings—and loving each other, of course. But during all this, Aries, using a technology of his own invention, stores in an app of his modem: a ... *virgin* personal assistant app we might call it. Bit by bit, the app learns her gestures and expressions, the colour of her imagination, the ways she thinks and speaks ... And when Leonor dies, Aries activates the app, the new Leonor, fearful he might have made an error somewhere, or that the final product might turn out to be no more than a cheap copy of his beloved wife."

"And what happens after?" I say, while noting that the little life I still have is seeping out of me in a torrent of confused memories.

"According to the myth, Leonor (who, obviously, Aries can only see inside his head) opens her eyes and says: 'Aries, my love, how frightened I've been! I couldn't find the way to get back to you!'"

I smile from ear to ear, although I know that from outside it would be seen more as a rictus than as a smile.

"It worked."

"It worked, Victor. It worked. When you began to notice that you, too, were losing your memory, you started to work like a madman in search of a cure. And I think you found it." The doctor indicated the table-screen. "You didn't even do it for yourself, but for mankind. It would have been the second Madrid Miracle. The *third* Hess Miracle. It's such a pity that you didn't have time to give me access to that information as well, that that synapsis has been lost. This is the nearest we've ever come to succeeding."

"Yes, it's a pity. But right now, I'm sorry, I don't really care that much." I cough, and again note how I'm getting weaker every second. I imagine I can see Aurora right in front of me. "Why didn't I pour Aurora's personality into the app? Because that's what you are, aren't you?"

The doctor nods, pleased.

"You said to hell with Aries and Leonor, that Leonor was unrepeatable."

I smile, in spite of the pain.

"Yes. *She is!*"

"And you implanted your own data instead, thinking that it would be difficult to take no notice of yourself when the time came. You even included a pile of protocols so that I wouldn't at once reveal who I was if it turned out that you didn't recognize me: recognize yourself, I mean."

"And look how it's served me right for trying to be so clever!"

The banging on the door announces the imminent arrival of the yellow creatures. But they're going to get here too late. I know that for sure.

"Oh, don't be hard on yourself. You're the best thing that's happened here in the last seven hundred years," he says, winking. "You're about to go, Victor. You asked me for two things for when this moment arrived."

I don't remember. And I'm beginning to forget the conversation I've just had with ... with myself, it would seem; with an app that looks like me, and shares some of my memories and my way of thinking. I mustn't forget this last point now that everything's starting to make sense.

"Tell me, what have you got ready for me?"

"The first thing is a song. You know which one, of course. Recently, it's the thing you've remembered best. The *second* thing you've remembered best!" It starts to play again, inside my head, Vermilion Moon's song, *You Will See the Moon Rise*. "The other can only be one thing: you wanted me to remind you ..."

"... That Aurora is waiting for me. I know. Thank you for everything."

"Thank *you*, my friend, in the name of all mankind. Bon voyage."

The doctor—my other self—vanishes the same time as everything else does. I can only see the sky, clouded over with pollution and the smoke from countless fires, and the moon just behind, smiling at me from high up. Perhaps it isn't even there, but I can see it. And it's Aurora who's singing to me, directly into my ears— without intermediaries, at long last.

We are particles, never-dying, everlasting,
Limpid eternal souls,
As we dance in the heart of the Whole
Alone you and I in the Cosmos

THE BARRETTE GIRLS BY SARA SAAB

Born in Lebanon and now living in the UK, Sara Saab's short fiction has appeared in *Interzone*, *Clarkesworld*, and many others publications.

———

When we get to Euston Station, we help them change trains, and the barrette girls do not resist us.

Andrew says, "They told us to be gentle with them, Sunday."

For his sake I touch them gingerly and coo to reassure them. I hand around the kind of water bottle you buy at a gas station, five liters in flimsy plastic, and they drink with the desperation of suckling cubs.

Andrew asks, "Where will they all sleep?"

I reply, "It's not supposed to rain tomorrow," because he should not be so obvious in public.

The station is full of people who watch us. They look at the orange knapsacks we have put on all the girls to make them seem part of an organized tour, here to learn English or ramble in the frosted countryside. Andrew and I wear orange hats. The girls' knapsacks are a different shade of orange to our hats. Andrew was late, so we bought the knapsacks in a rush from a TK Maxx near the pick-up point.

The barrette girls do not speak on the Tube. There is no place for every one of them to sit and so they stand. Andrew shrugs and sits down. The girls, who do not sit, bump each other with their orange decoy knapsacks, unwitting. Some girls catch a bag in the face but do not react, as if a bag is just a buffet of underground air.

They've never been on the Tube before, and all the passengers can see this. They are not nervous, not bored either. Their lips are not stretched bloodless dry over set teeth. They are uncanny in their calm.

"The next stop," I say to Andrew. He stands to grasp the hand of one of them, and he singsongs *come on*. The train doors piston open. They all follow without a word, the mother-of-pearl barrettes a spill of mercury in the nests of their hair.

———

You might accuse me of loathing the barrette girls because of my inherent similarity to them. Not *similarity* exactly—I am old enough to have raised them—but perhaps a kind of *parallel?* Between how the barrette girls have suffered and how I have suffered. But even our suffering is fundamentally dissimilar.

My suffering is because of how I've been wronged.

I have been wronged many times over. Patrick wronged me when we were children; I remember the smell of cigarettes on his fourteen-year-old fingers, fingers too young yet for tobacco stains. Dascha wronged me when she fucked me even though her heart had been hollow a long time. She let me love her; she leaked my love like a cheap thing. The Barthes wronged me by casting me out when I had nowhere to go. I stood on the stoop and shouted up at the bedroom window, my fingers fixed solid to the handle of my suitcase by the icy wind, but they did not let me in.

Society has not wronged the barrette girls. They are not the kinds of things that can be wronged. No one has ever dared touch them in a way they shouldn't. No one has ever *cheated* on them. *Evicted* them. These violent verbs could strain and strain and still do not a whit of harm to the barrette girls.

Andrew is gesturing to me: come on, Sunday, unlock the padlock, let us get out of the rain. This street is made beautiful by the brass instruments workshop. The saxophones and trombones and tubas in the display dazzle me. They are crisp and wondrous as Christmas ornaments in the light of the streetlamp. Across the street, I open our padlock and our door, squeeze past Andrew and the barrette girls.

So far, Andrew has not wronged me.

———

Consider what you know to be a person. Consider the most solid person you know, your brother Patrick; Dascha your ex-lover; Dr Ganesh, who drags you through your Mineral Sciences degree one grant, one research proposal, one data review meeting at a time. They are fully people; they are not modular, they do not come apart like a bedside lamp or a clock or a toy space shuttle built of blocks.

The fact that they are so very deeply people glues their parts together, makes it hard to imagine this next thing, but imagine it anyway:

Take away pieces from Patrick, Dascha, Dr Ganesh, miserly Asher Barthes and his wife. Take away a little finger first. It's still Patrick, a bit less tobacco-stained, his grip on your neck minutely softer. Patrick nonetheless. Venture inwards now, towards the so-fragile torso, and open up, and take pieces. Gape apart the ribs, take what you find beneath. The more inward, the more central, the more impossible it seems to be lifting away these segments of ones who were people, and all this blood is a curtain, for privacy, for sanctity, because without the blood it is all too obscene, to lift away lung heart gullet stomach, it should not be possible. But it is.

———

The barrette girls clump together on top of the overlap of sleeping bags Andrew laid out. They use each other as pillows, their configurations catlike, graceful. Each of them has taken their barrette out, let their hair hang loose as they offered the sharp, shining thing to us on upturned palms. The stacked barrettes are graceful, too. The stack leans against the exposed brick wall of the dining room: a compound jeweled insect. The barrette girls do not snore, or pass wind, or mumble the names of playground crushes in their sleep.

I find Andrew in the kitchen, where he is pouring a tall glass of water with tremendous care, as if measuring out ingredients. Andrew moves like a much older person, much older than himself, much older than me. I need to remind myself that he is fifteen years my junior, and that these are his first barrette girls, and that he is scared.

The house is dark except for the incongruous lamp with the green velvet shade on the rickety kitchen counter. It casts the white cupboards in dirty sea-foam. The kitchen smells like frying steak. There's no trace of food anywhere. I look out the window, see the brass instruments workshop across the street, see the wedges of shine on the great tuba in the main display.

"Do you play any instruments?" I ask Andrew.

He takes a sip in slow motion. His hands shake, his strong hands with their square palms and slender joints.

"No. The recorder. *Jingle Bells* on the recorder."

"I'd like to learn to play a big, heavy wind instrument," I say. I point out the window. "Just gas moving through a delicate vessel, a simple thing. But ethereal. Beautiful."

Andrew catches my crass analogy and sets his glass carefully down on marble, *clink*, stretches a steadying hand out beside it.

"I don't feel well, Sunday. I feel ill." He looks at me wild-eyed. His voice dips. "They said they were obvious fakes, just real enough to pass in a crowd. They're not fakes. They've got little eyelids with veins in them. They wet their lips. Their hands are warm and they hold with the exact grip of a—" Andrew flexes his free hand, "child."

"You were fine on the Tube."

"Was I? Okay." His voice cracks.

"Too loud, shh. You'll wake them up."

"Who cares, Sunday? Do they really need to sleep?"

"Handling instructions. You wouldn't store a bottle of wine on a sunlit windowsill."

Andrew moves his glass to the sink. Walks past me and up the stairs to the bedrooms in the dark. I've irked him. I suppose I wanted to, but not out of a personal vendetta. It simply feels right that we should both be that way. Irked.

———

Years ago. My first barrette girls. This was before I'd ever met Dascha. I was barely an adult. There were only two of them, experiments, and back then they would give them names to aid identification. Code names, yes, but still names, with the humanizing power of names. Officially, we called these two Monsoon and Typhoon. For the days that I had them, I called them Money and Ty.

I picked them up at St Pancras International. They'd been sent on the Eurostar with a minder; in their hands they each clasped a box of favors from the train. Cartoon lettering: *Conductor in Training*. I remember the word *Training* was rendered zooming along a track. The minder's name I've forgotten, even though it was the password we used in the pick-up.

To remember which girl was which I scratched an M and a T on respective wrists with a ballpoint pen. I talked to them the whole time. I told them my favorite bedtime story on the train to the house. My father had repeated it to Patrick and me so often I used to mouth the words falling asleep.

Money and Ty weren't interested in my story. Or anything over the next three days. Money wasn't interested when I accidentally clipped her lip with the shower head while—contrary to protocol—bathing her that night. Fat coins of blood appeared on ceramic. The blood was red, the blood looked real. Money did not cry. What I can say with confidence is that she did not *know*.

And one time I heard Ty make a high-pitched sound in her throat. It froze me in place. But I don't think Ty knew either.

They were experiments.

The loathing I feel now was germinating then, silently, a disease before the first symptom shows. And when I took my barrette girls to the location and saw how they worked I understood not to name them, not to ever, ever name them, and I fed the anger. Anger is a useful curtain, like blood. Anger is separate from my own hurt.

———

It's the morning of the day the barrette girls must be moved to the location. I go out among the people who watch, but they do not watch me because alone I am anonymous: a woman in a merino wool hat, a woman in a blue weatherproof jacket, a woman with short hair, a hard woman among all the hard women in London. Unwatched, I secure the street made beautiful by the brass instruments workshop. I send up drone cameras that look like cloudy marbles into the boughs of trees, and between designated trees I press my cold fingers against the warm winter softness of my belly.

Andrew has not come down from his bedroom yet. I heard the sharp in-breaths of crying when I stood at his door. My fingers hovered but did not knock.

Downstairs the barrette girls were awake. I'd handed back their barrettes in silence, but in my head was a litany of words. The words started out so harsh that my ears recoiled from the inside, assortments of four letters, one for each girl who stood before me, hands cupped. But I set my jaw and thought kinder words, words like *trombone*, *saxophone*, *horn*. These were not names. They were just words to ease the moment.

———

Dascha and I met at my first job. I was running routine statistical data for an energy firm, a job I could do with half my brain. The rest of me was unoccupied. That's the reason I fell in love.

The first thing I ever cared about as far as Dascha was that she was born four days before me, almost exactly half the world away. We were like barrette girls in that way, part of the same clutch of the planet's organic matter, nourished on the same zeitgeist and political vibrations and the same matrix of airborne pollutants and from the same global stocks of rice and corn and wheat.

She was a strategic analyst. She was too unconventionally beautiful for me. Her hair was straight and cut jagged; her lipstick was dark in the daytime; she never looked anyone in the eye. I should have known that meant she had a dishonest heart, but I was falling for her by then, wracked with a curiosity that strove to devour all her facts, full up with more questions than I'd ever had for myself.

We shared a cab after an office night out, celebrating a new shale gas contract, and when we pulled up in front of Dascha's house on a posh street in St John's Wood she said, "Do you want to come up for a minute? I've just renovated my kitchen and I sort of want to show it off."

I could smell a blend of whisky and craft ale—it could have been either of us or both. There was a heat in me everywhere.

"Yes," I said.

I went up and I saw the kitchen and also the couch and also the bed. I did not think of barrette girls the whole evening, which was a miracle. I was thinking about love. I did not know I was lining myself up for a terrible wound.

———

There's an unlikely bedtime story about a creature. This is my second-favorite bedtime story. It goes like this.

Deep, deep in the earth, right in the middle of the world, is a pit. Inside it, there's a creature. It's alive. There's no record of how it got there. There's no way for it to get out. It has been in this pit—more like the pit of a fruit than a pit in the ground—since the world began.

People drilled and drilled into the earth, and the plan was to breach only the surface, to access the good things pocketed just out of reach. People wanted good things faster than the pockets could replenish. The more people drilled, the less full the pockets were with good things.

Drills got sharper. Drilling got deeper. There were pockets deeper down, but not as many, and more expensive to reach. You'd think something like that would bring this project to a halt, would grind in its gears, but the opposite happened. People got more insistent. They set up more drills, and larger drills, and better drills.

That pit in the middle of the world? They eventually drill right into it. One person will tell you it was an accident; the measurements were wrong, they didn't know how close they were. Some people will tell you that scientists knew there was a pocket like no other down there, a seam of unadulterated fuel. A pocket the size of the moon, a pocket to last so long that greed would have to metastasize to exhaust it.

So the drills pierce the pit, and out flutter-scrabbles a creature. It's downy, colored a prismatic earth tone that's unknown to the earth's surface, and it's barely moving. The people are amazed. They call scientists in. The scientists bathe the creature in oxygen, which it cannot breathe. And when they do, the creature begins to change. Into a little girl, with a beautiful mother-of-pearl barrette in her hair.

That's the unlikely bedtime story about a creature.

———

I've been thinking about my death a lot. The more I think about it the more I realize that death is not a type of suffering. I think about the taxonomies of death: instantaneous oblivion, or slow death like the progression of disease, or an unraveling—I think of Patrick's hands around my neck and the dimming moment before my mother tears his leaden weight off my chest.

Andrew and I are getting the barrette girls ready for the trip to the location. Their faces are lit in the blue light of the surveillance stream projected against the living room wall. The street with the brass instruments workshop is mostly deserted under a sudden assault of freezing rain. One woman smokes a vape under the dripping awning of the off-license on the corner. With her free hand she's rearranging sickly imported papayas in the fruit display out front.

We put a tiny coat and an orange knapsack on each barrette girl. It is hard to maneuver their indifferent limbs into clothing.

"Give me your hand, honey," says Andrew to a barrette girl. "No, no, the other hand."

"Stop inventing things," I say.

Andrew stops moving. "Are you addressing me?" he asks after a moment.

"Who else would I be addressing?"

It's very silent in the room; it's nothing like a room with a group of girls in it. I wonder on a whim if the barrette girls are entertaining thoughts about death. What is death to them? Certainly not suffering. Perhaps a state change, solids melting, liquids evaporating. They contain the coiled potential of their deaths inside, but so do we all.

After the Barthes locked me out of their house I sat a long time against the fence of a council estate, hugging my suitcase in the rain, and I thought about what I would do with my next barrette girls. It could seem an accident; there could be an iron left face down in the next room, there could be a humongous fire, there could be no survivors. But I shivered so hard—my hands and feet got so numb— that some latent survival instinct kicked in. My next barrette girls came and went, and I nourished my anger, and I made a little money, and I found a new place to live.

"Let's go," Andrew says. "It's 2:58 and they said to move at three." The recipe-following exactness of the newly initiated.

"You take these ones." I nudge eight little orange knapsacks, strapped to eight pairs of shoulders, in the direction of the door. The floorboards creak drily under the carpet. The barrette girls I lead move with straight backs. If there's a preternatural bounce in their steps, only Andrew and I will notice it.

———

I suppose people like Andrew always want to make the world a better place. They must have seen this in Andrew right away, fed him the type of drivel that gets to people with morals. Chemistry textbook inserts laced with fairytales: not all natural resources are created equal, and this? This is the most noble of chemicals. Weep for the MRI magnets under threat, the precision manufacturing, the particle accelerators. They rely directly on you, Andrew. Do not falter.

Then there's the spiel everyone gets, earnest people like Andrew and tattered people like me. What a strange whimsy of civilization, that molding flesh has gone so easily for us, that it's cheap and ethical, that we've learned what no one else knows—that molding flesh generates so precious a byproduct.

It would have been criminal not to optimize for this, they'll have told him. All those imaging machines, silicon wafers, physics experiments that couldn't exist otherwise. Nobody—no *real person*, if you think about it—gets hurt. Nobody needs to know. By the time everything is in canisters and on the way to hospitals and manufacturing plants, there's no contamination at all. Nothing to show origins. No aerosols of blood. No spinal fluid. No eyelashes, hair, tears.

———

We've been given a decoy school bus for our trip to the location. It's a rental license plate, the kind of school bus mostly reserved for hen parties and frat boys on pub crawls, but the drive's not long, and Andrew has a kind face. We load the bus. Andrew pulls us out onto the road with his kind face and his orange hat, and he's sweating a dark ring into his shirt collar, but no one out there knows it's so cold in the bus that we can almost see our breath.

"Take a left at the end of the road," I tell Andrew.

"Sunday ..."

"Everything has been smooth so far. It's all we could have hoped for. Don't."

"We don't know what kind of people they might grow up to be. If we give them a chance." He whispers so that the barrette girls will not hear. Oh, Andrew. Those who better not hear have already heard.

"You're on the wrong track with this," I soothe.

"Where's your humanity? What have they done to you? I know you're not this person. These are little girls—they could grow to be people. I know you have a heart. I know it."

Andrew's driving slower, not faster, as his words speed up.

"Do you know what the hats are for?" I ask him.

"What?" He spares a glance away from the road, at me, at my orange hat. "What hats?"

I take the orange hat from my head, which is identical to the hat on his head, which is a little different to the knapsacks, and start unrolling the false lining. I expose the strip that looks like a short, red adhesive plaster. A barrette girl coughs behind me. I pause, until I remember that I've heard barrette girls cough before.

"They didn't tell you about the hats," I say, and I'm not thinking about Andrew wronging me, about the danger he's put me in, about the kind of death this adhesive plaster contains. I'm thinking I'm proud that they told me about the hats but didn't tell Andrew.

I peel the red plaster the way they taught me, pinching it with my nail so that I don't touch the sticky side, and I reach over like I'm fixing Andrew's collar as he drives, and I leave the plaster behind on the skin of his neck, over his jugular.

He looks over again. "What the fuck, Sunday."

"Get out of the seat, darling," I say. "You don't feel well. Get out of the seat."

"I knew you were crazy but—" he says, mournful. Then I see his right-hand-side slacken. His rubbery hand flops into the gap between the spokes of the flat steering wheel. "Shit. Oh, shit, oh God, oh shi —" he says. Too much drool gushes out of his mouth and onto his shirt, another dark stain.

"Come on, Andrew," I say. "Off you get, before you crash us into a wall."

He moves heavily, all dead weight and spasms. I take the driver's seat with a foot on the brake, then shift to the accelerator while Andrew's saying *oh-shi-oh-shi* in a heap in the bus aisle. I look back and some of the barrette girls are watching him. Involuntary nervous system tics: eye muscles tuned to motion in underdeveloped brains like sprouting cauliflowers.

It turns out that if you've been wronged enough times, you learn to assume it before you're sure it's coming.

"It's okay, girls. Everything is ready for you. You're nearly home now. It's nearly quiet time now. Let me tell us a story."

———

Helium is the most bountiful element in all of outer space. So, with all that helium inside, girls, you're built to the proportions of the whole universe. Cool, right?

I can be honest here? So close to the end? I like thinking of you as little space snow globes. I like thinking of you as bonsai galaxies. I like thinking of you as canisters of squirrelly giggles. These are the things I actually like when it comes to you.

You know what you're not missing out on? Pain. Pain, awareness, intentionality—the pillars of personhood. But girls, is personhood really worth the suffering?

Pain: that poor man wallowing on the dirty bus floor. Do you want to feel what he feels? No. Be bonsai galaxies. Don't wish to be him.

———

At the location, I unload the barrette girls in twos, like good school-children. They wait for me beside the bus. Tufts of breath come at synchronized intervals. Dr Ganesh is standing on the snow-salted sidewalk in a tailored grey peacoat. He's wearing a crooked yellow bowtie.

"Andrew is on the bus and you will need to remove him." I give Dr Ganesh a hug. His slighter frame makes our embrace seem brittle and forced.

"What happened, Sunday?" he asks. He does not sound especially sad, his question evidentiary.

"He snapped. Everyone I surround myself with ends up doing something crazy." I straighten Dr Ganesh's bowtie. "You know my history with people."

I don't know how long we hold each other's stares before Dr Ganesh looks away. He begins to lead the first pair of barrette girls by the hand. Their mother-of-pearl barrettes flash in the cold light of the season.

I catch up with Dr Ganesh at the door of the location. He shows me a grimace.

"We spend a long time training up someone like Andrew. Did you try to de-escalate?"

The frosted glass diamond in the door is covered in fingerprints. "He was a danger. He thought they were real."

Dr Ganesh leads the barrette girls into the location, counting them, a soft mantra (I think: *trombone, saxophone, horn*).

When he is done he says, "Andrew did *not* think they were real. They are so blatantly not real." He shoves a barrette girl on the side of her head. She corrects herself like a punch clown. "I do wonder sometimes who the danger is, Sunday."

"Dascha tried to phone me last month," I say. "She asked me if I was ready to leave this behind. She said I didn't need the money, that I have professional skills, the usual shit. Offered to pay my way if I quit."

"And what did you say?" Dr Ganesh asks.

"I told her I'm doing this because the world needs me to. And it helps to have something to focus on. A single bonfire of anger instead of the beginnings of forest fires everywhere. Did I ever tell you about my big brother Patrick?"

"Many, many times." His tone is acidic. He is the opposite of an inert entity. "We're here now, and we're a person down, so keep your musings to yourself. I need you to do twice the usual work."

I should have known Dr Ganesh was headed this way, too.

———

It's only uncomfortable to watch the first time. I wish they had no bones and drifted to the ground like feathers. I wish I did not have to heap them at the mouth of the incinerator.

There is a sucking noise when the machine has extracted all the helium and flesh begins to vibrate in the vacuum of cavernous torsos —that part is the hardest to become accustomed to. Andrew would not have liked that part at all.

The barrette girls approach the machine and, palms up, place their barrettes on a steel platform. Why do they do this? Is it bred into them? An instinct? A taught behavior from infancy? I watch them: their eyes are on the girl ahead, they see what happens, but still they come forward without hesitation.

Each barrette is genetically keyed. The machine reads a registration number from it and loads it in a mechanical arm. When twisted against the chest, the long edge of each barrette—molded tungsten carbide, sharp as anything—extracts an exactly round disc of flesh from below the sternum. Here the barrette girls uniformly emit a sort of sigh. The used barrette is swallowed into the extraction machine and clinks deep in its belly while a rubbery ring suckers onto the hole in the chest. The mat beneath the barrette girls' shoes is a massive, absorbent surgical pad. The chemical smell of this pad is on my fingers. I avoid putting my hands on my face.

There are five barrette girls left. Five girls are more than enough. Dr Ganesh has gone to the other room to watch those of us watching the surveillance stream.

There is a tangy sweetness to this happening while Dr Ganesh exercises his distrust.

"Come this way." I corral the last barrette girls towards the front door. Outside a wet-feeling wind has picked up. I arrange the girls along the porch; if we go onto the lawn the surveillance cameras will see.

There are different taxonomies of death and there are different taxonomies of personhood. There are people like me, and there are people like Dr Ganesh, Dascha, Patrick, Asher Barthes. There are no people like the barrette girls, but in spite of this, the barrette girls can be taken apart piece by piece, like Andrew can, like Dr Ganesh can, like I can.

"This way." I lead the barrette girls to the porch's side railing and pick each one up under the arms and put her down on the ground

below. Their clothes are warm and they are so, so light. Lighter full
than they are empty.

The surveillance drones do not see the side of the house, but Dr
Ganesh will know when he looks for me. Or when he counts the
barrette girls on the heap. I let us into the storage shack beside the
house. Fertilizer bags lend the space a noxious smell. There is very
little room, and though it is cold and tight, the girls do not know how
to huddle. They stand rod still.

"Bonsai galaxies, girls. Remember that. We've made our peace."

How do I pick one? Their eyes all look at me the same way. Five is
more than enough; five is too many. I only need one big, brave lungful
devoid of oxygen. I only need one.

I pick the one in the middle, for symmetry.

I go to my knees, put my hands out for the barrette. She removes
it from her hair and holds it out to me, palms up. Reflex, not intent.

I steady the shoulder and press the sharp barrette to the solar
plexus. I do not expect how easily fabric and flesh give beneath the
twisting cut. The barrette girl sighs. Even with my hand shaking, I
pull the disc of a body cleanly away on the barbs of the barrette and
slide my palm over the hole in a torso.

There's a lot of blood this way. I'm not precise like the machine.

I regard the barrette girl I have chosen. "Dying is the only human
thing you can do. Dying makes us similar."

The eyes are on me but not on me.

I lean in and replace my palm with my face and make a seal with
my cheeks and chin. It's awkward. Blood slides against my jaw. Blood
is a curtain. Anger is a curtain. The taste of blood in the round breach
of a chest is very strong. I wait to hear any words from this barrette
girl, or the others, or Dr Ganesh. But I suspect there are no words left
in the world. I breathe in long and luxurious, I breathe and breathe,
scentless bliss, until I fill my body with helium. I stop seeing and stop
feeling. The wronging melts away.

THE CALCULATIONS OF ARTIFICIALS BY CHI HUI
Translated from Chinese by John Chu

Chi Hui has been an editor and writer for *Science Fiction World,* China's premiere genre magazine. She has garnered numerous nominations and honours, including a 2016 Chinese Nebula Silver Award for her novel *Artificial Humanity 2075: Recombined Consciousness.*

———

Introduction: Some numbers

In the year 2042, 2,248 Actual people, but 11.26 million Artificial people, lived in the city of Mian on the continent of Asia. Meanwhile, 7.2 billion Artificials lived in the world, as opposed to only 1.44 million Actuals. Out of those, only 127 people knew the truth about the world.

1 - The solitary monitor of calculated behavior

Whenever the city suddenly got noisy, Aixia knew an Actual was nearby.

Through the special behavior monitor spectacles, he saw a somewhat stout, middle-aged man lead his wife and daughter across the street. A fluorescent green halo surrounded the man's body. It indicated that he was an Actual and his wife was an Artificial. His daughter was also an Artificial.

Without thinking about it, Aixia tapped his spectacles. A diagram of the city streets immediately superimposed itself onto his field of vision. It showed that 127 Artificials on this block had close ties to him, their behavior driven by advanced algorithms, as well as nine Artificials whose behavior was driven by the most advanced algorithms. The difference was his friends versus his family. Furthermore, there were over a thousand strongly interactive Artificials and over four thousand weakly interactive ones. They formed the entire world of this man's life.

One solitary Actual. He, naturally, knows nothing of his solitary existence. Lucky bastard.

Of course, around here, their calculations had already started to falter. The man could easily see a blank face, hear dull, halting syllables. It'd gotten to the point where some Artificials moved mechanically in non-human ways. The truth of the world was like a flimsy piece of window film, easily pierced by a few careless slips.

This was why Aixia came here.

He crossed the block, entered the neighborhood's public central square, then touched an old woman there. A stream of data danced in the air. The functions that had to do with her were revised. Her odd expression was restored again to a harmonious smile. It wasn't as easy, however, to make her stiff fingers nimble again. All in all, this Artificial had already been in service for too long.

After a moment of thought, he adjusted the "gossip function" to explain away the old woman's clumsiness as the result of a stroke. The internal harmony index for this block's behavior returned to normal.

The behavior monitor turned around. He slowly walked out of the man's scope of interaction. The surrounding city became silent again. Under the streetlights, a stream of people passed by as before, but their manner became stiff and mechanical. They weren't speaking or laughing anymore. Cars drove slowly down the street. The drivers' hands weren't even on the steering wheels. The algorithms for weakly interactive behavior had several hundred bugs, but in the name of conserving resources, no one had bothered to fix them. Since these areas didn't have any Actuals, no Actuals would ever discover these abnormal places. Only in those places that Actuals could observe did the world approach perfect behavior.

The behavior of Artificials was never intended to be one hundred percent perfect. What it sought was to be highly efficient and strongly interactive, to give the world's 1,440,000 Actuals a stable world, a stable life.

He walked down the street. Dim lights and a stream of clumsy people stretched across the silent block. Through his behavior monitor spectacles, he examined the behavior of Artificials everywhere in the world, their mistuned functions, misassigned values, not to mention some simply unfortunate accidents. As the behavior monitor, he fixed those faulty data and calculations to make the façade of this world even more realistic.

Aixia didn't remember how long he'd been wandering around like this. Artificials were installed here as though they had sprung up out of the ground. By the time the first batch of Actual children arrived, he had already come to this city. His work was to monitor the Artificials' behavior, a job he could do from anywhere. He still decided, however, to settle down in an Artificial city. Day and night, he wandered aimlessly, deceiving himself, looking at the behavior of Artificials as though it were real life.

He had an apartment, a quiet, deserted apartment. He rarely returned there unless he was physically and emotionally exhausted and desperately needed sleep. Because the solitude there cocooned him, reality could take him by surprise ... make him face the ice-cold world alone.

He crossed a block of the weakly interactive, who used a minimum of resources and computational power. Painstakingly, he searched for those places where the strongly interactive congregated, like supermarkets, food stalls, bars, night markets ... the sorts of places where Actuals always went. As a result, the Artificials there would improve their behavior, work with high efficiency. For a short while, the world would seem truly alive, as though every passing encounter with someone were real. In times like those, he let himself forget about the existence of Artificials and just tried his best to live.

He walked into the night market. A stall was selling small pets. He stopped in front of it for a moment and tried to buy a pair of hamsters, but the hamster cage was much too expensive. After he failed to haggle down the price, Aixia had no choice but to leave the two hamsters, whose small black eyes had filled with anticipation.

"Was the peddler who haggled with me an Artificial?" he thought.

His fingers felt for the behavior monitor spectacles in his bag. Finally, he gave up trying to tell the difference.

He walked aimlessly. As he did, he guessed at who were Actuals, but he was in a strongly interactive block. With only the naked eye, he had practically no way to distinguish between the Actuals and the Artificials here. They had the same smile and the same attentive gaze. They spoke the same way and had the same demeanor. From time to time, they'd burst into laughter, argue at the top of their lungs, whisper in confidence ...

It was now two in the morning at the night market, and Aixia felt somewhat tired and sleepy. In his line of sight, many Artificials had dropped their behavior level, becoming the dull and slow of the weakly interactive. Some had even stopped moving completely. This meant, maybe, that all the Actuals in the vicinity had left, Aixia thought.

No, he corrected himself. There was still one Actual. The behavior monitor didn't factor into the behavior of Artificials per se. This made him able to glimpse the actual state of the world and grab it as it spun.

A smile spilled across his thin lips. He got on a sputtering bus. The driver was a cross-eyed Artificial. Right now, one eye always stared right, one eye stared at the ground. As always, his hands gripped the steering wheel steadily. He drove the bus in the direction of Aixia's apartment.

The night swept past the bus's windows. The city beyond it was occasionally sharp and clever, occasionally dull and calm. Very few Actuals moved about the streets at night. The city was divided into tiny pieces by each and every highly interactive district. Most of the weakly interactive districts between them had already settled down completely. Aixia placidly looked out a bus window. By his side, an old Artificial woman sat perfectly straight, as stiff as a wax dummy.

One stop before his apartment, the bus erupted with a terrifying creaking noise. It rocked back and forth before finally stopping by the side of the road.

"It's broken. Get out," the driver mumbled stiffly. No computational resources were wasted to give this voice any intonation. Aixia forced a laugh. A slow stream of dull people got off the bus.

Where he lived wasn't too far from here, if he cut through a sparsely lit park. Aixia hesitated for a moment before he decided to walk straight through. Although the city wasn't very safe at night, he was too tired and sleepy to care whether he'd be robbed. Artificials wouldn't engage with a behavior monitor. As for Actuals ... He glanced at his map. There were no Actuals here for now.

He cut through the park. Streetlamps dimly lit the path. A pair of lovers sat mechanically, one stacked on top of the other, on a long bench to the side. They looked exactly like department store mannequins.

Suddenly, the two Artificials started to move. They emitted hushed murmurs, whispered sweet nothings. On another path, an Artificial standing dumbly with a dog on a leash started to jog and, at the same time, shout the dog's name. Within a millisecond, the entire park shifted from weakly interactive to strongly interactive behavior.

An Actual has shown up.

Aixia put on his monitoring spectacles, but all around he saw only the yellow haloes of Artificials, not even one green halo of an Actual.

Where is he?

He heard, in the distance, shouting and the sounds of kicking and punching. Even more disconcerting, he heard sounds of Artificials fleeing. On the monitoring spectacle's map, the words "Grade A retribution" in red caught his eye.

Oh, no.

Aixia began to run. A hedge, as tall as man, separated the two paths that he and that green dot were on. He simply crashed through, not feeling the pain as twigs lashed his face.

Grade A retribution meant one or more Artificials were attacking an Actual. Moreover, they'd already acquired permission from the algorithms that drove them to kill the Actual.

He crossed the path, then turned the corner to see three young people beating a scrawny figure.

"Stop!" he shouted.

Artificial Behavior Restriction 424: the monitor's order overrides a retribution directive.

The three Artificials halted. Their algorithms quickly decided on the flight reaction. The three glanced at each other, then with an unusually realistic look of panic, they turned around to rush out of the dark alley. In the blink of an eye, they disappeared out the other end.

The scrawny figure on the ground didn't move. Viewed through the monitor spectacles, a weak green halo surrounded him.

Aixia crouched next to the body. He reached for a hot, trembling arm, trying to support the person up, to stand. The figure stirred, lifting his young, smudged face to look at him. Black eyes revealed a stubbornness and alertness. His cheeks were bruised, but there were no traces of tears.

An Actual child, not yet fully grown, fourteen years old? Maybe fifteen? But, through the monitor spectacles, a red halo surrounded the child's immature face. Next to it, a row of text read: Monitor for violence, grade A danger.

2 - Senile and willful twins

"Why don't I take you home?" Aixia asked.

The youngster stared at him warily.

"You can have a bath, eat something. Change your clothes," Aixia said.

"Go away!"

"If I go away, those three bastards will find you, then beat you to death," Aixia stated calmly. This was one hundred percent fact. The boy was already branded "Monitor for violence, grade A danger." This meant any Artificial whose calculated behavior qualified could kill him. He could have died at the hands of those three thugs just now, been caught by the police, or died from some car suddenly rounding the corner.

He knew that every Actual was precious, but death, murder, and accidents were woven into the calculations of Artificials as indispensable parts of a "real world."

The youngster glanced at Aixia then looked at the head of the alley. The three thugs' shadows had disappeared, but they could be hiding somewhere, waiting for Aixia to leave. The monitor knew these Artificials were "locked into retribution." In other words, they wouldn't leave because they'd become stupid when they got too far away from him. Instead, they'd follow the youngster until he became an ice cold corpse.

"They won't give up on you, but you can hide for a while at my place," Aixia said.

This time, the youngster's expression wasn't defiant. "Is your place far away?"

"It's right nearby," Aixia said.

"I can't walk. My leg might be broken." The youngster's brow furrowed.

Aixia felt the youngster's ankle. It was swollen, but it didn't seem broken. "Do you want to go to the hospital?"

"No!" the youngster blurted. His tone couldn't contain his panic.

Aixia studied the youngster's face. He couldn't make out the expression in the dim streetlamp light. A moment later, he sighed. "I'll carry you home."

As soon as they got home, Aixia put the youngster on the sofa. He ran to the refrigerator and got out some ham sausage. The cupboard had two packs of instant noodles. He and the youngster had a late night snack. Afterward, he carried the youngster into the bathroom—with the result that he wrestled with the youngster's tangled hair and the dirt on his body for a hour.

"Why don't you get some sleep?" he said to the youngster. "The bedroom's all prepared for you. You take the bed."

"What about you?"

"I have to work tonight."

"Are you leaving?"

"No. SOHO, I work from home."

The youngster didn't respond at first. Black eyes stared deeply into him. "Why are you being so kind to me?"

For a moment, Aixia was dumbfounded.

"I don't know either," he replied. "Perhaps it's because I've been alone for too long."

He waited for an hour, until he was sure the youngster was asleep, before he turned on his computer. A complicated pattern of light and shadow filled his study. A rotating image of a starry sky covered a wall. He placed himself among the mirage of myriad constellations.

"Aixia here. Calling Rui An," he said. The computer responded to his voice. Right away, the image of a highly capable woman wearing a short jacket, combing her short hair, appeared in his field of view.

"Rui An here," a cold, female voice sounded. It seemed to carry the faint hint of fury. "I've been waiting for you to call me, Aixia. You've recently interfered with a retribution operation?"

"With the Artificials as my witnesses, I have the right," he answered.

"Do you know—" Rui An's image rippled. It settled into a face of rage. "Do you know what sort of person the kid you have laid up in your bedroom is?"

"Please, I beseech you to allow humble me to know the details."

"You're fucking trying to piss me off, aren't you ...?" Rui An curled her lips and bared her teeth, forming an expression that was absolutely not a smile. Her eyes, though, held the hint of one. "Fine, every night I want to give my Artificial servant a sound beating. It's rare to see an Actual face. I might as well waste my precious time explaining things to you, Aixia." She dragged out a chair he couldn't see, then sat down. Graceful crossed legs swung back and forth. "The kid is a grade A danger. He has four counts of burglary, one count of looting, not to mention one charge of murder."

"Murder of an Actual?"

"Murder of an Artificial."

"That doesn't justify retribution. As far as I'm concerned, only the murder of an Actual justifies retribution."

"The examination committee thinks he's a disruptive influence on society. Aixia, the youngster's parents are Actuals."

Aixia whistled lightly. "The Actual socialization plan."

"Exactly, that failed plan. Twelve couples. We let Actuals form households with Actuals, then let them bear children, rather than form families with Artificials—as you can imagine, good heavens, Actuals with Actuals ... out-of-control violent impulses, obsessions, lust for power, desire for control. They all clashed with each other in their cramped families to the point where not even an Artificial child could ease their pain. All of the frenzy landed onto the Actual children of those couples ..." Rui An paused for a moment. "As for this kid, his father abused his mother for ten years, then killed her. He witnessed the entire chain of events. When his father tried to kill him, he ran out the door ... where, by chance, his father was killed by a car rounding the corner. Unfortunately, he witnessed that, too."

"You all think he's become a destructive factor." Aixia's voice lowered. "That car was no coincidence, was it ...?"

"No, it wasn't. Artificial Behavior Edict 799: Retaliate against the murder of an Actual at the first opportunity. After this incident, we rewrote this edict to add the restriction 'within the vicinity of an under-aged Actual, permission to carry out retribution is not granted.' But for this kid ..." Rui An shook her head. "It was too late. We marked him, followed him, and tried to arrange for an Artificial to take care of him, but after he murdered the Artificial, we decided ..." The administrator's voice revealed a bitterness and hardship. "We decided to eliminate him."

"Can I keep him for the time being?"

"You're mad!" Rui An betrayed an extreme astonishment and deep dread. "You ... You are an Actual, Aixia. So is that kid. An Actual and an Actual living under the same roof. Artificials be damned, do you understand what you're saying?"

"The households you're talking about are all extreme cases, Rui An. Aren't you and I good friends?" As Aixia said this, he wasn't so sure.

She shook her head forcefully. The image of competence and determination disappeared. She now looked worried and restless. "That's not the same, Aixia. It's really not the same. Damn it. How many times do we get in touch a year? Three? Four? What you're suggesting is to keep the kid with you. He's not even fully ... How many years has it been since someone did that? Artificials be damned, at first we had a reason for filling the world with Artificials. Have you forgotten?"

"I haven't forgotten," Aixia said softly. "I can never forget. We are the first generation, Rui An. It's been 120 years ... We've worked together for 120 years. Now, I'm asking you to allow me one tiny indulgence. Can I?"

The corners of her mouth twitched a little, betraying an aged expression ill-matched to her youthful face.

"Very well," she said in a low voice. "In the end, you have a right to an indulgence. But, the area around you is a behavior vacuum. You don't draw the attention of Artificials. That kid does. The conflict must be resolved before everything will be all right."

"Their interest in him swamping their lack in me is just fine." Aixia started to laugh. He'd never felt so happy. "I've been forgotten by the world for too long. Why not have some excitement around me every once in a while?"

"That may not be a good excitement. The interactivity algorithms for the kid contains lots of negative functions, including police, riot, theft, gang, not to mention fighting," Rui An warned.

"I can handle it."

Rui An shrugged. "You'd better be able to, Aixia."

3 - They contained fire with paper to survive

He was the youngest survivor of the settlement.

On this piece of desolate wasteland, underneath the cold, gray sky, the crowd gathered to try to rebuild a new world on this land after nuclear war. They still had the knowledge. They still had the technology and the ability. It was nothing like post-apocalyptic fiction, where people pushed rough-hewn carts in ragged clothes as they pioneered farming and industry from first principles to reestablish human civilization.

As a matter of fact, within thirty short years they'd recovered everything, all that the world before nuclear war had had, as well as technology, knowledge, wisdom, and power that that world had never had.

They quickly grew powerful and arrogant. They exploded into quarrels. They fell into indescribable rage. They grew stubborn beyond reasoning. They split into distinct, walled-off factions. Their impulses couldn't be controlled ...

Then there was a second nuclear war.

They'd always believed that the first nuclear war broke out because of overpopulation, shortage of natural resources, as well as competing ideologies. It never occurred to them that the world they rebuilt, this world that had already conquered age and death, that could already build lifelike anthropomorphic robots, that had already pressed onward into space ... would still erupt into the second nuclear war.

Two nuclear wars within thirty brief years almost destroyed everything, but they still had the ability to rebuild the world from its ruins. They also feared endlessly their own abilities.

"We are too powerful. Even just one person can destroy the world," Rui An said.

"We are too impulsive. Even just one quarrel can spark a war," Kyoko Yamashita said.

"We have no way to restrain the violent tendencies in our souls.

We pour violence on each other, so it's best if we stay far apart from each other," Aixia said.

But a woman raised questions they had no way to avoid.

"What about families? What about children? We are so powerful, one person can destroy the world. The jealousies of one couple can destroy the world, destroy each other, destroy their children. What about us as a species? How will we reproduce?"

"Weaken them," Will Senna said.

"But raise our descendants on this piece of land? Let them continue to multiply without end? Let them rapidly grow old and die and not do anything for them?"

"Weaken them. Deceive them. Soften them. Deploy Artificials. A lion brought up around a hundred sheep will not grow into a lion. We have to engrain peace into the depth of their souls and, after that, awaken them into our midst."

"You're talking about raising them, raising our progeny! Is this something people are capable of?"

"But ... are we ... still human?"

Aixia opened his eyes. The motley pattern of light and dark on the apartment's ceiling reflected into his eyes. It was already ten in the morning. Unexpectedly, he'd over-slept ...

Recently, memories of the past had barged uninvited into his dreams. The doctor on the Star Trail had said that this was an inevitable side-effect of being over two hundred years old. Memories calcified, and yet the body stayed young. He worried that, after some time, he'd need surgery to implant memory crystals to get by.

He shrugged, got up from the sofa, then washed his face in the bathroom. There were no sounds coming from the bedroom. Perhaps the boy hadn't gotten out of bed yet. As he brushed his teeth, he thought about the question he recalled about humanity.

At the time, no one had answered him.

Even afterwards, after the plan of Artificial behavior and the Artificial world had been completely carried out, still no one answered the question.

Children these days grew into adulthood in safety, brought up by Artificial parents. They married Artificials and grew old in the company of Artificials. With the exception of Actuals with violent tendencies, who were retaliated against, the rest of the Actuals live safely until the appropriate age, after which they are received on the Star Trail.

But ...

He shook his head lightly, cast off the chaotic thoughts from his mind.

"Thank you," the youngster's voice rang out.

Startled, he jumped.

"Ah? Oh, no problem. Are you awake? Can you walk?"

"I only twisted it." He rotated his foot a little. "... thank you. I want to go."

"You want to go home?"

The youngster's body swayed a little. He ignored the question of "home."

"Staying here will just bring you trouble."

"Trouble?" Aixia knew the youngster had killed an Artificial. The police would certainly order his arrest. This was part of the retribution sequence. But, on purpose, he pretended he didn't know.

"No big deal ... those thugs." His voice grew tense. His body grew tense as well.

"They'll never find their way here," Aixia said with an intentional casualness. "This neighborhood is extremely secure. If they actually come to harass you, you can dial 110 for emergencies. You don't need to be afraid. Do you intend to go home?"

The youngster's lips trembled. "I don't want to go home."

"Then stay a while." Aixia patted the youngster's shoulder. "Be my roommate."

This time, the youngster didn't refuse. Soon, the two sat on the sofa next to the tea table, sharing what little milk and bread was left in the refrigerator as an early lunch.

"Oh, right, what's your name?" Aixia asked.

"... I'm Farrell."

"Hmm ... okay, Farrell, I have to go out this afternoon. It might be late before I get back. There are instant noodles in the cupboard. You should be able to make them yourself. I'll bring home KFC when I come back tonight."

"I want to have McDonald's."

Aixia stood dumbfounded for a moment, then started to laugh. "McDonald's it is, then," he said.

He wandered around as he always did, but his mood today seemed to change somewhat. Memories of the past appeared and vanished in the recesses of his thinking. He remembered the past, yes, before the second nuclear war erupted. Once, he'd had a huge cabin on the Star Trail, as well as many companions. They chatted with each other, had fun together, made all sorts of trinkets together, and craved the tons of trouble that got their parents involved.

That was a long time ago. One hundred years? One hundred and fifty years? Afterward, everything was destroyed. People hid behind Artificials, hid between flickering façades of the world. They forgot each other, kept far away from each other. Him deciding not to let the youngster go was completely on impulse. It wasn't that he didn't realize the danger of an Actual coming into contact with another Actual ...

But he couldn't contain himself, the soft touch of the youngster's hair awakened a speck of something that had survived in the depths of his soul. It was only by depending on that tiny bit of memory that he felt that he, himself, was someone truly alive, that he could remove himself from this world filled with the calculated behavior of Artificials.

A forced smile spilled across Aixia's thin lips as he laughed at himself. This was crazy. In this world filled with façades, the truth was cruel and dangerous.

Suddenly, the monitor spectacles in his pocket started to vibrate.

He put on the spectacles and skimmed the projected map. Red dots twinkled in a few places on the map of the world. They were all marked "Actual murders" and "Grade A retribution."

Aixia raised his eyebrows in puzzlement.

This was not normal. Actual murders took place, on average, once a month, and Artificial murders did not cause Grade A retribution.

He tapped the map a few times, zooming in on the nearest red dot. One, no, a pair of red dots were in this city, 17 Nanhang Road.

He hailed a taxi and hurried there just in time to see a policeman cordon the area off with yellow tape and a body bag being carried out.

"What happened here?" he asked an old Artificial woman next to him.

"Murder. A delivery person and the resident—I don't know why—

started to argue, so he killed the resident!" The old woman waved her hands wildly.

Aixia hid the uneasiness deep in his heart. The old woman lamented for a while about the degradation of public morals, then walked away.

Another red dot appeared on the map of this city on Qingzhao East Lane.

He took a half an hour to rush there by taxi. The police had already cordoned off the area. He didn't find anything out from the crowd of Artificials watching, but he saw a trail of blood at the head of the lane.

According to the behavior monitor display, this was yet another case of Actual-on-Actual violence, one person dead, one person seriously injured.

There was a problem somewhere. Aixia knit his brows. As he walked towards home, he examined the behavior code function by function.

The problem was in the primary function that broke up crowds.

This function originally kept Actuals apart. It used every sort of stochastic and every sort of rational, non-stochastic event to divide their work, lives, entertainment ... so that they wouldn't meet one another. The violent tendencies of Actuals would only hurt Artificials or, in a very few circumstances, they'd be hurt by the retribution of Artificials—but now, this function was being perverted by someone.

For a long time, the calculation of Artificials had always been to use Artificials to cocoon Actuals. Prudent and cautious, it was like using paper to contain a fire. As long as there wasn't permission for retribution, Artificials were essentially gentle and well-mannered. They effectively eased the tendency of Actuals to violence. But once the function was perverted, those stochastic events once used to separate Actuals were turned around to promote Actuals approaching each other, to the extent that they met ...

Only people on the Star Trail could modify a primary function. Aixia anxiously picked up his pace. He called Rui An—but no one answered.

A harsh car horn blared behind him. A car struck the sidewalk. It missed Aixia by only a few centimeters. Quickly, it rushed away.

He was scared into a cold sweat. Indescribable fury welled in his chest. He gave the car the middle finger.

The car suddenly stopped.

Then, abruptly, it turned around.

Aixia absolutely could not hide in time. Dealing with a person was one thing, dealing with a recklessly driven car was another. He leapt hastily to the side, but his left arm was swiped by the car. The world spun. His body flew, crashing into a dumpster on the sidewalk.

He tried to get up, but his left arm hurt so much that he couldn't prop himself up. The car stopped. A burly man howled as he kicked the car door open and then jumped out. Through the spectacles, Aixia saw a green halo.

An Actual.

Aixia tried to stand. The brute kicked him to the ground. Futilely, he raised his right arm to block the brute's blows. Disgusting curses mixed with the sound of fists hitting a body in his buzzing ears.

An Actual came across an Actual. One calculated behavior affected another calculated behavior ... This might originally have been what the kid had run into, but the calculations had been perverted. The Actual brought his violent desire, and was drawn together with Aixia.

Oh, fuck. I thought I could handle this.

He felt nauseous. He wanted to vomit. Out of sheer pain, he tried to escape from the brute's punches, but he was caught in the corner between the dumpster and a wall.

A weird rumbling sound.

The brute stopped all of a sudden. Then he fell over like a log.

Farrell. The youngster's figure emerged from behind the brute. A bloodstained brick was in his hand.

He was crying. Tears flowed down his young face. He gritted his teeth, as though he was ready to hit the brute's head again.

"This beating hasn't made me cry yet. You cried first." Aixia laughed. Slowly, he got up. The youngster ran to support him. He gratefully accepted the help. "What are you doing here?"

"I was following you," Farrell mumbled.

"You were afraid that I'd go to the police?" Aixia thought. What he said, though, was, "You were afraid I wouldn't buy you McDonald's?"

The youngster started to laugh.

Aixia looked at the brute. The latter's eyes had rolled back in his head. His breathing was even, though.

"Farrell, can you support me as we go home?" he asked.

The youngster nodded.

4 - Destiny is some sort of inverted calculation

All night, police sirens whistled through the entire city of Mian. A series of Actual altercations broke out, one after another. They included fights, murders, brutal slayings of entire families.

That night, only 1,924 Actuals remained in the city of Mian. Over two hundred died from every manner of murder. Functions were still guiding Actuals towards each other. When an Actual came across an Actual, catastrophes and violence increased geometrically. Death seemed like a time bomb lit, then finally going *boom*.

Aixia spent all night trying to contact Rui An, but never got an answer until three in morning, when he received a brief dispatch on his terminal.

"Come to the Star Trail." Rui An looked pale and exhausted. "Come immediately, as fast as possible."

"What?" Aixia raised his voice.

"I don't have time to explain, Aixia, just come quickly."

Having finished, Rui An broke off communications.

There were lots of ways to get to the Star Trail, but Aixia chose to pilot his own spacecraft. It was easy, fast, and convenient. Also, it could carry an additional passenger. He considered over and over again whether to bring Farrell with him. Although it would have been easy to leave without him knowing, he didn't want to leave the youngster in a suddenly chaotic city.

When he saw the spacecraft, Farrell's jaw dropped.

"Are you an alien?" he asked.

"No. I'll explain later. This is my spacecraft. Get on board."

Farrell hesitated for a moment then quickly caught up with Aixia.

As they flew to the Star Trail, he explained to Farrell the entire history of what had happened, as well as the calculations of Artificials that kept the modern world turning.

"So everything is fake?" Farrell kept looking at his own thin fingers. "Am I an Artificial?"

"No, you are an Actual."

"Really? How do I know you're not lying?"

"I have no way to prove it." Aixia started to laugh. "I wonder, myself, sometimes, whether I'm an Artificial."

"Oh."

They were silent for a while, then Farrell asked another question.

"Were my parents Actuals?"

"Yes."

"Both of them?"

"Both of them."

"But you just said that you worked hard to prevent people from coming into contact with each other."

"Yes."

"They never faced each other?"

"Never. Even my doctor gives me my physical exams through telepresence."

"What about my parents, then? And what about all the things happening today?"

"Inverted calculations."

"I don't understand."

"... about fifteen years ago, we conducted an experiment. We wanted to see whether Actuals could truly get along with each other. So, we inverted the calculations in the Artificials' crowd separation function. That function was originally used for separating Actuals, but we perverted it to use all sorts of excuses to bring men and women together, to facilitate their marriages. But the results ... they were simply catastrophic."

This time, the silence was even longer.

"They were unhappy," the youngster finally said softly. "They were truly unhappy, Aixia. You don't understand. They fought. They were miserable, but they didn't know whose fault it was. All sorts of people pushed them into marriage. All sorts of people praised their marriage. Everyone. It got to the point where if you were unhappy, you must be guilty of something. But they knew ... even if they didn't know about Artificials, they still knew the marriage wasn't something they actually wanted, still knew each wasn't the one the other one wanted. Just like I knew they weren't the parents I wanted. I didn't know who I could hate. They were my parents. That is ... I had no way to choose. It's like fate. You didn't know who to yell at. You didn't know who to complain to. You just knew the situation had become like this, and it wasn't anyone's fault. So then you can only hate yourself, hate everything ... just like nothing that was decided for you could really bring happiness. They simply had no other choice. Neither did I. I knew that feeling, the feeling of being reared and having things being decided for you ..." He suddenly raised his head, and said hoarsely through gritted teeth, "I hate you! I hate you all!"

Aixia didn't say anything. He just docked his spacecraft in the Star Trail.

The interior of the Star Trail was just as empty as Aixia's apartment. The Artificial servants passing by didn't bother to simulate the appearance of humanity, each and every one walking back and forth crowned with a round, metal head. He led the youngster through long corridors. Flickering lamps lit the way in front of them.

"Are there Actuals here?" Farrell couldn't help asking.

"We live scattered through the Star Trail. This place is huge. There are only just over a hundred of us. So we are extremely scattered," Aixia explained.

"What about those people on the world below who die of old age? You said that they are all received on the Star Trail."

"Hmm." Aixia nodded. "This is the problem. They've all been frozen. Not even one has been thawed."

"Why?"

"We don't dare."

With that, the two reached the control room. Aixia pushed open the door, then entered. He ordered the Artificial servants to repair the communication system. For a long time, no one could reach him. It'd made him feel odd and restless. And the message Rui An left behind had an ominous tone.

He breathed deeply, sat down, then turned on the communication system.

In an instant, a virtual image filled the entire room.

5 - The fruits of humanity

"What is that?" Farrell clutched Aixia's hand. Right before their eyes, the control room transformed in an instant into a spacious virtual conference room. The 127 who first established the Artificial world all gathered here to meet. And one solitary figure stood at the lectern. His youthful eyes, filled with passion, studied everyone below.

That was Aixia, himself, when he was young. Yes, young. That didn't just refer to the leather bag people call the human body. At the time, he actually was a young man, twenty-six years old, the youngest of the survivors.

He remembered this meeting. He could never forget this meeting. Because afterwards, he exiled himself semi-permanently from the Star Trail to the Artificial world, and took a different path than the other Actuals. Except for Rui An, he'd severed ties with practically everyone.

That image began to speak. "I am Aixia Ross," he said.

"I am Aixia, Aixia Ross. I am the youngest of the survivors, but I ask for the floor.

"Standing here, I can only see your likenesses. We all live so incredibly far from each other. On the Star Trail, we are, on average, 120 kilometers away from each other. Some even live alone like hermits in orbit at the outer reaches of the solar system.

"I understand your fear. You're afraid of yourselves, afraid of Actuals, afraid that even speaking to each other could spark violence. We exile ourselves, cocoon ourselves with Artificial servants, deny ourselves any connection with the rest of the Actuals.

"But, today, I must speak with you, and I beg that you listen.

"I know the Artificial world has already been built, but I continue to think that the calculations of Artificials won't actually be useful in controlling our violent tendencies, and the situation could get even more disastrous. A person, of course, should be responsible for their own behavior, including violent behavior. We use the Artificial world to take care of everything for our descendants, from freedom to their surroundings, and they rob them of the chance for individual responsibility.

"We were, at first, so afraid of our violent impulses, but we forgot to ask whether these impulses are innate within us, as well as whether we can really remove them from others.

"I beg you to abandon the Artificial world. I beg you that we raise our offspring by our side. I beg you to face yourselves, to face your own violent impulses and desires. Honestly confront yourselves, confront your family, confront your children.

"I beg you give everyone the truth, including yourselves.

"There will be death, heroic death and sorrowful death. But there will also be hope. We need fresh blood, new thought, and new vigor. It's already been dozens of years without any new inventions and improvements. We need to walk together, gather together, awaken the Star Trail. We must establish for ourselves new cities on each major planet. We must replenish our colonies, cultivate our successors. We must continue forward, toss our violent shadows behind us.

"There will be war.

"There will be death, famine, pestilence, and catastrophe.

"But if we evade them blindly, and not meet them head-on to defeat them, then we will not deserve to be known as humanity.

"I beg you respond to me.

"I beg you respond to me.

"I beg you respond to me ..."

That solitary figure begged again and again. Such a large conference room, however, held only silence, as though it'd been thus since ancient times and continued to be so for hundreds of millions of years.

"Everyone, please vote now on the proposal." A mechanical female voice reverberated through the meeting room.

One bulb, two bulb, many bulbs behind the young man lit red indicating, "No." Only the bulb representing Aixia, himself, eventually flickered green among the 126 red lights, as though it were a weak but stubborn seedling among a prairie fire.

The young man turned around, then walked away from the lectern. In an instant, he seemed a feeble one hundred years old, at last looking as he did now.

"That was you," the youngster said softly. His small, sweaty hand clutched Aixia's large one.

"Yes." Aixia stared at the unreal image of the past. "That was me."

"Aixia, perhaps we should have listened to you in the first place."

The two turned their heads. Rui An's tall and slender figure appeared at the door like a ghost.

"What is the meaning of this, Rui An? Who rewrote the function?

What is showing me this recording of the past supposed to do?" Aixia stared coldly at the woman before him.

"We rewrote the function. Aixia, I just wanted to tell you that you were right and we had no choice but to correct these mistakes," she said softly. "You two, follow me."

They passed through an endless corridor, passing by residential district after residential district. Many districts were covered by a thin layer of dust. Other districts also looked like they'd been vacant for a long time.

"Where did everyone else go?" Aixia asked. The uneasy youngster gripped his hand tightly.

Rui An didn't answer.

Finally, she stopped before a huge cabin door. About ten meters tall and twenty meters wide, that was enough to estimate the size of the cabin behind it.

The door slowly slid open.

Separated from them by a transparent glass wall, they could see in the dull blue light every single sparkling container. Inside were brains, smooth, round, and white as though they were full and ripe fruit. Huge and yet numerous, countless numbers of brains were submerged in a culture solution. They were crammed into the cabin in tidy rows. One side was reserved as a passageway, waiting to be filled by new brains. It was as though they were the rich fruit human civilization bore.

"They are all here. The earliest and most recent. Our ancestors and our descendants," Rui An said softly. "It included those people we gathered from the Artificial world as well as those who first established that world."

"... why?" Aixia finally choked out the question.

"Because of fear," Rui An answered. "If they have no limbs, they can't injure others. If feelings can be controlled through a culture solution, then there can't be any anger. If all of their thoughts are linked together so they can't tell whose thoughts are whose, then they won't hate."

"All of their thoughts?"

"All of their thoughts."

"Why hide this from me?" He grabbed Rui An's collar.

"We are all afraid of you, just like we fear how we once were. You were the only dissenter. You were ... the only Actual."

He suddenly realized Rui An used that word.

"All of you," Aixia said softly.

"All of us." Rui An nodded. Her face gradually transformed into an Artificial's emotionless face. "All of us."

Aixia wanted to say something, but nothing would come out.

"What you asked for over one hundred years ago, we'll now give you. We were the ones who rewrote the separation function. It was rewritten so that the kid," Rui An nodded at Farrell, "was someone we led to you. What has happened over the past few days ... was just a test, like the test with his family many years ago. The test results show that the Actuals' violent tendencies increased drastically within the Artificial world. You were absolutely right. So, we chose to leave the solar system." Rui An recounted calmly. "We've already mastered the technology to nurture the young mind from the embryo stage. Thus, we don't need Actuals any more, only Artificials. See you, Aixia. No, we'll never meet again. We leave you the Star Trail. We leave you the whole of the solar system as well as some Artificial servants. You'll become the emperor of an empty world. You'll control everyone's behavior. Whatever you intend to give the people of the world, they'll follow you ... Freedom is fine. Being Artificial is fine. They'll follow you ... but it's your choice, your responsibility."

As she spoke, that large cabin receded into the distance and Rui An's voice also gradually faded into indistinct noise. Finally, she transformed into an expressionless, Artificial statue.

Weakly interactive calculated behavior. What crossed his mind was: he was powerless to kneel, his face buried in both hands.

No, this isn't of my choosing. Why do they want me to take on the burden now? If the calculations of Artificials had not gone into effect in the first place, then the world wouldn't have become like this.

In his monitor spectacles, the calculations were still ongoing. Death and violence were still being incited constantly. Yes, he was absolutely right. He still remembered, before Artificial behavior was first established, the violent tendencies of Actuals approached ten percent. But nowadays ... it already approached sixty percent.

When someone is lost inside an illusion and he doesn't know whom to hate, he'll hate everyone. When his freedom is destroyed by his circumstances, he'll want to destroy everything ... just like Farrell's parents. The calculations of Artificials never truly eliminated the violent tendencies of Actuals. On the contrary, it intensified how their impetuousness manifested.

Can I give them the truth? After Actuals themselves have been distorted? Or, should I continue to deceive them, continue the deception to maintain the peace?

Futilely, he sought some solace from the descendants on Earth, from those free people about to sink into violence, murder, destruction, war, and death. Or, perhaps, he'd find some from those oblivious people manipulated by calculated behavior living peacefully among Artificials.

No, he couldn't find any. He closed his eyes. An abyss lay both ahead and behind him. Freedom and deception were both in his grasp, but any choice was a weight he couldn't bear.

The world became some sort of gigantic, spacious thing. It quickly disappeared into the distance, surrounding him in cold and silence.

"Aixia?"

The youngster's bony hand fell lightly onto his trembling shoulder.

Postscript

It all started in a QQ group. We laughed at the mention of the latest idea: suppose there was only one real person in the world, and the entire world had been established just for him. This would be quite extravagant, right?

Mikoyan Salabaji (I have to conceal the young person's real name) came out of nowhere to say, no, it actually wouldn't consume so many natural resources because the actions of one person are extremely limited.

Black Cat suddenly remembered a novel by Wesley. In this novel, Wesley compared humanity to insects in an unbounded world forever walking a closed loop.

It really wouldn't require very many computational resources, Mikoyan said. In so many games, it's blurry when you look in the distance, but you never feel uncomfortable because in real life, we also can't see things that are extremely far away. So simulating the world only as far as one person can see was enough. The behavior of everyone else can be economized.

Thus, Black Cat and Mikoyan, as well as friends in the "Eight Copper Coins Inn" QQ group, began to discuss it further, thinking about whether it was possible to be frugal with environmental resources. What about the "Artificials" surrounding the "Actual?" These androids who converse with him and live their daily lives with him ought to require lots of simulation resources to sustain, right? However, how many people can one person stay in contact with at once? Get together with three? Chat with a group? Shoot the breeze with fifty in a QQ group?

It doesn't need to be fifty. An active QQ group doesn't have more than twenty.

So we suddenly realized it really wasn't all that extravagant to counterfeit a world. And the Actual would have no way to realize any of this because everything he perceives around him was extremely normal and true to life.

Actually, this is an old paradox: you'll never know. In the world outside the limits of your perception, in a given moment, what has actually happened?

EL CÓNDOR DEL MACHÁNGARA BY ANA HURTADO

Ana Hurtado is a Venezuelan writer living in Ecuador, where she works as a professor of English. Her poetry and short fiction have appeared in *Strange Horizons* and elsewhere.

———

Papi throws our potatoes at the birds. White socks and sandals, long jean shorts with big pockets, brown leather belt, purple golf shirt, a black moustache that doesn't move when he talks. It all shakes as he grabs two or three potatoes with his long hands and pitches them at the black vultures that like to drink water from our backyard pool. They also like to shit on our windows and cars, and on the basil and cilantro Mami grows next to the pool. Papi has joked before about buying a gun and shooting down the vultures: "Una escopeta," he says as he holds an imaginary gun aimed at the birds whose feathers adorn my bedroom window, "y PUM! desaparecen." The heavy bag of papa chola I helped Mami place in our grocery cart a week ago ends up opened, plastic bag lost with the wind, potatoes spread around our backyard, a few decorating the downhill of the cliff, and some, even, swimming in the Machángara River that encircles our neighborhood.

"Don't you end up just feeding them?" my brother Carlos asks my dad as we spend a day outside, bird shit smell lingering.

"No, they only eat what's already dead," I respond.

We don't know much about the black vultures, except that they remind us of other beings: a giant black chicken, a mean dog, a snake that likes to linger under the sun after it's fed, a resentful cat, a pig that eats too much, and the Ecuadorian condor, a majestic and endangered bird that flies so high only clouds can witness its splendor.

I don't want my father to kill them.

———

The myth of the condor of Galope Kaka takes place in the Andes. The fable occurs before the Incas dominated the pre-Columbian cultures that resided in the long city we now call San Francisco de Quito. In the páramo of Galope Kaka, yellow flowers sprout from the riverbed and sometimes stay still when the night is too cold. It is the type of place where pulling a fistful of grass only produces another. Where the Andean wind is a vessel for secrets, chants, songs about love and curiosity, claims about life. Those who dipped cupped hands inside the river were immediately cleansed from pain. The water streaming down their throats is a liquid mystery, curing illnesses beyond physical ache. A river that cleans curses. It is the river of the condor and, as such, its powers are immeasurable.

———

My father says these birds are plotting something huge. We haven't seen them in a while. Potatoes intact. From our backyard, we look for clues around the swimming pool. "Anything that seems suspicious," Papi says from the other corner of the lawn. I spot pieces of feathers near my bare feet. The plumes are so small, almost rectangular. Borders sharp, yet soft to the touch. Grey, white, and all the shades in between. Rainbows of black that disappear with the moving clouds above me. These feathers belong to baby birds. Perhaps they were born here. Or maybe they flew above this specific spot a while ago, guided by their parents. The feathers are entrenched within the sharp grass and little bits of dandelion that flew from this morning's winds. I hope Mami doesn't see me touching the little feathers. Anytime Papi throws potatoes at the birds, she turns away, places her colorful apron over her mouth, and closes her eyes. "We have no business with those animals," she says as I, too, turn away and approach her. It's as if she doesn't want them or any part of them entering her. Mouth closed, eyes locked, nose open, "But my nose hairs will catch it all." I look over at our kitchen. Right now, Mami's cooking lunch. She's not watching. I then turn my head to the river down in the crevasse and remember the meeting spot of these beings: the giant rock that almost splits the river in two. We don't know how all the birds—all of them, no being left behind—fit on this rock. We also don't know what they do on it. But it's one of the few places in our landscape that's not covered in white shit.

Several of the neighborhood children—stupid boys who like to chase rabbits, wild rabbits they call them, but they are just the pets of our neighbor Juanjo—have tried to climb down the quebrada. They don't want to touch the water (nobody does. The water is dark brown and, from what we can tell, thick as yogurt). Kids wearing expensive clothes want to jump from the little river beach onto the bird rock as a dare. From what I've heard, no child has ever made it. They fall into the brown yogurt, cry for help, and the neighborhood guards—with shotguns strapped to their chests—climb down and rescue them. Ecuadorian law prohibits people from tampering with rivers, but our neighborhood knows others don't follow these regulations.

The Machángara River carries plastic bags and bottles, sometimes several car tires at once, used baby diapers, our poop, and, once, a baby some woman didn't want. The infant floated on the river and his journey went unnoticed until the river ended in Esmeraldas. The baby —now a child living happily on the beaches of Esmeraldas, he sells seashells to tourists—took several weeks to reach the coast. It is still a mystery how he fought the pollution, animals, and other dangers in his way. He—Roberto is his name—was featured as a headliner in *El Comercio* for five days straight. Then the next news trumped him: an American visa was granted to the indigenous man suing Shell.

The black vultures could be mutants. They were born in dirt water and fed with chlorine water from our pool. My brother says this is why they haunt our neighborhood: they are animals that don't know how to act naturally. This is his working theory.

Papi and I give up on our search. I don't tell him about the baby feathers I found. As we enter the kitchen we are welcomed by Mami's cooking. Mami cooks too much food for lunch today: coconut shrimp, baby spinach salad, spicy chicken, meat with garlic and purple onion,

rice, menestras, caldo de pollo, and two different juices, both made
with azúcar morena, my nickname.

"What's with the feast?" I ask her, helping her put away some of
the ingredients she already used.

"Viene Nicolás," she says. My tongue burns with the shrimp I grab
from the serving plate. Coconut bubbles sizzling at the tip of my
tongue. Nicolás is one of Papi's friends. Like Father, he's an aficionado
of golf, Scotch whiskey, rum and coke with too much lime, and homophobic jokes when inebriated. What they don't have in common,
however, is Nicolás's obsession with birds and bats. Over brunches
and dinners, Christmases and summers, Nicolás looks out of the
terrace of every house we're in, examining branches and leaves,
looking for winged things. And what he doesn't see he imagines, like
the Galápagos penguin or the great curassow, both beings lurking in
his brain and around our kitchen table. He discusses their behavior
and how it matches ours, their beaks and eyes, how they take flight.
He moves his hand—pink and dry—as he mimics a bird taking flight,
how his pinky is so distant from his thumb, how his cuticles are mani-
cured, how his palm could grab and suffocate all the black vultures
residing in our neighborhood. The lines on his hands tell stories of
golf sessions with Papi, of his trips to the Amazon for work on the oil
fields, of the birds he wishes he could cage.

"Why is Nicolás coming for lunch?" I ask Papi.

Papi dismisses me with a hand motion that means, your worries
are silly, mija.

"We're going to talk about los pajarracos," he says while helping
Mami toss the salad.

"There are none," I say back.

"Yeah, you killed them all with your potatoes," Carlos says as he
enters the kitchen. He too burns his tongue with the coconut shrimp.
I forgot to warn him.

"He never even hit one," Mami says. She laughs at Papi.

Papi's face gets serious. This is the same look he gets when he
stares at the golf ball that missed the hole after he putted. The same
stare he gives me when I ask too many questions. And the same
expression he gives anyone—including Mami—who hurts his pride.

"We can't keep living like this, haunted by giant black birds," he
says, moustache not moving.

———

The myth of Galope Kaka is about an adolescent girl. This oral narrative didn't give her a name, but I think that if no one is willing to assign her one, I will. I'll name her after me. Her name is Ana. Ana, like most girls my age, was going through a breakup. She hadn't officially broken up with her boyfriend, but she knew she had to. He was flirting with too many girls. Ana couldn't keep count of them with her two hands. Jealousy took over her actions: she dismissed her mother's advice, told her boyfriend's secrets to others, and imagined her escape from Galope Kaka to a place beyond the mountains, maybe to the place where all the blue and purple seashells come from. Instead of dirt she wants to taste the salt entrenched within the conchs her culture trades for obsidian. She no longer wants to see her reflection in the clouds above her but in a space where her boyfriend does not exist.

Ana's long hair touches the floor; she can't cut it unless a full moon lingers in the sky for days. But every time a full moon takes over the landscape, she decides she's not ready. Her breath smells like flowers. Eyes the color of the dirt when wet. Her skin is a soft leaf with tiny thorns which, when touched, makes men bleed. Ana's heart is heavy, and she can feel it through her breasts: they ache as she cries for him.

She knows the cure for her heartache is the river of the condor. Her mother once bathed her in it when her body would not stop trembling; days later, hair still wet from the river, her body stopped shivering. Today Ana wonders if the river of the condor will save her broken heart.

———

I eat lunch quickly. I don't even sit down at the table; I hover over the kitchen counter like an eagle cutting the air with my wings and barely dipping my claws into the water. I let my tongue burn with everything straight out of the frying pan and cool it with lettuce and juice. I eat it all and fast because I don't want to see Nicolás. Mami looks at me with confused eyes.

"Mijita, you'll burn your mouth," she says to me.

"And you're not leaving much for the rest of us," Carlos says.

"I don't like Nicolás," I say.

"¿Y eso por qué?" Papi asks as he washes his hands before lunch.

"Last time you both got drunk on the terrace he was being too loud," I tell him. And this is the partial truth. The entire truth is they were both so drunk and vulgar, Mami had left them alone hours ago. They sat out on the terrace, whiskey glasses never empty, talking about their coworker Andrés and his husband. Their homophobic rants echoed throughout our neighborhood. I'm sure even the pajarracos heard it. Their jokes about penises probably reached the outer corners of Cumbayá, the places yet to be gentrified. And when I went inside Mami's room to complain, she was wide awake sitting at the edge of her bed. Mami can't sleep either, I thought as I approached her. Mami was crying, mascara goops forming at the edges of her eyes, black tears running down her cheek and settling in the riverbed above her upper lip. Our conversation didn't make much sense because she didn't want to talk to me—all her answers were lies—and I assumed she was crying because our grandmother had passed away recently and this was a constant scene, her hiding from us to cry—Papi doesn't console her, a side effect of having friends like Nicolás.

Nicolás is the type of man who doesn't bring his wife with him when he's invited to lunch or dinner at our house. This has been happening for years. We sometimes theorize that she doesn't exist because every time Papi asks him about her—her name is Luciana—he says she's ill or busy, often dismissing the question with his hand, just like Papi does with my questions: your worries are silly, mija. But we have met Luciana and, from what I can remember, her tres leches cake is delicious. Now Papi, too, after years of friendship with Nicolás, has been leaving Mami behind at home while he attends company dinners and other festivities.

I sat next to Mami and heard her lies about our maid, Marianita, and her growing belly. "She is pregnant," Mami cried. "She will leave us." Marianita, an eighteen-year-old Mormon, had gotten pregnant, and mornings without Marianita seemed impossible: the cooking, cleaning, bird shit wiping, and plant watering all at once were too much for one person, and it is, but who else would help? Not us. Mami's tears felt cold on my neck. This is when I spotted Nicolás walking up our stairs.

The guest bathroom is downstairs, next to the kitchen entrance. At that moment, I wondered where Papi was—was he occupying the guest bathroom? But I doubt even a drunk Papi would do so. What bathroom was Nicolás planning on using? What if he wasn't planning on using a bathroom? Mami's tears streamed down my chest as I held her head near mine. Nicolás popped his head inside my bedroom, staring at the darkness, perhaps trying to decipher if the lump of blankets and comforter was me, the child of his good friend, his good, drunk friend whose laughs still echoed beyond the Machángara River, beyond the birth of the black vultures. Nicolás closed the door behind him.

About fifteen seconds later he walked out looking disappointed, his steps betraying him, hands strapping back the brown leather belt he unbuckled. My blankets warm and displaced, half of their body cascading down towards my bedroom floor. He looked at me as he walked downstairs. And today Nicolás is visiting our home and lunching in our dining room. He's going to use the guest bathroom, plant bombs or poison or venom in our backyard to scare or kill the big black vultures, and kiss my cheek when he says Hola. It all angers me. I let the food burn my tongue and my gums. I down the juice with the excess of azúcar morena. I tell Mami gracias and head upstairs to my room where I hide. I'm still chewing the coconut shrimp. Here no Nicolás enters, ni ningún otro hombre.

———

Ana leaves in the middle of the night. Stars stare at the crescent moon quickly traveling the sky. Ana, too. She secures her long hair from it. Ana carries some seeds tucked beneath her breasts, life close to her skin. She carries them with her because she wants Pachamama close to her now, skin-deep, in case the river has other plans for her. Her toes pull grass as she walks. She turns around and memorizes her life in this community: a guiding mother fast asleep, a father who trades obsidian for Spondylus, a man who is gone too much for far too long, five brothers and sisters who would love to watch the river of the condor fail her. The páramo's yellow flowers are drenched in moonlight and all kinds of blues. A scene frozen in time. Ana walks with determination. She doesn't want her heart to ache any longer because her whole body aches with it: her knees hurt when she runs, her back when she lies down, her eyes when she laughs. If the river of the condor does not heal her, she will have to live with the disappointment that perhaps her heartbreak is not important, perhaps the river only cures real issues, like her illness when she was a child, and she will have to live with this secret, too, because Ana doesn't want others to know the river refused her. What a disappointment. She is sure they'll call her a liar—the river cures all aches and people, maybe Ana is cursed beyond repair, maybe Ana never stepped foot in it, why would she bring us such shame.

———

Mami knocks on my door. I know this because her knocks are rough —they shake the rosary she herself hung above my bed. Not even Papi, with his long hands, knocks like this.

"Entra," I tell her.

Mami tells me about Papi's plans to kill the birds. They will all die tonight. Obsidian feathers will float around Cumbayá and land on muck, feathers replacing the shit on our windshields. And the feathers on my window will remain, remnants of a night caller, a being who feeds on the dead. She often points at the feathers embellishing my window when referring to the big black vultures Papi and Nicolás will envenom. This is all I will have to remember them by. Weeks ago, I heard some scratching on my window while I slept; something was grazing it roughly. I got up, turned on the ceiling light, and spotted one of the birds leaning on my window frame. A beak that could pierce glass. Claws, orange and strange, held together like bones without cartilage. Eyes that looked out into the river with hope. And a featherless grey head—cracked skin and mountain ranges. My own condor. I didn't know what it wanted: I didn't have any dead animals in my room. So, it just left a few of its feathers behind, perhaps as a reminder that it is the size of my bedroom window, it is large and grand and majestic, its feathers infectious.

Mami leaves after she complains that I have not folded the laundry she placed near my bed four days ago. I nod as she reprimands my behavior, focusing specifically on today's lunch. Whose daughter am I that I don't lunch with the family, that I eat standing up, hovering and flying over the sink taking care of the crumbs that fall?

"Perdóname, Mami," I ask her. She nods, and I read the worries swimming in her brown irises—she doesn't like Nicolás either, or at least what Nicolás does to Papi: he transforms him, and he hatches a new self.

She leaves after she folds all my laundry and tucks it away in my closet. I lie on my bed thinking about the vultures that dominate our neighborhood, the children who one day would like to crown the bird rock theirs, the Machángara River and its smells, the hours until bedtime, Nicolás, when will he leave, Nicolás, will he stay for dinner, Nicolás, poison, venom, bombs.

————

Ana's feet feel like roots; they now penetrate the land below her, grabbing the soil molded by the river and the purple flowers that died years ago. She's reached it. The river of the condor flows in front of her—it carries wisdom and secrets and a million stories of salvation. Ana is petrified. She hides her breasts from the river and stares at its waves: small tornadoes and hurricanes created by rocks, moonlight reflections and wind, how many universes contained within this water, how it's travelled from the peak of the Andes down to the edge of her toes, how it's shifted landscapes, healed the broken, astonished her. Ana feels small. The pumamaqui tree that hovers over the river smells like serenity; her mother boils and drinks its paw-like leaves to calm her nerves and worries, especially all her concerns about Ana—she's young and fragile, big breasts and little knowledge of what's around her, she's dating a young boy, too, who is lost in space and time. Ana's mother wishes she'd focus more on her gifts and less on boys.

She lays her back on a stone embedded in the riverbank, her toes buried in yellow and green shards of grass. The sharp grass tries to breathe but the almohadilla, a sea of grass that covers the entire mountain rage, prevents it. Ana can feel the tiny páramo sacha amor white flowers closing at the sight of the moon. The petals move inwards so slowly, the river seems to lose its speed, too. Her back is cold. The rock's humidity seeps into her skin, and as the cold reaches the echo chambers of her broken heart, she steps inside the river of the condor.

———

I hear them talking downstairs as I braid my wet hair until there's nothing left, only thin orquetillas I used to claim were orquídeas, but a black mane with split ends is not an orchid, Papi once assured me. Now my hair smells like coconut shrimp, the smell of Mami's cooking seeping from my fingerprints shaped like swaying volcanoes. The braid that rests on my chest smells like the tiny orange bubbles of used oil sprinkled around our kitchen counter, like the sea animal Mami deveined and dipped in eggs and panko salted with white shreds of coconut, fried until brown, blotted with paper towels and torn apart by the teeth of a predator.

Papi calls my name, and I don't say anything in response—I'm sure his moustache quivers with disappointment. He calls it again, and I throw my braid back, the weight of my hair bruising my lower back. The ceramic floor feels cold, but the warmth emanating from my soles leaves no sweaty footprints. Before I reach our kitchen, I step out onto the terrace. Another night of drinking is set: two wooden lounge chairs, a side table, two bottles of imported whiskey, the kind Papi asks Carlos to purchase at aduanas when he comes home from college, and a bucket of ice.

I don't see them, the birds who will die tonight. I smell the Machángara River and the constellation of trash it carries this evening. The moonlight fights gray and deep-blue clouds and brightens up the river. The river trails around our neighborhood, separating houses protected by guards—security guards who live well beyond the boundaries of Cumbayá, out in Puembo, out by the red rose plantations—from a parroquia of sculptors and veterinarians. These men and women live on a hill that constantly implodes with every month of heavy rain. Mami fears the hill will definitely disappear this year during abril aguas mil. "Where will all those people go?" Mami wonders, hands over nostrils, Machángara River smells putrid. The dust from the cement sculptures—lions and fountains, tiny babies with wings—has inundated the puppy mills from time to time, this tragedy making it to the starting segments of the eight o'clock news.

"Buenas tardes, Ana," Nicolás says to me.

———

Ana swims in a river that's not deep. In fact, the river of the condor only reaches her knees. But it deepens for her. It is wide and bottomless. Ana washes away her resentment and frustrations, the pain her boyfriend caused her. She feels her heart weaving back together, chamber to chamber, vessel to muscle. Certain memories come back to her: her brothers exploring a cave with her, the color of pumpkin squash and the taste of chicha, her mother's hands as big and as long as the pumamaqui tree hovering over her, watching her bathe. Ana comes up for air and sees him.

A man wearing a thin and long black poncho gazes at Ana, llama fibers swaying with the gusts. He steps forward as Ana swims away a bit.

"Come forward," he says, voice similar to her boyfriend's. "Who are you?"

The clouds blocking most of the moonlight part, and she really sees him. What smooth skin, what brown eyes, what puckered lips, what face. Ana's renewed heart beats faster. She exits the river, the water that healed her clinging to her pores. Ana walks to the man, who now stands still, pumamaqui leaves turning away. The river is loud. It washes over rocks, muds, and flowers, these noises echo the Andes and unsettle the lava hiding underneath volcanoes.

"What are you doing here?" Ana asks the man. But Ana doesn't get a response. As she steps out of the river, water trickling down her spine and legs, he steps closer to her, grabbing her by the waist. Her heart beats loudly in response. This is the gift from the river, a boy who holds her like she's the only one for him. He begins to stroke her long hair with his palms, removing bits of dirt.

"How soft, your touch," Ana says.

The smooth touch turns into rough rasping. The man's fingers pull Ana's uncombed hair, multiple knots once undone by the river of the condor now reappearing, locks twisting. The sky turns darker. And the man's fingernails grow into sharp claws, his poncho into black wings, his puckered lips into a beak. The condor raptures Ana into his control, and they fly away, bird and woman, into the distant open mouths of volcanoes.

———

From the terrace, I can see my mother. Mami walks up to the fence that divides our backyard and pool from the cliff and the river, sandals struggling through our newly cut lawn. She places her hands on the gray rail and admires the river's strength. How it avoids the rock of the birds, how it carries Quito's waste, how it defines us. Papi, next to her, raises his index finger and soars it across the equatorial sky. The stars shine above them, twinkling messages to each other. Words travel above us and leave us. I hear Carlos shutting our front door. He unlocks the car, enters, and drives away from us, out to Quito for a night out. And Nicolás places his hands on my shoulders, he has me, he's reached me, I am his, claws sinking into my skin.

———

Galope Kaka is divided. There are those who blame Ana's disappearance on herself: she left us, she played with the river, and the river won. And then there's Ana's family. Her mother who stands under the pumamaqui tree and awaits its response. Where is my daughter? The páramo responds with noiselessness and apathy.

The oral narrative skips eight months. The time it takes to grow a child in a womb. I don't know what she ate or where she slept, if the condor protected her from evil energies. If she cut her hair or if it reaches her toes. And when the culture residing in the Galope Kaka páramo watch Ana—the girl who left a trail of seeds, the girl who never came back—walk up a blossoming hill of sacha amor, they become unresponsive. Weeks later, inside her adobe house and next to an illuminating fire, Ana gives birth to the child of the condor, a zoomorphic baby with belly button and wings, with legs and skin like a mountain range, with puckered lips and hopeful eyes.

ALONE, ON THE WIND BY KARLA SCHMIDT

Translated from German by Lara M. Harmon

Karla Schmidt is the author of several novels in German, and is a winner of the German Science Fiction
Prize for best short fiction. She teaches novel writing and edited the anthology *Hinterland*.

———

I am the first wingbeat; I started the stones rolling. But now I need
help. We can't keep cowering here like hens on their nests. We have to
act, and soon, because my memories have started sinking into *now* and
we; I need to share them before they stop meaning anything at all. But
you shy away from me. Why?

*We have enough to do with the Dance of Stones. Folding dimensions so that
the Stones do not drift away demands all we are. Memory tips the world out of
balance too easily. Memory comes from regret.*

But what if there won't be a future without these memories?

The future comes from fear. It, too, tips the world out of balance.

But the world's long out of balance! Now that I've given you the
chance to share in events through me, you have to become part of
them. We need to change something!

Change is eternal. Even without our help.

And what about life? Is that eternal, too?

Life must grow, to exist. If it does not grow, it falls back into death.

Exactly! That's it. We're falling. It's already begun. Please, let me
tell my story and then—then you can make your decision.

It begins with a youth named Tuela. Tuela was too fearful for a life among the Dancing Stones.

————

"Tuela!" called Rasn. "Come back!"

Rasn had always stood by me, even though I was the most difficult youth in eir group. If I stopped now and went back, ey would lay eir arm on my shoulder comfortingly, would explain to me that my siblings loved me and hadn't meant it that way. And ey would've been right, because their laughter wasn't mean. They laughed to hide their concern. They laughed to give me courage.

I didn't know why Rasn hadn't followed me that time, why ey hadn't pulled me aside under some salt-glittering, moss-overgrown rock and, with a mixture of disappointment, anger, and pity on eir face, brought me back. I was almost grown, but I still behaved like someone freshly hatched.

The trail faded away under my feet as I ran ever higher, up against the bird-gravity. Finally I couldn't go any further. Dizziness seized me as I looked around, and I clung to an overhanging rock.

Above me, only blank, black space, but if I leaned far enough forward and peeked over the path's edge: at my feet, the Dancing Stones. I hated being so far out on their edge; there were no hand-ropes here, no bridges. No buildings to protect you. Despite all of that, I let go of the rock overhang as I felt the whole mountain tilt and tip forward, positioning the Dancing Stones directly in front of me. I wouldn't fall; the mountain would hold me down as long as I kept my feet on the earth. Still, I felt my stomach lurch, and I had to suppress the impulse to throw myself flat on the ground and cling to it with every cell in my body. I took another shaking step, the tips of my toes jutted out over the trail edge, and I spread my featherless arms out like wings.

The wind snatched at the channels in my flight suit and flared them out, ready to carry me away. Only one more short step and it would happen.

I breathed deliberately, slowly, felt the fear, and watched the first birds I saw as they lifted from their nests, circled a few times in the air, and began to check the orbits of the Stones in their territories.

The Stones' complex movements looked completely different from this vantage point on their outskirts than they did closer to the center, where my school was. Where I felt safe. Yet, seen from out here, it was the center that looked hopelessly dangerous. The boulders seemed to cluster far too close to each other. Some were so big that, over the course of generations, glittering cities had grown up on them, and some had only one or two pink huts clinging to them among the waving salt-grass. Here and there a few boulders drifted faster, others slower; some turned on a shared axis, others just around their own. Most were bunched together in stable groups by a flock's bird-gravity, and between them drop-seas hung in the air like iridescent eggs, the smallest just big enough that a group of youths could bathe in them, others as big as the mountain on which I stood.

I'd never enjoyed being outside. Wherever you went you looked into the abyss, into dizzying depths, always finding yourself at the center of that baffling, twisting and turning drift-flow, and everything everywhere seemed to only just scrape along without colliding. Beyond this controlled chaos, there lurked either profound nothingness or the fierce, smiling face of the Yellow World, hanging sometimes over and sometimes under us. Unlike my siblings, I'd never picked up the knack of always knowing which direction to look in when leaving home.

As always when I watched the Dancing Stones, I waited against my will for a convulsion, a collision, explosions and wreckage, the screams of the dying. But nothing like that happened. Of course it didn't. The birds had everything under control, by instinct, and unlike conscious thought, instinct never broke down. Ever. The sun bathed the craggy meadow a few flight-minutes below me in a golden glow, and I saw the cloud-shadow of the mountain I stood on drift across it. I closed my eyes.

It was really only a step. Most youths did it as soon as they could walk steadily. I wiped away the tears that had forced their way out from under my eyelids. If I didn't do it now, I would have to go on living like this: hobbled, always relying on help. Until the day I died.

Not far below me my siblings, with their crash helmets and their wind-flared, colorful flight suits, passed by in close formation. I saw how two of them let themselves fall behind and drop into the ripple between manipulated gravity fields, shrieking and relishing the acceleration before Rasn called them back into line and they let an updraft catch them. Despite their quick pace, the group's movement seemed almost stately as they wheeled through a passage between two Stones turning counter to each other.

And then they were gone. Rasn had left me out here alone, and I stood on the edge of a cliff with outspread arms, knocking knees, and flapping flight suit. It was the thought of the scornful and pitying looks I'd receive if I had to return to school riding piggyback again that let me finally act.

I jumped.

———

An air current seized my body and pulled me head-first inexorably toward the center. Use your arms and legs. Don't lose your nerve. Keep your goal in sight. Use the changing gravitational foci, torque, and any passages between the Stones that emerge. Theoretically, I knew the right responses—I'd certainly read more about aerodynamics, bird neurology, the inverse square law, localized dimensional distortion, and heightened gravity than even Rasn—or any of the other teachers.

But the texts hadn't told me what it's like when you almost soil your flight pants for fear, or when your own vomit flies past your ears and you can hardly hold your eyes open because you're in a headwind without protective goggles. They didn't say what happened when you suddenly forgot all the theories. When you no longer had any idea how to spread or bend your arms and legs to use a current, to steer, to dodge an obstacle. Or to land.

In spite of everything, I hit the field I'd aimed for. Or the field hit me. The landing broke my right knee and the pain was so sharp that I waited, yearning, for unconsciousness. But it didn't come, and I began to explore the pain and accept it. And even though I couldn't get to my feet to leave without help, a feeling of elation suddenly seized me.

It happens, youths breaking something on their first flight attempt. I could count myself lucky that nothing worse had happened, as I hadn't taken my helmet with me when I'd run away from flight lessons. I'd done it. I'd bested the airspace between two Stones under my own power and my injury would prove it. Despite my broken bones, now I wanted to stand up at any cost and make the rest of my trek back the same way: alone! On the wind!

———

The attack came the same moment I'd made this resolution. An old, bedraggled bird swept down on me, biting at my head and ripping off tufts of my hair and shreds of my skin with her long talons. A few steps away another pair of birds stirred in the morning sun; the female rattled an egg into place under her blue-black feathered belly and yawned hugely, while the male eyed me with distrust and stuck his violet penis out of his mouth in a threatening gesture. The bird above me spat out wild, inarticulate noises and aimed her talons at my eyes.

I acted from pure instinct, striking out, getting a hold of the bird's lower jaw, gripping under her upper row of teeth with my other hand at the same time. And I tore with all my might, until she cracked and my fingers bled from her sharp teeth, until her lower jaw hung loose and she made gurgling sounds. But she still wouldn't leave me alone, and as I got hold of her pink feet, I smacked her against the rocks over and over until she was finally quiet and her age-grayed wings hung limp around her. The bird was dead and I was alive. Stupid animal.

———

We feel a hint of outrage. We shift anxiously on our feet. We remember; we were there. We could have intervened. But we knew what was done was done. We felt it as the egg shattered. As the child shattered. It was her last egg. She could lay no more. She was ready to move on. No being should ever hold back another who moves on.

———

The less thickly settled edges of the Dancing Stones, with their salt marshes full of juicy mussels, have been bird territory since this small world shattered. That's longer ago than we can even imagine. Here they live, and with the seven-layered kernel in their bird-brains create the Dance of Stones; here they nest in the ten thousands on every single boulder, and the child-catchers prowl their territories and search the nests for newborns.

But I was no child-catcher; I had never, in conscious memory, seen a nest up close. Only as I cautiously straightened up did I realize why the bird had attacked.

The nest was old, the grass in it brown and slimy, and it was just as tattered as the bird now lying dead at my side. The pale-blue egg was hidden beneath tufts of grass. It looked like there was no longer any male to go with the dead female, and likely she had covered the egg to protect it against the hot sun at the beginning of the day, or from cooling off during the night while she was away.

The egg was shattered. The youth inside was brown-skinned and very blond, just like me. It could've hatched any day. A tiny creature, lying before me in the frail blue shell as if it were sleeping, with little legs pulled up and balled fists. On its head was the egg tooth, pale blue and gleaming, with which it would've opened the eggshell. Many youths came to school with their egg teeth hanging on grass bands around their necks as good-luck charms. I still had mine, myself, and felt for it, as if with only a little luck I could take back what had happened. I'd smashed in the youth's tiny ribcage with my fall. My triumph had dissolved into nothing, transformed into two small, dead bodies that lay near me in the grass.

———

On the first day I did nothing. On the second day, early in the morning, I licked the salty dew from the grass. I needed a freshwater drop-sea, but I couldn't find one. With great effort and pain, I hid the corpses in a hollow in the stone that I covered over with moss, so the child-catchers wouldn't find them. Then I scattered the nest to the winds. The second night I spent shivering and alone under the open sky. I could die out here. That would be fair. I could hope for rescue. Rasn knew where they'd left me behind. They would search for me. But maybe they would come too late. I could try to make my way back to civilized regions on my own. All in all, this option seemed to offer not only the greatest chance of survival, but also the greatest chance that my crime against society wouldn't be discovered. I had to try to move a few Stones further at least. To somewhere where there were water and people. I crawled around, found a place I could push off from, and started on my way.

While I worked onwards Stone by Stone, I realized this was exactly why Rasn had left me behind: to force me to learn to fly if I wanted to survive. When I reached school on the fourth day, I was received like a hero. But I didn't feel triumph. I only felt guilt.

———

Guilt means keeping the past alive. Regret.

Yes, I couldn't forget what I'd done.

We had forgotten, until you told us about it again.

And now the memory makes us angry. Anger exerts too much gravity; the Stones could crash into one another. We do not want to hear any more. We must keep the balance.

Wait! Stay! I promise, at the end, equilibrium will be restored again.

———

In the eyes of Rasn and the others I would have been a sibling-killer if I'd explained what had happened. And if I hadn't been so obstinate, weak, and self-absorbed, things would never have gone so far. I was too much of a coward to face the consequences. But I atoned in my own way—by becoming the best flyer in my group. At any time of the day or night, I was out and about among the Stones, and out in space, too. I wanted to become a water-carrier, and that required the hardest training you could imagine.

Rasn supported me. Ey was proud of me and of emself, because ey thought ey had awakened such courage and drive in me. But I distanced myself from em internally. Ey didn't know how deeply ey was mistaken about me and eir fear for my life filled me with contempt.

But the Yellow World didn't make only em afraid. Everyone feared the desert sands of our big sibling, which are so acidic they eat flesh from bones. Everyone feared the heat and the storms that raged over the lowlands and ground the mountain ranges down to glass-smooth whispers. The gravity there dragged at us, making breathing a torture.

Only close to the poles were the storms less frequent and the days not quite so hot. There, water gathered under the surface where we could reach it. And there, cliffs rose up out of the sand, and in the cliffs were settlements of wild tribes, up to a thousand head strong: heavy, thickset people with black eyes peering out from the eye-slits in their protective sand-masks. They killed without scruple. And they ate their dead.

In school I'd learned it was the inhabitants of the Yellow World who'd shot to pieces their own little brother-world, moving hand-in-hand with them through the heavens. Yet we'd survived and still danced in all of our wreckage, right under their noses, while the Yellow pulled jealous faces at us. They wanted to destroy us, but in the end we'd fared better than they had. Our world is green and warm and the air the bird-gravity holds around us is salty and mild. The only thing we're missing is fresh water.

And the Yellow's only riches gather under the surface. Oceans of fresh water filtered through thick strata of earth and stone, rid of the ever-replenishing acid on the surface. They drilled for it, built caverns, moved ahead of the storms in their caravans to tap new wells.

In secret, by night, we took only what they'd taken from us. And when they stood in our way, we killed them.

———

It was my fourth mission, and I was proud to be with the water-carriers. I hadn't killed so far, but a part of me hoped I would get the chance to prove myself this time. The more I put myself at risk, the less guilt I felt.

Like every other time, I was nervous before we set out. Seven of us, plus ten birds on their tough grass leads we stood at one of the outposts currently facing the Yellow World, the invisible outer limits of the atmosphere a bare ten minutes distant.

The plan was always the same: we would fall toward the Yellow World and rely on our gliding skills, in the shadows of the night.

The birds determined our course, they made sure we had air, and with the uncanny sureness of sleepwalkers, they found the places that gave access to water. Under the protection of night we would search for an entryway, would kill the watch, would keep watch ourselves.

The birds did the real work. They would smell the water, would seek it out. They would unfurl as much of our spacetime as needed to draw the water up through wells, halls, and stairways, and let it flow up into the air. There it would gather, a new drop-sea hanging shivering over our heads, swelling and never overflowing. And before the morning dawned, the birds would let themselves and us fall up, back home, with our shimmering, priceless spoils. We would disappear over the horizon and the settlers down below would never discover who'd killed their watch and taken their water. So we had always done, and we'd never lost a water-carrier or been caught.

My flight companion had gleaming brown plumage and scuttled restlessly here and there on my back while we waited for the order to begin the mission. It was no comfort, the thought that he could bite me or drive his talons into my flesh at any moment. Bound together, we were at each other's mercy. If I fell, the bird on his lead would be dragged down with me, and if he saved himself by rolling space together, making himself dart back upwards, he would have no choice but to save me, too, taking me with him. Most of the birds were well-trained and cooperative. Despite that, I didn't like them so close to me, didn't like their appraising, cold bird-gaze. My companion produced smacking, guttural noises and stuck his penis in my ear. I knew that he only wanted to be friendly, but I didn't like that sort of affection. I put my helmet on quickly and made certain the visor was shut securely against wind and sand.

Judging by feel, the Yellow World was below us now. Very far below. And between us and the Yellow World was nothing but a little vapor glistening in the sunlight.

"Ready?" cried Utjok.

I worshipped our squadron leader even more than I'd worshipped Rasn as a youth. Utjok was stronger, harder. Ey was considered one of the best.

We gave em the thumbs-up sign and I felt my bird clamp tight to my back. Utjok raised eir arm and as ey let emself fall, we pushed off one after another from the mossy outpost and dove headfirst toward the Yellow.

———

On my first three missions I'd had my fear under control, had almost savored it, like a well-deserved punishment I had to endure. But this time it was worse. As I felt us leaving the atmosphere of the Dancing Stones, the panic built into a massive wave and broke over me. It was worse than my first catastrophic flight attempt. I screamed in mortal terror, as though seized by a horrific premonition—one which would turn out to be accurate. The bird on my back had no pity for my distress. He was a dumb animal that, aside from the breeding instinct, was guided only by careful training. He bit me until he drew blood, and brought me to my senses.

When I could think halfway clearly again, I found myself drifting aimlessly between the Dancing and the Yellow, surrounded by my atmosphere, which the bird had pulled out of the larger atmosphere as one pulls drops out of a drop-sea. The other members of the squadron were a good ways ahead; Utjok looked back at me. I corrected my course, joined up with them, and let myself fall into formation.

————

Two meager mealtimes later, we reached the first layer of Yellow's atmosphere. I hadn't had the energy to shake with fear the entire time, and I already had enough flight experience to get myself back under control. So despite the bird skittering restlessly on my back, I'd even managed to catch a little sleep here and there.

"We need to get out of the sun," called Utjok eventually.

I shivered and wished we could fall a little further through day-lit regions to warm up. But light might drastically reduce our chances of going unseen; we didn't know how far their telescopes reached. So we moved along a wide-flung arc in the diffuse area between day and night, toward the point where, together with the desert stronghold we were aiming for, we would turn with the planet into the dark night.

As soon as the planet's atmosphere was thick enough, we let our formation's atmosphere go; the wind struck us unchecked and the air smelled metallic. My bird let go of my shoulders and glided with a pleased smile on his face only two arm-lengths above me, free. For a moment I was happy not to feel his talons any longer, yet suddenly I felt alone. In the palpably stronger gravity, without the support of the kernel in his bird-brain, I found it hard to keep my balance in my flight suit, and the wind howled so loudly around my helmet that I felt as though I'd gone deaf. Whenever our goal took shape in the distance, we dove deeper still, until it disappeared just below the horizon again.

Utjok pointed behind us. "Something's brewing back there. Make sure you don't fall into a downdraft," ey bellowed over the noise of flight.

I threw a glance back over my shoulder. It was true, the night behind us was pulling together into still blacker night, and our smooth, gliding flight picked up a tailwind; the birds let out uneasy noises as the wind began to rip at their tails and wings and their tethers. We kept picking up speed.

"A storm!"

Utjok made signs that we should shift course to the left. And then behind us, next to us, and, in the next second, right in front of us, a series of poisonous yellow flashes struck out of the blackness into the sand and opened our eyes to something we hadn't planned on:

Riders—at least five hundred—in a long line, one after the other. The animals they rode they called armor-mules. Their hooves, eaten away by the acidic sand, oozed downwards into cone shapes like melted fat. The riders were wrapped against the storm, squatting on their animals like black ghosts; and we shot towards them at a speed that made controlled maneuvering almost impossible.

As one of the mules sheered off to run up a dune and the rider on his back stiffened, I knew we'd been spotted. One moment he looked like a playing piece on a broad game board, and the next, I could already make out the folds on the wraps he wore and what he was pointing at us—which could only be a firearm. In that moment, the best we could hope for was to stay in the air.

"Up! Higher up!" bellowed Utjok and gave the birds a sign. I felt us bear up against the wind that was trying to press us down, carried by a wave the birds hurled behind us. And the storm rose with us, and the sand, and the riders on their mules.

I caught a last glimpse of the rider from the dune's crest as he was thrown through the air. I'd flown too low. I tried to throw myself into the upswell, but coasted right under it instead. I felt my bird fish for me, but the Yellow World's gravity was stronger; it grabbed me, tore my bird's lead, and left me spinning while, around

me, sand and riders and my squadron, too, plunged towards the
ground.

———

You couldn't say I regained consciousness. I regained pain. I couldn't
move my legs, and my arms stood at wrong angles to my body. My left
hand lay unprotected in the sand, the skin red, weeping, and the
burning was so piercing I retched bile that ran out of the corners of
my mouth into my helmet. The sun stood high in the iron-gray sky,
and all around me was nothing but sand. On Yellow, very little grew
that could cope with the acid in the ground, and from school I knew
that without armor-mules or the right footwear, you had no chance in
the desert. Where my flight suit was torn away, my raw flesh baked in
the sun; my tongue was swollen and my throat too dry to swallow.
After a while, I discovered one single clear thought buried under all
the agony: I would die down here.

The hope of returning back home as myself shrank down to nothing, just like my brain would shrink under the sun to a fraction of its
present size. My vocal cords and my tongue would waste away, my
ability to think would collapse, and I thought I could already feel my
body fluids gathering together and concentrating to keep alive the
part of me that wanted to survive at any cost. That wanted to go
home. That was already thinking about laying eggs. I lay dying.

———

Is that all? How does this story justify change?

No, I'm not finished. Tuela didn't die down there.

Why not?

Maybe because the chain of events hadn't yet led to the change we
need. Maybe I was saved so I could bring it to that end.

*We reject that. There is no higher power. If there is, then we are that power,
or a part of it. We do not know. It does not matter to us. But still, we want to
know why Tuela lived on.*

Unfortunately, I can't remember. I wasn't conscious. But there is
someone who was. Pierre told me about it. Let's remember what he
recalled.

———

Pierre paused at the kitchen gateway and looked up into the sky. The evening was still bathed in pale-green light emanating from the Heights hanging slantwise over the horizon, but soon it would be pitch black. The wind drove sand and small stones and leaves before it.

As a boy, Pierre had been afraid of the Heights, of the ghosts that dwelt there. Elder Rock had told him about them. Many generations ago, it was said, the Heights had been a small planet, and this world had been covered in thick forests. But the tribes quarreled with the Deathbirds, there was war, and the acid that had rained from the sky had made a dead sand world out of the dark-green jungle world. Only a few had survived, and even for these, what was left over was barely enough. It was then that the Deathbirds left the world and took the small world for themselves, and the tribes cursed them because they were trapped here below. After the last cataclysmic acid storm, so the legends said, the surviving tribes looked into the sky, searching for the small world and found only rubble remaining. The Heights were shattered; the Deathbirds had gotten their punishment.

At this point Elder Rock always dropped his voice and whispered, "But their ghosts still fly up there among the rubble. On especially dark nights, they descend. And if they catch anyone not keeping a close enough eye on the sky, they rip off his head and take it back up with them."

Then Elder Rock would pull on Pierre's ear and laugh. And afterward, Pierre would lie awake and stare at the sky through the open sand-shutters, not daring to sleep.

Today, now that he was an adult, he welcomed the Heights in the sky in the evenings because on any normal night they afforded a few meters of visibility in the blackness. It was only on nights like this that you couldn't see them at all. The wind kept intensifying, whirling dust and sand into the upper layers of the atmosphere. Light emanated now only from the ever fiercer lightning strikes forking down.

The men and women from Pierre's tribe ran across the stronghold's courtyard. Their scarves and masks pressed against their faces, they fought against the wind hurling acidic sand at them, tied the animals fast in their stalls, and secured hatches and doors.

Pierre turned his gaze away from the black sky and ran over to one of the greenhouses to stack sandbags that would shield the milky glass from the impact of the wind and windblown debris. Then—a dry thunderclap and a new cluster of lightning strikes beyond the wall, hitting one on top of the other, first far out in the desert and then, instantly, right near Pierre. And then one of them crashed into the cripple-palm whose fronds spread over the courtyard and the green-house. It burned, burned blazingly, while the lightning strikes moved on. Pierre's eyes ran, his ears were deafened by the roaring flames, and he groped his way along the ground, hands protected by thick gloves, ignoring the sand burning where it forced itself under his clothes as he crept towards the place where he had last seen the boy.

He lay so close to the trunk of the palm that the flames had singed his hair away. It was Jen's son, still too young to have been given a name, though his nickname was Cakes, the word he said most often. He must have followed Pierre outside.

Pierre lifted the boy up, carried him, heart racing, into the second courtyard, where the fires were kept alive in high glass chimneys, and climbed up the outer steps with him. Inside the walls, the howling of the storm became high and wailing.

Jen was, as expected, in the upstairs hall, tending to cuts and acid-burned eyes. Her breasts swayed under the thin cloth of her night-shirt, her hair spread heavy and black over her back.

As she spotted Pierre, she abandoned her patients. He laid the boy carefully in her arms. Some glanced over, curious. Most found it easier to avoid looking at them.

"I'm sorry. A lightning strike. He had ..."

Jen didn't look at Pierre, turning her back to him and laying the boy on one of the smooth-polished stone benches that ran the length of the walls. She covered him up as though he could still feel cold.

It hurt Pierre to his soul. All of it. That he couldn't help. That he couldn't touch her. That the boy lay there. He felt guilty, although he knew it wasn't his fault. He turned away and ran out again, into the raging night.

———

It was dangerous to go up on the wall then, but Pierre had to check the telescopes. If they weren't carefully wrapped and tied up, the sand would grind the lenses blind within an hour.

He pulled his mask over his face-scarf, hooked his belt into the safety line, and pulled himself along against the storm, hand over hand, until he reached the first telescope. Through the thick dust shimmered a last greenish hint of the Heights that Pierre used for orientation. At the second telescope the wrapping flapped loose against its bindings, and it was pure luck that it hadn't yet been ripped away. Pierre cast a glance through the telescope before he wrapped it, more out of habit than hope that he would be able to see anything in this weather.

But he did see something. A snaking line of points of light. A caravan. A big one, with many mules shoving their armored feet along and just as many swathed riders.

But they weren't expecting any caravans. An unexpected rain of this size could mean only one thing: an exodus. And that meant war. In a day at most.

Pierre looked out, screening his eyes behind their protective goggles with his hands and staring intently in the direction where he had seen the caravan. Nothing but darkness. Again a series of lightning strikes flashed across the sky and Pierre used the opportunity to look once more through the telescope. Nothing. He waited. But even in the harsh light of the next storm-fire, the desert remained empty. Not a single mule and not a man to be seen. There was nothing but sand and blackness out there.

———

It is hard for us to remember. But if we let ourselves fall far enough, we know the Dancing Stones were a sphere. That is true.

There was war. That is true, too.

They hunted us in their woods, slaughtered us, stole our eggs. The woods were all-concealing, and we liked the trees. In trees you sleep well. We would have gladly stayed there.

But they were everywhere and we never heard them coming. Only as the trees first disappeared did we truly see them. And we sallied forth.

There was much anger and bitterness and fear and destruction and death and no balance at all. We refuse to think about it any longer.

———

The kitchen gate into the courtyard stood open so that the first sunlight shone in and warmed Pierre's hands. With him at the table sat Jen and Elder Rock. They blew silently on their mugs of tea, shoved dried fruit in their mouths and chewed, sucking it entirely dry of sweetness and flavor before swallowing the fibers. They were dirty and exhausted; they'd been on their feet the entire night. Jen's eyes were swollen. Pierre didn't dare look at her.

"There's nothing out there," said Elder Rock. "Lor was on the wall the entire night and kept watch."

"But I'm certain. It was an exodus, an entire tribe. We have maybe half a day to prepare."

Rock sank into himself just a little more.

"We'll never manage it. Not after this past night."

"Are you certain?" asked Jen. She seemed calm.

"I'm certain," said Pierre.

Then no one said anything more, no one moved, until Jen suddenly stood up and clapped her hands.

"Well then. To work!"

If Jen said, "To work," then to work she would go and prepare for a battle. Five hundred in the desert against two hundred in the stronghold. They had a real chance. At least Pierre hoped so.

Elder Rock stood up as well.

"I'll give the alarm," he said tiredly and left the kitchen.

As the bright sound of the bells broke the air, Pierre asked, "How are you?"

Jen didn't answer. Pierre suspected that in her silence she blamed him, just as he did himself. Because the boy had been with him. He stood up to take her in his arms. She let him.

"Oh, to hell with you," she said sadly.

She sounded as exhausted as Pierre felt.

She'd never let him come to her bed since they'd married, hadn't once allowed him to show tenderness and comfort her. Her first husband had been murdered as he stood waterwatch below in the outer entrance on a lightless night. His throat had been sliced so cleanly through that his head just barely remained resting on his shoulders. Her marriage to Pierre wasn't going to improve now that her son from that old marriage was dead, too. Pierre let the hug go.

"I'll have them double the watch on the reservoir."

Jen nodded.

———

The day passed and no one believed any longer in the exodus Pierre claimed to have seen. There was no one out in the desert. Jen rounded up some children to help her prepare the death meal. And shortly afterward the inner courtyard was full of people sitting on the carpets, crying and talking in low voices about the dead boy. It was the first shared meal since the storm, and they ate it quietly. Pierre sat alone on a carpet under the palm, where the boy had died whose bones, gnawed clean, now lay on plates and platters all around.

Jen went around and collected what the tribe had respectfully left over, to gather it into a bundle and hang it on the burned-up palm. Sand and wind would break down the remains over time, and when that was done, the mourning period would be over.

The sky took on the green shimmer of evening. Pierre sighed. Maybe in the end, the storm had brought them not misfortune but rescue. If there had been an exodus, then the storm had buried it in the sand.

A shadow fell across his face. Jen stood near him, the bundle with her son's bones pressed to her breast.

"You can come to me tonight, if you want," she said. For a moment a trembling smile played over her lips.

Pierre felt as if he'd waited half a lifetime for this invitation. But he shook his head.

"I can't. Not tonight. I have to go out and search for them. Maybe there's still something left."

No one else would go. No one believed him. It wasn't just a matter of the spoils that the sand would quickly dissolve. His credibility was at stake.

Jen nodded. She'd clearly expected this response, but her smile reverted to its usual hardness.

"Can I ... come to you afterwards?"

She shook her head. "Maybe it's better if we wait a while longer. Until I've ... recovered."

Pierre forced himself to nod shortly, then stood up and left.

———

He got a mule out of its stall and watered it generously before he loaded it with water pouches, ropes, blankets, a shovel, two lamps with milky glass, and his armored boots. At last he mounted up and drove the great bleating animal on with his heels. If his luck was bad, he would spend the whole night awake in vain. If his luck was good, he would bring spoils back with him. And if his luck was really against him and he stumbled into an ambush, than this would be his last foray out into the night.

But in the green light of the Heights, it looked as though the sand actually had swallowed everything: there was no hint that there had ever been a caravan there. Despite that, Pierre couldn't bring himself to go back home, back to Jen, who would turn away from him again; back to the mocking looks if he returned empty-handed. His eyes burned from the traces of acid in the air, and he'd had nosebleeds for two hours. He wouldn't be able to stay awake much longer. It was the second night he hadn't slept.

Only when the pale light of dawn arrived did Pierre's gaze find an irregularity in the landscape. The fluttering of a shining blue scrap of fabric in the wind. He remained standing a stone's throw away, waiting to be certain that what he was seeing wouldn't turn out to be a mirage and evaporate. But the fluttering held steady, and he rode closer.

In the sand before him lay a tall adult form in a blue coverall, arms and legs much too long and thin, no breasts but still so delicate he had to believe it was a woman. The skin on her hands was gold-colored, the hair that poured from under her tight-fitting helmet almost white. Pierre put his boots on and slid down from his mule into the sand.

As he opened the helmet's sand-blinded visor, he saw narrow features with a wide, soft mouth and long eyelashes lying like feathers on her cheeks. Her arms and legs were clearly broken in multiple places.

Pierre took a step back, waiting to see if the form noticed his arrival, if she would move. He could tell that she lived because her chest rose and fell convulsively. If he waited just a little longer, her breathing might stop. He stood there and stared, uncertain what to do. He knew no tribe whose people looked like this girl. The pockets of her suit were empty, and beyond that he found no clue to her origins. He knew he should kill her to end her agony. But he couldn't bring himself to do it.

Her body felt very light despite his exhaustion, and she groaned weakly as he laid her prone across the mule's back. On her back, the fabric of the suit had already been eaten away by the sand and had fused with her dissolving skin. She might heal, but only slowly.

Before he gave the mule a slap to start it forward, he stuck a piece of fabric he'd soaked with water in the girl's mouth. Her raw back he left open to the still-cool morning air.

The caravan he'd seen last night had been giant. But this white, lanky being on his mule seemed to be the last of her tribe. Suddenly the full force of her tragic fate hit Pierre and he began sobbing softly, throat dry. Killing her would be more merciful, even if she could survive. Somehow, he would have to try to make up for his weakness.

———

As I awoke, I was still me. It was cool and dark; I lay on my side and ached, but the ache was still dull, in the background. Directly in front of me a face hung in darkness; in that first moment I thought it was a bird. Its skin was almost black, and its head and chin were covered in hair of the same color. The face smiled and floated upwards and then I saw that it sat on a broad, massive body. I heard its voice, deep and rumbling, but it was articulate sounds that I heard, not the meaningless stammer of a bird.

Only then did I truly take in my surroundings. Stone walls hung with colorful carpets, two glass chimneys where small fires burned, a low roof, a wide door, and instead of a window, a closed hatch in the wall.

I'd fallen into the enemy's hands. I was at their mercy. Apart from my injuries, the gravity of the Yellow World pressed me down all on its own, making it impossible for me to move, or even to breathe deeply enough.

A massive dark hand was laid on my forehead. Strangely, this touch comforted me, and I shut my eyes and fell asleep again.

The next period is blurred in my memory. There were alternating phases of intense pain, deep darkness, and numbness. Other than the dark one with the deep voice, there was another thickset figure who attended me regularly. In front she had wobbling, heavy-looking appendages on her torso, and the thickest, blackest hair I had ever seen fell down her back. She washed me and fed me salty broth and a spicy gruel that lay heavily in my stomach. With a set expression, she stretched my arms and legs into the right shapes and splinted them while the bearded figure held my screaming body down. She spread salve on my back and encouraged me with noises and gestures to move my broken bones, to bend, stretch, and lift. But she never smiled.

Only the bearded man did that. He smiled wide, with white teeth and with tears in his eyes when he looked at me. And after what seemed like a lifetime, I could hold a spoon myself, and even if I took a long time and spilled, I was full when I was done eating. I lived like a just-hatched youth, fragile and barely strong enough to bear eir own weight. And as with a youth, there was someone near me most of the time, too, keeping me company and watching out for me. Nights, the bearded one often sat on my bed and spoke in his strange, rolling language, listening to me as I told him everything that went through my head. We smiled a lot and occasionally we exchanged gestures, and one night he took my hand for the first time and pressed it cautiously, as if he was afraid he might shatter it.

His strength was unsettling, and at the same time aroused a strange elation in me. I felt I trusted him, trusted the enemy, and I told him my name.

"Tuela."

"Tu-e-la?"

"I'm Tuela."

He laughed, long and booming, until my own belly resonated with it and I had to laugh, too.

"And I'm Pierre," he said in his language. I understood him.

———

Nights. It would be too easy to say I loved him because he was the only one who was friendly and took any interest in me. It was more than that. It was a tension between us, something strange, exciting. We talked for hours; he helped me train my muscles, massaging them devotedly when I lay sweating and exhausted on my bed after strength training, and I felt this satisfied me just as little as it did him, without knowing what it was I longed for. And one night we pressed ourselves against one another on my bed, entangled ourselves in our ankle-length shirts, and pressed our open mouths against one another like birds shortly before nesting time. This was the night I discovered Pierre had a penis. I'd never—not even once—thought that I could regret not being an animal.

———

The next morning, led by Pierre's hand, I passed through long, cool halls and several stairways, out into bright sunlight for the first time, still uncertain on my legs and fearful of the strange world outside my small room. There, I'd often shoved the sand-shutter to the side and looked over an endless yellow plain to a far-distant horizon. And nights I'd gazed up at the Dancing Stones and longed for their green buoyancy.

Now we stepped out into a stone gallery and looked into an inner courtyard with white sand, colorful carpets, large hairy animals, and green plants three times as tall as me, spreading their wide, green leaves out like a roof under the glaring sky. Everything here was fixed in place, nothing drifted or spun or shifted around anything else, everything I saw was oriented around the same reference point, just as if we still stood in a room in a solidly-built house. Between the trunks of the largest trees stretched hammocks where people lay and dozed in shadows; and at a hearth something was suspended over the open embers, exuding a delicious savory scent. Around this wide hall, under the open sky, were solid walls built out of solid cliffs, and even the sky with its even, steely blue seemed solid and immovable. I can't describe that moment as anything but the feeling of having come home, where you could depend on your feet and the direction of gravity. I fell in love with the Yellow World the first moment I set foot on it awake and aware. Pierre stood next to me, small but twice as wide and ten times as strong as I; I clung to him hard and laughed and cried at once, and he laughed his sustained booming laugh.

We searched out a free carpet, and before Pierre sat with me he rang a bundle of bright bells hanging from a tree branch. Then he disappeared into the dark behind an open gate and came back with fresh water, dried fruit, and bread.

He began to eat slowly and methodically. While I, in accordance with the custom of his tribe, kept him silent company, the courtyard filled with ever more dark, thickset people who scrubbed their hands in a sand-basin, sat down to eat, and eyed me curiously. Finally, a good two hundred faces were turned to me, expectant, and Pierre said quietly:

"Very rarely do so many come to eat at the same time. They knew I would bring you with me today."

He stood up.

"I know you want to find out more about Tuela. Ask your questions."

The first to rise was an old man.

"Rock, do you want to begin?"

The elder nodded and turned to me, but asked the question loud enough for all those present to hear.

"You were on an exodus, yes?"

I didn't know this word and shook my head, helpless.

"You wanted to invade."

"Yes," I said truthfully and felt ashamed. I stood up with Pierre's help.

"I'm sorry. We're trying to survive."

"We all want to survive," retorted a young woman. "But *we* manage it without raiding."

"We don't have fresh water. We're not interested in your land. We need water."

"And how did you want to transport water for so many people? On your mules somehow?"

For the first time I realized they took me for someone from the caravan I'd seen in the storm, and I glanced at Pierre for help. We'd never explicitly talked about it; I'd just always taken it for granted he knew what I was talking about when I spoke about the Dancing Stones. He nodded at me encouragingly.

"The birds would've carried it for us. They make things light or heavy."

The surrounding faces looked at me without comprehension and I'd no idea how to begin to explain. Or if I even ought to explain. Strictly speaking, I would betray Utjok if I did.

While I hesitated, Pierre spoke for me.

"She doesn't belong to the lost caravan. She comes from the Heights. She belongs to the ancient tribe of the Deathbirds."

My heart beat wildly, fear-filled. I saw their doubt. And then I saw their fear. Fear of us.

"But how?"

"They can fly. Like in the old legends."

"No one can fly."

"She has to prove it first."

"Look at her. She's so different from us."

"And what if she's come to destroy us once and for all this time?"

Pierre lifted his hands in an appeasing gesture and the people stopped speaking over one another. He counted off on his fingers:

"She crashed. Her flight suit is torn to shreds. She has no weapons. She's alone. She can't do anything to us."

"What does she want here?"

"What she said: she wanted to get water because her tribe up there in the Heights is dying of thirst."

"I told you so! A raid!"

"Would we have given them water of our own free will, then?"

No one answered, and again Pierre did it himself.

"No. Because anyone who doesn't belong to us is, obviously, our enemy. But I tell you this way of thinking is a mistake! Since I found Tuela, I've thought a lot. About our lives and about the old stories. No one knows exactly what happened then. Why the little world shattered, why we live in a desert. We blame them and they blame us, and that's the only thing that tells us for certain anything even happened back then. But that was then. And now is now. We have to stop this. We have to learn from each other so we can make our lives easier, together. Tuela's stranded here. She can't go back. I want us to take her into our tribe. That would be a tiny beginning, a small change."

Pierre paused before he spoke further, looked me in the eyes, saw the pain that had balled up in me like a fist at his words, that choked me and weighed me down.

"I want to take her to wife."

In the courtyard was silence, and Pierre stood there with out-flung arms and waited for a reaction.

It was Jen who was the first to speak.

"But I won't let you go."

Pierre let his arms sink, astonished.

"I thought you'd be pleased. I thought I disgusted you."

"You're right. I've no desire for a man to lie beside me. And I'd let you go with pleasure. But—" Jen pointed at me. "I've seen her naked. She's strange, she's ... not even a woman. If I can prevent her mixing with us through my refusal, I'll accept being your wife." Then she turned to me. "I've nothing against you personally. But you can't be a man's wife."

"I want some proof," said Elder Rock, quiet but clearly audible. "I want some proof that she isn't human."

And Jen tore my long white shirt down the front. And I felt their eyes on me like burning ice.

"It's completely flat. It doesn't even have nipples," said Jen matter-of-factly. The simple observation sufficed as proof that Pierre and I could never be a couple. I lowered my head, asking myself how I could have let myself hope for even a second.

"Pierre, she can't bear children," said Rock.

"Of course I can't bear children. No one can do that before they've died," I said, tired.

Pierre's face remained earnest as he turned to me.

"But I still want to marry you." Then he turned again to his tribe. "I found her in the desert. It should be left to my decision."

"You owe us children, Pierre," said Rock softly.

"I know. But I ask this of you, nevertheless. Jen, I ask you as a friend: Let me go."

Jen's lips were narrow and she had her arms crossed over her breasts.

"Just the thought makes me sick. And Rock is right. You owe me a son."

With that, she turned and walked away.

And I stood there shivering in the evening air that was quickly turning cold, two hundred pairs of eyes fixed on me.

Elder Rock laid a drape around my shoulders so I could cover what I didn't possess. He clapped me on the shoulder as if he wanted to apologize.

"We aren't done yet. There will be further questions," he said. "About your homeland and how we can defend ourselves against you."

Pierre brought me inside again. I saw fear in his eyes and felt it begin to clutch at me, too.

———

In the following days, I stayed in my room and Pierre came by only occasionally, for a few minutes. He said there were difficult times ahead for us and he'd stave off the worst.

I'd be neither killed nor chased into the desert. But Pierre couldn't prevent them from piecing the rest together, too, from connecting the dead waterwatchers with my appearance. They blamed me, and Jen, who'd nursed me back to health, was particularly furious. True, I hadn't killed her husband or any of the others. But I'd taken part in the missions during which they were murdered. I couldn't deny my complicity, and so they debated over me and passed judgment.

Later, Pierre explained to me it was Elder Rock who'd had the idea that I should get a chance to settle my debt—and I was beyond grateful to him. But I recognized the real thinking behind this, too: should my people send water-carriers here again, I'd have a chance to return home. And perhaps to begin then what had become Pierre's and my greatest wish: To live together. I didn't explain to Pierre that for me there was yet another way home. Because I feared that way far too much.

So it was decided that deep in the mountain under the stronghold, I would change filters, work pumps, keep reservoirs clean, and sound alarms if anyone tried to invade.

It wasn't, as I'd hoped, Pierre and Rock who took me below. I hadn't seen Pierre for days; he kept himself away or was kept away. Two men I didn't know accompanied me. They stared grimly ahead and positioned me between them like a prisoner who threatened to fly away at any moment. Inside the stronghold we went down countless steps; the entire mountain the stronghold was enthroned on must be shot through with tunnels and halls, which generations of inhabitants had driven down ever deeper until they had finally struck water.

The deeper we went, the colder and damper it became, and I began to shiver in my shirt. The walls were slick with algae and fungus, and the halls we passed through at the end were so narrow that we could only shove ourselves forward single-file, sideways.

Then finally the pathway opened onto a round reservoir; the walls were brick, the roof was arched, and after the tallow-lamp-lit darkness of the halls, harsh sunlight fell in through a row of narrow embrasures on one side. A catwalk the width of a man ran along the circumference of the reservoir, and at regular intervals in the walls were set brick-lined niches where rations, weapons, blankets, clothing, filter screens, buckets, poles, brooms, and other equipment waited to be called into service.

The waterwatcher received us in front of the reservoir's opposite exit. His niche was furnished with a large sack laid flat, stuffed with sand and rags, a couple of blankets, and a mule-grease lamp smoldering in its glass cylinder. Overhead was a leather cord that disappeared into a hole in the wall.

"The alarm pull," the watcher explained, brusque, and I nodded.

As he gathered up his personal belongings, he threw suspicious glances at me, as if I might attack him from behind and cut off his head without a sound as we did on our missions. Then he climbed back up into the stronghold with both of my escorts. Only now did I notice the bars of sturdy bone which they pulled closed behind them. I was alone.

Sunlight reflections painted swarming snakes on the walls. Unable to think clearly, I watched them until they faded. Only then did I fill the oil lamp out of a leather bucket and set about taking a closer look at my new home.

The second exit I'd noticed earlier was not barred. The hall behind it was as narrow as the one we'd come through, but it was dry. After some minutes spent stumbling over stony ground, I stood in a stairwell leading up. At its end, I stood at a second set of bars separating me from a long cavern where a second waterwatcher wrapped in a blanket lay on his rag sack and snored. Over the watcher's camp was fixed an alarm pull just like the one below in my niche. The light of the Dancing Stones shone in through the entrance and drenched the view in a sickly sheen. The scene was familiar to me; I'd already been here once before, and I asked myself how the watcher could sleep so peacefully. It was no wonder it was so easy for us to steal from them, when you could simply murder them in their sleep. I would've liked to have woken the man and reproached him for his carelessness. Instead I climbed down again, to sleep a little myself.

And then I had nothing else to do but make my rounds regularly, scrape algae from the stones, sustain myself on dried fruit, meat, and fresh water, and throw my waste out through the light embrasures. Occasionally, someone came to supplement my supplies, and several times during the day I made a pilgrimage to the upper bars. But none of the watchers on duty ever spoke with me. They all stared past me, and many spat on the floor contemptuously when I appeared. As time passed, I realized that they weren't guarding their water so much as guarding me.

When Pierre finally came, I was already at the point where I was talking to myself.

"Tuela," he said simply as he appeared at the lower bars. I recognized the deep rumble of his voice more with my gut than with my ears, and a tingling shot through my limbs that couldn't be explained by just surprise.

He unlocked the bars and stepped in, bringing cheese and fresh, soft bread and a pouch of hot tea that did my throat good, sore as it was from constant coughing.

"You're too thin," he said as he sat next to me on the rim of the reservoir and watched me eat.

"I was always this thin," I replied, chewing.

"No, you weren't. You've got to get out of here. Very soon."

Pierre took my hand and looked at me out of great, sad eyes.

"Should you be here with me at all?" I asked.

After all, I was someone put here to atone for the murder of several watchers. I coughed drily.

Pierre grinned. "I cheated a little." Then he shook his head. "You really don't look good."

"Thanks," I said. I wanted it to sound coquettish and carefree, but I didn't manage. It came out as a true thank you, one that acknowledged how much he worried about me.

"Can you swim?" I asked and wondered at myself for not having had the idea before. At home in the Heights I'd often swum in the drop-seas.

Pierre shook his head. "What's swimming?"

"Letting yourself be held up by water. Moving through water."

"Yourself? All of you?"

I nodded. "Come, I'll show you!"

In a quick motion, I stripped off the fur vest and my unlaundered, greasy shirt, and stepped up to the rim of the reservoir. The water we had at home originated on this world, maybe even from this reservoir. But at home the water was bright and transparent. You could see all the way through and laugh over the strangely wobbling boulders on the other side. Here below, the water was opaque and black and you didn't know how deep it was. Or what was under there. I hesitated. But then Pierre stood next to me, his penis erect, aroused and full of anticipation. And we let ourselves slip together into the icy water and I showed him how it held us up. At first he was a little fearful, holding onto the edge, but soon he swam with powerful, spluttering strokes and savored the gliding motion. After that, we lay wrapped in my blanket and made love while golden snakes danced over the walls and Pierre's black shoulders gleamed in the light that reflected off of the water.

And again I described for him our Dancing Stones: the sky's depths, the blue of eggs, and how the child-catchers collect the youths as soon as they leave their nests and threaten to fall over the Stones' edges.

"Don't the parents pay proper attention to them?" he murmured, sleepy.

I didn't have an answer for that, because that question had never occurred to me. What would happen if you left the youths to the birds? What would they become? I shook my head.

"Who would they learn to speak from? How would they leave their Stones without flight suits? When the Dancing Stones were still all one piece, it might have been possible. But now ..."

I described how we grow up with our siblings. How we play. How we learn to fly. But I didn't describe how we die to him. The thought frightened me. For the first time in my life it was actually important to me that I live. Because I wanted to be together with Pierre, because I wanted something we could call "our life." Pierre didn't tell me what would happen if someone caught us. He'd gone to sleep.

———

And they did catch us. There were eight of them, and they appeared, heads glistening, gasping for air, in the middle of the reservoir. There must have been a hidden inlet below, perhaps a brick channel or a crack in the stone. The water had to come from somewhere, after all. They swam better than Pierre; they were practiced. Their arms cut with quiet, liquid noise through the water and pulled their heavy bodies up onto the catwalk, where they smacked their shivering bellies and backs to warm themselves. They laughed until someone ordered them tightly to lower their voices. I knew the voice.

It belonged to Utjok, who was the last to get out of the water, slender, and shivering just as much as the thickset men ey had come with. Ey was, as always, the leader.

I wanted to jump up, wanted to hurl myself at em. But Pierre held me tight, shaking his head silently. We were only two. Utjok pulled a sack out of the water by a long rope one of the men had bound about his hips, and passed out pickaxes and knives to eir new squadron. I'd no doubt ey would kill Pierre if ey discovered him, just as we'd killed without hesitation on our missions. And suddenly I was uncertain ey wouldn't kill me, too, when ey realized we no longer stood on the same side.

Pierre and I pulled ourselves further back into the shadows of my niche silently and waited. They took the path down through the inner bars, tearing them right off their hinges with the help of a pickaxe and a rope.

As soon as the last man had disappeared, I reached up and tore at the alarm pull. The leather cord was rotted through; its end came loose in my hand.

Pierre didn't even take the time to throw on a shirt.

"I'll go around outside. Rock's there! He can give the alarm."

I held tight to his arm. "They belong to the lost caravan. I know it —we saw them on our approach."

Pierre nodded. "I know, let me go!"

"Utjok was leader of my squadron. Somehow, under the surface, they must have ..."

"I know! There's no time for this now."

Pierre pulled away without kissing me.

"And me?" I called after him. "What if more of them come? If they discover me?"

Pierre paused. "Come with me," he said and we went together, shoving ourselves as fast as possible through the narrow passage, naked.

The upper bars were locked. Rock lay not even an arm's length from us. The alarm pull was sliced through, just like his throat. His wrinkled face lay in an already congealing pool of blood. He must have been dead for hours. In his fist, Pierre found the key.

"Why didn't they just come in through here?"

"Eight of them? We would've seen them from the wall. The Heights stand in the sky." Pierre pointed to the full bags and saddles standing ready in the cave. "Early tomorrow morning we three would have been gone. On our way north," he said sadly.

So that was what he'd meant when he'd said I had to get out. He and Rock had had a plan.

Despite the fear taking hold of me, I rejoiced inside. For the first time in countless days, I breathed the fresh metallic-tasting air of the surface; for the first time in days I felt the wind on my skin. We ran on, naked and barefoot, through the acidic sand. By the time we reached the narrow outer steps, our soles were bleeding, but there was no time left to worry about that. I struggled upwards against the gravity, Pierre hauling me after him and cursing because we were so slow. When I realized he'd signed his own death warrant by taking me up along with him it was already too late.

I knew the wallwatcher awaiting us above. He'd spat in a pouch of dried meat before handing it through the bars to me with a smile. And I'd spat back, hitting him on the chin. He spotted me before he saw Pierre. And while they overpowered us on this side of the stronghold, the strangers invaded from inside and killed more than fifty sleeping people before they were stopped.

Again they blamed me. No matter how Pierre and I stated our case, I'd killed Elder Rock, I'd let the strangers in. As evidence, it sufficed that their leader was a white, gangling freak like me. Naturally

I'd been in contact with em the entire time and planned everything out long beforehand.

Utjok, eir new squadron, and I were all sentenced to a dishonorable death. We would be pitched from the stronghold wall. The sand would quickly dispose of our remains. The tribe could afford it; there were more than enough other dead to consume. But there was worse in store for Pierre. He would be sent into the desert on foot with enough water to last only a few days. His chances of survival were far slimmer than mine.

When the moment came I begged to be allowed to wear my old helmet. Utjok had lost eirs in the vast labyrinth under the surface, and someone had removed the blinded visor from mine. But it was better than nothing.

I felt no fear as I stood on the battlements, naked and chained next to Utjok and eir people. The survivors from Pierre's tribe stood close behind us in their full number, robes fluttering. I would die, and I didn't mind. In those last moments of my life I felt only gratitude at being allowed to see the soft shine of the Dancing Stones one more time with my own eyes, and the longing to finally return suffused me.

There was no ceremony, no pronouncement of the sentence. A row of people stepped forward, spiked staves held tight in their hands. With astonishment I recognized Jen among the executioners. In a moment of rage I considered grabbing her stave and dragging her with me into the depths. But it was unlikely that would work. The wall was too high; Jen's center of gravity was far too low.

I concentrated. More important than revenge was somehow managing to control my fall. Even without a suit and the chance to lie as spread-eagle as possible on the wind. Jen shoved first Utjok and then me down with one hard, focused strike apiece.

And we flew, flew too fast; I saw the strange men and my former squadron leader tumble down before and beside me, rebound off of stones, saw as they dashed against the ground far out, naked like the child whose ribcage I'd squashed more than a lifetime ago. The same thing would happen to us now.

I didn't lose consciousness, although the breakneck fall tore the breath from my lips, although my instincts balked against experiencing my death while conscious. Despite everything, I stayed with myself as my backbone broke, as my organs burst, as my lungs

collapsed. Around me, eight bodies struck the ground with dull final-
ity. Utjok didn't manage it. Eir skull was smashed to pieces.

---

*Do we remember the first moments after our birth? They fade so quickly and
there are no words for them because we experience entirely new feelings that we
have to learn first. None of us still remember the day of our birth.*

*But a piece of Tuela remembers, a piece that we retain until it is time to
reach a decision whose necessity we begin to divine. We remember.*

At first there was a distant many-voiced whisper. Then eyes
opened and looked into a familiar face. The name that belonged to it
wanted to be spoken. But there was no throat any longer, no vocal
cords, and the tongue had retracted, had begun to turn into a tract
deep in the throat which felt an unprecedented, sensual itch at the
sight of this face. Greedily the bird-mouth gaped open to receive its
lover, and a demanding gurgle rose from it.

But he did not understand us and shrank back, letting Tuela's
helmet fall into the sand, and we slid from his lap into the biting sand
and screamed in pain.

Quickly, Pierre picked us back up, shoved a scarf under us that
would protect us for a while, and dripped water in our mouth. A hot
wind stroked over the feathers already shoving through the skin of our
cheeks. The separation took place quickly. Our new feet kicked out of
the old neck, wings unfolded themselves, and last of all, the spine
binding us to the old body dissolved with a quiet, definitive pain.

*In that moment Tuela began to fade and she had to hold herself together
with effort. She holds on now, still, and we help her by encapsulating her life in
this story. We begin to feel the urgency she felt. We want her plan to work.*

Pierre picked up our new body carefully, wrapping it loosely in his
scarf, and we slept as he carried us away from the stronghold, deeper
into the desert. He went to his own death, but that did not bother us.
We just needed a little peace. We slept lulled by the soft swing of his
steps, slept until agonizing thirst woke us and he gave us water. We
beat our wings, fluttered up, and turned our first reeling rounds on the
steady wind of the Yellow World.

Seated on a stone, Pierre watched us, full of astonishment. And as
we landed in his lap, a little clumsy and awkward yet, he let us quiet

the other longing, too, let us drink our fill from him as birds do. He shook as he gave us semen and, after, we watched him cry many salty tears that mixed, bubbling, with the sand.

When he had cried himself out, the Dancing Stones stood slanting over the horizon, and his mouth moved. He spoke, but we no longer had ears that could hear him. We heard now only our own distant whisper deep in our skull, but we heard no wind, no hiss of sand. Not his booming voice that had moved Tuela to laughter. The world was silent and Pierre's lip movements struck us as ridiculous and lewd and we tried to laugh. Pierre stopped talking, staring at us.

What must he have seen? Tuela's head without the body he had loved sat before him on bird feet and blinked at him. The hair had fallen out of that head. Instead it grew light-colored feathers. She wanted to say that he shouldn't speak, that there were more important things now, but his expression told her she uttered only sounds, meaningless, guttural bird sounds, wet and ugly, that made them both sad.

Tuela felt it would be a relief to give up the past; the temptation was great, the promise of the eternal moment enticing. She could have turned around and flown away, back home. Forever. She was tired, as dying is hard work against which one cannot shield oneself. But although we suffered growth pains, the pain of rejection, and the pain of loss, we were not really dismayed and we felt that home would accept us.

But there is something still better than forgetting—more life! Togetherness! Trees to sleep in!

The realization of how simple it would be to have all of this forced Tuela anew to hoarse laughter. Our lung volume had shrunk and pulled back into the inside of our cranial cavity. That chamber of bone was still there and in its interior there was a new pitch-black dot with seven layers, one for each dimension, harder than stone and as all-encompassing as an entire universe. We felt its pulse, felt how our thoughts reached for it. This awareness was what made us heavier or lighter; suddenly the gravity of the Yellow World no longer pressed us down. We weighed less than nothing; our flight was elegant and we savored it. We understood the Dance of Stones and how we brought it about; we saw the warping of space in and around us, and it pleased us.

Once, in school, Tuela had dissected a dead bird. She had removed the cherry-sized seven-hulled kernel from its brainstem, had cut it open. She had found a smaller cherry inside, and inside one smaller yet, and so on to infinity. Life is exactly as large inside as outside, and the flight to the center of a molecule takes just as long as that to the edge of the galaxy. They do not realize everything is just as light as it is heavy, just as large as small. Just as sweet as sour. It is easier than thinking. It is easier than wanting. It simply happens.

Pierre no longer sat on his weathered stone. Instead he hung help-less in the air under us with his arms paddling; we had picked him up with us, and we admit, his fear amused us. And then we started on our way. We hoped we would be welcome.

———

The *we* seemed so self-evident to us now that the interest in every-thing single and separate quickly faded. Only not in Pierre. We took him with us, we rescued him from the desert as he had rescued Tuela, and now we are responsible for him. We watch him as he lies in the salt meadow of a Dancing Stone and looks down at the Yellow World. He teaches us writing and we drink from him still, and he lets us. Although Tuela no longer hears his rumbling and booming, she does not lose herself and stays near him. Why? Why am I still interested in him?

Because I still feel somewhat to blame for him? Because we both owe our tribes a child? Or because nothing of him will remain if he dies, not even his dream of a life together. His kind die so much more thoroughly than we do.

———

Pierre is not dead. You are together, so far as it is possible. What more could he and Tuela wish for?

We said already: more life! What we all strive for as soon as we die. We want to create life!

Only you are not biologically compatible.

Right. But we've learned life emerges from death, as Tuela died in the desert.

Think about it, feel it: our power to hold the Dancing Stones is just as big as small.

There are no boundaries in any direction.

Stone that grinds to salt under its own weight.

Pierre's tears that sizzle in acid sand.

Dancing Stones and the Yellow World.

Water gushing out of the dark in shimmering seas.

We could sleep in trees again, under a steady sky.

We could make one living world out of two dying ones.

———

Sun gave way to shadow, the wind came up, and suddenly it was cool. Pierre awoke as the storm tore at his hair, and instinctively he shielded his face with his arms. But it was no storm like Yellow's. It was the thundering of millions of wings around him. The smiling mouths, winking eyes, and shimmering feathers of the Deathbirds were everywhere, surrounding him. He stood up cautiously, so as not to startle them; he walked around the Stone on which his tiny, hand-built hut of tough grass stood. Nothing but whirring, calling, rejoicing birds everywhere.

Pierre ducked, covering his head as they came nearer and their wings brushed his shoulders. He thought about the old story: if you don't watch out, they'll take your head!

Then he felt himself lose contact with the ground, felt as he began to drift away from his Stone. He tried to hold tight to the roof of his hut, but his hands missed their grip. Dammit, did you have to wear your flight suit here even when you were sleeping?

Then the bird that had been Tuela sat down on his back, bent over his shoulder, blinked, and kissed him tenderly. He hadn't seen Tuela for days; she'd been troubled and preoccupied, but now she looked as though she'd never in her earlier or her present life been so happy. She let a little piece of grass paper fall into his hand.

We go below. We go home, stood there in her still-uncertain scrawling child's script.

THE SEVENTH BY ELIZA VICTORIA

Eliza Victoria is the author of several books, including the Philippine National Book Award-winning *Dwellers* (2014) and the graphic novel *After Lambana* (2016, a collaboration with Mervin Malonzo). Born and raised in the Philippines, she currently lives in Sidney, Australia, pursuing a postgraduate degree.

———

She arrived at the house on a perfect morning—gentle sunlight, light breeze, the pleasant smell of coming rain. She knew, somehow, that it wouldn't be a destructive downpour, just a wispy shower to water the flowers. She knocked on the back gate, and the caretaker's wrinkled face appeared to greet her through the peep hole. "Oh," the old man said. "It's you. Did you have a nice walk?"

She smiled and ignored the old man's strange remark. She got here straight off the bus, what walk was the old man talking about? Inside the kitchen, she saw a tray with two plates by the sink. One of the plates contained half an omelette and a slice of bread, the other had traces of ketchup and a spoonful or two of rice. Leftovers.

"Is there someone else here?" She wondered who else could be there. Her siblings? Her cousins? The caretaker looked confused, mystified.

"What do you mean?" the old man asked.

She pointed at the tray. "You have a guest?" She didn't mean to sound obnoxious. Her grandmother had that tone with the help, but then, the caretaker was not supposed to have guests in the house.

The caretaker took a moment to answer. She noticed him looking at her shoes, the hardened mud like brush strokes, the dried leaves stuck to the soles. Instinctively, she lifted one foot to check what he found so interesting there.

"Are you all right, Julia?" he said.

She frowned. "I am," she said slowly, putting her foot down again. "Why?"

"Those are our plates," the old man said. "From earlier today? Remember? We had breakfast."

She shook her head. "I just got here."

"You've been here seven days."

Silence, then she started to laugh. "No. I just got here. I literally just got off the bus fifteen minutes ago."

"No." The caretaker looked perplexed, and a little frightened.

She sighed. Her father was right. The old man was getting confused. Just like her grandmother before she died. "It's okay. You can go home now. I'll just call you when I need anything."

"You've been here seven days," the caretaker said.

She was starting to feel irritated. "No," she said.

"You have. You were up there and you were studying. Then after breakfast you went out for a walk."

She counted to ten in her head. Took a deep breath. "I'll just call if I need anything," she said, and steered him out through the kitchen door.

———

It was a beautiful house with a flourishing back garden and expensive furniture. Her family wasn't rich, but her grandmother was, so the house with the flat screen TV and the hot shower and central air and a soft couch that didn't vomit its cotton stuffing was where she threw her birthday parties, where she took her boyfriends, where she stayed for nights on end when she needed some time alone.

The bedroom upstairs was neat and smelled of disinfectant spray —a tangy, lemony odor—and certainly didn't look or smell like a room where someone had slept for a week. She wondered how the caretaker was doing, if he was still thinking, *If that wasn't you, then who have I been talking to for seven days?*

She shivered and stood by the window. The window overlooked the garden, with its white chairs and white table. Beneath the table was something she had never seen or noticed before: an opening of a water well, covered with a slab of plywood. Was it new? She had been coming to this house for years and had never seen that well before.

She started unpacking, placing her clothes in the closet, placing the books and her notepad on the study table. She was studying for the engineering board exams, and passing the board would mean she would be able to follow one of her uncles to Qatar, an impossible place where water was more expensive than gasoline. They'd probably give everything for that well outside, she thought.

She didn't want to become an engineer, and she didn't really want to go to Qatar or anywhere, but the job paid a lot of money. When she was younger she thought she would become a scholar, a professor, unpacking theories, learning new languages, travelling to give presentations about her view of the world. In the end, it turned out all she ever really wanted was a house with a flat screen TV and a hot shower and central air and a good couch.

———

Often, she would wonder why she even tried so hard. Either she would be in a freak accident, or she would live until the ripe old age of ninety. Either she would be injured, or she would forget all of it, in the end, like her grandmother who died at eighty-eight with her memory jumbled up. Confused, unwanted, moved from one son's house to another. Whatever brightness her grandmother had, Julia was never able to witness, which was a tragedy in itself. Lucky number eighty-eight. *I still have sixty-eight years of lucidity left,* Julia thought, sitting at her desk with her structure formulas and her design methods. Sixty-eight years didn't feel like such a long time.

———

She was wrong about the rain. When it fell that night, it fell hard, hammering on the table and the chairs and the flowers, the wind whistling through the gaps in the windows and the doors, through the floorboards, the cold banisters. She tossed and turned in her sleep, hearing something moaning in pain, hearing a clear voice saying, *First a warm bath, then you will be left hanging here until your bones are dislocated.* In her dreams, she was sure the moans were coming from the covered well.

———

She woke up later that night to the sound of banging coming from the back of the house. Someone was knocking on the kitchen door. An urgent, insistent knock, like the knock of someone who was being pursued.

But the only person standing outside was a woman in a shirt and a pair of jeans, waiting with her hands folded in front of her chest, like an orator or an opera singer. Julia had never seen her before.

The woman was searching Julia's face for something, and when she didn't see it, she dropped her hands and her shoulders, and put on a worried expression. Julia noticed the flashlight sticking out of the pocket of the woman's jeans. "I'm so sorry to bother you," she said, "but I think a kitten of ours fell into your well? I've been hearing it for hours, but I'm not sure if it's real or just my imagination."

Oh, how terrible, Julia thought, but then she remembered the sounds from a few hours ago, the moans cutting through the rain. That wasn't a kitten.

"Can we," the woman said, pointing with her flashlight to the well under the table, "can we check? I'm sorry. I'm too scared to check on my own."

Julia would be terrified, but not at that moment. The terror would come later, much later, after she had returned the woman's smile, after she had said "Yes, of course," after she had walked through the garden, after they had pushed the table aside, after she had knelt by the well's weather-beaten plywood covering and pushed it off with the heels of her palms.

First there was the smell. Putrid, overwhelming, a smell that reminded her of hospitals and animal cages, of powerlessness and shame. It was the smell of feces, urine, vomit. The woman swung her flashlight's beam to the well and Julia absorbed the scene in bits and pieces: a tattered shirt, a stained piece of fabric fashioned like a hammock, a scalp covered in scabs, a hand reaching up toward the opening, toward her, toward light, and Julia screamed and scrambled across the ground, scraping the palms of her hands, hitting her forehead on the kitchen door. The woman's shadow fell across her like an eclipse. Julia ran deeper into the house.

———

"Should we go through this again, Julia?" the woman said. The woman's name was Sylvia, a name that floated out of the ether. Why does she know the woman's name? Julia, who had locked herself up in the bedroom, could hear herself huffing like a dog. She couldn't breathe. She crumpled to the floor and hugged her knees, covered her mouth with both hands to stop herself from screaming. She had never before felt terror like this, a terror that seized her insides and made her shiver as though she were pushed into a vat of ice.

"Julia," Sylvia said. The knob turned and Julia screamed.

"Julia," she said again. "You know what you saw."

There was a woman in the well, and the woman was wearing her face. She looked the way Julia would have looked if her teeth were kicked in, if her hair and fingernails were torn out, if she were dehydrated and starved and tortured for hours. The woman in the well was unrecognizable as Julia, but Julia recognized her with one glance.

"You go into the well and your new version that appears in this house goes through the same stages of fear and denial," Sylvia said on the other side of the door. "Over and over. You are the seventh version now. What does this tell us, Julia? That perfection does not require memory?"

Sylvia had a key. The door opened and Julia rushed at her, shoving her aside. Julia ran down the stairs and tripped on something—a chair leg, the edge of the carpet, her shoelaces. She fell hard. She sobbed with her face against the floor and couldn't get up.

"You have legs now," Sylvia said. "Use them and sit at the table with me."

Why was she doing what the woman told her? She should be running now. She should be attacking her. She should be—

"It will come to you," Sylvia said, disappearing into the kitchen.

She came back a few minutes later, carrying a tray. On it was a cheese sandwich, a bowl of cookies, and iced tea. Sylvia placed the tray in front of her.

"During your last hour in the well, you always start singing," Sylvia said. "It's a simple tune, and it's always the same tune, but it's in a language I don't recognize. Maybe one day you will be able to tell me what you're singing about."

"I don't understand," Julia said, crying. Wasn't she just studying a few hours ago, figuring out the logistics of living abroad, listening to the rain fall as she fell asleep?

"What did you notice in the sixth version?" Sylvia said. "Hm? What did you notice when you saw the Julia in the well?"

I am not a version, Julia thought but couldn't say. There is no Julia in the well because I am the only Julia.

Sylvia said, "What was she missing?"

Julia didn't know what Sylvia was talking about. Then she was reminded again of the smell that hit her when she uncovered the well, the emotions she associated with it. Shame. Powerlessness. Disgust. Why was she reminded of hospitals? Why did the caretaker stare at her feet, why that brilliant smile, that pride in his voice when he asked, *Did you have a nice walk?*

"She didn't have any legs," Julia said, and the world tilted slowly, like a leaf on a placid lake.

"It was late at night," Sylvia began, and continued to tell the story in the bored tone of someone who had been telling the same story over and over and over, "and it was dark and you were hurrying down the street from work and you didn't see the opening in the ground, the drain grate without the grate, and you fell and you injured your legs. The fall was only ten feet. You would have been able to shake that off, but there was debris at the bottom, sharp glass, rusty, rotten things, and you struck them, and you weren't found for hours." Sylvia sighed, shrugged. *Oh well.* "The doctors had to amputate from the knees down."

"No," Julia whispered to herself, touching her legs, but the world was still tilting to fit this new perspective, and the world was telling her, *Yes.*

"You wanted your suffering to mean something," Sylvia said. "It always means something in stories, doesn't it? Your own Catholic parents had faith that an individual's suffering can cleanse the world and rid the rest of us of further pain. There are people who refuse medical treatment because they believe suffering has a purpose. If your suffering could bring your legs back, if it could make you better, then the pain would be worth it. Right? That's what you told her, and she said she could do that, she could show you."

"Her?" Julia said.

"Or him," Sylvia said. "Or it. The one you found at the bottom of the drain, the one who held your hand after you got tired of screaming for help."

Julia felt fear like an electric shock.

"I don't remember any of this," she said.

"That's what all the other versions say," Sylvia said.

"I don't know who you are."

"But you know my name, right? I was there at the hospital, and you told me this story. I was there because my entire family died in a bus crash; what else was there left to believe? But I believed you." Sylvia glanced at the clock on the wall. "Hour before midnight. Sooner or later you're going to climb back into the well. I can't wait to meet your eighth version. You came back with both legs on the seventh day. Maybe on the eighth you will be calmer." She smiled as though this were a long-standing joke between them.

"I am not going in there," Julia said.

"I know," Sylvia said. She grabbed the cheese sandwich from her plate and took a bite. "You always say that, and yet before midnight you'll have lowered yourself in the hammock, begging me to cover the well."

"What happens in there?" Julia asked, at the same time parsing together a path out of this house, down the road, her legs taking her to the bus station and away.

"Suffering that has meaning," Sylvia said. She was quiet for a moment. "But you never tell me the specifics. Once, you told me there is someone waiting at the bottom of the well."

"I want to get out of here," Julia said, and found herself crying again.

"You always say that, but you never do," Sylvia said. "Look, I'm not stopping you. Get up and leave if you want."

Julia wanted to, but her legs felt leaden. Sylvia wore a triumphant smile. *See?* that smile said.

"Remember your grandmother telling your family that she didn't want to end up like her mother?" Sylvia said. "And her mother before her, and her mother before her. It runs in your family, that awful disease. She said she'd rather die than inflict that kind of burden on her children. Remember how that broke your heart? If only she were still alive. If only we could put her in the well."

Julia thought of her grandmother sitting at the table and touching her arm to say, "Who bought this? This food looks expensive." The food came from their kitchen and was cooked by her mother, but in the ruins of her grandmother's mind she believed she was in a restaurant, enjoying an expensive meal with a bunch of strangers who looked vaguely familiar. *Who bought this?* And Julia, who knew there was no need or time to reason or explain, said, "I did, Lola. I bought this for you."

There was no need or time to reason or explain.

"What version are you, Sylvia?" Julia asked, changing her tone, making her sound sweeter.

Sylvia wiped crumbs from the corners of her lips. It took a while for her to reply. She looked ashamed. And hungry. "I have never been in the well."

"But you wanted to go?"

There was no hesitation. "Of course."

Julia nodded. "Why don't you go this time, Sylvia?" she said. "I will wait for your new version. I'm sure she will need someone here to explain things to her."

Sylvia's eyes filled with tears. "You will do this for me?" she said.

———

Sylvia chattered on as they walked to the well. The midnight air was cold, and Julia could hear nothing but Sylvia's voice, as though everyone else in town had died. "I wonder, does your consciousness move from the old version to the new, like water, or does one, the superior one, just obliterate the other?"

"Aren't you afraid of the pain?" Julia asked. She remembered again the lacerations on the arms of the person in the well, the blood in her mouth.

"I've been through worse," Sylvia said. "Imagine, a driver who fell asleep at the wheel, just three seconds out of his many hours on the expressway, and he obliterates my entire family. Imagine that. Imagine the senselessness of that. At least in the well, my pain would amount to something."

The well was empty. A new hammock was strung up in the middle of it, white and pure. Beneath this white fabric was darkness that went on and on and on.

Sylvia took off her shoes. She sat on the edge of the mouth of the well, and with Julia's hands in hers, slowly lowered herself to place her bare feet on the fabric.

"Do you think I will also sing?" Sylvia asked, her face white as the moon inside the well. "Do you think you'll be able to understand the words?"

Before Julia could think of an answer, Sylvia glanced back and suddenly tightened her grip on Julia's hands. "Wait," she said. "Wait. No. Get me out of here. Get me out of here! *Get me out of here!*"

She pulled Sylvia up without a word. Sylvia's grip relaxed, and Julia opened her hands and let go.

Sylvia did not scream, or did not have the chance to. Julia waited for several minutes for the sound of water, for the sound of impact, but it did not come.

She replaced the cover and turned to run back into the house, to get her clothes, to gather her books, to leave this place. She looked up at the last minute and saw the curtain twitch behind her bedroom window. She threw herself at the back gate, for a horrible second thinking it was locked, but the gate yielded, and she burst out of the garden onto the dark road, running as fast and as far as her legs could take her.

SCREAMERS BY TOCHI ONYEBUCHI

Tochi Onyebuchi is the author of the YA novel *Beasts Made of Night* and the holder of multiple degrees. His short fiction appeared in *Asimov's*, *Omenana*, and elsewhere.

———

When Dad talked about the Screamers, I thought maybe he could've been a writer. We were different like that. I was never too good at metaphor myself.

———

I'd brought homework with me so I could get some done in the back seat of the cruiser while Dad answered the call. He was working Homicide at the time, and I could tell what kind of case it would be by how he came back into the car. If the case was going to be a quick clearance, Dad was all purpose, and it showed in his stride. If the case was going to be slow-going, so was he.

"Bad case, Dad?" I asked from the back of the cruiser one night.

He'd been in the driver's seat for a while, long enough that the body had been carted off to the morgue and the crowd had dispersed. He had pinched the bridge of his nose and had even undone his cufflinks and loosened his tie. He looked at me in the mirror and smirked. "It's all right," he said. "Just need a couple base hits is all." He talked like that sometimes, like he was America-born. He took their metaphors, their imagery. I figure he thought I liked it.

This was usually around the time Dad would pull out another notebook and, with a pencil, scribble something down. A line or two, sometimes an entire paragraph. He'd tuck it back into his breast pocket, and then he'd transform himself into the Super Detective he'd always been, his lapse in confidence all but forgotten.

———

With Dad taking me on occasional runs, it was only a matter of time before we ran into our first Screamer. There had been blood everywhere.

Body parts littered the alley floor like a bomb had gone off. In the flashing light from the cruisers, the fingers and pant legs shone blue and purple in their sanguine coat. Chunks of scalp hung from the fire escape, strands of silver clinging to the rails like spider webbing.

Nobody knew whether the whole thing should go on the board in the office as a homicide or if this had been some sort of terror job, but the absence of evidence left it in the no-man's land of accidental death.

Dad had come back into the cruiser with that going-into-overtime shuffle and stared ahead for a long while, and when I reached out from the back seat to touch his shoulder, he didn't move.

He hadn't once reached for the tiny notebook in his pocket.

———

Soon, the office board was entirely covered in the red ink of open cases. One by one, detectives would come in, shake their heads, and slump into their seats, marveling at the bad luck of a perfect crime committed with as comprehensive a lack of physical evidence as ever.

Afterwards, they'd retreat to a nearby Irish pub called McLarney's and compare notes. We all gathered in the back. Nigerians, mostly, with some Ghanaians and a few Senegalese detectives. I sometimes sat with Dad, with my ginger ale and his pint of Guinness, and watched him scribble in that notebook while the other detectives reminisced about old cases.

"He is practically a boy, nah. No hair on his chin even. And he comes in smiling like a—a—a Cheshire cat. He says he solved the case. It took him three weeks! Eh-heh, clap for yourself."

Someone else waves their hand dismissively. "If they are raised here, they think they deserve a prize for every mystery they solve."

"These children. Give them a gun and a badge, and suddenly, they are talking to you as if you're their age-mate."

Then a more conciliatory voice: "It is not easy o. Any proper police knows all you need is a jury of these, these just-blacks, to ruin a perfectly good case."

"Where is the lie?"

On and on they went, about the woes of training this new generation of immigrant police, about how often the just-blacks refused to cooperate and accept their policing, about how this land had inured them to common sense so that each generation of ancestry that could be traced to a plot in Georgia or North Carolina or Missouri was another stone in the mountain of their stupidity. But beneath it all was wonderment at why African-Americans made it so difficult for the Africans who had been brought in to police them.

"But these new things, these bombings in the projects with no witnesses—"

"That's not news, now."

"No motive."

"That's not news o."

"No nothing. Except a pile of mismatched limbs. I'm telling you, eh, it makes me want to scream."

Dad looked up at that, but only I had noticed. A moment later, he was scribbling again. I wouldn't find out till later that what had happened in that moment was a bit of serendipity, a two-step in what Dad liked to call the cosmic choreography of his existence.

Someone's phone chirruped, and the detectives were off again. Dad was a little slow getting up, but when I tried to follow, he said, "Go home." The way he said it was enough to keep any protest I had in my gut where it belonged.

———

The victim was identified by his teeth, and when the hits came back for a kid whose dad was a banker, the rest of the city seemed to want in on the investigation.

I didn't ride along with Dad as much anymore. Some college buddies and I would trawl the abandoned neighborhoods of foreclosed houses, and stare at them from hilltops with a case of Coors between us. Sometimes we would toss our empties and try to hit a few windows.

By then, more squatters had filled the vacant homes and occasionally I'd watch some of my dad's old partners make their rounds, rousting the kids who always shouted that they were protesting, though they never said what; that they had rights, though they never mentioned which. With their iPhones and their hoodies and their braided hair, they'd shout and cry until the whole block was quiet again.

I saw Dad roust a few, but he was never rough with them like his partners were. His heart didn't seem in it, and when I'd watch him get back into his car from the hill, I'd wait to see if he pulled out his notebook to scribble out some lines. But, nothing. Just the protestors in the back seat as his cruiser sped off, and I finished another Coors. Like he'd just tucked the neighborhood in and couldn't be bothered to see if we were all asleep or just pretending.

———

All the base hits in the world couldn't turn up a clearance in the case of the erupted banker's kid. The city threw the entire force at it, but the most closure the kid's divorced parents could hope for was that it had been an accidental death. A freebase session gone wrong.

The case forced a few retirements, and I hung back, against Dad's wishes, to watch some of those guys who'd given him company at the bar pack up their desks before their pension could join them. A couple of them went into private security, but I never heard from most of the departed. Even when the protests started up again, and tents lined the streets and sidewalks of those foreclosed neighborhoods and vagrancies went up by double digits, the department slimmed.

So maybe it was a sense of duty that made me take the cadet's exam. Or maybe it was my inability to see something so full get gutted and made irrelevant. Maybe it was the reverence in the voices of those detectives as they'd swap stories at the bar and talk about their profession like it was a religious calling, like you could actually see God, or something like Him, in the titanic folly that made up a single evening's work. Maybe it was because I'd just wanted Dad to tell me what he was writing all that time in that damn book of his.

She had silver hair and silver eyes to match. And I was coming for early relief when they brought her into the box. By the time I'd arrived, she'd already dropped names on perps involved in fourteen open cases. I watched from the other side of the one-way glass of the interrogation room as she closed a dozen more cases for us.

When Dele started in on the details, she filled it all in, describing each scene as though she'd been there herself. Some of the Number Twos on those investigations went scurrying back to their files, to match the little physical evidence they had to her statements and everyone came back green. The board went from blood-red to night-black in a single shift. Dele went on with her for hours, but when he finally asked about cause of death, she told him they were suicides. Each and every one of them. Including the banker's kid.

The whole place went still; detectives crowded around the partition holding their breath.

I'll never forget what she did next. She closed her eyes, almost like she was praying, and she opened her mouth. And the entire world went white.

When I woke up, the whole floor was in pieces, chunks of wall were missing, desks split in half, glass all over the floor like hail. My ears wouldn't stop ringing, and when I put my hand to my face, it came back bloody. Someone had the sense to call it in as a terrorist attack. My body felt like I'd been laid on some train tracks right before the 4:30 uptown came through, but I managed to sit up enough to see what remained of the interrogation room.

Blood had sprayed over the entire place, with no body part large enough to use for identification. Intestines hung in ropes from the overhead lamp and the metal table between Dele and the girl had crumpled in on itself like tin foil. In the uppermost corners of the chamber, silver hair splayed like webbing.

———

I saw Dad at the funerals, and then the memorials afterwards, and though he never reeked of Guinness or looked at me with the blurry-eyed semi-lucidity of the day drinker, I knew he was on the slide. It showed in his shuffle.

Routine, after that, meant showing up to support the grieving families of the slain officers, holding our own wake at McLarney's, singing a few songs from back home and knocking back shots in honor of our fallen comrades. We clung to that because there was nothing else to cling to, no explanation, no motive. At least, until the first silent protests started.

———

Lining the protest tents in the wasteland of foreclosed homes, they stood like columns of soldiers: just-blacks, men and women with their hair uniformly silver, duck tape over their mouths. We'd gotten so used to hearing them chant about police brutality and hoist their ensloganed placards and shout and rage against anything they could blame, but we'd never seen them silent before.

The first time I saw them, I'd been on the hillside with Detective Kolade and we'd had a case of Coors between us. When he saw the columns form, saggy-jean kids spilling out of the empty houses, an electric current passed through him. Before I knew what he was doing, he'd gone back to the cruiser for his nightstick and had marched down the hillside. I waited for the inevitable confrontation, for that one kid to break ranks and charge him, or to say something stupid, but there was only silence, then the accusatory thunk of nightstick cracking jaw. I don't know why I did nothing as he beat that poor kid, but I think a part of me saw my father in that moment, saw him grasping at answers to a thing, a type of killing that he could not explain, among a group of people who, though we looked so much alike, were as inscrutable as night. Kolade had no notebook, but he had a nightstick and who was I to stop him?

———

We locked up a few more silver-haired just-blacks after that first run-in, mostly from downtown protests gone awry, but when we brought them to the box, they lost all usefulness. Almost anything they took credit for was proven false a few minutes later. None of them had left behind an ensanguined crime scene. None of them even had natural silver hair. After a few hours of interrogation, they were quick to confess to that lie. They had dyed their hair in solidarity with whoever had committed these crimes.

But soon after the silent protests started up and home vacancies spread even further, the first envelope came in. Witnesses would later report a high-risk analyst at a securities firm had been sorting through his mail when he came across an envelope marked with his name and nothing else, no postmark, not even a stamp. He'd turned it over, then opened it, and in the next moment, his two halves had traveled in opposite directions the length of the trading floor. Witness reports vary on just what happened the moment he opened that envelope, whether the cry was one of anguish or rage, whether it was even he who had screamed or someone else who, knowing something was wrong, had emitted the cry. But everyone there agreed that there had been one. That it had been pained and laced with injustice, and that it had been like nothing they'd ever heard before.

———

Dad took a few more of those cases, but he was never Number One anymore. Most nights, when my shift ended, Mom would call and tell me that Dad still hadn't come home and I'd crawl his familiar haunts until I eventually found him wearing a groove into a barstool, head and shoulders hunched over his notebook, a pint of Guinness at his elbow.

I'd wait till he finished scribbling before I'd sidle onto the stool next to him and tell him how much Mom worried. But it always took me a few moments to work up the courage.

Dad looked more like a stage-four cancer patient than a veteran cop. His balding head had pits in it. His cheeks had hollowed out, and the joints of his fingers were knotted with arthritis. Scribble, scribble, drink. Scribble, scribble, drink.

"My son," Folasade the proprietress said, smiling with all the sadness in the world. She knew why I was here, but she'd still ask, "What are you drinking tonight?"

And I'd say, "I'm fine, Sade, but thanks." And she'd walk away and leave me and Dad alone.

"We're like priests," Dad said one time when I'd come to pick him up, "and this, all this, is our battlefield. And you have the angels on one side and the demons on the other side, and us taking care of what's in the middle. What is encased in all the glass and steel? That supernova that is getting dimmer and dimmer and dimmer until one soldier from either side accidentally kicks dirt over it and, pfft, the fire is out forever."

This was senility, and I recognized in myself the fury at my own powerlessness. People said that would happen. Dad was crumbling in front of me and every misspoken metaphor was another brick coming lose, another rusted beam creaking against the weight it supported, another moment before inevitable gravity caused the whole thing to collapse on itself.

———

The cancer we all knew was coming finally had Dad bedridden.

He refused treatment and contented himself with having his loved ones near for his final months.

In the room Mom and I set up for him, the lights were left dim, like he preferred. We'd filled it with his effects from the old house in his village back home: his writing desk, the standing lamp that looked like an upright tree branch, the hollowed-out calabash bowls I used as a helmet when I was a child.

In the beginning, when I took up my post at his bedside, I filled the air between us with news of his contemporaries, his "war buddies." Nneka was sitting pretty at a university security gig. Chidi retired to a place in Fort Worth, where his whiskey and his porch could keep him company. Babatunde finally patched things up with his wife and was seeing his kids again. Israel couldn't cure the policing itch, so a routine traffic stop gone wrong cured it for him.

Since the departmental reshuffle and the creation of a new unit specifically for Scream-related crimes, most of the veterans had been put out to pasture. It didn't take long for me to run out of news.

Dad seemed content enough with silence anyway.

"Strange," he said one night.

I must've been sleeping. Or halfway there.

"When I was a child, my mama was the woman in the village to whom others came to resolve disputes." Smiling, "Her reputation was unimpeachable. On one occasion, she was told something that someone else had said about her behind her back. She went to the offender's home to confront her, and the woman was nowhere to be found. Her husband was, however, and by the end, the poor man had begged your grandmother to understand that this was simply his poor wife's nature. She loved Sunday School, your grandmother, because that is how she learned to read. Your grandmother could only read words as they were written in the Bible. If they were arranged in any other order, or formed any sentence not written in Scripture, she lost her ability to read. When I told her I was coming to America to become a detective, she looked up from her Bible and the look on her face ..."

The cancer had broken down his American-ness, rendered him unrecognizable. He no longer spoke in colloquialisms, no longer talked or sighed or laughed like an American. And I wished I'd seen this part of him sooner.

"Was as if ..." His voice carried off, and we settled into our familiar silence. That was when I got the notion to ask about his notebook. Before I could get a word in, though, Dad said, "... as if ..." and this time, his voice was little more than a whisper. I felt as though I should have done something, adjusted his blankets, turned down the lighting, raised the heat a little, but I didn't want to interrupt whatever communion he was carrying on in that moment.

"As if ..."

The muscles in his face shifted. Light flared briefly in his eyes. His wrinkles smoothed and everything sort of loosened. I knew what had happened and part of me was happy that I'd been with him for it. But the smirk on his face angered me. It was like he'd finally figured out the perfect metaphor, seen in his mind's eye the perfect image to describe what he felt and decided in that final moment, as with that damned notebook, to keep it to himself.

I transferred out of Homicide soon after we buried him.

————

In the Scream unit, they'd discovered, after some very expensive failures, a way of corralling the weaponized envelopes. They weren't hard to notice. Their targets were obvious, and despite the infighting amongst the growing number of protestors, the message the envelopes were meant to send was quite clear. It was only a matter of time before law enforcement adapted.

The envelope disposal rooms were steel-reinforced and soundproofed and the suits they made us wear began as bulky encasements of plastic armor and were soon slimmed down so that we could fit our entire bodies in the upright chamber where the bravest of us took the things apart with our own hands.

They trained you for half a year before they let you open your first envelope. Meditation techniques. A slew of controlled exercises in disassociation. By the end, you could watch yourself from several angles at once with clinical distance. Tedium became a shield against the explosion sealed in the envelope, ennui a rampart.

That's what the Screams were. Entire souls encased in folded paper. Lived existences laced with every weaving of emotions so that when the encasement was opened, the entirety of someone else's anguish and joy and hope and fear and hatred assaulted the victim, resonated with the swirling emotions within them so that the matched frequency overrode the physical confines of flesh and bone and sinew and the human body came apart.

To battle such a thing, you had to give it nothing to resonate with. You had to still the tuning fork in your own body. And once you did that, a Scream could tear a metal desk in two, topple an entire skyscraper, level an apartment block, but it would leave you untouched.

————

Dad had been two years buried when I finally found the notebook.

It'd been nestled near the bottom of a cardboard box, the soggy bottom of which gave out when I tried to lift it. Mom's basement had flooded in the spring thaw and I'd come along to help her out.

The little thing had plopped into a small puddle, but when I took it out, none of the ink had smudged.

... like how a sunrise would taste if such a thing could be tasted. The scribble trailed off after that, and I flipped back to the beginning of the paragraph to find what looked like a description of Mom when she'd been younger. I skipped a few pages and found another line: *the smokestacks like minarets and the church spires like watchtowers all arrayed like some steel mill blue-collar kingdom where workers lived with the dignity of kings and the hope of paupers and where cops policed less like people and more like forces of nature, stalking the edges of paradise and eliminating anything that would disrupt the rhythm of peacefully-lived life.*

I sat on an upturned milk crate and turned to another page.

... less like the aftermath of a massacre and more like the alley had been built in reverse, like the architect used the very act of destruction to construct it, stacking broken bricks on top of each other and carving large pocks into the concrete to catch blood or whatever might leak there, metal staircases twisted like balloon animals on each side of the passageway expanded by the blast, the walls half-coated in blood-paint, the whole thing unfinished.

As I read, I found fewer and fewer complete sentences. Instead, the metaphors grew more wrought, extended over entire pages, mapped out like a cartographer's first draft, and Dad turned, in my mind, from some unknowable specter into that frontiersman I always imagined he was, an explorer skirting the edges of known experience, peering into the blackness, the unknown, and shining a light for someone else to follow.

The Screams grew new texture. Like marijuana laced with PCP, or a cocktail with an extra kiss of vodka layering the top. Some Screams managed to break through the defenses we erected in ourselves.

I remember the beads of sweat on Obiwu's forehead more than anything else. His fingers were deft, his movement smooth, and his eyelids didn't flutter like they used to. His poise was erect and he moved like he did during every other disposal, but the beads of sweat beneath his visor told me that his concentration had been bent and would soon be broken. The next instant, the disposal chamber had acquired a new coat of paint. The clean-bots went to work preparing the sturdy contraption for its next victim. For those of us with enough training, we could look at Obiwu's death with the clinical distance of a scientist marking a failed experiment. We were already recalibrating our ingredients. For those ready to crack, those whose hands had already begun to shake, whose distance between soul and body was too easily bridged, the chamber became less a place of work and more a coffin, a sarcophagus they would never be comfortable stepping into.

––––––

I started carrying Dad's notebook into the chamber with me. Slipped it into a little fold by my left hip, about where my holster used to go.

After my shift, I carried it home, and in the empty pages Dad didn't have the time or energy to fill, I'd describe my own crime scenes. I'd climb into the interior of each Scream. I'd traverse each river, crawl along every thread of every emotion braided together, and I would write down what they sounded like. One sounded like a chorus of angels that, for the duration of the blast, fancied themselves demons. Another sounded, at its apex, like a massive log the size of the Earth was being chopped inside my head, and when the wave passed, it sounded like how a sunset might sound if such a thing could be heard, a red and blue and purple and golden thing that slid along the underbellies of clouds before the entire world was engulfed in darkness.

I would return to some of Dad's earlier metaphors to buttress my own. And in those moments, I felt like I was right alongside him on the edge of the darkness, his sidekick, his Number Two, the both of us metabolizing the psychological trauma of the just-blacks into a shining light for others to follow.

––––––

I was sent in to handle the third envelope we'd collected that day and in the chamber, my hands on the envelope, ready to open it, my heart quickened. Not with fear or worry, but with excitement. What would

I write in that notebook when I finished? How many generations of racialized violence would this Scream sound like? How many forced prison sterilizations would fuel this Scream's tenor? What specific brand of injustice, colored by equal measures loss and never-having-had, would tint the timbre of what awaited me in this envelope?

A sweat-drop plopped against the inside of my plastic visor.

My fingers froze, and I could hear fear stampeding towards me in the distance. I thought of Obiwu, remembered the look of frozen calm on his face just before the envelope in his hands had detonated. But this—this was different. This was possibility sealed tightly between my fingers.

The part of me governed by my training told me to put down the envelope, step out of the chamber and hand this one off to another officer. But I couldn't. What tapestry of experiences and feelings could I walk into by opening this one? What if this one held that perfect combination of rage and joy, that perfect amalgam of loss and gain?

I heard voices through the muffle of the chamber's walls, then an alarm sound as personnel began to evacuate. And I don't know why they did it, or why they thought I would do what I would do.

Because I was the only one in that room who had in his mind's eye the image of my father smirking at the ceiling of his study. Like he'd finally answered a lifelong riddle, like he had solved the mystery of the just-blacks, had understood them, and could at last quiet the rumbling in his own heart.

THE BOIS BY R.S.A. GARCIA

R.S.A. Garcia's debut novel was *Lex Talionis*. She lives in Trinidad and Tobago, where she is currently working on a sequel and a new high fantasy novel inspired by Caribbean and African folklore.

———

I rest Mags down on the lavender grass and kneel beside she. My hands cover with blood, dark and hot. She breathing with a whistle, chest rising and falling in fits. When her lips part, I see teeth that stain red. A fist squeeze my heart and I run my wired hand over she cold cheeks. I avoid the little clump of plants lying next to her arm; try not to see the pulsing fluorescent trails that make a sick light under she skin from the tips of she fingers to she elbow. The lavender grass almost shadowed in the glow. I can feel the azure tendrils of the trees above me waving like extended fingers.

"Girl, why you do that? Why?"

I don't expect she to speak, but she surprise me with a whisper. I lean down to hear.

"... wasn't ... wasn't suppose to be like this."

———

"What wasn't?" I ask. Mags sit on the barstool next to me, big smile on she face, black hair held back by the rag tied 'round she forehead.

She dark brown eyes too pretty and I hide the flutter in my stomach behind a sip of my beer.

"We first date." She motion to Chester behind the bar and a mug appear in front she like magic. She hold it with long, slender fingers; her skin light-brown and prettier than mine.

"You smoke or what? This ain't no date." My wired hand steady but my left side tremors as she pulls her stool nearer, forcing me to look at her.

"No, is not," she agree softly. "Next time, we go be more private."

For the first time in my life, I don't know what to say. I am Tantie. I know the Law and I know the History. I don't know this. The accident take my hair, so I bald. Is only synthskin cover my wired parts. I'm a good few years older than Mags, too. Men don't chase me, far less girls.

"Mags, be serious. I not for you. Besides, your father go kill you."

She smile slow like molasses from a bottle. "He could go to hell." She pause. "I'm grown. I know what I want."

Panic rise in me like the tide. I stand up so fast, the stool slam into the wooden floor. Chester glance up, frowning. Mags continue to smile, she gaze taking in all of me, resting finally on the gun at my hip. I can't speak so I just walk away, heart thumping and skin fevered.

———

I walk till I reach the only place they come near me at all. Trees stand around a purple clearing, reaching scaly blue tendrils toward the pale sky. Their shade don't hide the thing standing in the centre of the patch. It must have heard the commotion. Terror sweep over me, like the day I lose my arm and face, but I think of Mags lying alone in the forest behind me, dying, and I fall to my knees and bend my forehead to the ground.

"Good day to you, Papa Bois."

It don't speak. The Bois don't have language. But impressions and emotions push against my mind and the metallic taste of them fill my mouth. It's angry, disgusted, but curious too. I grab hold of that feeling like a life-line.

"We didn't intend disrespect, Papa. She didn't know you was here. I never tell nobody. She didn't know the forest is yours."

That every piece of it is separate and the Bois, at the same time. That she can't harvest plants because when she hurt one part, she hurt all. I only hear a rustle as it moves; the thick grass muffle the sound. It over me now, but I don't look up. Somehow, I know Papa Bois would take that as disrespect. Its beard touches my shoulder, slippery vines cold like Mags skin. It still mad, but it ask the question.

"Help," I say, tears welling without warning. "Please. She innocent and good and she go die."

It's dismissive; all things die.

"If she die, is my fault. I can't take that."

It pause, considering.

"Please," I whisper.

Long seconds go by. I feel every one as blood dripping from Mags' mouth.

My emotions amaze and confuse it. But it have new understanding. Beneath its resolve, cruelty prick at me. It want something.

"A sacrifice?" I confused. But it determined—it want something I can't afford to lose. Something I value. My heart thumping, but I don't hesitate.

I look up.

———

Mags smile down at me. "I tell you I soon come."

My heart skip a beat. Is months now Mags coming to my hut near the forest. I try to discourage her, but she wear me down like water on stone. She sits down beside me as I calibrate my gun on the bench outside my home. It's quiet here with nothing but the blue trees of the Bois forest in front us. The wind too light to move the tocsin hanging above my head. Not that it need to ring. It quiet for weeks now, with no trouble in the colony.

She nod toward the forest. "What you does see in there so? You always staring at it."

I shrug, looking up at the waving branches to avoid she face. "It pretty," I lie. "Peaceful. Is just me and the forest. Anybody come here either looking to leave, or to get me to leave. The forest just let me be."

It accept me because I don't belong, I think, but don't say. I keep my secret from Mags because no one can know. It too dangerous still. The colony young and foolish and the forest can't be fucked with. But to tell people "no" is to tell people "go."

I glance at the deepening indigo twilight of the trees to make sure nothing watching us together. So is a shock when she take the gun from me and fold my wired fingers into hers.

I am an Outcast. A freak. Everybody always avoid me. Nobody ever touch my synthskin so before. It tingle and jump and I try to pull back, but she lips cover mine and just like that, I lost.

When the sun go down, it was a long time before I light my lamp. But maybe something see. Maybe something mark we. This planet cruel—hard and dry with a sea that eat flesh.

I should have guess the forest would devour we, sooner or later.

———

The Bois face not human. It have no features I could name. Just twisting fronds. They fold and turn and bend over each other. Thousands and thousands of them. Some thin as threads, some thick as fingers. A few trail toward the seething mass of the lower body, which is just a column of vibrating tentacles.

It should be disturbing, but it not, and that's because of the colours. Shifting and changing all the time, colours run through the tentacles and tissues, blending and tumbling into each other like waves in the ocean. Is a terrible, beautiful sight.

I could only see it out of my wired eye.

Is the only reason people don't know 'bout the Bois. They blind to them. Everyone just know to avoid the forest. Sometimes, is as if they could sense them. It make everybody uncomfortable to come by my house on Law matters. They always grumble about why I live so far outside the colony.

But since I first catch a glimpse of them as a child, I drawn to the Bois. I know better than to approach them or try to talk to them. But I see them—and they know it. Is like a truce for a war that never happen. I stay out they way and they let me see them as they flit through the trees. Keep me company where no one else willing to come.

Until Mags.

Poor, sweet Mags, who don't 'fraid nothing and decide to go exploring today, despite the fact that every fool in Diego know the forest is no place to go and it have nothing in it but darkness and bad juju.

I don't know how I know what happen or where she was. I just know I wake up from a deep sleep, she voice in my ears, and the bed cold on she side. I never dress so fast. I never run so quick. Every human part of me was trembling with panic.

The wired part was cold and calm as ever.

When I find her, she have some fading orange growths next to her. The forest version of flowers. Only they not pretty harmless things. I can see the twisting trail of poison running through the veins of she arm, a flame of orange under she cappuccino skin. The wired part of me jolt like I get an electric shock, because I know what she was trying to do and I know why and is my fault.

I never tell nobody my birthday before.

I also never tell nobody what I see the Bois do. How sometimes a tree would be turning dark, like a bruise, bending its head to the ground, weary with life. And then one special Bois would come. Bigger than the others. Brighter. It would pass it rainbow tentacles over the tree—caress it for hours—and days later, the tree standing tall again. Pale blue and full of life.

Mags need life now. This creature I call Papa Bois, after the protector of the forest Tantie Pearl tell me about as a child—it could help. It could save Mags like it save the trees.

If it want to.

If the sacrifice big enough, and given willingly.

So I don't flinch as it bend over me, tentacles sliding down my shoulders like ice water. I look straight into the rainbow face as cold amusement scorch my mind.

Hurry, I think, blood beating in my ears.

And it does. Papa Bois beard whip toward my face and pluck both my eyes out of my skull before the scream could swell my throat.

———

Weeks later I sit on the bench outside my home and listen to the wind in the trees. I alone and these days, only Lucretia from the clinic does check me, to see if I healing okay. She don't make no talk really. Just check the bandages and help me bathe and so on. Today, before she leave, she tell me the doctor go come and take off the bandages tomorrow. Is the only good news in a long time.

Everybody avoid me because I kill Mags. They don't know how, but they know she dead because of me. It don't matter that the flowers poison her; what kill she was the stupid idea to go in the forest in the first place. Despite the fact that it have nothing in there. Despite the fact that the first generation off the ship tell stories about how when the *Diego Martin* crash-landed, the Captain himself went in there with some of the crew, and nobody ever come back.

I bewitch she. I make she throw away good sense. I take her in the forest then bring she body out. Blind and bleeding, I ring the tocsin for help, and I wouldn't say what happen to we. You don't see I guilty?

I hear from Lucretia when they tell Mags' father, he lock himself in he house and drink. That he still drinking.

I think that good though. A drunk man in a house can't make no trouble. And the less trouble the better because I can't carry out the Law for a while. Not until my new eyes ready.

It go be hard. I treasured my one human eye. I treasure all the normal parts. I see things different, but that was good for a Tantie.

Papa Bois take that from me. He take the sunsets, and the emotions on people face. The tears I cry for Mags. He leave calibrations and scrolling menus. X-ray and night vision. A wired eye is a complex thing—accurate and full of features, like a flight deck on a starship. But it can't see humanity. It can't see ordinary.

Tonight, I sit on my bench and I sense them. Hear the whisper of emotions in my head. The Bois here, watching—waiting. They curious. Surprised. Something new happen.

A solitary emotion detach itself from the Bois and drift toward me, a tendril on the wind. It settles on me, a loose thread around my thoughts and heart just before something touch me. Chilly threads slide under and between my fingers, but warmth explodes inside me— I can almost taste secret kisses and feel tight arms around me.

Papa Bois keep he promise. It was too late for Mags' body. But she energy—she soul—it was still there. And Papa take it, along with my sacrifice.

The Bois don't die, you see. They is energy and energy don't really end. It does just change form. And that change take a long time. Almost as long as a wired woman like me have to live.

I will never kiss Mags on she soft lips again. But I will never lose her either. I have the feel of tendrils between my fingers and the presence of a spirit that nothing like the alien Bois to keep me company in my home at the forest's edge.

I can't cry anymore, so I smile instead and tilt my face into the evening breeze. I let the fronds move against my hand while a new world flood my mind with colours and impressions and emotions I never dream 'bout.

Tomorrow my bandages come off.

Tomorrow, I will see.

UGO BY GIOVANNI DE FEO

Giovanni De Feo is the author of two novels in Italian and several stories in English published in *Conjunctions, Lightspeed,* and elsewhere. He was born in Rome, lives in Siena, and teaches Italian literature.

———

That's how Cynthia and Ugo met.

The Easter egg hunt had just started when little Cynthia noticed a dark, short-haired nine-year-old boy, all alone, sitting by the church steps. Her first impression of him was his quietness, and the way he stared at her. When she told him (well, shouted) that it was impolite to stare at strangers, and why wasn't he running like all others?—the dark-haired boy walked quietly over and told her that they didn't need to hurry, for the grand prize, three enormous chocolate eggs, was located right under the picnic table that was set up for lunch.

And as for the staring, she was no stranger to him.

"No? What is my name then?"

"Your name is Cinzia[1], and we will marry ten years and one month from today, in this very church, on an April's day."

———

Of course after that she was too scared to want to see him ever again, especially since the three chocolate eggs *were* found under the table. Then summer came. Not many families in Caversham West could afford to go to the seaside. So old Mr. Brown—the owner of the White Trout—organized badminton matches at the church on Sundays. It was mostly an excuse to be outdoors, as none of us were big enthusiasts. But we did have a lot of time on our own. Especially Ugo. He was almost always alone and off to the side, "just watching."

Every time Cynthia saw him, she missed the ball. Her blunders sent waves of mirth through the opposing team. This went on for quite a while until—ears red—she marched up to Ugo and asked him to leave.

Suddenly his cool was gone like a blanket snatched by the wind. Behind it, he looked red-faced, raw and trembling. It was painful to watch. He left without a word. But his reaction had so impressed her that, after the match, she went to look for him.

She found him sitting on the top of a wall like a child Humpty Dumpty, looking every bit as fragile. Years later, Cynthia had only a vague recollection of what they talked about that day, probably cartoons they both liked. He told her he had a bike that could go faster than the wind. She, in turn, told him about ice skating, her passion; her mother said she would become a star, one day. At that, Ugo glanced at her sideways, as if he wanted to say something but couldn't. When she asked him why he got so upset when she asked him to leave, Ugo smiled. He couldn't figure out how, in just an hour's time, they would end up here, considering what would happen next.

Cynthia frowned. What would happen next?

"This," he said, and kissed her on the mouth.

It was an adult kiss, with lips and tongue and teeth, one so shocking, so unexpected for a nine-year-old that Cynthia froze on the spot. When it was finished, he quietly hugged her. They stayed like this for so long that Cynthia felt her feet growing numb. His body was thin, and yet it was so warm she felt scorched down to her bones.

"Now we are together," he said.

———

It turned out the whole kissing business had been a Leap.

That's why he had behaved with such certainty: he had to play his part to the end. This was the really unsettling bit of Leaping. For when he came to the moment in time he had experienced beforehand, he still felt—in his mind—the presence of his younger self, watching.

Later on, Ugo developed a theory about it. He said that, in reality, everybody Leaps all the time. The proof? Déjà vu. The feeling of having already experienced what is in fact happening for the first time was for him the ultimate, definitive evidence of Leaping. The only difference between Ugo and everyone else was that he remembered, while we don't. Why? Because our brains are incapable of retaining the memory of the future. But then how was he able to? He didn't know. Bit by bit, Cinzia came to the conclusion that his mind could hold the future because deep down he was so desperate to escape the present.

Ugo moved to Cinzia's neighbourhood when he was eight. His parents had just divorced, after the failure of Ugo's father's sports career (he was a basketball pro). His mother was an Italian meteorologist who held a PhD from Reading University but didn't have a job in her field. She got by translating cookbooks, which I always found quite amusing since she couldn't fry an egg to save her life. She came from a large family from a town near Naples, and spoke with a strong Italian accent Ugo had somehow inherited, though to a lesser extent.

By the time his family moved, two years had passed since his first Leap at the age of six. The first time Ugo skipped ahead in time happened in a parking lot, right after his father hit him for losing a soccer match. Since then, Ugo had Leaped twenty-three times. Most Leaps were short, lasting a couple of minutes. But three had been quite long, and one huge. Ugo called those bigger spells "vacations" (I will tell you everything about them later). They lasted instants in "base-time," but weeks or even months in his mind. Not only that, they put a mark on him, a feeling of otherness that never left him entirely.

There was something in Ugo that was always out of place. Sometimes people didn't react to his presence, as if he weren't there at all. Even at his best, he was always out of sync, a creature caught between two worlds. Sometimes he struggled to talk like a child. School came easily to him, especially math. What was really difficult for him was social interaction. He could only warm up to people he had "seen" in his future, of whom there were very few. With the others, he behaved as if they were ghosts. Which in a way, for him, they were.

With time, Cinzia experienced both sides of Ugo's Leaps. She was there when his mind *fugued,* and she was there when he was possessed by the younger version of himself. With the latter, usually, there was a hesitation she had learned to recognize. The worst, though, was when he came back from his longer explorations. These were his "vacations." In these cases, he had got stuck in his future-self. Until something triggered a memory of the exact time period when his Leap started. Right at that very moment, he came back. Violently.

Before their marriage, Cinzia had experienced only two of these episodes. One, in middle school, was really nasty. They were at the Berkshire Spring Fair, bargaining for new ice-skate blades when Ugo's eyes rolled back and he collapsed. She caught him easily, thin as he was. He came around quickly; cold and rigid at first, then all of a sudden warm again, hugging her so tight it hurt.

"Oh my God, you are still here," he said, "you are still you."

He never explained what he meant, or his out-of-character display of public affection. For they had agreed since the first kiss to hide their relationship. Adults don't believe in the loves of children. They would show their mutual affection later on, so that their parents could gradually adjust to the idea of their early marriage.

———

For months after that episode Ugo acted more strangely than ever. He snapped easily, at home as well as school, at other students and even at teachers. Only Cinzia understood what was really the matter. He was resentful of being treated like a child again.

"It's like all of a sudden you've become a baby. To everyone, you look normal because they think this is how you should look. So they put you with the other babies. And you should feel all right because they *do* look like you. Only they really are babies, and you're not. So you have to pretend. You learn to pretend so well that you forget what it was like, to be free, not having to ask permission just to exist. And when you have finally forgotten, then you Leap again."

"Is that what we look like to you? Little babies?" said Cinzia.

"There are some," he said after a while, "who are always them-selves, no matter where in time they are. It's like people are trees. As they grow, they start to lose their shape, and become so different from what they once were that if you saw them, you wouldn't recognize them. I am not talking about the way they look, it's something deeper than that. The way they talk to dogs, the way they laugh, the way they look at the sky, the way they shut their eyes against a sudden wind. These secret ways show their inner shape. Most people lose it almost entirely, but some don't. It's not like they stay the same, they do change, they evolve, but because they've kept their shape, they always grow in the same direction, skyward. That's how you recognize them: Their branches are the tallest."

"And me—?"

"You are the tallest and brightest I have ever seen."

On the last day of middle school, while we were celebrating with a furious battle of water-balloons, one of our classmates, a boy called Norwitz, darted out of the parking lot and was hit by a lorry.

While we waited for the ambulance, we sat in shock on the curb. The teachers did their best to calm us. Many of my classmates were crying, boys and girls alike. It was then that Cinzia saw Ugo. There was a funny expression on his face, something she had seen before.

"You're Leaping, aren't you? Right now."

Ugo didn't say a word but his eyes looked frantic, trapped.

"So you knew this would happen, all along. Why didn't you try to stop it?"

"I-it doesn't work like that," he said, slurring his words.

She wondered who was talking, the older or the younger Ugo?

"No? How does it work then?"

"What happened, happened. And I can't speak of it, or ..."

"Or?"

"... if I speak *to* change it, I'll come undone. I know, it's nothing I can prove to you, but I know it's true. I will cease to be."

"Okay, let's say I believe you. Then tell me: Why is your life more precious than Norwitz's?"

"I never said it was."

"You didn't, but you think so. Because you are oh-so-special, and we are just babies. You never even tell me what you see. You say we are going to be married, but I don't know how many children we'll have, what kind of woman I'll be, what kind of man *you'll* be. You see how unfair all this is?"

"Of course it's unfair," he said, "more so since you don't know what this knowledge would do to you, while I do."

"Then tell me, will I keep on ice skating? Will I? Now listen: Why would I even bother to work my butt off every day, six hours a day, if I knew that ten years from now my skating won't matter? Why?"

He said nothing, but she could feel the anguish in his eyes, the impotence of his silence. She turned away from him.

"Ugo, I'll make it simple," she said, "we won't ever marry for the very simple fact that I'm breaking it off now, and I won't change my mind, ever. So you see, your time-jumping was good for nothing."

"It is *always* good for nothing," he said, and his voice was so full of despair that she was almost pleased. But then she realized. The frightened look belonged to the younger Ugo, watching. But the one talking, this one knew. In fact, he had always known they would break up on the last day of middle school. She turned and broke into a run.

They would not speak to each other again for three years.

———

High school came in like a storm. More and more she felt she understood what it felt like to be trapped among babies. Only in her case the babies were boys, while the Tall Ones were girls. And they didn't look like children anymore either: they branched out under the boys' eyes, taller, fuller, their shapes changing, shifting, blooming.

Hormones came, and so did her first blood. Her father chortled his amusement at lunch when they told him, and her little brother moved into her small room and she took her big sister's, who moved out to Christchurch. She remembered the pains of trigonometry, her discovery of the Romantics (oh Byron! and Shelley!), Laura expelled for smoking hash, the first time she really *felt* her breasts. She had her own group of friends outside school, mostly girls who figure skated. The competition was terrifying, but she kept on winning. She had something to prove, and not just to herself. Ugo had never come to see her skate when they were together. Now he didn't miss a single practice. He would sit here with his red cap and stare. But now, under his gaze, she didn't trip. She was tall, muscular, strong; her clumsiness had melted away, while he still looked so fragile, almost brittle.

She had lots of boys, of course. The first high-school kisses were such a disappointment. She became notorious as "the tiger." Well, if they couldn't kiss, at least she could bite them back. After all, Cynthia had been French-kissing since she was nine. Those bubble-gum smooches tasted like water to someone accustomed to spirits. She felt the same insipidness in their tentative touches, in their "grown-up" talks. They were the opposite of Ugo, pretending to be adults when they were really just children. At times she wondered why she bothered. But she knew why. Because, if she stopped, she would go back to him.

Patryck was in Year Twelve and was different from anyone she had dated. He didn't pretend to be older; he was just himself, a boy with a witty talent for language and a weird sense of humour. All the class talked of how he had once stood on a table in the canteen and recited in full a poem he had written himself. Cynthia loved him for that, especially because the last lines were about her.

Together they went to Oxford for picnics, to Jericho, by the river barges, her arms all white with mosquito cream, as he stood up and read poems to the swaying willows. His kisses were different from Ugo's: tender, soft. In spite of his Celtic brooding, there was no anxiety about him. In this regard he was quite the opposite of her time-traveller, edgy on the outside and quiet within.

In her last year, Cynthia decided she wouldn't continue to Uni. She wanted to become an athlete, not a scholar. Of course her parents didn't agree. Her dad was a German teacher, her mum worked in university administration. They said she needed to "keep her options open," an expression she despised. Patryck, though, was very supportive. He said that, for example, in poetry only losers get PhDs. Like those who added "PhD graduate" on the back covers of their books, as if it mattered. He was all riot and turmoil, her sweet poet.

On the day of the selection for the European Figure Skating, Patryck didn't show up. It was a very important competition, and for the first time, she failed. She was seventeen, young for many other disciplines, but almost too old to reach peak performance in ice skating. The horrible part was that nothing had gone wrong; there were simply too many others who were better. When she left the rink, she was trembling all over. Why wasn't Patryck there? She kept looking for him until she saw Ugo, by the exit. They hadn't seen each other for over a year. The clumsy adolescent was gone, replaced by a tall, dark-haired stranger. It was like his body had finally caught up with his eyes.

"I'm so sorry," he said.

Was he sorry for her failure or apologizing for his behaviour? Both, maybe. But there was a third meaning that she would only understand later. She found out through friends they had in common. On that very day, Patryck had sat the tests for prep school and passed. He was going to Uni after all. When Patryck finally showed up at her house to apologize, with a bouquet of flowers and a poem on his lips— Cynthia's little brother was laughing himself to death—she opened her window and threw a bucket of cold water on him. He sputtered and cursed and then left, his Celtic pride wounded, never to be seen again.

Had Ugo known about all this? Probably.

That night, she phoned him. They stayed up until five o'clock in the morning, Cinzia (who was not Cynthia any more) whispering into the receiver under the bed sheet, pretending he was there with her.

"Do you want me to come over now?" he asked.

"No. First I want to want you so much it hurts. And anyway, you already know you won't come tonight, don't you?"

"I don't know everything. Not always."

"What about this: will we make love soon?"

His silence was an answer.

"Good. So you know it won't be my first time."

She could feel his silent laughter pressing on the receiver.

"Whatever you say," he finally responded.

"God, you are impossible! Of course you know! How can you live like that?"

"I don't live: I watch. That's why it's so important you don't become like me. Do you understand now?"

"So you won't tell me anything, ever."

A long, slow sigh.

"I've thought it over. I can, but it can only be really small things. Trivial details, things that don't matter."

"So you still won't tell me if I'll succeed as an ice skater."

"No."

"Why? I could dedicate my life to something else. Maybe my parents are right, I should get a degree, I could do the right thing."

"Of course not. What would happen is that you'd watch yourself as you do the wrong thing, trapped in that choice anyway."

"But how could you possibly know for sure?"

"Because that's *exactly* what I have done."

His voice cracked, she could hear the splinters in his throat.

"I knew ... I knew I would lose you for three years if I replied the way I did that day outside school ... and yet I had no choice, I had to. Do you understand what that felt like? Three years Cinzia and I—"

"Oh!"

"—what's so funny?"

"I almost forgot. The way you say my name. Say it again."

"Cinzia."

"So nice. I like the soft 'ch' sound. You know it's three years."

"Since I've said it?"

"No, till we marry. That will take everyone by surprise, won't it? We'd better start working on it, don't you think?"

———

There had always been two of her, Cynthia and Cinzia.

The former was how she would have been if she hadn't she met Ugo. In the months following that phone call, she realized that being Cynthia had been only a "vacation," like one of his, only to a parallel universe where Ugo's presence was unaccounted for. Which, of course, was impossible. Cynthia and Cinzia were two very separate identities. Still, they were part of a unity, a unity that stretched over time. Cynthia had not known how her life could turn out. But Cinzia *knew* they would marry. And knowing made all the difference.

"Will we have children?" she asked him.

"Yes."

"How many? Boys or girls?"

A begrudging silence.

"Okay, will we stay in Reading or move out of Berkshire?"

"Both."

"I knew it! I knew you were going to say that!"

In time, she learned a good deal about the small things. They would have a dog, a German shepherd named Jericho. Their first house would have a huge hawthorn bush that would catch fire at their first barbecue. She would buy a second-hand Vespa from the Sixties that she would paint pink (Cinzia was too masculine to be afraid of pink).

Bit by bit, all these things came to pass. Cinzia wondered: did they choose the flat with the hawthorn bush because he had told her about it or because it was meant to be? Did she buy an Italian scooter to fulfill his prophecy? Did any of it matter at all?

High school ended on a rainy June day that left them soaked and kissing fiercely on her porch. They had both decided to get jobs, temporary job manager, him and council clerk, her. That was earlier than almost everyone they knew, but that independence went with the early marriage they had always foreseen for themselves. Sometimes her parents complained; they called her new apartment "her room," as if she were still the reclusive teenager they knew before. Yes, her daily routine was complicated by ice skating, and she always came home very late, knackered, incapable of speech but for some low grunts. But the truth was, she loved her adult life, even her strife; it was her own.

Ugo took care of her tenderly, taking her clothes off, carrying her to the steaming bathtub. On Sundays, they stayed in bed until noon, eating sweets and letting the sunlight slowly fill their bedroom.

At the end of their first year of living together, they announced their marriage. Their parents were still surprised, but in the end, they didn't resist, not as much as she had thought. Ugo's mother, in fact, was more than happy to have a daughter-in-law. She hadn't remarried and—coming from a big family—felt the need to connect with an extended family. As for Cinzia's family, they had always liked Ugo. Her father especially was intrigued by the smart boy's mind. Why didn't he apply for computer science at Oxbridge? Yet when he was confronted with such questions, Ugo flashed his sphinx-like smile, and quietly said:

"It was not meant to be."

———

They married in the church where they had met ten years and one month earlier. Later, Cinzia would remember a day full of light, even if all her friends told her that it had rained in fact. She didn't care. That day there was enough light for all the rainy days to come.

———

They struggled with money, but most of all Cinzia battled with the constant stress of her sport. She had come to resent it so much that she sometimes talked of quitting. He would shake his head and tell her that skating was her life, she would feel empty without it.

"So you know it's going to be part of my future."

"I know it's part of your present," he said, stroking Jericho.

"And of my future," she said, frowning at the dog's antics.

"We've been over this countless times. I won't tell you, sorry."

"Okay, then I quit."

"No you won't."

"Why? It's my choice! You can't decide for me."

"Do you know how rare it is to have your gift? I've seen all the little girls watching you skate. You inspire them."

He was always right, as if he had seen how it would end. And actually, he had.

———

Things started to change soon after that. In six months, Cinzia won three European skating competitions. The money was sufficient to pay for her training, so she quit her temp job. An important skater, Davor Timuresku, invited her to train at his rink. Cinzia commuted to London every day, taking the seven o'clock train. It was still dark when Ugo helped her pack her cucumber sandwiches, Jericho licking his hands. When they kissed at the train track, she felt like one of those war-spouses saying goodbye to her husband.

There was some tension, too, of course. Her parents said she was stressing out too much, that she slept way too little. Ugo, too. Some-times his support seemed less enthusiastic, like something that was expected of him, something he had to do. In those moments she had a hard time fighting back her irritation. Was Ugo behaving like that because he knew she would fail? Or was he resentful of her success?

Finally, the big selection to enter the new Winter Games came. The International Skating Union would choose a team of six female figure skaters to represent the UK in Turin at the Olympics. Her dreams had never been so close, never so terrifying.

Sometimes she stayed up at night, unable to sleep, watching Ugo's white body afloat in the deep waters of a dream. Knowing that her husband *knew,* that inside he was preparing either to celebrate or to console her, was unbearable. At times she wanted to rip his dreams open and look inside them, to see the colour of their blood.

———

The day of the ISU selection, Cinzia looked at Ugo like the citizens of Delphi must have looked at their Oracle just before a battle. The way he dressed, the way he spoke, the way he moved, were all harbingers of her success. It's not like she didn't understand or appreciate his efforts. But he knew. He knew whether her passion would carry her far or if she would just stay behind. The selection started. She performed a combination of loop jumps and a cherry flip, scoring very high on the Grade of Execution Table. When the applause started she was beaming, her parents in the stands in tears. She looked at Ugo, but his smile was that of a sphinx, a mirthful bow to eternity.

In spite of this, Cinzia was relaxed. The second contest was a series of axel jumps, with two extra rotations, something she excelled in. She started well, storming her opponents with her flawless tempo. Yet as she landed on her last axel, she suddenly lost her balance and fell. A deep sigh from the crowd. She grimaced. Not only had she lost vital points, she felt her ankle swelling up.

She started to cry. Not out of pain but out of fear. In the infirmary, Timuresku was implacable. If she continued, she could damage her ankle. Permanently. It was her choice, her risk. She looked up in despair, only to find Ugo at her side, staring at her.

"I'm so very sorry," he said, "I really am."

So that was it. She quietly asked Timerusku and the nurse to leave. Her coach gave her a sharp look and walked out. As soon as the door closed, she let it out. It wasn't a scream but rage liquefied, turning to sound just outside her mouth. Ugo jerked back, or rather, the small kid in him did. After that she spoke in a low, coarse voice.

"Are you happy now? I know you are. It's all come to pass, finally. Finally we can go back to our little lives, have our children, grow our vegetables in the backyard. I see it now, I see it in your eyes. This was the turning point, wasn't it? The moment when I almost escaped your small-town dreams. You were right: in the end, we have no choice. But if this is my last act of free will, then I will make full use of it by spitting on your small-town happiness. For, apart from your Leaps, you are a mediocre human being, Ugo Forster. There is *nothing* in you but a wide-eyed spectator, ready to judge other people's talents, incapable of having any of your own."

Even before she finished, Ugo's features were seized by such a violent anguish that it seemed his face was coming undone. He had the same raw nakedness she had first seen on the badminton field, only on an adult it looked obscene. His voice was also different, not just slurred but child-like. When he made an effort to speak it was as if every word was a shard of glass, it sent tiny shivers all through his face.

"I-it's not like you said," he croaked, "it is far worse. For you are right, when you say I have no talent but my time Leaps. But you are also wrong in that regard, because—in fact—I don't even have that."

"What do you mean," I said, slowly standing up.

"I knew your name that day because I asked the priest. And I knew where the chocolate eggs were because I was the one who hid them. This is my secret. I lied to you. I've always lied. Always. There is no time travelling, there are no Leaps. If there is one talent I truly had, it was making up stories. I have fainting spells, that's all. All the rest is a make-believe story. A story I told first to myself, to have the confidence to kiss you that day, and then to convince you we would be together. That was the only way I could keep a person as extraordinary as you. I could tell you now that I'm sorry for what I have done, but I am not, because all these years I had you, which was more than enough of a victory for me. As for your future, I can't tell you what it is for the simple reason that I don't know it. I never did.

You are free, Cinzia, as you always have been. Go out there then, and win."

————

And this I did.

It wasn't easy, with the searing pain in my ankle, but I had too much to prove. I couldn't afford to lose; and I didn't.

The young woman who came out of the infirmary was certainly not Cinzia, but not even Cynthia, for even the latter had lived only in the absence of Ugo. And he was gone now, gone so completely it felt like he had never been there. I wasn't surprised when I didn't see him in the cheering crowd, nor with my parents later on, when we celebrated with Timuresku and our staff. For, in the end, he was right. The moment I was freed from his future, I could realize my own. I had won. I would compete in the Olympics. My life was on course.

I was happy my parents were tactful enough never to mention Ugo. As for me, my feelings were tangled. There was a mix of regret, guilt, but most of all relief. I felt a terrible anger for having being deceived by such childish nonsense, and for so long. And yet, I had to admit that my husband's exit had come at the best time.

When I finally returned to our apartment, I was astonished by how thoroughly he had removed himself from my life. Not one picture, not one shirt, not even his smell remained. I wasn't surprised he had also taken Jericho; the dog had always been more his than mine.

So I went back to live with my parents. No one ever talked about Ugo, I think not to upset me. I was in fact so concentrated on the task ahead I might not have noticed if they did. The frantic six months before the Olympics were the most terrible time of my life. I lived the life of a monk. The only things that existed were the rink, my skates.

It's not that I never missed him, but his revelation had become suspended inside me, like a kite in a glass sky. Had it really happened? Had I married a man because I believed him to be a time traveller? Was he insane? Or was I? Sometimes even my memories of him seemed unreal. My wedding ring had left no mark. That's how I felt: unwritten, a frozen lake before the first skater scarred its surface.

What is it like to realize one's childhood dream?

Very few people find out, and I should feel fortunate. And yet, how bitter is it to know that by achieving something, you have to lose something else. And how harsh, knowing you won't be able to share your discovery. For the loneliness of a winner may make a good story, but only a winner himself would want to listen to it.

So in the end, I went to the Olympics and won two medals, one bronze and one silver. On the last day, I had seventeen job offers, the weirdest of which was to be the ice skating trainer of an Emir. Do they have ice in Arabia? I had won, but in the process my soul had grown thin, like the last of the butter spread over too much bread. Exhaustion was my second name. I kept falling asleep in the most embarrassing places. When the plane from Milan landed in Gatwick, I wanted nothing else but to get into a hot shower. And yet, in Reading, there were journalists waiting at the train station. I was answering their questions when I suddenly realized that I had expected him to be there.

Hadn't my victory also been his? In the days right after the competition, I had come to see Ugo's revelation differently. For, in the end, he hadn't lied to me, but to the little girl I had been. And to what end? To woo me, to make me believe a story that we shared together. His withdrawal had been so complete it was startling. Not a phone call, not an email, not a text message; not even after my victory. So when I saw that he was not there, I started to feel a strange, pulsing dread.

I kept dozing in the taxi, something that alarmed my sister (I had slept fifteen hours just the day before) until we finally passed through my neighbourhood. I had a brief glimpse of Ugo's flat. Had he already moved out? I asked my sister, but she frowned at me and didn't answer. Apparently his name was still taboo.

I was happy to hear so many friends' voices on the answering machine. Yet his wasn't there. When I finished my shower, I finally felt ready. I dialled his number. A recorded voice told me the line was disconnected. That was a bit of a surprise. I called the landline. Nine rings; nothing. A slithering anguish began to crawl around my neck. Still in my robe, I went down and asked my mother what had happened to Ugo. It was the first time I had mentioned him in seven months. What horrified me was not her answer, but her blank stare.

"Oh ... you mean Gilbert's second son? Oh, bless you, that's so sweet of you to ask. He is doing all right, I guess. He will be more than happy to meet his auntie now that she has become all famous."

I was not amused. No, I didn't mean my nephew, I meant my *husband*. Mother blinked twice and asked me to repeat the question. I did. At that, she spun around and said to no one in particular:

"Oh dear, that's ... Oh dear. Roger, can you come in for a sec?"

My father came in, bespectacled and scruffy.

"What is it?" he said.

"Cynthia is ... well, see it for yourself."

"What is it darling?"

"I want to know where my husband is. Is that too much to ask?"

"Your ... Honey, are you all right? Do you want to sit down?"

Then I knew. All that followed was just a part I had to play, excruciating and unnecessary. I told them I didn't feel the need to sit, and where was my husband, *please*. My voice had already begun to shoot up; little bro and big sis came down immediately. I knew what they believed, but their unwillingness to address the subject maddened me. So I became more and more insistent, until finally, my mother said it. There was no husband. I had never known a boy called Ugo, I never dated him, I never married him. There was no Ugo.

I fled upstairs. In my room, I took off my robe and—naked—I started to look for my old pictures. I rummaged desperately, looking for a picture of Ugo when we were little. There were so many photos, saved from our shared flat. Yet I couldn't find him. I was in all the pictures; he wasn't. I kept on looking until I found the Easter egg hunt picture. That was our very first picture together, one so clear in my brain I could have drawn it with eyes closed. But when I opened them, there was only me.

————

This is where I would love to tell you that—the following day—I filled my bathtub with hot water and slashed both my wrists. It would have been appropriate, at the very least. But I am a Brit and in our despair we are often underwhelming. It was worse, of course, the slow dark tide trapping me in a corner of my room where I rocked back and forth, gnawing at my fingertips till they bled. It lasted nine weeks. When at last I came out of it I didn't need to be told I needed to see a doctor: I went to the hospital on my own.

Dr. Buchanan was a tall black woman of fifty-five, and I liked her immediately. She knew who I was even before I began to explain what had happened to me. Afterward, she told me that she had read in the local papers that I had had a breakdown because of the Olympics. I asked her what she thought of it. She smiled at my directness.

"I think you had a psychotic episode, my dear," she said. "What is peculiar is that you didn't hallucinate a presence, but an absence."

In the days that followed, my life was put under a magnifying glass. Dr. Buchanan listened attentively to my side of the story. She was not only very surprised at how extensive my memory of my "imaginary husband" was, but that often while I told my story I spoke about myself in the third person, and even called myself two different names.

I shrugged. That didn't feel special to me. I had done it so since kindergarten. This, she said, was typical of schizo-affective behaviour. I associated that word with split personalities and homicidal rages. It turned out it meant the inability to see thoughts for what they were, mistaking them for perceptions: voices, smells. Sometimes these intrusions became coherent, bringing on sub-personalities. However, such a detailed delusion, an entire past with an imaginary human being, was uncommon. That's why she wanted to consult with some colleagues, and could I be admitted for observation?

So here I am, the self-hospitalized athlete, estranged from family and friends. I spend my days in this room reading and writing, as Dr. Buchanan has encouraged me to. By writing Ugo's story, I might not only remember it better, but give it a new meaning, she said. That's why she told me to write it all down as if it was a story. I know what she wants to get at. She wants me to write his story so that I can see it is a fiction. I won't tell you that I'm not tempted.

Maybe it's the medication they are giving me, but remembering Ugo has become more difficult. What did his hair smell like? What did it feel like when he was inside of me? Did he talk when we made love? I have this image of a boy whispering in my ears. I know what the doctor would say, that this is a personification of schizophrenia, murmuring intrusive thoughts I've taken for memories.

It's like waking up. So many flashes come to my mind now.

The way, sometimes, people reacted to Ugo, ignoring him completely. My friends' surprise when I talked about him. The plain fact I didn't have any friends in common with him. I can't remember a single time when I was with a friend and with Ugo. How is that possible? And my wedding day: How is it I can't remember any details except that it was a sunny day? And then our shared apartment, our daily lives. My parents told me I never left home. How could I in fact hold a job, train for ice skating, and pay the rent at nineteen? How likely is that? The doctor says I didn't just "make up" a person. A part of my mind created a whole parallel life, the ideal way I wanted to live my youth. In love, independent, married, with a future that was mine alone.

Until, on the day of the Olympic selections, the ideal world of my childhood came into conflict with my ambition. Why did I want to talk with Ugo alone? Because there was no one there but me.

But no. That's what *they* want me to believe. That Ugo was the invisible companion I conjured up from my lonely childhood. This is where his imperfections save me. His aloofness, his infuriating smile, all those traits I'd always resented: How could I have made them up? The greatest objection to his existence came from my sister. If, in his Leaps, he couldn't change the future, and if he saw we had a lifetime together, why had he made his revelation? And why did he disappear after that?

Oh, but can't you see? This is exactly why I still cling to him. Only now I understand what he did. The moment he realized the Olympics were my life's dream, he fought to change what he had seen, to reshape my future so that I could win. But why did he do that? He had already seen that in the end we would be happy together, that my words were just a momentary fit of anger. Or maybe ... maybe what awaited us was not what I thought. That was my idea of romantic marriage, as a teenager would imagine it. But Ugo saw what it really would be like. All our dreams fulfilled and then broken, one by one. Can you imagine what this could do to a child? Seeing how love will end, how routine slowly would erode everything you believe in?

Is that the reason why he hugged me at the Fair, after his long

Leap? Was it because he missed the girl I had been, replaced by the acerbic wife I would be? In the end, he acted like the romantic he truly was. Instead of giving me our shared happiness, however brief, he gave me its absence. I'll never know what our shared life would have been like; and therefore it will stay intact, an untouched horizon inside me.

Cover art by Sarah Anne Langton.

ISBN 978-1-937009-74-8 (TPB)

Apex Publications
PO Box 24323
Lexington, KY 40524

Visit us online at ApexBookCompany.com.

ABOUT THE EDITORS

Lavie Tidhar is the author of the Jerwood Fiction Uncovered Prize winning *A Man Lies Dreaming*, the World Fantasy Award winning *Osama* and of the critically-acclaimed *The Violent Century*. His other works include the *Bookman Histories* trilogy, several novellas, two collections, and a forthcoming comics mini-series, *Adler*. He currently lives in London.

Cristina Jurado is a bilingual author and editor who writes in Spanish and English. She studied Advertising at the Universidad de Sevilla (Spain) and holds a Master's degree in Rhetoric from Northwestern University (USA).

TRANSLATOR BIOGRAPHIES

Jim Hubbert is a Tokyo-based translator of Japanese science fiction stories, including *The Next Continent* by Issui Ogawa and *Gene Mapper* by Taiyo Fujii. He also serves as a script consultant for Japanese versions of films.

Matthew David Goodwin is an Assistant Professor in the Department of English at the University of Puerto Rico at Cayey. He is the editor of *Latin@ Rising: An Anthology of Latin@ Science Fiction and Fantasy*.

Jessica Sequeira is a writer, journalist, and translator living in Buenos Aires. She has been published in the *Boston Review*, *Time Out*, *Litro Magazine*, *Palabras Errantes*, and *Ventana Latina*.

Steve Redwood is an English writer and translator living in Spain. He translated the first Spanish cyberpunk novel, *Cat's Whirld* by Rodolfo Martínez. His latest novel is *Los sanadores* through Editorial Cerbero.

John Chu is a microprocessor architect by day, a writer, translator, and podcast narrator by night. His work has appeared in *Uncanny Magazine, Clarkesworld,* and *Tor.com.* His story "The Water That Falls on You from Nowhere" won the 2014 Hugo Award.

Lara Harmon is an online community manager and occasional translator of German science fiction. She has translated a second short story by Karla Schmidt and is working on a third.

Gord Sellar and **Jihyun Park** are a collaborative translation team. Sellar's writing has appeared in many SF venues while Park's debut short film, the award-winning "The Music of Jo Hyeja" (2012), was South Korea's first cinematic Lovecraft adaptation.

Elisabeth Jaquette is a translator from the Arabic and Executive Director of the American Literary Translators Association. Her work has been shortlisted for the TA First Translation Prize and her forthcoming translations include *The Frightened Ones* by Dima Wannous (Harvill Secker) and *Thirteen Months of Sunrise* by Rania Mamoun (Comma Press).

ALSO AVAILABLE FROM APEX BOOK COMPANY

The Apex Book of World SF: Volume 1
The Apex Book of World SF: Volume 2
The Apex Book of World SF: Volume 3
The Apex Book of World SF: Volume 4